More Praise for *The Kingdoms*

"Speculative fiction and historical fiction are closer cousins than one might think, and alternate-history novels can give enterprising writers the chance to work in both genres at once. Fans of such stories will be richly entertained by the lavish world-building and breakneck plotting of Natasha Pulley's *The Kingdoms* . . . Beautiful, surreal imagery appears throughout the novel, too . . . Clear a weekend if you can, and let yourself be absorbed."

—*The New York Times Book Review*

"As scenes spiral back and forth between centuries, the book's emotional center crystallizes around a fundamental mystery: Who, in fact, is Joe? All time-travel plots are fraught with paradox, but not all rise to Pulley's level of tricky cleverness, and few of those trickily clever books rise to her level of emotional intensity. Suspenseful, philosophical, and inventive, this sparkling novel explores the power of memory and love."

—*Kirkus Reviews* (starred review)

"Natasha Pulley poses such a beguiling set of questions at the opening of *The Kingdoms* that even readers who are resistant to speculative fiction will barrel forward to discover the answers . . . *The Kingdoms* is interested not only in the adventure of its historical and imaginative plot, but also in what it would actually feel like to slip out of time . . . Thoughtful, inventive, and moody . . . an insightful meditation on how a sense of oneself can be lost—and found."

—*USA Today*

"Pulley's latest genre-bending feat (after *The Lost Future of Pepperharrow*) masterfully combines history, speculative fiction, queer romance, and more into an unputdownable whole . . . This is a stunner."

—*Publishers Weekly* (starred review)

"This book is a bit of a hodgepodge of a few different genres as there's time travel and it's obviously historical fiction, but there's also elements of fantasy so seamlessly weaved throughout the story that they almost blend in with the very essence of reality. Pulley's prose feels ethereal even as it sizzles with dry humour. Pieces of the story take place at multiple places and times, and Pulley paints every single one of those settings with utmost veracity and vividness. Every single aspect of this book was indeed sheer perfection to me, but the romance at the core of the story—that blossomed even amidst all the uncertainty and carnage and hopelessness of war—really was the most beautiful thing about this book."

—*The Nerd Daily*

"Pulley balances the topsy-turvy nature of time travel by grounding her story in tidbits of naval history and a gradually unfolding queer love story."

—*BookPage*

"*The Kingdoms* contains multitudes: it is a love story, a seafaring war novel, a time-travel mystery, an alternative history tale, and more. And while each description in the previous sentence is accurate, each description fails to capture all that the book encompasses . . . The book is as much about trauma as it is about love, and Pulley doesn't flinch away from showing how the impacts of trauma reverberate throughout history."

—Tor.com

"I loved the vivid and intricate alternate universes of *The Kingdoms*, and the flawed and complicated people who inhabit them."

—Katherine Addison, author of *The Goblin Emperor*

"Natasha Pulley's *The Kingdoms* is an intricate plot, for sure, but you get swept up in the narrative. I appreciated how this time travel story deals with shifting futures, when little actions have big impacts. Anyway, I am going to tie myself in knots trying to explain this plot further, but if this sounds like the type of book you're drawn to—epic! time travel! history!—you know who you are. Read if you're into: time travel, queer love, historical fiction, alternative history."

—Alma

"This one is really, really not a mystery, but I loved it too much to not include on this list. Also, it's got mystery-esque elements to it!"

—CrimeReads, "Most Anticipated Crime Books of Summer"

"Pulley successfully tackles time travel with both humor and fine detail . . . Exploring time, chance, identity, love of all manners, loss and destiny, this is a novel in which to immerse yourself. At heart a love story, a sweeping and strange romance, it is also a grand adventure and a writerly feat of achievement."

—Bookreporter

"*The Kingdoms* is a complicated tale with plenty of twists and turns that will keep readers enthralled all the way to the last pages."

—*Washington Independent Review of Books*

"This riveting story keeps the reader hoping that Joe can rebuild his family in the best time line."

—*Booklist*

"Natasha Pulley has an uncanny ability to make me feel some kind of way about the concept of time. Honestly, I'd be mad if I didn't love it so much. The interplay of time and memory in her newest novel, *The Kingdoms*, wows to astounding and gut-wrenching effect. Truly it has everything: alternate history, naval warfare, a yearning-filled love story, and temporally displaced tortoises. I did yell out loud alone in my apartment as I neared the end, which is about as glowing an endorsement as I can give. Please read this and then everything else she's ever written so next time we can yell together."

—Sarah Reif, Powell's Books, BuzzFeed's "58 Great Books to Read This Summer, Recommended By Our Favorite Indie Booksellers"

THE KINGDOMS

The Watchmaker of Filigree Street
The Bedlam Stacks
The Lost Future of Pepperharrow

THE KINGDOMS

Natasha Pulley

BLOOMSBURY PUBLISHING

NEW YORK · LONDON · OXFORD · NEW DELHI · SYDNEY

BLOOMSBURY PUBLISHING
Bloomsbury Publishing Inc.
1385 Broadway, New York, NY 10018, USA

BLOOMSBURY, BLOOMSBURY PUBLISHING, and the Diana logo are trademarks of
Bloomsbury Publishing Plc

First published in 2021 in Great Britain
First published in the United States 2021
This edition published 2022

ISBN: HB: 978-1-63557-608-5; PB: 978-1-63557-952-9; EBOOK: 978-1-63557-609-2

Library of Congress Cataloging-in-Publication Data is available.

2 4 6 8 10 9 7 5 3 1

Typeset by Integra Software Services Pvt. Ltd.
Printed and bound in the U.S.A.

To find out more about our authors and books visit www.bloomsbury.com
and sign up for our newsletters.

Bloomsbury books may be purchased for business or promotional use. For information
on bulk purchases please contact Macmillan Corporate and Premium Sales Department at
specialmarkets@macmillan.com.

To the crew of *Pelican of London*

Part I
LONDRES

I

Londres, 1898 (ninety-three years after Trafalgar)

Most people have trouble recalling their first memory, because they have to stretch for it, like trying to touch their toes; but Joe didn't. This was because it was a memory formed a week after his forty-third birthday.

He stepped down off the train. That was it, the very first thing he remembered, but the second was something less straightforward. It was the slow, eerie feeling that everything was doing just what it should be, minding its own business, but that at the same time, it was all wrong.

It was early in the morning, and cursedly cold. Vapour hissed on the black engine right above him. Because the platform was only a couple of inches above the tracks, the double pistons of the wheels were level with his waist. He was so close he could hear the water boiling above the furnace. He stepped well away, feeling tight with the certainty it was about to lurch forward.

The train had just come in. The platform was full of people looking slow and stiff from the journey, all moving towards the concourse. The sweet carbon smell of coal smoke was everywhere. Because it was only just light outside, the round lamps of the station gave everything a pale glow, and cast long, hazy shadows; even the steam had a shadow, a shy devil trying to decide whether to be solid or not.

Joe had no idea what he was doing there.

He waited, because railway stations were internationally the same and they were a logical place to get confused, if there was ever a logical place. But nothing came. He couldn't remember coming here, or going anywhere. He looked down at himself. With a writhe of horror, he found he couldn't even remember getting dressed. His clothes were unfamiliar. A heavy coat lined with tartan. A plain waistcoat with interesting buttons, stamped with laurel patterns.

A sign on the wall said that this was platform three. Behind him on the train, a conductor was going along the carriages, saying the same thing again and again, quiet and respectful, because he was having to wake people up in first class.

'Londres Gare du Roi, all change please, Londres Gare du Roi ...'

Joe wondered why the hell the train company was giving London station names in French, and then wondered helplessly why he'd wondered. All the London station names *were* French. Everyone knew that.

Someone touched his arm and asked in English if he was all right. It made him jump so badly that he twanged the nerve in the back of his skull. White pain shot down his neck.

'Sorry – could you tell me where we are?' he asked, and heard how ridiculous it sounded.

The man didn't seem to think it was extraordinary to find an amnesiac at a railway station. 'London,' he said. 'The Gare du Roi.'

Joe wasn't sure why he'd been hoping for something other than what he'd heard the conductor say. He swallowed and looked away. The steam was clearing. There were signs everywhere; for the Colonial Library, the Musée Britannique, the Métro. There was a board not far away that said the Desmoulins line was closed because of the drilling below, and beyond that, elaborate iron gates that led out into the fog. 'Definitely ... London in England?' he asked eventually.

'It is,' the man said.

'Oh,' said Joe.

The train breathed steam again and made the man into a ghost. Through all the bubbling panic, Joe thought he must have been a doctor, because he still didn't seem surprised. 'What's your name?' the man asked. Either he had a young voice, or he looked older than he was.

'Joe.' He had to reach for it, but he did know; that was a thump of a relief. 'Tournier.'

'Do you know where you live?'

'No,' he said, feeling like he might collapse.

'Let's get you to a hospital then,' the man said.

So the man paid for a cab. Joe expected him to leave it at that, but he came too and said there was no reason why not, since he wasn't busy. A thousand times in the following months, Joe tried to remember what the man had looked like. He couldn't, even though he spent the whole cab ride opposite him; all he remembered later was that the man had sat without leaning back, and that something about him seemed foreign, even though he spoke English in the hard straight way that old people did, the belligerent ones who'd always refused to learn French and scowled at you if you tried to call them monsieur.

It was maddening, that little but total failure of observation, because he took in everything else perfectly. The cab was a new one, all fresh leather and smelling of polish that was still waxy to touch. Later, he could even remember how steam had risen from the backs of the horses, and the creak of the wheel springs when they moved from the cobbles outside the station to the smoother-paved way down Rue Euston.

But not the man. It was as though the forgetfulness wasn't so much an absence of memory, but a shroud that clung to him.

The road looked familiar and not. Whenever they came to a corner Joe thought he knew, there was a different shop there to the one he'd expected, or no building at all. Other cabs clopped past. Brown fog pawed at the shop windows. The sky was grey. In the background, he wondered if the man wasn't being kind at all but taking advantage of things somehow, but he couldn't think what for.

Not far away, monster towers pumped fumes into that gun-metal sky. They were spidered about with gantries and chutes, and in the flues, tiny flames burned. On the side of an enormous silo, he could just make out BLAST FURNACE 5 stamped in white letters in French. Joe swallowed. He knew exactly what they were – steelworks – but at the same time, they filled him with the dream-sense of wrongness that the Métro signs at the station had done. He shut his eyes and tried to chase down what he knew. Steelworks; yes, London was famous for that, that was what London was for. Seven blast furnaces up around Farringdon and Clerkenwell, hauling steel out to the whole Republic. If you bought a postcard of London, it always looked amazing, because of that towering tangle of pipework and coal chutes and chimneys in the middle of it. It was a square mile that had turned everything black with soot: the ruin of St Paul's, the leaning old buildings round Chancery Lane, everything. That was why London was the Black City.

But all that might as well have come from an encyclopaedia. He didn't know how he knew it. He didn't remember walking in those black streets or around the steelworks, or any of it.

'Did you get off the same train as me?' he asked the man, hoping that if he focused on one particular thing, he might feel less sick.

'Yes. It came from Glasgow. We were in the same carriage.' The man had a clipped way of talking, but his whole body was full of compassion. He looked like he was stopping himself

6

leaning forward and taking Joe's hands. Joe was glad about that. He would have burst into tears.

He couldn't remember being on the train. The man tried to tell him things that had been memorable, like the funny snootiness of the conductor and the way the fold-down beds tried to eat you if you didn't push them down properly, but none of it was there. He confirmed that Joe hadn't fallen or bumped anything, just started to look disorientated early this morning. It was nine o'clock now.

Joe had to let his head bow. He'd never been scared like it. He opened the window, just to inhale properly. Everything smelled of soot. That was familiar, at least. On the pavements, droves of men in black coats and black hats poured from the iron gates of the Métro stations. They all looked the same. The cab stopped for a minute or so, waiting at a railway crossing. The train was a coal cargo, chuntering towards the steelworks. The whistle howled as the driver tried to scare off some kids on the line; there were ten or twelve, foraging for the bits of coal that fell off the carriages.

'You'll be all right,' the man said quietly. It was the last thing he said; while Joe was seeing the doctor, he vanished. None of the nurses had seen him go, or seen him at all, and Joe started to think he had got himself to the hospital alone, and that the man had been a benign hallucination.

There were two hospitals. The first was the Colonial Free, which was a dark, frozen place where all the windows stayed open to air the wards, and an exhausted doctor referred him, urgently, to an asylum over the river. Then there was another cab ride, by himself, paid for by the hospital. He curled up under his coat on the way, cold right to the marrow now. More of the black streets glided by, the terraces like widow's lace. Then there was the Tamise: black too, and so packed with cargo ships that a limber

7

person could have got across the whole breadth of it jumping from deck to deck. Normal, all normal. Except he felt like someone had left him on the surface of Mars.

The second hospital was called La Nouvelle Salpêtrière. It was a much nicer place than Joe had expected. South of the river, in Southwark, it was an impressive building that looked much more like a museum or a bank than a hospital. He had imagined it would be grim and white inside, but in fact it was hard to tell that it was an asylum at all. The entrance hall was all marble and pillars, nice couches, and chandeliers of electric lights. Someone deep in the building was playing the piano.

On the way upstairs to the consultant's office, the nurse took him past two cells lined with cork, but the doors were open and nobody was inside. There was, said the nurse, a criminal wing, where the cases were far more serious, but it was separate. The only other sign that perhaps not everyone was to be trusted was the cages around the fireplaces.

While he was waiting outside the consultant's office, a man lent him a copy of *Le Monde* and claimed to control the weather. Joe sat holding the paper, looking at the words and the typeface, and trying to trace why it was all wrong. It didn't say anything extraordinary. There was the weather in one column – it didn't match what the man predicted – an advert for silk shirts, one for a M. d'Leuve's brand-new invention, an electric corset which was apparently very good for feminine discomforts. He wondered at that, because Madeline had never seemed so uncomfortable that she would need electrifying. He frowned at his knees when he realised he had remembered a name, and her face; a small woman with dark hair, who suited dark green. He couldn't think of a last name, or if she was a sister or a wife, or neither.

The doctor's office was airy, with a bleak, beautiful view over the hospital's frosty lawns. On the wall was a certificate from an academy in Paris. The desk had bite marks on one leg, near the top. Joe looked round for the dog that must have done that but couldn't see one, which was a lot more disconcerting than it should have been. All the details landed in his mind like bright pins, sharp and pricking and very unpleasant.

The doctor explained that he would be there for a week, on the understanding that the accommodation fees would be waived. 'Now, you've been referred from the Colonial Free, I see. I can tell you now exactly what you're suffering from. It's a seizure; a form of epilepsy. With any luck, it will go off soon.'

'A seizure?'

The doctor set the notes down and smiled. He was young and smartly turned out, Parisian; on colonial placement, probably, to rack up experience before returning to France. Joe felt hopeless. The more he thought about it, the more he realised he knew general things, but nothing specific.

'Yes,' the doctor said. 'I'm personally very interested in this particular epilepsy type, so I've been asking for cases, hence your referral. It's what we're calling silent epilepsy; it doesn't come with convulsions, only the symptoms we would usually associate with an epileptic aura – amnesia, paramnesia, visions. Had anything of the latter two?'

'What does paramnesia mean?' Joe asked. The doctor's voice was so posh that he could feel himself furling up inside with the urge to keep his answers short, and not to ask questions or to waste time.

'The blurring of something imaginary and something real. Most commonly, déjà vu; the sense you've seen something new before. And its opposite, jamais vu, which is when something that should be familiar feels wholly alien.'

'Yes!' Joe said fast, and felt his eyes burn, desperately grateful to hear someone name the feeling. 'Yes, that second one, ever since that man found me at the station! I didn't think the Gare du Roi was in London, all the streets looked wrong, the – *newspapers* look wrong …'

'Textbook,' the doctor said gently. 'Absolutely. Now, I can promise you that you *do* know Londres, because you've got a very strong Clerkenwell accent.' He smiled again. 'Let's see what happens if we keep you here in the quiet for a few days. I'm putting you down as a curable,' he added, motioning at the form in front of him.

'What if it doesn't go away?' Joe said. He was having to speak carefully. It felt like he hadn't spoken for a long, long time, which was absurd, because he had spoken before, at the other hospital, and the train station. But the order of words felt wrong. French, they were speaking French of course, and the man at the station had spoken English; maybe it was just the switchover.

'Well, let's talk about that in the—'

'No, let's talk about it now, please.'

'There's no need to be aggressive,' the doctor said, sharp. He drew back in his chair a few inches, as though he thought Joe might punch him.

Joe frowned. 'I'm not being aggressive, I'm really scared.'

The honesty seemed to take the doctor by surprise. He had the grace to look awkward. 'You understand my caution. Your notes say you arrived at the Colonial Free speaking English, and that coat you're wearing now has a tartan lining. The train you were on came from Glasgow.' His tone turned from questioning to accusatory by the end.

'Sorry?' said Joe, lost.

'If I say the Saints to you, does that ring a bell?'

Joe searched for it, but got nothing. 'Is that a church?'

'No, it's a terrorist group that makes a habit of bombing trains and random sections of the Republic.'

'Oh. And they …'

'Speak English and wear tartan and occupy Edinburgh, which does not have a railway connection, for obvious reasons, to Londres. They use Glasgow.'

Joe stared down at the lining of his coat sleeve. 'I ... can't see myself bombing anything. I think I'd go to pieces under pressure. I *am* going to pieces. Have ... gone.'

The doctor must have thought so too, because he relented. '*If* it doesn't go away, it means that there may be a lesion or a tumour pressing on part of your brain, in which case, there's very little we can do, and it will probably prove fatal eventually.' He said it bluntly, punishment for Joe's having scared him before. 'Meanwhile, we're putting your details and description in the papers. See if we can find you some relatives.'

Joe knew he should say thank you, but it was an uphill struggle to say anything now. 'And if no one comes?'

'The county asylum is free, so you could go there.' The doctor winced at the idea, and Joe tried not to imagine what the county asylum was like. 'But as I say, we're putting you up for the week, so we have until next Tuesday.'

'Right.'

A huge dog padded in and put its head on Joe's lap, and looked at him hopefully until he stroked its ears. It was a relief to see that there really was a dog, and that it wasn't a patient who'd gnawed on the table leg.

'Don't mind Napoleon, he's very friendly. However,' the doctor continued, as if he hadn't mentioned the dog, 'I've never seen a case that hasn't cleared in a few days, if not a few hours. And it's an incredibly common condition. We had a rush of people with it a couple of months ago and they all recovered perfectly. Not so bad as this, but precisely the same thing.'

Joe looked up from the dog. 'A group of people with the same thing in the same timeframe implies an external cause that affects all of them. Doesn't it?'

The doctor widened his eyes, then laughed, as if it was surprising that Joe would know words like implies and external. 'Well, yes. A cluster does imply an external cause. But there is no geographical cluster. Patients from right across the Republic have experienced it, from Rome to Dublin. We're looking into all sorts: weather, water tables, crops, air miasma. But don't worry yourself. We'll work it out.'

Joe nodded.

'Settle down, have a game of tennis with someone. Plenty of veterans here, wonderful fellows, they just don't get on so well with sudden noises. I'll see you in a few days.'

Joe wanted to ask more, but that was that, because a woman drifted in holding a doll too tightly and pointed at the dog, and the doctor hurried up to ease her away again. The dog followed them.

2

The nurse, a thin white lady, was brusque. Most of the other patients were educated people, so he should mind his manners, thank you. A Clerkenwell accent, the doctor had said; that must have been code for scummy. She put him in a narrow room with a bed and a desk and a view over the gardens, berating him all the while.

He thought she was just being rude at first, but then realised that he was making her nervous, so he put himself in a corner and tried to think small thoughts while she explained where everything was and what time meals were. He felt disconcerted, because he wasn't a big enough man to loom. What the doctor had said about the tartan lining of his coat chimed again. Carefully, like it might be on a fuse, he took out the idea that he might have something to do with terrorists. It still didn't sound right. He was pretty sure hardened terrorists would have to be angry people, and though he wasn't confident of many things, he knew he had about as much inclination towards explosive rage as a Joe-shaped pile of salt. Not everyone would want a lot of it, but it was, basically, neutral.

That, part of his mind pointed out, was a chemistry joke. How does English scum of the earth from Clerkenwell know chemistry?

No use wondering that for now.

'Um,' he ventured, 'are there any books?' If he couldn't get away from it all, going somewhere imaginary seemed like the next best thing.

'There's a library. It's designed to be improving.' Her whole posture made it clear he could do with improving. 'French classics of course.'

Classic sounded a lot like it would be about the horrors of life in slums, and Fallen Women who were never interesting enough to actually fall off anything. 'Anything English?' he said, not with much hope.

The nurse stared at him. 'What kind of place do you think this *is*?'

She didn't let him speculate before she strode to the open door and vanished into the corridor with a disgusted huff.

He put his hands into his pockets and turned them out on the desk.

He had a few francs, new-minted, with Napoleon IV looking the age he was. There was a case of cigarettes. They were home-made, but the tobacco smelled good. From the same pocket came a tin with an enamel lid and a tiny picture of a ship on the front. He thought it was a snuffbox until he opened it and found matches inside. Last, from his inside pocket, there were two train tickets. They were both singles to the Gare du Roi, from Glasgow. The ticket inspector had clipped out the 'Glas'.

His heart missed a gear and crunched. Two tickets.

He turned towards the door, meaning to go after the nurse, but then realised he didn't know who he wanted her to look for. He put the tickets aside uneasily and tried to let it go like the doctor had said, and went downstairs to explore. But no matter how often he reasoned that the man who had helped him would have noticed someone else, or that it was possible he had just picked up a stray ticket by accident, he couldn't shift the certainty that he had wandered off oblivious from someone who had been looking for him. The more he thought about it, the more certain he was.

He strained again to think of the train, the carriage, whether there had been a woman with dark hair who suited green, but he couldn't remember a single person.

'Madeline, come on, she's called Madeline,' he said aloud, trying to trick his brain into letting just a corner of that forgetting-shroud slip.

Nothing.

He hoped she was looking for him.

Feeling only half there, he spent the rest of the day ghosting around the open rooms downstairs and the gardens, which were full of cherry trees. That he was taken with the latter made him think he wasn't used to gardens, but it was only a guess. He tried to read a book later, unsuccessfully, because the tight feeling in his chest wouldn't go away for long enough to gather up much concentration. He stuck to the papers. They were full of ordinary things. The Emperor was in residence at Buckingham Palace for the season, having just arrived from Paris; there were festivities open to the public at St Jacques' Park all week, with fireworks. After a lot of work underground to properly heat the vineyards, the price of plantations in Cornwall was rocketing, and so was the price of slaves because the owners got through so many, what with the digging and maintenance of the hot air flow; the usually thriving Truro slave market was quite empty. He found himself in the evening classifieds. *Joseph Tournier, memory-loss patient at La Salpêtrière, seeks relatives.*

There was no change. He sat awake through the night, trying to listen to his own memory. The more he listened, the more hollow it rang. But that tiny recollection of Madeline was right. He could see her if he thought about it, so he did think about it, hard. He told her name to the doctor. The doctor promised to pass it along to the police, but looked grim when Joe said he still didn't know where he lived. Tuesday, the deadline of his stay, loomed taller.

On Saturday morning, someone did come, and it was an unexpected someone: a pin-sharp, purple-cravatted gentleman. When the doctor showed the man into the visiting room Joe froze, wondering who he could have offended, but the man let his breath out and smiled.

'It is you! Oh, Joe. Do you recognise me?' French, Paris French.

'No,' Joe said softly. His stomach screwed itself into a knot. There was no way he could have any normal business with someone like this. God, what if the doctor had been right, what if he *had* been involved with the Saints? This man was easily well-dressed enough to be a police commissioner, or one of those government people who introduced themselves politely, showed you the red badge, and then took you away to what they called an inquiries facility.

He had a surge of anger with himself. How could he know about red badges and inquiry facilities but not who Madeline was or where he bloody belonged?

'I'm M. Saint-Marie. I'm your master. You've been in my household since you were a little boy.' He said it kindly. 'I hear you're having a few problems remembering.'

Joe's lungs hitched, because his instinct had been to say 'Pleased to meet you', which of course was wrong. 'I'm sorry, I don't ...' He trailed off uselessly. The man was too grand for the visiting room.

'Never mind for now,' the doctor said quickly. 'Perhaps Mme Tournier?'

Joe looked up fast. Maybe it was Madeline.

Every atom of him wanted it to be. He still didn't remember her properly, but it would be something, and seeing her would help, he knew it would – and *she* would help too, because if there was a single thing he did know about her, it was that she could help with anything. She was one of those people who could blast through walls and barely notice.

The observer voice in the back of his mind pointed out that, in its humble opinion, he sounded awfully like he was spinning a fairy-tale woman for himself.

Shut up, *shut up*.

She *was* real. Maybe she was just outside.

'Mme Tournier?' he asked. His voice came out tight.

'Yes,' the gentleman agreed. He looked worried, but he didn't say anything about it. 'I'll fetch her.'

Joe waited, feeling like he might burst. Neither he nor the doctor spoke. The details of the room kept scratching at him. The only sound was glass scraping near the window, because the gardener had come in to water the ferns some of the patients were growing in bell jars. He flipped the bell up, sprayed the ferns with a perfume puffer, eased it down again. Outside, the man who said he controlled the weather was talking to a cherry tree.

The doctor was playing with his fountain pen, clicking the lid off and clicking it back on again. For a red-hot second, Joe thought he deserved a hand grenade in the face.

Well, said the voice, maybe you could manage the Saints after all.

Steps groaned just outside the door.

'Hello again,' said the gentleman as he came back in. He held the door open for someone else. 'Here's Mme Tournier.'

Joe's heart swelled, and then crumbled.

It wasn't her. There was nothing familiar about the woman called Mme Tournier. Her clothes were plain but well-ironed, and when she offered a quiet good morning, she spoke with a Jamaican swing. The way she moved was so quick and precise it made Joe wonder if she might be a governess, or a nurse.

'I'm Alice. Do you know me?' she asked. She was very young. Joe looked from her to the gentleman and wanted to demand how in the world either of them imagined he could possibly be married to her – he must have been twice her age – but neither of them seemed to think it was ridiculous. They only looked expectant, the gentleman nervously so, and Mme Tournier tiredly. Joe could see that she didn't care whether he knew her or not.

'No,' he said. It came out indignant.

The gentleman looked even more nervous and Alice Tournier looked even more tired.

'Well, you do,' she told him.

Joe wanted to argue, or even run out. She was a child. The doctor was already beside him, though, holding his shoulder to keep him still.

Alice had even brought a photograph. Later, when the doctor had sent her back to the waiting room, Joe stared down at it. It was their wedding day. It must have been taken with a decent camera, because they didn't have the stiff look people did when they'd had to keep exactly still for three or four minutes. Neither of them looked happy either. He couldn't read his own face. Closed down, neutral. It wasn't his resting expression, which was a kind of drilling attention that made him look like he was reading a physics textbook even when he was shaving.

'Joe,' the doctor said when he came back, grave. 'M. Saint-Marie has informed us that you are a slave. You disappeared two months ago. The gendarmes have been looking for you. This is very serious.' With each word, he tapped the end of his pen against one of the gold pins on the arm of his chair. The chairs were all grand but ancient. Someone had said they'd been donated by a gentleman's club, which seemed right; if you sat down too heavily in one, it puffed cigar smoke. 'I need you to tell me the truth. Is your memory gone, or did you run away and then change your mind? You can tell me if it's the latter. M. Saint-Marie doesn't want to press charges. He just wants you home.'

'No!' Joe said, and then had to force himself to calm down, because the doctor hardened and looked like he might call in the burly nurse with the tranquillisers. 'No. I – can see what it looks like, but ...'

'I choose,' the doctor said slowly, 'to believe you. And that is what I will put on your medical records, a copy of which will go to the gendarmes. It will keep you from being prosecuted even should your master change his mind.' He didn't look like he believed it for a second. There was something hurt in his expression.

Joe nodded, feeling like he'd lost his grip on everything all over again. A slave. Escaped, maybe. He swallowed. 'Listen – I've never seen that woman before. My wife is called Madeline. I'm sure ...'

'False memories are common. It is *very* unlikely that Madeline is real, Joe. The feeling of remembering her – that's a hallucination.'

'But I had *two* train tickets—'

'Joe, we have put your case in every national and local newspaper. You don't think she would have found you by now, if she had been looking?'

Joe had to stare at the carpet.

The doctor studied him for a while. 'Mme Tournier has a photograph; that seems like proof to me. And you must consider that if you turn these people away, it couldn't look more like an escape attempt if you tried. No medical report could stop the gendarmes investigating then.'

'But—'

'I will tell you,' the doctor snapped, angry now, 'exactly what the gendarmes will say. They will say that you are one of the *many* English slaves who decided it would be a good idea to join the Saints in Edinburgh. You escaped, you got there, you found it was not the wondrous Promised Land but a hideous mess well-supplied with zealots but not with proper food, and you decided to come home again and make up an amnesia story from knowledge of a very common disorder, which you could have heard about from anyone, or read about in any newspaper. At best, they would say, you have been extremely stupid; at worst, you didn't get fed up and leave, but were *posted* south with some horrible mission to blow up a train. And frankly, I really couldn't blame anyone who thought that was exactly what you'd done.'

Joe felt caged. M. Saint-Marie and Alice could have been anyone – it could have been some kind of scam, and he'd end up sold on a plantation somewhere in Cornwall.

But if he refused to go with them and he vanished into a gendarmerie, he would never come out. He had no clear idea about what happened to slaves who had run away, but he did know that he was walking a narrow, narrow bridge above a black gulf, and he could hear things shifting down in the deep places. He found himself twisting his head to one side, trying to get away from the thought. He wanted very much not to investigate those things too closely.

He looked up at the doctor again when he realised that if he wasn't a slave, he wouldn't feel like that. People who were safe didn't have chasms like that in the bases of their minds. They just had a nice wine cellar.

'I'll go with them,' he said.

The doctor lifted his eyebrows. 'Good choice.'

So Joe went with Alice Tournier and M. Saint-Marie to a house he didn't know. It was in a down-at-heel part of Clerkenwell, and the rooms had high ceilings and furniture that would have been expensive sixty years ago. M. Saint-Marie threw his arms round Joe and welcomed him home, a bit tearfully. More than anything, he put Joe in mind of a hen who had just rediscovered a lost chick, all bustle and cluck.

'I didn't run away,' Joe said. His whole ribcage was crushing inward. 'Or I don't think I did.'

M. Saint-Marie shook his head while Joe was still talking. 'Of course you didn't. You're such a beautiful boy; someone will have stolen you and given you a crack on the head in just the wrong place.'

Joe felt unbalanced by that. He had a charming smile, he'd worked that out at the hospital – the nurses had turned out to be extraordinarily nice once he started smiling – but it hadn't occurred to him that he might have been stolen. He was, he'd thought all week, an odd-looking person; he had brown hair, straight, but the set of his bones wasn't European, and he was two shades too sunny for all his ingredients to have come from this far north. One of the other patients had assumed he was from the south of France, one of the doctors had wondered if he might be Persian, and someone else again had said he had a bit of a Slavic look and did he know her cousin Ivan.

'You'd be very valuable on the black market, even without a pedigree certificate,' M. Saint-Marie was saying. 'It's *flooded* with Welshmen; you wouldn't believe how ugly they are. No, you got yourself home. Thank God. If the gendarmes want to whinge about it, leave them to me. I'm responsible for you, I'm the one at fault.'

21

'Um – do I *have* a pedigree certificate?' asked Joe, who would have liked to know where he was from, if only because it might have explained where he had been, before the train station.

'No, I'm sorry. You came from an ... er, an unofficial breeder. Just a nice girl in Whitechapel.'

Whitechapel was not near Glasgow, that much he knew. He should have been interested; he should have fastened onto the idea of his parents like a bloodhound, but it was just another corner of the edifice of things he didn't know.

'We got your brother from her too, of course. I never did meet her husband,' M. Saint-Marie said, embarrassed. 'I rather think she was having children to order. All crossbreeds, all very lovely – she had photographs. Toby had quite an Oriental look, but you might not have shared a father, so I couldn't really say ... But never mind that now. How do you feel?'

He looked hopeful. Alice looked shattered. Joe looked around the living room. There were sun-faded silk rugs on the floor, and a Regency couch that was probably more for dusting than sitting, with holes in the upholstery. Pipes cackled in the walls. He didn't recognise a single inch of it.

He promised aloud that it looked dead familiar now he was here.

3

The memories didn't come back.

Joe tried to go back to La Salpêtrière, was told that slaves couldn't make appointments without their responsible citizen, and he had to ask M. Saint-Marie. Thankfully, M. Saint-Marie went with him straight away. The doctor suspected a tumour, but there was no way to find out without surgery, and the mortality rate was so high it was more like a very expensive execution. The good news was that there had been no more amnesia bouts, so it probably wasn't going to be fatal. The doctor delivered all this in the arch way of a person who didn't believe for a minute that Joe had a problem at all. M. Saint-Marie lodged a formal complaint against the doctor for being a prick.

It didn't matter as much as it could have, the not remembering. M. Saint-Marie was sweet and even more chickeny than Joe had thought at first. Alice he was never really sure of, but M. Saint-Marie said that was only to be expected. Alice was supposed to have married Joe's brother, but Toby had been killed in action near Glasgow six months ago; and marrying Joe instead, it seemed, had been the only way to escape *her* horrible mistress and stay in the household of sedate, untroublesome M. Saint-Marie, who had only agreed to buy her on some kind of spousal licence Joe didn't understand but which would have been void if she didn't marry someone.

Joe turned that information over and over for a long time, but he still couldn't remember a brother or the wedding.

He was glad of Alice and M. Saint-Marie. The outside world made him nervous. Joe knew Londres, and he didn't. He could navigate well enough, and he knew where all the Métro stations were and how to buy tickets and all the boring necessary stuff – but he didn't know street names or station names, and the first time M. Saint-Marie asked him to go up to the market for groceries, he had a nasty bolt of real fear. Saint-Marie saw it.

'Oh, Joe,' he said. 'You're not going by yourself; you couldn't anyway, it's illegal. You're going with Henrique from across the road; you know, Mme Finault's kitchen slave? You can look after each other.'

'Oh, right,' Joe managed, relieved. Henrique was an easily worried German and they chatted sometimes if they were putting out the washing at the same time, mainly about an on-going fight Henrique's mistress was having with someone else's mistress about local council elections and whether or not it was going to escalate to the point that Henrique would have to find out how to get red wine out of silk.

M. Saint-Marie showed him an official-looking card, with spaces for stamps. Joe's name was printed at the top, and a long slave's registration number. 'So, this is a Responsibility Card. What you do is, you show it to the newsagent – her stall is on the corner of the market, Henrique knows where – and she gives you a stamp to show you got there safely. If anything happens to a slave, you see, and they turn up lost, the gendarmes have a look at the Responsibility Card to see where they've been. And it's got my name and address on it, so they'll know where you belong.'

Joe nodded. 'Like a passport.'

'Exactly.' M. Saint-Marie rubbed the small of Joe's back. 'We shan't lose you again. And don't worry about forgetting. You can't buy anything until you show the stall-owners the stamp. And on the back here – that's the official list of things you're not allowed to buy. No alcohol and nothing sharp. I mean, not that there's anything like that on your shopping list, but you know.' Joe saw him scramble for a reason that was nothing to do with trying to escape. Saint-Marie had been contorting himself into knots to make sure Joe knew he didn't think that was what had happened. 'If kids ask you to get something for them, or something like that.'

'Right.'

'Good boy.' He grasped Joe's arms, his eyes watery. 'Sure you'll be all right with Henrique?'

Joe smiled. He could see why Alice hated it, but in the state of mind he was in lately, it was good to know that there would be plenty of people making sure he was in the right place and properly accounted for. 'I will.'

'Wonderful. Here's the list. If you're not back in an hour, I'll call the gendarmes out to look for you. Give me a kiss, lovely boy.'

Joe did as he was told, though he wanted to duck away. Up close, Saint-Marie was like crêpe paper someone had scrunched up, ironed, and then left out in the sun too long. He smelled of old cologne, and it had a way of sticking to you a good while after you'd touched him. Idiotic to get on his wrong side, though. The gendarmes were never far away.

Henrique was unsympathetic. His mistress wanted unreasonable things all the time and he would have been very grateful, he said, if all she'd wanted was the odd peck on the cheek. He could swap if Joe wanted, but darkly, he opined that Joe would want Saint-Marie back on pain of death after he'd had a week trying to find where in God's name you could buy hummingbird down for a doll's-house cushion.

'Mallard ducks have got feathers the same colour,' Joe said, which surprised him. He was still getting to know himself, and he hadn't realised he was that crafty.

Henrique told him that if he was too sharp he'd cut himself, but Joe caught him looking speculatively into the butcher's window.

On the wall of the butcher's shop, there was graffiti in English. It said,

WHERE IS EVERYONE??

Joe had a strange drop right in his stomach. He didn't know what did the dropping, but some internal lift-shaft had just gone wrong. 'What does that mean?'

Henrique only glanced at it. 'Uh. Crackpots,' he said crossly. 'It's election time. You know what happened to you, the epilepsy, and then the remembering things wrong? Happens to a lot of people. Except some of them are too stupid to understand what epilepsy is. They think they're missing relatives and the government has drugged them and erased all the records.'

'Could they have, though? Been drugged, or …'

Henrique snorted. 'Well, my mistress is seeing a gentleman who sits in the Senate, and if he's anything to judge by, the government couldn't get opium to a Chinaman, never mind drug all of England.' He gave Joe's shoulder a squeeze and said nothing else about it.

Joe had to admit he couldn't see how or why anyone might have pulled that off. But now that he had seen the writing on the wall once, he kept seeing it in other places: on the sides of old carts, in public toilets (there was a stamp on the Responsibility Card even for that) and then, once, outside St Paul's Cathedral. Every single time he saw it, he wondered about Madeline.

After another three months, the mortgage labour on the attic was all paid off, and Joe was officially free after thirty-five years of service. M. Saint-Marie threw a small party and cried over his wine. Joe hugged him, feeling guilty. Saint-Marie was getting older, and poorer, and he didn't go to Paris for the season any more. Most of his friends had left him behind, and now it must have felt like his household was doing the same thing.

'I know you're a grown man now, I *know*, but I've had you since you were tiny. I hate the idea of booting you out in the world and no one responsible for you but yourself ...'

'You silly hen,' Joe said, touched. 'You're not booting me anywhere. I'll still be living in the attic. I worked long enough for it.'

'You won't leave?'

'No,' Joe said, and smiled when Saint-Marie let out a relieved laugh. It was the first time since the Gare du Roi that he felt like he belonged.

Alice was overjoyed with freedom — she burned all her old Responsibility Cards in a pot on the windowsill and then dyed her grey day dress maroon with wine — but Joe didn't like it. He felt exposed going out without the stamp card or Henrique. In the week he went out job hunting, just as the weather turned bitter, he was stopped and searched twice by the gendarmes for no reason. On the second occasion, he got a baton in the ribs for asking why. When he told Saint-Marie, Saint-Marie cut out the tartan lining of his coat. Losing it upset Joe a lot more than he wanted to say — that tartan was one of the few things that had been with him, wherever he'd gone in that lost time — but the gendarmes didn't stop him again after that.

He didn't want to leave the house for the next couple of days, but he had to gut up and do it on the following Monday. It was the middle of December, dim even at nine o'clock in the morning. The fires that burned at the top of the steelworks chimneys made an orange constellation above the weak street lamps, which were popping; there was always something wrong with the gas line.

Just outside the back door, he walked straight into the postman, who squeaked. The postman looked annoyed to have made such an unmanly noise, and thrust a piece of paper and a pen into Joe's chest.

'M. Tournier? Sign.'

'What for?' said Joe, who hadn't ordered anything and didn't know anyone. He squinted at the form. There was a line to sign on, and underneath in small transparent letters, *recipient/recipient's responsible citizen*. He hesitated, because he didn't have a signature yet, and just wrote J. Tournier in his normal writing.

'A letter,' the postman said unhelpfully. He did look curious, though. 'They've been holding it for ages at the sorting office. Ninety-three years.'

'What? Why would ...?'

'Because it was to be posted on the date specified and now it's the date specified,' he snapped, and stamped off once Joe had signed, as if giving in to curiosity would have been even worse than the unmanly squeak.

Perplexed, Joe looked down at the letter. The envelope was old enough to have yellowed. He opened it as neatly as he could. Inside was the front page of an old news-sheet. The date on it said 1805. It was one of those very early editions, from just after the Invasion, when they'd first started printing in French and they'd had to keep all the words short and easy because English people hadn't understood yet.

And then there was a postcard. The picture on the front was an etching of a lighthouse. Beneath it, a label in neat copper-plate read,

EILEAN MÒR LIGHTHOUSE
OUTER HEBRIDES

The message on the postcard was short, in looping, old-fashioned writing that Joe could only just read. He had to stare at it for a while, because he never saw written English except in graffiti.

Dearest Joe,
Come home, if you remember.
M

Without meaning to, he looked left and right down the street, and flinched when he saw a gendarme on beat not far away. He swung back inside and snapped the door shut, and had to lean against the edge of the kitchen table for a while. If the postman had stayed and chatted, if he'd seen the postcard with English written on it and a Scottish place on the front, that gendarme would be pounding down the street now.

M; perhaps for Madeline. Except, he knew Madeline *now*, not from a book or a painting a century old.

The lighthouse in the picture was so familiar he was sure he could have named it even without the label. Eilean Mòr; he knew that. He knew the shape of it. And more than that, something in him had been looking for that shape for a long time now.

He turned the postcard over again and touched the handwriting on the back. His instinct was to say that it couldn't possibly have been posted over ninety years ago, and that it was some kind of odd mistake. He was not ninety years old and the Joe Tournier on the envelope couldn't have been him. Half of London was called Joe Tournier. Tournier was what all the old gentry had changed their surnames to, during the Terror. It was the commonest slave name in the Republic now.

But he *knew* that lighthouse.

He took down the business directory from the high shelf. For half an hour, he searched it for anyone who might know anything about a lighthouse: architects, shipping companies, anything. He'd written down a few names and addresses when he came to a M. de Méritens, maker of engines and generators for the running of lighthouses. Not sure what exactly he wanted to ask, just that he had to ask, he set out. He kept the postcard in his pocket. He would have felt safer carrying a bomb, but he couldn't bring himself to leave it behind.

M. de Méritens, originally of the Rue Boursault in Paris and now also of Clerkenwell, held a government contract for every lighthouse in the Republic. It said so on the gilded sign above the workshop – *at the pleasure of His Majesty Napoleon IV* – and on the wall below was a poster. The generators provided electricity for arc lamps of up to 800,000 candlepower, and they were guaranteed for a hundred years.

As Joe approached the main yard, steam poured out of the double gates and sparks rained down where someone was welding. The machines were monstrous, and in the vapour, some of the angles of their pipes and girders looked like elbows or spines. One of them hissed as a boy passed an experimental jet of steam through the pistons, which shot down hard. A shipment of steel floated low over Joe's head, the crane invisible in the smoke. The smell of hot metal and coal was stronger nearer the workshop, and patches of light glowed through where the furnaces were. He asked someone about the main office and was pointed to a glass door.

M. de Méritens himself was behind a broad desk, sifting through a chaos of papers and machine parts with the determined expression of a man who insists he has a system. He was a cloudpuff of a person who must have put on weight recently, because he was still wearing a waistcoat that was too small for him. He was mumbling under his breath, a kind of gravelly bumble that didn't sound like he knew he was doing it.

'Hello,' he said when Joe stepped in. 'Here about the welding job? I'll tell you now, it's yours if you're sober and you speak in sentences.'

'No.' Joe hesitated. 'I have a funny thing to ask. Do you … happen to know this place?' He showed de Méritens the postcard. He kept hold of it, his thumb covering the English message on the back.

De Méritens put on a pair of glasses. 'The Eilean Mòr light, yes. Why is that a funny question?'

'Do you know if anything – has happened there recently? Three months ago, say.'

'Happened? No. It's only just been built. How do you mean? Have you got a complaint? Christ, if you're from the Lighthouse Board—'

'I'm not, I'm not,' Joe said, embarrassed. It was bizarre to talk to someone who spoke to him as though he knew things. He felt like a fraud. 'I'm nothing to do with anything, my name's Joe Tournier. I was found at the Gare du Roi three months ago with no memory of anything until then. But this morning, someone sent me this, and I think I know it.'

De Méritens looked intrigued. 'You're one of those amnesia cases? Remarkable. I don't think I can help you, though, it's … as I say, it's a brand-new light. It was only finished six months ago.'

Joe frowned. 'Brand new. Was there another lighthouse there before this one?'

'No. Why?'

'The …' He had to laugh. 'The postcard is from eighteen hundred and five.'

De Méritens had a brilliant laugh; he actually said *ho ho ho*. 'Someone's having you on, I'm afraid,' he said.

Joe folded the postcard back into his pocket, still smiling the cinders of that first laugh. He'd known it would never be so easy as looking up an address and asking someone. He hadn't expected anything enough to feel too disappointed. 'Well. Thank you anyway, sir, I'll – hang on. Did you say welding job?'

4

Londres, 1900 (two years later)

The Psychical Society sent Joe an invitation to their annual
dinner, again. It was tomorrow.

Apparently the Society, who had heard about his case from
La Salpêtrière, were ever so interested in people with his kind of
epilepsy. They'd invited him last year too, and the year before.
They always sent him a free copy of their quarterly journal.
He couldn't look at them at home. It made Alice think he was
dwelling on things he shouldn't. Instead he stuffed the journals
in the spanner drawer at work to read in tentative snatches over
lunch. Everyone else hid dirty magazines there. The invitation,
though, was too suspect even for that, so it stayed in his pocket,
along with the postcard of Eilean Mòr.

The invitation had sharp corners that kept catching his
hand all week. He didn't know why he'd kept it. The Society
was based in Pont du Cam, so he couldn't go. It was seventy
miles and half a day on the train away, and train tickets cost
too much. And he would have had to come back here on the
midnight train to make it to work on Friday. But he kept
thinking about it. He didn't normally go in for anything that
called itself 'psychical', but the doctor at La Salpêtrière was
no use, and these people did seem like proper scientists. He
had ten of their journals now and everything in them seemed
sensible.

He couldn't believe it had been two and a half years since that morning at the Gare du Roi. He still felt like he was hurrying to catch up with himself and all the things he didn't know.

Two and a half years since the Gare du Roi. Two years and two months since he'd started work for M. de Méritens. Sixteen months since Lily had been born.

It was only just light as Joe walked into the workshop yard, Lily in his arms because he couldn't stand the idea of letting her walk through all the men and machines. Whenever she shifted, the corner of the Society invitation nicked his hip. The whine of saws and welding torches was tempered, sometimes, by the shouts of the stonemasons on the broken dome of St Paul's. When the scaffolding had gone up there last year he'd wondered if they might be rebuilding it, but in fact they were only cleaning, which seemed silly. The Farringdon steelworks would only turn it black again; Blast Furnace Four towered over the ruin only a hundred yards to the north, a skeleton of a rig only just showing through the smoke and the hazy dawn. Fires flickered above the flues. He pointed up at them to make Lily look.

'See? Fairies. Told you.'

She laughed. Joe kissed her springy hair. She looked just like Alice, all chestnut-coloured and perfect. Bundled up in her coat, she was spherical. He opened the workshop door with his elbow.

Inside, there was a snap and a blue flash of light, then a bang and swearing.

'Morning, sir,' Joe said to a heap by the door, which was de Méritens. Having his name above the workshop had never stopped de Méritens working in it, although Joe sometimes thought it might not have been a bad idea. He set Lily down so that he could help.

De Méritens clamped one hand around his to haul himself up, which gave Joe a brutal static shock.

34

'Ow, Christ—'

'Yes, morning,' de Méritens said cheerfully. Then, 'Is that a child? Good God! Where's your *wife*?'

Joe was caught between snorting and feeling offended. He wasn't brilliant with children, but the way M. Saint-Marie and M. de Méritens behaved, anyone would have thought they were worried he would get confused and eat her.

'She'll be by soon,' lied Joe. Alice was on the day shift at the hospital. She couldn't admit to being married there, so she couldn't take Lily, or ask around for anyone who might be willing to look after her. In a way which made Joe worry about them, the senior doctors and nurses seemed to think that married women shouldn't work, as though husbands were nervy creatures one shouldn't leave unsupervised for too long. Middle-class people, Alice explained, hadn't been in the world enough to know anything, and it was best to smile and nod and ignore them.

Usually Lily stayed with M. Saint-Marie in the daytime, but he went to his bridge club on Wednesdays.

Joe scooped Lily up again. She opened and closed her hand, which was how she waved.

'How come you're not in Paris, sir?' he asked, hoping he didn't sound too strained. Everyone liked M. de Méritens, but everyone did also look forward to Tuesday and Wednesday, when he was generally in France. He didn't have to be, as far as Joe could tell; the Paris office ran itself, but the brand-new tunnel crossing between London and Paris was de Méritens' favourite thing in the world, and he always came back thrumming with the wonders of modern engineering, and exactly the same story about how the mathematics behind its building had been so accurate that when the two teams of diggers – one from Dover, one from Calais – had met in the middle, they'd only missed each other by a foot. Everyone suspected a mistress in France.

De Méritens waved back at Lily, then seemed to remember what he was saying. 'I'm not in Paris: no, I'm not. Because. We've had a letter about an engine from the Lighthouse Board …' He trailed off, like he often did, into mumbling. He could keep up an incomprehensible background buzz for hours at a time. Joe had had to teach himself not to listen. De Méritens was fishing around his desk now.

'… coffin for two hundred francs.'

'Pardon?' Joe said.

De Méritens didn't hear. 'Here we are. An engine has broken down. They want an engineer out there.' He paused, reading over the letter again. It was watermarked, and the hazy light behind him filtered through the government's eagle crest at the top. 'It's urgent. It's on a shipping route and we must send some-one soon, or we'll hit the winter and the sea freezes out there.'

Joe frowned. 'Where is it?'

'The Outer Hebrides.'

Frost went down his spine. 'That's the Eilean Mòr light.'

'Quite.' De Méritens looked uncomfortable. 'I've got to send Atelier, but he's already cross with me because I got drunk at his wife's party – do me a favour and break it to him, will you? You're all …' he motioned at Joe generally '… charm-ing. And you've got your special charm baby. So it should be easy, hey? Just, um – tell him he'll have to leave on Friday. Back by mid-March. Long haul, but the sea freezes, you see. And it is rather foolish to have an unmanned lighthouse over winter. Our machines would generally look after themselves, but the temperatures up there – that's steel-fissuring cold.' He pattered his fingertips over his own stomach, which was his way of saying that he was pretty certain he had made an inarguable point, but then he crumpled. 'You're laughing,' he said defeatedly.

Joe was. 'I am not charming enough to persuade M. Atelier that he wants to go to an island off Scotland for three months.'

He was laughing, too, partly to cover over just how much his entire soul had snapped to attention. His free hand clamped of its own accord over the Eilean Mòr postcard in his pocket. This was it, the reason he had wanted to work here; the chance to go, to see if there was anything in the north that he remembered, or maybe even to find the person who had sent the postcard, why it was a hundred years old, all of it. Maybe Madeline was still there. If she had waited – he didn't even know. The idea of seeing the lighthouse had so much gravity he already felt like he was falling towards it.

He had to concentrate to keep smiling. If he could just make it sound casual, it might work. 'Can I go instead?'

De Méritens took a breath, stopped, then tried again. 'Can you what?'

The postcard was much softer and more dog-eared than the Psychical Society invitation. Every morning, he thought he should get rid of it. Carrying written English around was stupid. Every morning, he put it off.

He hugged Lily nearer, because holding her made him feel obscurely protected. 'I don't know if you remember, but I came here asking you about that lighthouse. I ... would like to go and see it, if it's all right to send me. I passed the keeper's exam,' he added, his insides screwing tight with anticipation of being brushed aside. It wasn't normal practice to send out an ex-slave. Ex-slave sounded a lot like 'unqualified' to most people, even if that ex-slave had passed all the same exams as everyone else and spent a lot of his time quietly talking the citizen engineers through the harder mathematics.

But de Méritens really did look like he was thinking about it. 'Listen,' he said. 'Before you decide one way or another, there's something else. That lighthouse shouldn't be unmanned. It should have three keepers. But they're missing.'

Joe lifted his eyebrows. 'Was it the Saints?'

'I said that,' de Méritens said, a touch defensive. 'But the Board says not. It's the Outer Hebrides, there's bugger all there. No one to terrorise, nothing to steal. The Saints concentrate on the docks at Newcastle. Other side of the country.' He paused. 'Given all that, are you sure you want to volunteer, on your salary? I can't promote you. We'll pay expenses and all that, but ...' His eyes flickered over Lily.

'No, I want to go.' Joe's heart was straining against his breast-bone as though it thought it could go by itself even if the rest of him didn't. 'I know it sounds mad, but ... I don't know. If I see it, I might remember something.'

De Méritens gave him a half-sympathetic, half-wary look. It was a familiar one; Alice aimed it at him all the time. People could see it was a nasty thing to live with, damn all memory of anything prior to a couple of years ago, but it made Joe different, in an unsettling way. He was living the thing that people feared, and they worried it might rub off on them.

'Well. I won't forget this, pun intended. It's very good of you to volunteer, whatever the reason. You're a braver man than me. Mme de Méritens would give me hell.'

Joe stopped himself before he could say aloud that Alice wouldn't mind one way or another, because he would sound like he was complaining, even though he wasn't. The idea of living with a twenty-four-year-old who was in love with him was much worse than being married to one who perceived him more as a piece of useful furniture. If she had been in love with him, he would have felt terrible for not loving her back. He couldn't. Part of his mind was always waiting for someone else, whoever he had left behind, Madeline, or ... whoever.

'Alice is happy by herself,' he said.

De Méritens nodded and faded into his background buzz as he looked over his desk for the paperwork.

Lily twisted to watch sparks fly down from a welding torch. Joe put his nose against her hair. He could take her with him. Alice wouldn't mind; she wasn't keen on motherhood. And then even if there was nothing for him at Eilean Mòr, it wouldn't matter, because Lily would love a lighthouse, and it was a real chance to get her used to being around machinery.

Joe had strictly unspoken hopes about Lily. He wanted his own workshop one day, even if it was just fixing bits and pieces. Then he could employ whoever he liked, and then Lily could have a trade.

It stayed unspoken because he was frightened Alice would call it exactly what it was: idiotic. If he didn't manage to open his own workshop, he would have wasted Lily's childhood on something no one would ever employ her for. It would be better for her to be a midwife, like Alice, or a seamstress, something steady, and not surrounded by territorial men who would happily beat up a woman for getting above herself. But the hill Joe would die on was that any chance not to deliver babies for a living was worth it. Midwifery was horrendous. He knew that. He'd delivered Lily. That had gouged harrows through his soul in a way no exploding engine ever would. She deserved a choice, at least.

It all sounded very noble if he said it like that, but the other reason it all stayed unspoken was that he knew bloody well it was really just a way of keeping her with him. Lily was the only person in the world for whom he was just himself, not the ruin of who he used to be. And she showed every sign of quite liking him. That was a stupid, simple thing, but it was everything. Half the dismay he felt at the idea of letting her work at the godforsaken hospital was that it would mean she left him behind.

He came back to himself when he realised de Méritens' background bumble was coming up to normal speech again.

'Can you imagine, living in a lighthouse in the Outer Hebrides?' de Méritens said, shaking his head. 'I bet the poor bastards did a bunk. Place sounds one human sacrifice away from gibbering barbarism.'

'Well, if I come back wearing skulls and a kilt you'll know,' Joe smiled, because he liked de Méritens and his tactlessness.

As de Méritens pottered off, looking happy, a man with a long coat and a straight bearing walked through the testing yard.

Joe's heart lurched so hard it hurt. He set Lily down and ran out after him.

He felt the epilepsy coming. It had happened often in the last two years, but it wasn't amnesia any more. It was euphoria. His chest felt like it was full of sunlight, so much it was confusing to look down and not see it beaming through his ribcage. He had to push one hand over his mouth, because it was making him cry. The ordinary world was only a curtain, which had been twitched aside. He could still see the engines and the yard gates, but they seemed gauzy. Only the man was really there.

'Hey – hey.' Joe caught his arm. He was shaking with happiness. 'It's you. What are you doing here, what ...'

But then the man turned around, and he was only a stranger and Joe couldn't remember for his life who he had thought he was.

'God, I'm sorry. I thought you were ... someone else.'

The man looked amicable enough and went on his way. Joe touched his own chest, trying to snatch at the memory as it trickled away, but it was gone. The testing yard was just the yard. The world wasn't a curtain but the world, and whatever he had seen through it had vanished. He had to stand still through an anvil crash of disappointment. It happened every time, and every vision was the same, but it didn't come any easier with familiarity.

It was the fourth time in two months. They were getting more frequent.

He hadn't told anyone. There wasn't money for any more doctors.

'Tournier, you *fucking idiot*, *what* is a baby doing out here by her*fucking*self!'

He swung back and saw it without sound, though the welder was still shouting at him. Lily had come out after him. She had stopped right in front of one of the train engines to look at the welding, square between the test tracks and completely out of sight of the mechanics who had just begun to ease the whole thing forward in a mist of steam. It was inching towards her, too slowly for her to have noticed.

He snatched her up. The engine hissed past them, and in the future that hadn't happened, he saw the beak shape of the air-breaker knock her over, and then a shattering noise he would never forget, even though, really, he had never heard it. He didn't realise he had been backing away until he bumped into the wall of the coal shed. It was corrugated iron, so it juddered and whooped.

Lily was staring at him, shocked to have been grabbed like that.

'Don't put her down or I'll punch you in the face,' the welder snarled. He was shaking too. As he spoke, he slung a mallet so hard onto the floor that it bounced twice, even though it must have weighed as much as a cannonball. Lily jumped.

Joe jolted back from him, sorry and furious at the same time. 'Jesus, you're scaring her!'

'*I'm* scaring her? Get her *out* of here! You *stupid bastard*!'

He hurried to the gate and stood by the road, waiting to calm down, but it didn't come and he still couldn't remember, even under the steam-powered panic pressure, who he had thought the man was. He never could.

5

Joe lay looking at the gas lamp, which had been stuttering lately. It smelled chemical even when it was off. They kept the window open now, just in case, and so the long attic room was always cold.

The headboard bumped the wall. He had to concentrate not to wince. M. Saint-Marie could hear downstairs, he was sure. Alice pushed her hands under his shirt, pressing down on his collarbones. It added nastily to the feeling that there was a breeze-block right over his heart. He tried to think about something else.

He'd gone to St Paul's on the way home, still shaken up about Lily and the engine. The inside of the cathedral had been loud with the work on the dome, and through the weave of the scaffolding, dull light from the steelworks' lamps came down in tines. Pinned to the confession booths were printed signs that said, *Confession available between the hours of 3.30 p.m. and 6 p.m.* He was too late for it, which was a relief. M. Saint-Marie always wanted him to go, but Joe couldn't look Père Philippe in the face these days.

He wished Alice would hurry up.

The cathedral had new electrical wiring. The dean had gone a bit far; the shrine of Maria had an electric halo now. But Joe liked the new prayer-candle set-up. Instead of lighting a taper and candle, you put a coin through a slot and an electric candle lit automatically. He'd put in a centime and prayed, like always, that he wasn't going mad.

Alice stopped and sighed. There was a tiny moment when she saw him properly and looked sad, because he wasn't Toby. She had never said that, but he knew it was true. He had spent a long time studying photographs, and he and Toby looked uncannily alike, or at least, they did if you could see past Joe's being older and smaller. It must have been pronounced in twilight, because twilight was always when Alice seemed to catch the similarity strongly enough to want to see if he was like Toby to touch as well as to look at.

He wished she wouldn't, but he wished for a lot of things and you couldn't go round getting your own way all the time.

'Is there any kind of insurance?' she said, which was only a continuation of the previous conversation. 'For if anything happens to you out there?'

'No. But I'll be all right.'

She hmmed as she got up. 'You've got to wonder what it's like up there, haven't you,' she said pensively. 'No slavery. Women allowed to work properly. Everyone with their own choices. They can't be how the papers say they are.'

Joe sat up slowly, not wanting to seem in a rush, though like always, he felt filthy. Alice smiled to say she was only complaining, not trying to say he shouldn't go, and disappeared into the next room. The sound of running water exchanged places with her. He looked sideways at the floor while he righted his clothes and looped his scarf back on, and then gloves, so that he wouldn't be able to feel anything.

Being married to someone he didn't know had been fine at first. They'd been polite to each other and kept everything meticulously tidy, and that was it. But then Alice had started to see Toby in him. He'd said no; even the idea had scared him in a way he couldn't trace. It would be betraying whoever he had left behind, and it wouldn't be any less a betrayal just because he'd forgotten who that was, but it was more visceral even than that.

She'd told Père Philippe, who had dragged Joe to the doctor for pills and an examination, and then all but supervised. And then afterwards Joe had had to go outside and cry for a while.

He couldn't understand why. Alice was beautiful, and he should have been glad, but all he felt was dirty. He had tried to explain. She'd been furious. She even asked him coldly if he just hated women, if he couldn't bear to be near one. That had made him want to scream, because she would have punched him if he'd accused her of hating all men just because she didn't want to sleep with one in particular. He had wanted to know how *she'd* feel if someone she'd only met a few times had demanded sex and called in the Church when she said no. There were whole societies for women who objected to that.

He didn't say that. Père Philippe said that it was unnatural in a man, and anyway, you had to want to do it in order to do it, right? Joe had had to murder the urge to say that actually, it could be pretty bloody involuntary, which you would know if you weren't professionally celibate.

But more than any of that, he stayed quiet because none of it was Alice's fault. Toby was dead and she missed him, and she missed him alone, because Joe couldn't remember him. It must have felt like being abandoned. Whatever Joe thought about it, they *were* married, she was *his* wife, before God, and he owed her anything that could make it better, even if it was only better for ten minutes. His own bizarre feelings on the subject were irrelevant.

He realised he hadn't said anything yet. 'No. I doubt they are.'

'It just makes me angrier, the older I get. I don't understand why the government can't just see that if they admitted the Saints are what they are – this … amazing tiny shard of England like it used to be before the invasion – we wouldn't be so bloody furious all the time. If they just said, yes, they're not *terrorists*, or pirates, or criminals; they're the last of a proper nation with its own laws and those laws are different to ours ... are you listening?'

All Joe could think was that she sounded young. 'It doesn't matter if you're furious when you can't vote.'

She leaned around the door. She had taken her hair out of its daytime knot, and now it was a tawny halo. Anyone normal couldn't have kept his hands off her. 'We, Joe, not *you*. It's your life too; you might like to start giving a fuck what happens in it.'

He nodded and didn't say that it still didn't feel like his life.

'Speaking of your life, do you know anyone who can look after Lily on Wednesdays?'

He looked up. 'No, I'll take her with me.'

Alice gave him the look she usually deployed when she caught him gazing at someone imaginary. 'To a lighthouse where the sea freezes, where the previous keepers might have been killed.'

He frowned. 'I – thought you'd be happy for the break.'

'You're insane,' she said factually. 'You're not taking a baby to Scotland.'

'I'm not insane,' he said, struggling, because he knew she didn't mean it to stab so deep as it had. 'It will be fine, we'll be fine—'

'No,' she said. 'She stays here.'

'But you ...' He trailed off, because he couldn't think of any tactful way to say that Alice had never put Lily to bed, never given her a bath; that they both knew Alice resented Lily for not being Toby's, in an involuntary way that clearly upset her as much as it did Joe. 'She doesn't know you very well,' he tried.

'Well, she'll have to get used to me, won't she. Because she damn well isn't going off to Scotland with you. Joe, come on. You don't understand the world enough to take her into it. You

45

trust anyone who's kind to you. You can't do that, not with a little girl. I don't mind the workshop, the people there keep an eye on you, but not Scotland.'

There was nothing he could say to that. She was right.

He got up and washed when she came out of the bathroom, looked in on Lily, who was asleep, then went to sit in the kitchen, which was really just the far side of the bedroom. The floor there was just the boards, so he could see down into the study below through the gaps. M. Saint-Marie must have heard every word Joe and Alice said, but he had never complained.

He leaned forward against one elbow and held the other shoulder, which was sore. It took him a while to notice that he was digging his nails hard into the space above his collarbone and that it hurt. When he stopped, he could feel the crescent marks.

Three months without Lily. God, he was stupid. He should tell de Méritens he couldn't go after all.

Only, he had to. He had to, or he'd go mad with not knowing. He would sink deeper and deeper into this certainty that nothing was right and he didn't belong. He would keep racing after visions until one day he chased them in front of a carriage and killed himself.

'Moo,' said Lily, who was biting the rail of her crib and looking like she might explode if she didn't tell her joke. She flapped her arms.

'A flying cow?' he smiled, glad she was awake. Alice had gone to bed, curled up in a ball. '*Are* there flying cows?'

Lily grinned and hid. She wasn't too good at hiding, because she had a perpetual snuffle from the smog. He pretended to have lost her and he hunted around, then knelt down to settle her again once he'd found her under the blanket. He stayed there a good while after she'd gone to sleep, his back against his own bed and one hand on her chest to feel her ribs lift and fall. He'd sewn a picture of a duck on her nightshirt and the stitches were already faded, because she kept stroking it as if it were a real duck. Looking at her made him feel clean.

He heard that crack again, the sound of her going under the engine, clear as any other memory for all it hadn't happened.

Maybe three months away from her was for the best.

Like always, he jerked awake at quarter past four in the morning with raging panic kneeling on his chest. He sat up and lit a cigarette, the base of his skull resting on the steel bar at the top of the bedstead. Nothing helped, but smoking was something to do.

The night-time panics had come on after that first epileptic attack at the Gare du Roi and never improved. Aching, he wished, again, that the man from the hallucination would reappear. Nothing was forthcoming. The purple electric lights from the club over the road flashed on the gloss paint on the skirting board.

He felt sick of the way the epilepsy infected everything. He left a baby girl to be run over by steam engines, he'd chosen a whole career because of a postcard, he pined for people he didn't know and couldn't bring himself to love the ones he did. It was cancerous.

A flash from the club caught on the gilt invitation poking from his coat pocket where it hung from the door. He could just make out *RSVP Prof. E. Sidgwick, Secretary.* If he set out in the morning and went north to Eilean Mòr straight from Pont du Cam, he would be able to go. He could find out why they were so interested in epileptic amnesia. Even better if they could help.

He wished Lily would wake up so he could have something to do, but she had slept like a rock since she'd been ten weeks old and now she scowled if you disturbed her before eight.

He calmed down after a couple of hours, and like he had done every few months, he dreamed about the man from his visions. He was always in the same place. It was a beach, cold and misty. The shore was full of old flotsam – bits of rope that had turned the same colour as the dull pebbles, pale spars – and black weed. The man was waiting on the tideline up ahead, and though there was nothing at all to say so, the dream always came with the perfect certainty that he was waiting for Joe.

6

Pont du Cam, 1900

Pont du Cam was much colder than Londres. The land changed on the way, from hills and dips to flat, flat fen. The fields were flooded. There were no trees, no walls; only drowned hedgerows. When the train pulled in, the station looked run-down, and in places the water had puddled between the tracks. The whole place looked like it had only been reclaimed lately from the fen, which was doing its best to take everything back again.

Joe had never been this far from home. As he stepped down on to the platform, he expected the station guard to demand to see his freedom papers and then declare that for whatever reason he wasn't allowed to travel, but no one stopped him. The engine blew steam around disembarking passengers. People here looked much less smart than they did in Londres. Londres might have been the Black City, but it was alive, and busy, and full of people like de Méritens, with their expensive suits and brisk walks. Here, there was no one like that. Everyone was very English; all lumpy bones and clayish skin, wearing heavy shapeless clothes and the graven expressions of people who still had miles to go before they could sit down. In his properly tailored coat – he still couldn't remember where it was from and he still missed the tartan lining – Joe stood out.

Wooden houses lined the station road, covered in graffiti so thick there were layers of it, like it had grown and died and grown again, a sort of ivy of paint; old English flags, scrawls of GOD SAVE THE KING, gang tags, and just like in Londres, *Where is everyone?*

From every roof protruded a short pole with a scrap of calico tied to it. The scraps were yellow, red, and blue. Yellow for a place that sold beer, red for a spare bed, blue for food. M. Saint-Marie had told him not to stop for any of it, looking like he did.

'Like what?' Joe had said, not understanding.

'Valuable.'

He walked well away from the house fronts.

There were women outside, a good few of them, older ladies, selling meat on skewers and waving them at passers-by. Fried chicken hearts, tripe in paper cups. Behind them, children and younger women sat propped against the walls of the houses, with baskets of vegetables arranged on the pavement in front of them. Potatoes and swedes mainly, which they weighed out on rope scales hanging on hooks from the window ledges. At the cooking stalls, doomed chickens cocked their heads and scratched inside little cages. The air smelled of animals and damp, and hessian sacking. Discarded vegetables floated in the puddles.

Joe had memorised the route so that he wouldn't have to keep stopping and looking at his map; that, said M. Saint-Marie, was asking to be mugged or worse. Town was to the right. It was about a mile, but M. Saint-Marie had forbidden him to take a Pont du Cam cab. There were all kinds of stories and they all ended up face down in the river.

Parts of the way were flooded. People had made ramshackle bridges with old crates. There were no street lights. Children with lamps skittered to and fro instead. A whole firefly swarm of them shone from the shell of what had once been a post office, where they must have had their headquarters. In ghost letters still visible on the brickwork, probably upwards of a hundred years old now, the facade said in English, *Cambridge Sorting Office.* Joe smiled at that. Pont du Cam; obviously it meant Cambridge, but he'd never translated it in his head.

The streets between the colleges were tiny. All the signposts were still in English, even though on the map the names of the colleges were the modern ones. The Sidgwicks – there were two – were professors at Napoleon College, and he'd assumed it wouldn't be hard to find an entire college, but he got lost twice. It took him a while to work out that Napoleon College used to be Queen's.

The address Mme Sidgwick had given him wasn't only hard to find, but hard to get to. Their part of the college looked straight onto the river, the front door only a foot above the water. The invitation said to show it to the man who rented out punts on the millpond. When he did, the man saw him on to the far end of a river tour with five students polite enough to offer him some of their beer, and who laughed when the riverman stopped to let Joe climb out on to the broad step that served as a landing bay. He knocked, then waited with his back to the door.

On the opposite bank, the willow trees stirred and a pair of swans settled down near the roots. There must have been a lot of birds, because the grass was thin and full of down. Along from him, bay windows that came to Turkish points painted their own shapes in light on the water.

The door opened inward and a woman in a rich blue dress smiled.

'You must be Monsieur Tournier,' she said. 'You've come at exactly the right time, the place is populated but not crowded. I'm Eleanor Sidgwick.' She put her hand out and he didn't understand why for a second, then did and shook it. 'May I ask if you speak English?'

'Yes. I do.'

'Because we're having something of a revivalist fad. Some of the linguistics men are getting quite tendentious about it.'

Joe frowned. 'Are they sure the gendarmes won't think you're recruiting for the Saints?'

'Yes, now you see, you and I are in exact agreement, but I can't say that because then I'd seem ignorant and not in support of the Cause.' She must have seen him tip back, because she touched his arm. 'Not that kind of cause, I'm being facetious. Good heavens, is that bag all you've brought? I thought you said in your telegram you were going to Scotland after this?'

'I am, but I didn't want to carry too much on the train. Um – Mrs Sidgwick,' he said, and it felt rude to say Mrs and not Madame. 'Why am I here?'

'Mainly for dinner. Come in, let's find my husband. He wanted to meet you.'

'I see,' said Joe, wondering if he ever would, but then decided that if he didn't find out it would be funnier when he told Alice.

The house was as interesting inside as it was out. A stone staircase coiled up into the dark, the banisters carved into little columns like a diagonal cloister. One was an oak tree, with brown glass beads for acorns. The contrast between that, which must have been an echo of how the whole university had once been, and the abject poverty outside was bizarre. Joe hadn't known that places like this still existed.

'You teach here?' he asked, amazed.

She laughed. 'Oh, God, no. All the old college buildings are hotels now, this one included. The teaching is done at the faculties – all very ordinary, I'm afraid. We've rented this place for the night.' She led him through to the next room, a wide space where clusters of people in gowns and evening jackets were talking in the animated way of friends who didn't often get the chance to see each other. In passing, he heard someone say, 'And my *ninth* point ...'

'Oh, there's Henry,' she added, and rose on to her toes to wave.

The other Professor Sidgwick was a handsome man whose hand enveloped Joe's when he shook it.

'Mr Tournier, what a pleasure. Yours is a fascinating case, it really is.'

'Is it,' said Joe, feeling strange to be 'mister', and to hear so many well-dressed people speaking English. He had an urge to tell them to stop being so silly. You couldn't *do* nice conversation in English. English was for yelling at omnibus drivers and getting drunk behind dodgy clubs.

The dinner bell rang.

'I thought we said eight?' Mrs Sidgwick said.

The butler ghosted up. 'If Madame wishes to use College slaves for the occasion, Madame will have to put up with *College* time,' he said, in what sounded to Joe like rather deliberate French, with the hint of an eyebrow at just what he thought about all the English. It was a relief to find a normal person in among everything else. Joe wanted to hurry away with him. 'Suspect they've only the one setting on the old clockwork. But I shall usher guests through as they arrive.'

'Usher,' said Sidgwick.

'Usher, my dear,' the butler said firmly, then glided away.

'Fair enough. Can't complain; on we go, everybody.'

In the dining room was the finest spread Joe had ever seen.

Sidgwick pulled out a chair for his wife and put Joe between them. Four slaves appeared from a narrow side door to serve. They were all matching blond men. Among the plates and serving bowls, flowers cascaded.

Joe looked along the table and realised uncomfortably that some people were still watching him. 'I feel like a new giraffe at the zoo,' he said.

'Well,' said Mrs Sidgwick, but her husband talked over her and she looked amused into her salad.

'We'd like to talk to you about your epilepsy.'

'Right,' said Joe, not seeing what that could possibly have to do with these people. Some of them, having noticed the College slaves, were talking now about the pedigree of their own.

'We'd like to know what you remember about the attack you had two years ago.'

'If you don't mind talking about it,' Mme Sidgwick put in, more towards Sidgwick than Joe himself.

Sidgwick dipped his head. 'Yes, of course, pardon me.'

'How do you know about it?'

'You were in the papers. Would you prefer not …?'

'No, it's all right,' Joe said. 'I … was found in Londres, at the Gare du Roi. I don't remember getting there. I didn't remember anything on the day, except my name. After a few hours I realised I knew general things; like, I knew how to read, how to speak English and French, I sort of knew Londres geography. But nothing specific. I still don't remember anything from before that day. The doctor says it was a seizure. Funny but not … this kind of funny, I'd have thought,' he said, nodding down the table.

'No, no, no, it is *quite* our kind of funny. You say you were confused. Our information is that … pardon me, but that in fact you were in an asylum. You swore that you were married to someone who didn't turn out to be your real wife.'

'How do you know that?'

'We asked for the files,' Sidgwick said blankly. 'You're a slave, it's all quite easy to come by, there's none of the usual medical privacy nonsense. We looked into buying you, but then your service tenure was up and it was too late.' He seemed annoyed.

Joe felt on edge. If Sidgwick still wanted him, really wanted him, there was nothing but social convention to stop the man slapping a blue band on Joe's sleeve, taking away his papers and claiming to have found him wandering about outside the tobacconist's for anyone to pick up.

'Henry, you're making him nervous,' Mrs Sidgwick said.

'I'm what?'

'Ignore him,' she said to Joe. 'Do you remember the name you gave to the doctor?'

Joe had to struggle to remember what they'd been talking about. 'Yes, I – but it was a false memory. They said at the asylum that epileptic paramnesia is common,' he said, looking between them. He wanted to stop. The sooner Sidgwick decided he was boring, the better. 'Why is it interesting? What's it to do with all this?'

'It is relatively common. In fact, it's happened to everyone in this room,' Sidgwick said. 'Every one of these people experienced exactly what you've just described, but usually for a much shorter time. An hour, two hours. The same intense disorientation, feeling convinced that their families were not their families, only to recover later the same day. So far we've found it affects men and women equally. It's nothing to do with gendered neuroses or any nonsense like that. Some people have even suggested that the same phenomena would explain erratic periods of behaviour in dogs.'

'R ... ight, good.' It did make Joe feel better to hear again that it wasn't a unique piece of insanity, but not much. 'Am I missing something? You're the Psychical Society, not the Psychiatric Society.'

Mrs Sidgwick smiled. 'Some of the stories link up.'

'What?' he said slowly. He felt as if she had thrown a pebble at him and, instead of bouncing off, it had gone straight through, and now it clattered as it fell down inside him. 'Link up how?'

She sat forward. 'The reason we contacted you is that we've been playing games of mix and match. We invited people to write to the Society about their experiences. When the letters came in, we found that occasionally, the same name would appear. Of course, only a few people wrote in. But then we started to visit asylums, looking for cases of this syndrome, and we stumbled on yours. The name you gave, for the woman you thought you were married to. Madeline Shale. Is that right?'

Joe didn't say anything, because he had no memory of having given the doctor a surname. He must have held that in mind only for a little while, just like the memory of the man from the railway station, the one who had taken him to hospital. It was such a tiny thing, but it brought on a blast of despair. He could have forgotten God knew what since then, without even noticing.

'Now, we had an Albert d'Vigny write to us, saying that for an entire morning he was convinced he was really called Albert Shale and he had a sister called Madeline, who had gone missing along with her son and no one was looking for her. It happened to him about five weeks before it happened to you. He's that gentleman over there. If it's the same Madeline, he would have been your brother-in-law. Do you recognise him?'

Joe looked. 'No,' he said quietly.

Her son.

His son too?

'No, and he didn't recognise you. But, same name. A woman of the same age, from the same place; it's simply too much of a coincidence that you produced identical information.'

'It – well, we probably both read something in the same newspaper.'

'No. There's never been any such person. We checked newspapers, parish records, we spoke to Albert's parents. She never was.'

Joe stared down at his wine. 'Are you telling me it was – real?'

'Oh, yes,' she said, as if it wasn't important. 'What we find of particular interest in your case is that you felt it far more, and much later than the main cluster of cases. Everyone else remembered their real lives again after a few hours. But your memory never came back. At all?'

'No.'

Sidgwick adjusted his glasses. 'Because the thing is, you see – what all this implies is that something very particular happened, and that it happened in or around the end of October two years ago. That's when the first set of these episodes cluster, almost to the day. There have been waves of it since but not much to speak of before.'

'What could do that?'

He saw them both shift, now that they were having to say it aloud and unshrouded in academic language. He understood now why the dons were pushing to use English. Science words were French words. English was a test to see if an idea made sense without decoration.

'We don't know.' Mrs Sidgwick paused. 'Nothing like it has ever been recorded before.'

'Your case is unique,' her husband said. He spoke like he was talking to students, slightly too loudly. 'Something was different, for you. Either you yourself are far more susceptible, or the circumstances were different somehow.'

Joe felt drunk, but he hadn't taken more than a sip of wine. His eyes kept slipping to the man across the room, Albert. This time they slipped at the same time Albert's did. All he saw was the blankness that must have been in his own face too. There was nothing familiar about the man.

'Do you remember anything?' Sidgwick was saying. 'Anything at all, of what you were told were false memories?'

'No – I'm sorry.' He hesitated. The man in the visions was too precious to hand over like an old library book. More than that, he did not want to give Sidgwick any more reason to imagine it was worth talking to him. 'Look, I'm sorry, but I don't understand what you're trying to say.'

Mrs Sidgwick put her hand on his arm. A flicker of alarm went across her face when Joe flinched. 'What we're saying is that the missing people must have gone somewhere.'

Joe had a strange, building urgency deep in his chest, the same as the kind that woke him up every night at four o'clock. 'Where?' he asked helplessly.

'We have no idea.' She was watching him too closely. 'But the scale of all this is astronomic. These epileptic episodes – or what's being called epilepsy – are common. We estimate about one in four people in England has experienced it. Which means we might be looking at hundreds of thousands of people missing, just like Madeline. Our counterparts in Chartres have collected similar data all through France too.'

Joe nodded. 'But they existed. In some ...' He didn't know how to finish. In some other place, so close to this one that people could remember it.

'Yes.' She was quiet for a moment. 'We have no idea what's happened, none at all. We were wondering ... if there was anything else you've remembered since you spoke to the doctors?'

Joe shook his head. He looked down at the reflection of his own eyes in his wine, and wondered if the man who waited by the sea had been real once too.

Or perhaps was still.

7

Scotland, 1900

The border was just north of Glasgow. The train stopped, and everyone had to queue at the checkpoints. Joe put his bag down while he waited, because no one was moving yet. A Senegalese soldier in the marines' winter uniform paced by, scanning the new arrivals.

Joe hoped that the marines were making the traditional rotation round random parts of the Republic – but the longer he let himself think about it, the more conspicuous it seemed, and the more logical to man the border with regiments who were unlikely to know the people they sometimes had to shoot. The same soldier pulled a pair of boys out of the queue. They hadn't been talking; he couldn't tell what they'd done. They were too sensible to argue. All three disappeared into a side office.

At the checkpoint, another soldier looked over Joe's papers, then asked with a grim politeness to see his letter from de Méritens. Joe kept quiet while it was handed back to another man, with more chevrons on his uniform. Like he'd known they would, they took him aside, but not to the same office as the boys a minute ago. He couldn't tell if that was good or bad.

'You're English,' the officer said, in that old-fashioned Senegal French that made them all sound so courtly.

'Yes, sir.'

'Freedman. How long have you been out of indenture?'

'Two years.'

'Explain the purpose of your visit again.'

The letter had already explained, but Joe nodded and explained again. Behind him, another soldier was looking through his bag. The lighthouse postcard was hidden in the lining. He couldn't believe he'd done that. It was beyond stupid to try and get that across the border, and he'd be arrested if anyone found it. That would be *possession of a document in handwritten English*, which was newspaper and government code for *in the Saints*. But he still hadn't been able to throw it away.

'Is it usual, for an English person to become an electrical engineer?'

Joe arranged his expression into the blandest he could make it. Alice had made him practise questions like this before he left, to make sure he wouldn't get flustered. He closed his hand round his rosary, to make sure the man had noticed he was wearing one. He had put a Latin bible in his bag, at the top. The soldier behind him had found it, and now he was flicking through to see if anything would fall out.

'There are plenty of English engineers, sir. Often we begin as welders.'

The officer studied him. His uniform coat had a fur trim. Joe was starting to feel the cold, even inside. 'Very specific thing, lighthouse engines. What else does the de Méritens workshop make?'

Joe swallowed. It was a famous enough workshop to be common knowledge. 'Locomotive engines. Artillery.'

'Are you involved in the production of artillery?'

'No.'

'Have you ever been?'

'No,' he lied. 'Never.'

The soldier behind him finally finished searching his bag. Joe tried not to look too relieved.

'Tell me once again about the problem at the lighthouse.'

Joe took a deep, slow breath. 'The lighthouse is very remote; it's off the coast of Lewis and Harris, on an island called Eilean Mòr. The lamp has been extinguished. It shouldn't be, not at this time of year. The locals went out to look. They found that the lighthouse keepers are missing, and that the lamp couldn't be turned on again. Someone then reported the problem to the Lighthouse Board. The Board administers all the lighthouses in the Republic, but the de Méritens workshop builds all the machinery, so when there's a technical fault, M. de Méritens sends a mechanic out. In this case, I'm supposed to fix the fault and stay at the lighthouse for the winter, as a temporary keeper.'

'Surely lighthouse keeping and mechanical work are quite different.'

'No, sir. All lighthouse keepers are qualified to maintain and repair lighthouse engines, and all of M. de Méritens' mechanics are qualified lighthouse keepers.'

'Why aren't they sending someone local, then? There must be qualified people in Glasgow.'

'I'm cheaper.'

'Why's that?'

'I'm a freedman, not a citizen. I'm on minimum wage.'

It went on and on, for another three hours and well after he'd lost any hope of getting through. There had been a man who was meant to meet him on the other side, with onward passage arranged on a ship up to the islands, but it was hard to imagine he would have waited so long. The questions stopped and they left Joe alone in the little room. The dark came down and the powerful searchlights came on. He saw one of them swing to the right. Then gunshots. He tried not to think about it.

A new trainload of people arrived. Doctors; the checkpoint soldiers let them straight through. They must have been going to the regiments fighting further east. He watched the train pull away, back to Glasgow. In another twenty minutes, the station was silent and empty again.

Joe sank forward against his arms on the table edge and shut his eyes. The lights were too bright. He saw greenish stars behind his eyelids. Carefully, he reconstructed the image of the man waiting for him by the sea. It had some borrowed calm in it.

He wished the Sidgwicks hadn't told him it might have been real. The thought that the man had been there, really there, only to be lost now, hurt much more than imagining he was just a thing Joe's misfiring brain had made for itself. Madeline too. But he couldn't picture her any more.

A younger soldier opened the door. Joe pulled his sleeve over his eyes. The shift must have changed; the man was much more junior than the original officer.

'You're staying overnight for more questioning. Come with me.'

Joe felt sick. 'I have to go. Please. I'm going to lose my job if I don't get to this lighthouse.'

'Not my problem,' the young man said.

Joe pulled out half the money he had for the rest of the whole three months. 'I'm not trying to say I have no respect for your position, I do. I wouldn't ask you for anything like this without paying properly.'

The young man looked happy and Joe realised, feeling stupid, that he had been waiting for an offer. 'All right. I'll shoot you if you breathe a word to the colonel.'

'I understand.'

He let Joe take his bag back, then showed him along a dull corridor, to a small door. When he opened it, the lights in the checkpoints were behind them.

Joe dipped his head. 'Thank you, sir.'

The young man nodded, trying and failing to hide how pleased he was to be called sir by someone twice his age, stamped Joe's papers, and closed the door again.

Even with the stamp on his papers, it was difficult to walk the stretch of unpaved no-man's-land between the two borders. A searchlight followed him all the way, throwing his shadow on to the frosted mud in front of him. His spine turned to glass. The night was so quiet that he heard the squeal of the search-light's base whenever the soldier behind it moved it to follow his path. He was afraid to breathe, in case he missed the clack of the machine-gun pin.

The Scottish checkpoint was nothing but a wooden hut. Above it loomed a guard tower made mostly of scaffolding. A woman, silhouetted, sat at the top with her arms resting on an old Gatling gun. Joe handed over his stamped papers silently. He could still feel the French machine gun pointing at the back of his neck. The searchlight beamed straight on to them.

'You're French,' the checkpoint guard said, in English. He was having to hold his hand up to block out the light.

'No, I'm from Londres.'

The man snorted, and glanced at de Méritens' letter. 'I don't speak French.'

Joe translated it. He wished the soldiers on the French side would turn off the searchlight.

'Ah, the lighthouse,' the guard said, suddenly cheerful. 'McGregor! Your man's here.'

McGregor was the name of the man who was meant to meet him.

McGregor ducked out from the little back room in a haze of smoke and brandy fumes. Before the door creaked shut, Joe saw a slice of what was inside: people sitting on the floor playing cards. McGregor was still holding a drink. It was in a jam jar.

He nodded, not as if he had been held up for an unexpectedly long time, and motioned Joe to follow him to where a cart and a sleepy horse waited.

The harbour wasn't far away. When they arrived, the sea was shushing and the whaling steamer on which Joe's passage was booked wasn't even set to sail for another two hours. No one seemed to think he was late and it was only little by little that he understood they hadn't expected him to get through quickly, and that it was always going to take three hours and a bribe. He couldn't understand their English well enough to ask why no one had told him that when they'd arranged it all over the telegraph. Maybe it was common knowledge.

He wasn't the last on to the boat. A young woman came just after him with a gun slung over her shoulder and a tartan scarf. The whalers, all heavyset, gave her a wide berth and anxious looks. One of them pushed Joe into the tiny cabin they'd given him and he jolted backward, but the whaler held up his hands.

'I'm not trying to hurt you. Are you carrying francs?' he said urgently. Joe only caught what he said on the second time round.

'Francs, yes—'

'Give them to me.'

'What?'

'We need to get rid of them, she can't catch you with francs. Now!'

Joe gave him the diminished roll of notes, fast. He thought he was just being robbed, but the second he had them, the whaler slung them over the side and came back looking shaken, like it wasn't money he'd thrown away but a live grenade.

'Why did you—'

'Shut *up*!' the whaler hissed.

The young woman with the tartan scarf glanced at him and the whaler nodded, too polite. When the whaler saw Joe watching bewildered from the doorway, he leaned on the door and whispered to keep inside till after they had dropped the woman off at Fort William.

Joe stayed on the edge of the bunk for a long time, rattled. But he was too tired to demand a different ship now, and eventually he sank back into a dead sleep that lasted, inevitably, only until four in the morning, when he read by candlelight for an hour and a half before he slept again, this time all the way to Lewis and Harris.

Part II

THE LIGHTHOUSE

8

The Outer Hebrides, 1900

The Eilean Mòr lighthouse wasn't on the coast, but on a tiny spray of islands ten miles from the nearest harbour, shrouded in rain. It was a gaunt tower that rose from the natural slope of the rocks like a whale rib. Even from a distance it looked like it was falling to ruin.

One of the lamp windows was smashed, a colony of white birds hopping in and out. Joe saw it more clearly as they came closer. Greenish streaks stained the side that faced the incoming tide. The steps were worn and barnacled. They plunged right into the sea, and the mooring hoops that should have been around the landing quay had been lost underwater.

It was hard to believe the surveyors could have been so wrong about the sea level or the weather, to have built something that fell apart after just two years. He would have to do a decent study of the thing, but if there were no windows, he couldn't stay for the season. Dismayed, he wondered what he was supposed to do then. Report to the Lighthouse Board, probably, but he didn't know where that was.

A deep part of him hated finding it in ruins, having seen it etched whole on that postcard for so long.

All along the shore of the mainland, points of light shone among the watchtowers, hundreds of feet up from the beach.

Joe had heard about the Harris Wall, which was even more ancient than Hadrian's, but he hadn't ever seen a picture. He stood up when he saw the real extent of it. All along the gullied cliffs, there were towers and walls. In some places they had been built from stone, and in others, the masons had cut into the cliff-face. Where the cliffs petered out, more walls bridged the gaps. Lookout towers stood in different stages of decay, some still with their roofs and some tumbled. He looked back out over the water. The next land on from here was America. He couldn't remember what it was the builders had been trying to keep out.

Someone shouted and the ship slewed to the right, which knocked him off balance. When he looked back, the captain pointed from the cabin to something beyond the rail. There were two pillars in the water, taller than the ship. They must originally have been rock stacks, but they had been carved smooth. Joe held onto the rail as they looped around. They hadn't needed to; they would have cleared the pillars easily, sailing between the two. It was an exaggerated horseshoe of a manoeuvre to go round the other side. Maybe they marked underwater rocks.

The harbour was on the west side of Lewis and Harris, looking out over the dark sea towards the pillars and Eilean Mòr. On the map, the town was called Aird Uig, but Joe couldn't work out how you were supposed to pronounce that. The whalers called it the Station. It crouched among the ruins of the wall, looking vulnerable.

One of the whalers told him that there should be rooms at the sailors' boarding house, which was also the pub, if he could commit to not swearing for the night. The landlord was strict. The whaler stopped, because Joe was staring at him hard, concentrating.

'What?' he said.

'Sorry. My English isn't so good,' Joe had to say. It seemed politer than 'Are you certain you aren't speaking Norwegian?'

The pebble beach smelled of seaweed and iron. A stairway led up to the boarding house, but the rail had rusted to nothing and someone had left an anchor there to hold on to instead. Joe, who had never been acquainted with any anchors before, was surprised to find it was at least three times as long as a person, and quite well-suited to its new job.

Music came from inside. When the door opened, heat rolled out. Joe and the whalers stopped in the broad entranceway to pull off their coats, slick from the misty rain. In the sudden warmth, the rainwater on Joe's skin felt unpleasantly like sweat.

Joe followed the others to the bar. A young man started to hand out keys, then paused over Joe and asked, looking doubtful, if he was new to the ship.

'I'm here for the lighthouse,' Joe said, for the first time. The whaler captain hadn't asked him what he wanted passage for and everyone else had seemed too tired to bother with questions. 'To fix the generator. I'll need to stay here tonight, though, if there's space.'

'Plenty of space,' the man said slowly. He looked Joe over more carefully than he had before. 'Five shillings. Firewood's sixpence per bucket and if you want to sit down here you have to eat something.'

'You took my money,' Joe said to the whaler, who sighed but paid for him, looking like he regretted not having handed Joe over to the woman from the Saints.

'Where are you from anyway?' the barman said. He looked sceptical.

'Clerkenwell.'

'Originally.'

'Clerkenwell,' Joe repeated, uneasy. Someone, he couldn't remember who now, had once said that he looked like he could have been from anywhere except where he was, which was exactly true. 'I'm not French.'

The barman gave him another unconvinced once-over, then some rum to be getting on with. The food – stew – would arrive when it did. Joe took himself off to a spare table. There were more tables than people to fill them. The place must have been built when the fishing was still good.

Everything was wooden, and there were dead birds and joints of meat hanging from the rafters. It looked how he imagined the frontier settlements would have looked in America. He pulled *The Count of Monte Cristo* out of his bag to read. He'd brought it because it was a brick and it would keep him going for a bit – or, that had been the theory – but it was exciting and he'd got through a quarter of it already on the train. It was a while before he became aware that some men at the next table were looking at him and his tool case, pushed under the chair now. He set the book down when one of them spoke.

'You're here for the lighthouse, you said?'

'That's right.'

'No one'll take you.'

Joe wondered if this was their way of asking for a bribe to put up with his accent for the duration of the trip across to Eilean Mòr. If it was, he couldn't see why they were bothering. They all knew he had no more money. He didn't see what there was to say otherwise either, so he only nodded. Whatever they said, he would have to get across somehow.

Something took a firm hold of the hem of his coat and pulled.

He expected a dog. In fact it was the biggest tortoise he had ever seen and, on its back, someone had painted '4' in white. It blinked at him, beak still fastened on his coat. Tentatively, he stroked its head. Apparently satisfied, the tortoise shuffled over towards the whalers. They seemed to know it well.

There were three other tortoises by the hearth. One had a blanket on. There was a man with them, feeding them pieces of cabbage. He saw Joe looking and lifted his eyebrows to ask what his problem was.

'Um,' said Joe, because although it was clearly a good idea to mind his own business in this place, four massive tortoises was going too far. 'Why have you got four ...?'

'It's bloody cold. Can't make them stay in the yard, can I?' the man said, and went back to shredding cabbage.

Maybe they ate them.

Joe worried about what would be in the stew.

When it came, though, it was just lamb, and he decided he should probably be grateful for small mercies.

The lodging rooms were meant to hold two people each, but there weren't enough people any more and so there was plenty of space. The window looked out over the sea, which was whipping itself into a fury now beneath a charcoal sky. It wasn't the kind of weather you ever saw in Londres. It was wild.

He wrote a letter for Alice and Lily and M. Saint-Marie. He didn't put in anything about the Psychical Society – Alice wouldn't like that – but he told them about the journey and the border, and the tortoises, and even that took up a couple of pages. He didn't seal up the envelope, in case there was a chance to add more tomorrow.

Lily would be wondering where he was by now. He had to scrub his hands over his face. Alice wouldn't understand Lily's jokes, the made-up animals. He was going to come back to find a sombre child who had been told to be quiet too much. His insides twisted with the already worn-out certainty that he shouldn't have left her. None of his reasons for coming looked very good now.

Still, it was only three months. Not the end of the world.

Three months for Lily, the mathematical part of him pointed out, was a fifth of her life. A fifth of Joe's life would be eight years.

Hail blasted the window.

The storm came in fast after that. The sea smashed right in against the cliffs and the walls. There was a deep hissing behind the boarding house: water receding in the caves and the broken doorways of the fortifications. He was sleepless as always, but he didn't mind this time. The longer the wind raved around the towers, the more he felt like he was on his way home.

9

In the morning, there was an unearthly quiet. It was the sound of ordinary quiet after the choirs of winds in the night and the smashing of the water on the walls. The sea was calm. Although his watch said nine o'clock, the dawn had only just come, and even then, it hadn't come all the way. The sky was doomsday mauve.

When Joe ventured downstairs, half the pub floor was covered with trout. That side of the room was too cold for anything to smell much. Two women had set up barrels, two each, one for fish and one for the parts of fish nobody wanted. He hesitated, but then decided there was nothing anyone could say that would persuade him to offer to help.

He edged around the fish towards the bar and the fire to see about coffee. The four giant tortoises were still there, asleep now. While he waited – the barman was grinding beans – he studied the sea from the window. It looked strangely thick; it was congealing. Plates of ice bobbed in the weak surf. No wonder nobody wanted to go out to the lighthouse. He'd have to persuade someone. After coffee, though.

Behind the bar, beyond a glass door that led out into what looked like a back yard, some men in dark blue uniforms slipped by, carrying sacks. The barman fixed Joe with a defensive look.

'You didn't see that.'

Smugglers, they must have been. 'See what?' Joe agreed.

A girl pattered down the stairs. She was in a wedding dress.

'Mam,' she said, and seemed as unworried by the fish as everyone else. Joe started to believe he might be the only one who could see them. She did stop, though, shy of the floor.

'Before you ask me, I don't have a telegraph line to God,' one of the fishwives said.

'Can you see out the window?' the girl asked Joe. 'Do you think the winter might come today?'

'I have ... no idea,' he said. It seemed like an odd thing to say, the winter coming *today*, as though it arrived all at once, but it must have just been a local turn of phrase. 'The sea's starting to freeze.'

She blinked. 'Where are you from then?'

'Londres. I'm here to fix the generator at the lighthouse. If I can make anyone take me over. Congratulations,' he added.

The girl's whole expression sharpened. 'Fix the generator,' she said. 'Are you good with technical bits and pieces then?'

'Pretty good.'

'How about a picture box?'

Her mother looked over at him too.

'A picture ... like a camera?'

'Right. The one at the church is broken. And if the winter *does* come in today, it would be such a shame not to ...'

Joe paused. 'Your father wouldn't be a sailor, would he?'

'And if he were?'

'I'll look at the camera if he takes me out to the lighthouse after.'

'That is not a gentlemanly thing to ask,' her mother said. 'It's the girl's wedding day, for—'

'Dad!' she shouted out the stairs. A faint voice said aye. 'If you take the French man to the lighthouse he'll fix the camera, say you will or I'll move to Skye and you'll never see me again!'

There was a quiet in which the girl winked at Joe and opened her hands in the way priests did when they were hoping for a well-timed sunbeam.

'Oh ... *fine*, all right then,' the voice from upstairs said.

'Ta dah,' the girl said. 'Sorted. Now you'll be going to the church, I want my bloody picture.'

'Don't swear at the man, Fiona,' her mother said absently.

'The church is on the left, you can't miss it,' the girl said to him. 'It's the only other building with glass windows.'

'Right,' Joe said tentatively, and leaned out the door to see if it was near. The cold tried to take his head off, but the steeple was just along from them. There was candlelight inside.

A steep, icy stairway led to the church, and he had to go up by inches. When he reached the doors, he had come up the wrong way somehow and arrived at the vestry rather than the nave, and he had to tap on the window. The priest was huddled by the fire. He bustled to the door tucking a scarf into the top of his surplice.

'Who will you be, then?'

'Fiona sent me,' Joe said, with a glance back towards the boarding house. On the little beach, just around the cove and only visible because the church was so high up, there was a small group of people in dark blue uniforms pushing a longboat into the sea. He shuddered, feeling sorry for them, even if they did look like they might be in the Saints. It was bone-eating cold. 'I might be able to fix your camera.'

'Oh!' The priest looked delighted. 'Well, you couldn't have better timing. They're saying on the wireless that the winter might come in this morning.'

Joe stepped gratefully into the warm. 'People keep saying that the winter will come in today, but seasons don't – generally arrive all at once. What does that mean?'

The priest sparkled. 'You don't know about the Harris winter?'

'No?'

'Well! You're in for a treat. Here's the camera.'

It was taking up most of the table. It was an ancient one, a box with a cloth across the back of it. Joe took it apart, careful of the plates. The spring had come off the shutter. There was nothing else the matter with it. He connected it up again. He was about to tell the priest that it was ready, but he didn't get the chance.

A siren rose up from the sea. It howled around the cliffs and echoed inside the church. Joe was flooded with the feeling that he had heard it before and that he would remember what it meant if he could just catch it right.

'It's coming!' the priest beamed. 'Quick, you take that outside. I'll fetch Fiona.'

'What's coming? Outside where?'

'The churchyard, it's round the other side!' the priest called back, already on his surprisingly fast way down the steps.

Joe took the camera and its wooden stand around to the church-yard, which was a natural pool of grass among all the stone. He was just fixing the tripod upright when the priest came back with Fiona's mother and some other women, all carrying bouquets of heather, all of them pink from the run up.

'Face it south, then you'll be able to get it coming in — that way,' someone called at Joe.

'What coming in?' Joe said helplessly.

'The winter, look! Is that thing ready?'

'Yes,' Joe said. 'But …' He trailed off, because he had finally seen what they were all talking about.

The winter was coming in at running pace over the sea. It swept in from the west, and in its wake, the water froze in a clear grey line. Joe went to the edge of the graveyard to see it hit the beach. It made a sound, a splintering that must have been forming frost. Fiona rushed up the steps and at last he understood what they were doing when her mother put her ten feet to the left of the camera. They were waiting so that she could run with the frost line, the summer ahead and the winter behind. Behind her, the trawlermen and their wives were running up too, laughing.

Joe stared at the sweep of the rushing frost. It was impossible; nowhere in the world, nowhere, was there weather like this. Not unless there was some sort of mad polar vortex, but there was no storm any more.

It was something to do with the pillars in the sea, though. The winter was radiating outward from those twin spars in the water, like they were sucking through the cold from somewhere else.

'It's about twenty seconds off!' the priest shouted.

'Ready?' Fiona said to Joe. She was holding handfuls of her wedding dress, ready to run. 'It's coming!'

'Right ...' He put his hand up, looking through the camera lens now. The frost line came up behind her.

'Go!' everyone shouted.

She didn't have to run fast to keep pace. She looked back at just the right second, and the magnesium flash went off in time to catch how she was laughing, and how the hem of her damp veil froze as it furled up on the wind. The congregation cheered. Someone threw rice at Joe and the priest clapped him on the shoulder when he straightened up.

'Welcome to Harris, lad. Get it? Right! Better get inside. Everyone back at eleven!'

The whaler from yesterday, Fiona's father, was waiting just behind him. He nodded to Joe. 'Time to take you out,' he said. He looked pleased, and aware of the debt. 'Just about.'

Joe went to fetch his tools, full of the fizzy joy that came from seeing something he couldn't explain.

I O

Eilean Mòr, 1900

The beach was glittering with frost. Whale ribcages made cloisters all across it, and on the bones perched dozens of cormorants, every single one of them dead, because they had been drying out their wings when the winter came, and now they had frozen.

Once Joe had climbed down on to the boat, the trawlerman set off straight away. The engine stuttered at first, and when they did move off, it was gradual, because they were cutting through ice. The hull was fitted with a steel harrow. They left a black wake. After about fifty yards, it started to freeze again. The cabin was tiny, so Joe sat outside on the bench beside some lobster pots and a collie, which edged across to put its head on his knee.

The little boat gained some speed in the open water. Away from the bay, there wasn't so much ice, the stronger currents still churning the water. Up ahead were the pillars they'd veered around yesterday, but the trawlerman didn't do that today. They chugged between them, into a blast of even colder air. The space was broad enough for a much wider ship. On the way past, Joe looked up to see the carvings. They were all chiselled names.

Trying to see where the pillars' foundations were, he leaned down to the water. So did the dog. The straight shapes of sunken masonry loomed a long way below. He caught a snatch of what might have been crenellations and then, close enough to the surface to touch, a weathervane. There must have been a whole town down there. Joe had a strange coil of nervousness. Maybe it was only because he had forgotten so much, but he couldn't help thinking that everyone might have forgotten something important here.

The dog whined and hid under the bench. He scuffed up its ears. It only snuffled unhappily and then, as if it could hear something frightening, it shot out and away from him. Before he could stop it, it had gone over the rail, onto the ice.

'Hey! Monsieur – your dog!'

The trawlerman didn't seem worried. 'She's light. She'll make it.'

Joe stood at the stern, not sure she would. The dog was tearing back to the beach much too fast to stop herself if she came to a thin patch of ice. She skittered around bumpy ice blocks twice, which made his insides lurch, but she didn't fall, and then, finally, she sprayed onto the pebbles and stood watching them, barking.

Joe sank down on the bench again. The cold was so sharp that it was biting through his coat despite the sealskin Fiona had lent him to wear inside it. He breathed into his hands. Now that they were through the pillars, there was mist, even though there had been none in the bay. The islands inched closer.

Eilean Mòr was the largest of the islands, and high on its flat top was the lighthouse. He could only just make it out through the mist. Nearer to them, talons of rock ploughed down into the water. The trawler crept further around. Beyond a spar was a miniature cove, hardly anything but a bite in the cliffside. A set of steep steps cut an uneven zigzag into the stone. There was a jetty and a winch to take supplies up the cliff.

The tower windows weren't broken. There were no birds in the lamp room, and no greenish gauge of the storm tides on the walls. The lighthouse was as whole as the morning it was finished. Something under his liver turned over. He had been sure, yesterday, that it was in ruins. He climbed over some lobster pots and a clutter of fishing floats to lean into the cabin. Touching them printed rust-coloured grime on his gloves.

'Monsieur. Are there two lighthouses here?'

'Two? No. This is it.'

'Because ... when we came in yesterday, I saw one that was ruined. This one is – new.'

'Same one,' the trawlerman said. He seemed to see that that was insufficient even by the short standards of this place. 'Sometimes it's old, sometimes it's new.'

'What does that mean?' Joe said. It should have been ridiculous, but the trawlerman had said it too seriously to laugh at. 'How can it be sometimes old and sometimes new?'

'Just is.'

Joe went back out again, expecting to come around to a weatherbeaten side, but there was none. They pulled up close to the jetty steps.

'Can you wait, while I check the supplies?' Joe said. 'The Lighthouse Board is meant to have stocked the place, but ...'

'I'm not missing my daughter's wedding. If anything's wrong, send up a flare and someone will come when they can.'

Joe wanted to say that was unreasonable, but it wasn't. Guilty that he had no money to give the man, he edged out, holding on to the mooring bollard in case he slipped. It was so cold his glove stuck to it. As soon as he was over the rail, the trawler looped away again, engines struggling to push it through the ice.

Joe climbed slowly, his left shoulder aching from the weight of his bag and his toolkit, but he wanted his right hand free if he slipped. The steps were irregular and the mist had made the weed on them slick. There was no rail, so he held the stiff grass that grew between the rocks. When he was halfway up, he looked back to watch the trawler. The wind blew a sheet of hail towards him. It stung. He turned his back to it again and carried on, and upward.

The top of the steps came out on the tower porch.

He turned the door handle. It was unlocked.

The tower was cold inside, and dark. The first room was a living room with an armchair set close to a hearth, where the floor was covered in furs and the windowpane was white with frost. Between him and that, the stairs were an ammonite spiral. They went all the way to the top, into dimness. The shutters on the lamp-chamber windows were down. He called, then listened, but nobody moved or spoke. Little echoes came back to him after a while, having explored by themselves.

The engines were usually in a separate outbuilding, but there were no outbuildings here; the architects probably hadn't wanted to spend any more time outside than strictly necessary. Here, the engine room was underground. The stairs plunged into blackness. He had to sort through his bag to find some matches. The scratch was loud, and so was the gunpowder fizz. He found a lamp just as the match bit his fingers. He shook it out. In the time it took him to light another, the dark raced at him and he felt panicky, certain there was someone here. But there wasn't. It was just him and the engines.

The new light made gruesome shadows from the belt of the steam engine and the sharp, cog-shaped magnets in the generator. He lit all the lamps he could find, four, and moved them close to the machines.

The steam engine was all right, but as soon as he looked at the generator, he saw what was wrong. One of the electromagnets was missing.

There was a clunk upstairs.

'Hello?' he called. He waited but there was nothing. His breath steamed. M. Saint-Marie's house settled loudly enough in winter. God knew what moved and snapped as the temperature here shot down low enough to freeze fuel lines.

He replaced the magnet – he had brought two – in half a minute. Once he had, he got down on his hands and knees to see under the generator. It had been built into the floor; generators were worth a thousand francs. The broken magnet was just underneath. It had cracked right in two, down a jagged line. He had to lie flat to reach the second piece.

He caught it with his fingertips and sat back, cross-legged on the cold floor, then fitted the two pieces together to make sure there were no shards left that might grind in the machinery. They matched perfectly, but he stopped when he saw the mark on the left one. Someone had smacked it with a hammer.

He rubbed his thumb over the bright dent. There were rigid specifications for the selection of lighthouse keepers; they had to be men below a certain age, because they had to be strong enough to go out on a stormy sea and haul sailors in from a wreck. He couldn't imagine Paris would send anyone to fetch a keeper for anything except a complete breakdown of food supply. Even that was probably your own problem. From what he had heard of the Lighthouse Board, it was a tight-fisted, pettifogging sort of organisation. They'd be no help even in an emergency.

Much better, if you knew how the contracts worked, to break the generator. Once the lamp went out, procedure was for the mainland to contact the Board urgently.

Joe lit the engine furnace. It only took a match. He stood next to it for a while, listening to the fuel line. It creaked, but didn't burst. As the engine built up heat, the pistons began to turn and so did the belt that led to the generator. He set his fingertips on it and let it run under them, feeling for tears, but it was new.

The light didn't come on by itself. Someone had turned off the switch in the lamp room. Not very much wanting to, he put his bag over his shoulder again and started up the spiral stairs.

The doors into the rooms were all propped open. The keepers had made it as cosy as it could be; there were armchairs and little heaters in the round sitting room, and someone's jumper folded over the back of a chair. The kitchen still smelled of baking. There were dense fruit cakes on a rack by the cold stove, beside an open bottle of brandy. He went in to see. All the cooking paraphernalia was still out on the drying rack. A jar of dried fruit and a scattering of currants on the worktop. When he touched one, it was still sticky. He opened the stove door. There were more cakes inside, burned. It was good to think that the man's last thought had a decent chance of being, not family or money or anything heart-rending, but *bugger I left them in the oven.* But not so good to think that whatever had happened, it had happened so fast that someone had run straight out of this kitchen with the oven still going, midway through clearing up.

At the top of the stairs, the lamp room was dark.

In the middle of the room was a small steel ladder that led up into the lamp. When he climbed up, he found that the lamp's two carbon rods had burned to black stubs. The clamps that held the rods in place were stiff, and he had to lean hard on them before they gave. The replacement rods were in a cardboard box by the ladder. They looked like javelins. Once they were into the clamps, he got them aligned, then threw the switch.

At first, the only sound was the clicking of the clockwork that would keep the rods at the same distance apart as they burned down. It took a minute or so for the electricity to heat the carbon enough for it to react. It began as a vague glow, then a hissing, and then an electric arc jumped between the rods. The hissing turned to cracking, and light brighter than any daylight flooded the lamp chamber. He smiled at nobody and felt better. The place felt more like his now that he'd fixed something in it. And now there was light, real light, the idea that someone else might be here didn't seem so looming.

Built into the lens was a narrow strip of red glass. It was a fixed light, not rotating; the red part of the beam was aimed back towards the mainland. He frowned, because there had been no dangerous shoals or sandbars that he'd seen on their way in. But he knew what it was pointing towards even before he went out onto the gantry. In the red strip stood the pillars in the sea.

Since it seemed better to do it sooner rather than later, he went back downstairs for water and then up again to clean the lamp-room windows. The wind screamed outside. He had to keep ducking back in to breathe, which was annoying, because for opaque reasons the door handles were wooden and the cold had already cracked them, so his gloves kept catching. Once it was done, he sank down at the table and puzzled over a box of four new wooden door handles, all neatly turned.

'Or you could just use ... metal ones,' he said aloud. Feeling picky about the windows now, he scratched off a mark on the inside and then hissed when he burned himself on the steel frame. It was so cold it tore off a rag of skin. 'Or wooden handles,' he said, feeling stupid. He put his gloves back on and changed the door handles. The last keepers had left a screwdriver in the box.

While he teased out the screws, the sea whitened. In the distance, the land was grey; the silhouettes of the ruined towers along the wall reached up into the weather, roofs invisible. Inside, though, the arc lamp made the little room warm.

Once the handles were done, he remembered about supplies. In that at least, the Lighthouse Board had been thorough: there was a pantry stocked with everything he could have needed and a good deal more. Fish in a generous icebox, smoked meat hanging along the rafters, jars of oats, barley, rice, ordinary basic things, but a lot of them, and seeing it gave him a rush of security that made him see afresh how close to the edge they always lived at home. This was three months' worth of food, all assured. He couldn't remember when he'd last felt sure about three months' time.

All at once it seemed less likely that anything odd was going on, and something in him relaxed. The night was twenty hours long now, so he moved a set of bedding up to the watch room and arranged it on the iron grille floor so that he would know if anything went wrong with the lamp. He took out *The Count of Monte Cristo*, basking in the quiet. He could feel it would make him edgy before he got used to it, but for now, the novelty was heady.

Something moved downstairs. It sounded like a chair being dragged across the floor. Without giving himself too much time to think about it, he went straight down, away from the noise of the lamp and into the gloom. Voices came from the bedroom. Not voices that might have been the mumbling of the sea or a chance of the wind around the ledges; close. He couldn't hear what they were saying, but he could hear that it was English. The door was open. He tapped on it anyway and went in. No one was there.

He stood in the empty room for a long time. The voices stopped at first, but then they began again. He spun slowly, trying to find where they were loudest, but couldn't decide. There was a smell too – rum, salt, wet clothes.

Maybe the sugar smugglers. It would make sense for them to stop here, if they were going any distance in that miserable little boat.

'I can hear you,' he called. 'Look, there's no need to hide, you can come out and we can have some tea. There's plenty.'

Silence again.

Annoyed, he went back down to the engine room for a tape measure and a notepad, and spent the next hour measuring every wall and beam in the tower, certain he was going to find a hidden space. He did find a couple of unexpected cupboards, the doors disguised in the wainscoting, but there was nothing in them except shoes and coat hangers. The rest of the place was exactly where it was meant to be. There wasn't an unaccounted inch, and where the walls or the floors were thick, they were solid.

When he came back to the bedroom, the voices were talking again. He didn't make a sound this time, only listened. They were laughing. He could smell smoke now. The grate was dead.

Something smashed right next to him. There was nothing there, not a solitary shard of glass.

He thunked the door shut after him and locked it. Silence came down on the other side again. Then, very quietly, scratching. Someone was sweeping up the glass that wasn't there.

Not knowing where he meant to go except that it had to be outside, he pulled on a heavy coat that the last keepers had left behind, and set out onto the path again, down through the rocks towards the stairs and the sea.

I I

Joe found a rock and sat there until the cold got into his joints. The tideline was full of lacy frost where foam had frozen along the sand. Rather than splashing, stray water drops clicked.

There were no voices here, only seagulls. It could only have been two in the afternoon, but it was full dark again already, with the ghost of the aurora above the horizon. The lighthouse lamp cut through the thickening night and shone on the sea. There was nothing else here but a few isolated rocks where nothing grew. The red strip drew a line straight between the pillars.

He had brought the notebook out. He went back over the measurements and the sketches he had done to go with them, expecting an obvious mistake. He couldn't find one.

No wonder the whalers had been uneasy about bringing him.

He was still too nervous to go back inside. He drew a little ghost on the corner of a page.

He caught the shape of a man in the water a while before he understood that it was a real man and not an illusion. The sea rolled in with a splintering of fine ice, and there was nothing.

The man surfaced and caught the edge of a rock. He lost his grip as the tide swelled again but, rather than struggle, he let himself spin. He must have been too tired to fight. Joe slid down to the edge of the rocks, balancing in the places where there was lichen instead of seaweed. He had never seen anyone swim before, or even float. He didn't know what he'd expected it to look like, but not like this. It was strange, and not quite human.

Then he came back to his senses. The water was freezing, literally freezing; he had no idea how long a person could last in temperatures like that, but it could only have been minutes.

'Hey – here.' He caught the man's arm. 'Get out, come on. Are you all right? I didn't see a shipwreck or I'd have come down straight away ...'

The man stared at Joe's hand, then looked up slowly. If he had been a murderer and Joe had banged down in an eddy of feathers and smoke, he couldn't have looked more hopeless. The light painted cinders in his eyes.

'I'm a mechanic,' Joe explained quickly, in English. If all the whalers and the people in Aird Uig had been nervous about the lighthouse because it was haunted, it was reasonable for a ship-wrecked sailor to imagine he'd just been snatched by a ghost. 'I came to fix the lighthouse, it's all right. Come on, let's get you out—'

The man wrenched his arm away. He was still looking at Joe as though he much preferred to freeze to death than climb out on to the island.

Joe wanted to just haul him out, but he didn't think he was strong enough, or sure enough of his footing. 'Look, are you a selkie?' he tried.

'No,' the man said, and it was a relief to hear that he under-stood and spoke. English too.

'Then please come up now, you're going to die.'

Joe had an itchy, wrong feeling that he was about to change his mind and disappear under the water again. In someone's drawing room, being polite over fine china, the man would have been ugly. There were burn scars down one side of his neck and around his eye. He had turned his head away from an explosion just out of time. In the sea, he was different, and however damaged, he didn't seem so much like a man as something else that only happened to be a similar shape, and perhaps one that belonged more in saltwater than on the land, but he let Joe help him out.

Once they were level, Joe pulled off his coat and put it round the man, quickly at first, but the man shied and Joe had to lift his hands to show what he was doing, then try again more slowly. If the man had ever had a coat, the sea had stolen it. His shirt was translucent from the water. Although he was powerful from the ribs up, his bones were near the surface. It was the hunger strength that miners and boxers had, not the healthy kind. There was already ice in his hair. When he did let Joe put the coat round him, he couldn't move his hands enough to fasten it, and only crossed his arms to lock it closed.

'Where did you come from?' Joe said, bewildered. The empty horizon was interrupted only by the lumps of forming sea ice.

The man was shivering too much to talk a lot, but he managed to say, 'I fell.'

Joe hurried him ahead, worried that he would collapse. Their shadows spun as the lantern swung. The man held his hand out to help Joe up the last stretch of steps, which had mainly crumbled away. His fingernails were blue, but he did manage to grip. That had to be a good sign.

'It's warm inside,' Joe promised. 'The furnace is going.'

He shoved the door shut behind them both and let his breath out, because the quiet roared after coming in from the wind. 'Let me find ...' He trailed off and turned away to hunt out a towel and some dry clothes. 'Go downstairs and stand by the steam engine, it's hot. Follow the noise.'

'Y-es,' the man said uncertainly. He looked apprehensive.

Joe didn't understand at first, but then wondered if perhaps people round here weren't used to machinery. The boats had engines, but the chances were that hardly anyone between here and Glasgow ever saw an industrially sized one, with a generator. Generators were unsettling things; the fan belts moved fast and the magnetised cogs were thick, spiky, and full of the potential to fly off. He could remember the first one he'd seen at M. de Méritens' workshop. He'd been nervous of it, for sure. 'It's all right, it's just an engine. It powers the generator. It's safe. And warm, go, go.'

When he met him there, the man was standing by the furnace, the window in the scuttle partially ajar and his back to it. Joe put the towel around him and made an uncertain sound about the size of the clothes. The last keepers had left everything and it was all still there in the dresser, ironed and smelling of wood.

'Thank you,' the man said.

'Welcome. I'm glad you're here.'

The man smiled. 'Have you been here long?'

'No, but the last keepers vanished and I spook more easily than I should.' Joe watched him change, because he was covered in marks. The worst were the burns. They went across one side of his face, right down his neck, his shoulder, his arm. Joe only noticed he was staring when the man flinched, self-conscious.

Joe arranged his now-wet coat over the near end of the engine instead, where it would catch the heat, and kept his back to the man.

'It's a strange place. When they first built the tower,' the man said, in a careful way that sketched out forgiveness, 'there were all sorts of stories. If you looked from the land, you could see the men building it. If you looked from the sea, the works looked like ruins.' He brushed Joe's elbow to say he was dressed again. Even out of the water, there was something foreign about him and his clear precise English, which wasn't Scottish, or the

Londres pidgin, or the bracken violent kind they spoke at the stations north of York. His voice was young; in fact, he was much younger than he looked, Joe realised, closer to thirty than forty.

'You've seen it too?' Joe said, absurdly grateful. 'I thought I was going mad. No one in town would tell me about it.'

'Oh, I've seen it plenty,' the man said, cutting his eyes to one side with a kind of wry tolerance. 'They've nothing better to do in town than be mysterious.'

Joe laughed, and felt far safer than he had an hour ago.

Once they had eaten – salmon, no less, from the cold stores – Joe gave him a tour, ending in the lamp room. The man came in slowly and hesitated in the doorway, skittish at the noise of the carbon rods. Joe showed him how they worked. The man looked into the screaming purple light without narrowing his eyes. The noise plainly didn't stop bothering him, although he said nothing about it, so they went back downstairs and played cards in the little living room, propped against the pipes that ran hot from the furnace. He lost good-naturedly and paid his losses in old money, English gold from a button-down pocket of his wet clothes, which were steaming now, draped over the broadest pipe. Joe stared at it and then pushed it back over the table.

'I can't take that. That's fifty francs' worth of gold, I—'

'Not here it's not,' the man said gently. He slid it back to Joe. Two of his fingers had been broken and set improperly; he couldn't move them as much as he should have been able to. 'Just take it. Use francs here and you'll be lynched. I prefer not to be.' He didn't have to show his teeth before the scars around his eyes made it clear he was on his way to smiling. 'I'm putting you to a lot of trouble, anyway.'

'There's nowhere else you can be. The sea isn't frozen enough to walk on properly yet. What do you expect to do, fly?'

The man opened his shoulders and cast a ball of awareness between them that he knew he looked like a thug and that he wouldn't have blamed Joe for yelling and shoving him back into the sea. 'Even so.'

Joe hesitated, because neither of them had introduced themselves yet, and he had an uncomfortable sense that this was not the kind of place where you pulled a mystery man from the sea and just trusted that he was going to be a nice person. There was something about him that wasn't right. You didn't get that many scars, and that much strength, from making a living as a stonemason or a bricklayer.

Joe felt very aware of his own voice, and how French he must sound. Lynched if you use francs. He thought of how urgent the sailor had been on the way here, when he slung Joe's money away before the Saints fighter could see.

Joe hadn't seen a ship nearby, even from the three-hundred-and-sixty-degree view from the tower. It was hard to hide like that unless you were trying to hide, surely.

'I don't mean to sound – but are you from the Saints? Because if you've got business round here, I'm not – I don't want any trouble.'

'The Saints?' The man sounded honestly mystified, but it couldn't have been honest. No one would really have thought it was an odd thing to ask. 'No.' But he didn't say what he was. He was watching Joe with some attention now. His eyes were green, very light. They made him look wolfish.

Joe swallowed. It must have been the isolation of the lighthouse and the ghostly feeling of lifting someone unexplained from the sea, but he had not clocked, before, that it might have been more dangerous to take a man like this inside than leave him in the water. 'As I say, whatever you're doing round here, it's none of my business. I'm just the lighthouse keeper.'

'I know. I'm not … going to hurt you.' The man seemed finally to understand. 'We were smuggling sugar, that's all. We were on our way out of the harbour when the lamp here came on. It made the helmsman jump, he knocked the tiller, we spun, I fell like an idiot into the rip.' He was making himself smaller, Joe realised; he didn't like the idea that he'd frightened anyone. His hands were clamped together in his lap.

The words sounded old in a way that Joe's own English didn't. 'Rip?'

'A fast current. They're dangerous, you can't swim against them.'

'Oh,' said Joe. Then he laughed, feeling silly. 'Right. Sugar – I saw you, when you brought it in. And today, on the beach.'

'Well-known income supplement round here,' the man said tentatively, as if he wasn't sure Joe was ready for a joke yet.

Joe smiled. 'Well, sorry for that little burst of hysteria. I'm Joe. It's nice to meet you. I should have said that before.'

The man's eyes ticked up again, not for long. 'Kite.' He didn't say if it was his first or last name, and Joe couldn't tell; north of the border, people had strange names, from old clans or kings no one had heard of any more. 'Can I ask how you ended up being a lighthouse keeper on a rock that's nearly in the Arctic?'

'I didn't end up, I applied,' Joe said. He paused. He had been going to say something bland about it just being his job, but he had a peculiar urge to be honest. 'I, um … long story, but I lost my memory a couple of years ago. Epilepsy seizure. And then someone sent me a postcard, of *this* lighthouse. It was mad; it had been held at the post office for a hundred years, and this place wasn't even built then, but it had my name on it. It must be a hoax, but I don't know why. I've got it here.' He pulled it from his pocket and handed it over. He must have sounded a lot less casual about it than he'd hoped, because Kite took it in the way he might have touched someone else's rosary. 'It's signed M, and I ... sort of remember a woman called Madeline. I think she was my wife. So I hunted out the engine workshop that made the parts for this place. Started work there. Then a week ago we got a message to say there was a fault here, so I volunteered. I wanted to see ... well, if any of it seemed familiar. So here I am.'

'And does it? Seem familiar.' Kite gave the postcard back as carefully as he had taken it. He had studied it front and back, even the postmark, his expression neutral. He was kind enough not to snort, or to agree that it had to be a hoax.

'Sort of,' Joe said wryly. 'I feel like I've been around here before. But epilepsy gives you raging déjà vu.'

Kite nodded slowly, still neutral. It was, Joe saw now, the breakable neutrality people aimed at the very ancient or the nascently lunatic.

'You've got the only mad lighthouse keeper in Scotland,' Joe said, wishing he hadn't said anything. He could feel himself going red with exactly the same boiling shame he'd had at the engine workshop. All he had to do to cope with the epilepsy was *not* run after strangers or blurt out random bollocks. It shouldn't have been this difficult.

'Epilepsy isn't madness, though, is it,' Kite said. 'That's collapsing sometimes. Stop pretending. You're not that glamorous.'

Joe laughed. 'I don't even collapse.'

Kite let his head bow and pretended to fall asleep. Joe prodded him, hot with relief to be teased. Not a single person at home had been easy enough with the idea to poke fun at it.

'Well. I hope you find out,' Kite said. He hesitated, and then seemed to decide something difficult. Joe saw him struggle with it for a good few seconds, catching himself on its more awkward angles. 'You shouldn't stay here long enough to investigate too much, though. It's not safe for you here. When the sea freezes, you should go back to Harris.'

'What?'

'This tower was dark for a week and now you've lit the lamp.' He was quiet then, but he had stopped on an unfinished uptone. 'The last lighthouse keepers are gone. Now you're out here by yourself and you know how all this machinery works. Someone's going to come for you; you're valuable. You shouldn't stay.' He was urgent without being loud.

Before Joe could say anything, something banged upstairs. They both fell quiet. For five or six seconds there was nothing but the wind and the hail on the window, but then other voices talked again. They were in the bedroom. Kite listened, then went to look. Joe went with him. No one was there.

Joe thought Kite would try to say it was some kind of extraordinary echo from Aird Uig, but he didn't. He rapped his knuckles against the wall hard, three times. The sound was hollow.

They both waited. Joe jumped when the wall knocked back three times. 'Jesus.'

'Hm,' Kite said, as unflustered as he had been in the sea.

'I went round with a tape measure, there's nowhere broad enough for anyone to hide in the walls,' Joe said. 'I was outside before because I was trying to work out what was going on.'

If Kite was angry not to have been told that he'd been bundled into a haunted lighthouse, he didn't show it. 'At least you haven't got anyone living here with you.'

'But I have got a haunted room. Don't suppose you know any exorcists?'

'No.' He glanced over again and Joe saw him pretend not to notice the panicky edge in the question. 'I met a part-time deliverance minister once in Glasgow.'

'What's a deliverance minister?' Joe said, grateful, and guilty to be leaning on a much younger man.

'An exorcist without the Latin. He just sort of mumbled at the stairs and then everyone was very impressed that the strange noises stopped right after the neighbours moved out.'

He touched the wall with his fingertips, then tapped it again, in more of a pattern than before, so particular it must have been the rhythm of song lyrics. There was a pause. Kite shied when the wall knocked at them again. It didn't sound like someone on the other side. It sounded exactly like it had when he had done it, as if there was an invisible person next to him. Joe didn't care as much as he could have. It was reassuring, very, to see someone else flinch. It made him feel less stupid.

'Let's go back downstairs,' Joe said. 'If we've got a ghost, we might as well leave him to it. He can knock on the door if he wants something.'

Kite nodded and closed the door behind them. The voices began again, as though they had been waiting for them to leave. They glanced at each other, but neither of them tried to touch the door again.

'You're coming in with me tonight if you want to sleep at all instead of being woken up at three in the morning by a hysterical mess,' Joe told him. He didn't feel embarrassed about asking. It was amazing what meeting in haunted isolation did to your capacity to trust someone. Just then, he would have trusted the man with his life, or even Lily's.

A cautious voice at the back of his mind said that this was not a good idea at all.

The mercury dropped and dropped, even inside. The barometer swung around to stormy, and the wind hammered at the bars of the lamp-room gantry. They went down to the furnace to stoke it for the night together, then back up together, to the nests of pillows and blankets they'd made on the floor by the pipes. Outside, snow slithered over the frozen sea in snake patterns. Where the light beamed, the ice sparkled. After an hour or so, the voices in the upstairs room went away. They looked up at each other over the newest card game – the betting was only matches this time – and neither of them said anything.

Something smashed against the wall. It took Joe a lot longer than it should have to understand that it was only one of the shutters, blown loose from its catch. It banged again.

'Are you all right?' Joe said, because Kite had let his neck bend and drawn both hands over his ears. It didn't look urgent – Kite was too measured a person to yelp and hide – but it didn't look like he had chosen to do it, either. Joe would have bet more than matches that he was hearing a worse noise than a bit of wood on a wall. The burn scars must have come from somewhere.

'Yes, sorry. Careful,' he added, because Joe had got up to open the window and close the shutter. Hail pinballed on to the floor. Having hauled the shutter into place, Joe had to stand for a second while he got his hearing back. Kite was still watching the shutters, tense.

'Was it bad?' Joe asked eventually.

'It ... you know,' Kite said. Although he was speaking quietly, there was pressure behind the words. He had put up a dam in his mind.

'I don't know,' Joe said, aware he was pressing. 'I hide in engine workshops, the closest I've come to war is artillery production.'

Joe could see Kite searching the dam for an extant fissure that wasn't doing too much damage by itself. He nodded once when he found one. 'We put sand on the deck before any action. It gets everywhere; it's like walking on a beach.'

Joe nodded. 'What are your feelings about beaches?'

'Dominated by passionate hatred,' he said, and they both laughed, and the pressure behind the dam seemed to ease.

Joe turned up their oil lamp. Even in ordinary light, not the monstrous brightness of the arc lamp, Kite was so white he was translucent in places. The veins showed electric blue in his wrists. Dry, his hair was red, but dark, a deep colour Joe had only seen before in church windows. He had let his hands drop around his own neck, as though he were imagining martyrdom. On his burned side, he kept his fingers just above the scars to keep from touching them. Joe gave him the deck of cards to deal.

Voices came from upstairs again. Joe stared at the ceiling. He looked down when Kite shuffled the cards, flicking two piles of them together with a zingy clatter. His eyes were on Joe, though, full of the silent recommendation to ignore whatever was happening upstairs. Joe settled down next to him, back to the wall, and arranged some matches into a pyramid.

Not long after that, the voices faded and left only the sound of the wind in the rocks and the sparse gorse, which made it whistle in a way that sounded morning-like, because it was just the pitch a kettle hit on the very edge of singing.

Joe fell asleep so quickly he was unaware of having done it. When he came to in the night to find himself alone in the blankets, it was disorientating, and he sat up trying to remember if the memory of the man in the water might only have been an over-hopeful epilepsy construction. But he heard voices again, then quiet steps on the stairs. When Kite slipped back in, Joe had a roll of sadness.

'You're a ghost too, aren't you?'

Kite knelt down next to him. 'Yes and no,' he said. 'Can I tell you in the morning?'

Joe agreed and sank back to sleep, thinking unhappily that whatever kind of ghost he was, he was at least a polite one.

12

S omeone shook his shoulder. Joe opened his eyes.
   'What's wrong?' he said softly. It was still dark and at first he thought it must be the middle of the night before he remembered that it was almost always night here. There was a lamp close to him, and dense shadows among the living-room furniture, warped strangely on the curving walls.

'It's morning. The ice is solid. We can go.'

'What?'

'It's six o'clock,' Kite tried again.

'You're joking.'

'No?'

Joe laughed, high with shock. 'I haven't slept properly for years. I'm taking you home with me, you're medicinal. All right, let's find some gear. There's a cupboard by the front door.' He paused halfway to the door, because he had a half-memory of waking in the night and feeling sad, but it was so brief that he was sure it must have been a dream.

After the wind in the night, the dark morning felt unnaturally still. There was no noise except the ice creaking. Sea spray had frozen on the stone jetty and on the steps, so getting down onto the ice took a fraught ten minutes.

Because the tower was so high above them on its rock, the light from the arc lamp cast the ice immediately on the shore into deep shade in a black hem all around the island. They had to walk through it for a good hundred feet before they reached the edge, where the light began to wink on the ice. Emerging from the island's shadow, their own shadows were distorted and mutant, like those gigantic carnival puppets at Mardi Gras.

Joe looked up when Kite pointed him more to the left.

'We have to take you back through the pillars.' He spoke quietly, as though there were someone close by, listening for them.

Confused, Joe looked round. The deep red strip from the lighthouse's stained lens traced an eerie, bloody road. A long way out of their way. 'What? I know they're interesting but I don't want to be out here for any longer than—'

'You sailed through them on the way here?'

'Yes?'

Kite nodded. 'If you don't go back through them, the harbour won't be the one you left.'

Joe slowed down. 'What?'

Kite's green eyes ticked over him and again they put Joe in mind of a hesitant wolf. 'I can't explain, I have to show you.'

It hadn't been a dream, in the night. He had woken up and Kite had said he was a ghost. He could remember now.

He had been walking all this way with a ghost.

A kind ghost, though. He swallowed and nodded, and followed him towards the pillars.

'Look at the land through them,' Kite said, 'and then look to either side of them.'

The ice was the same, the cold the same, the snow moving on the wind, but the harbour lights were different. There were fewer.

Lights that were there to the left and right of the pillars disappeared if he looked between them instead. It was like closing one eye and then the other and watching your finger move without moving. He did it standing exactly behind one, looking left and then right.

'You see it?' Kite asked.

'I don't – understand.'

'Go to the other side and look at the lighthouse. Through the pillars, then not.'

Joe hesitated, then went round to the other side, the land side, looking west. On the right, not through the pillars, the lighthouse was dark and ruined, and nobody waited for him three feet away. On the left, in the space between them, it was whole and new, the lamp lit, and Kite was leaning against the stone. Joe had to do it three times before he could convince himself that what he was seeing was real.

Joe realised he hadn't been seeing Kite properly either, or listening. Sand on the deck; ships weren't so fragile any more that shot tore them to bits and the gunners behind them, or not so that there would always be so much blood underfoot that you had to set down sand. Not even in Scotland. 'Where did you say you'd fought?'

'Trafalgar. London. Newcastle.'

Joe's stomach dropped until it bumped into the cradle of his pelvis. 'Is this ... am I seeing through time?'

Kite nodded. 'Yes. Your time is back through the pillars. This side is eighteen hundred and seven.'

Eighteen hundred and seven: ninety-three years ago. It was one thing to reason out a time difference, another to hear it from someone else, quite factually.

'But the lighthouse is brand new, how can ...' Joe began, and then finally understood. 'We built the lighthouse on the wrong side.'

'Yes. Your builders sailed straight through here without knowing what they were doing. We noticed on our side because the locals contacted the Admiralty. They thought the French were doing something strange on the island.'

'I see.'

Kite tilted his head down, and managed to communicate that it was still all right not to see. 'The ghosts in your attic are men of mine, they're just on the future side. The riptide must have pulled them off course after I fell.'

Joe found himself linking his hands behind his neck. The new ideas were making his head too heavy. 'And the fast winter, on my side. It's colder on *this* side, but the pillars are like a pressure valve, so ...'

'Right. It does seem to be warmer in the future, I don't know why.'

'And my – oh, my postcard.' His own voice sounded distant. It was amazing how fast you could accept something impossible. Or, maybe it was just Joe; everything in the world seemed pretty extraordinary to him, with no baseline memories about normal. 'Someone sent it to me from ... your side. Maybe I'm from your side, really? That would explain a lot.'

'Maybe,' Kite said softly.

Something inside Joe woke up again. 'Can you take me with you? I'm going crazy, not knowing what happened to me. If I'm really from—'

'No,' said Kite. 'No, I can't.' He looked like he was in pain. 'We came here, me and my crew, under orders to take you. To take whoever came to repair the lighthouse, I mean. There is a war, in our time, against France. You've ... heard about that?'

'The Napoleonic Wars, yes.'

'We're losing. The French have blockaded Edinburgh, and they're moving troops from inland; there'll be a full siege soon. The Admiralty, the English Admiralty, wants future inventions, to help. Guns, machines, anything—'

'Fine!'

Joe was shocked with himself. He didn't feel like *he* was talking. One part of his brain, the part that wondered unceasingly about

Madeline and the postcard and the man who waited by that black shore, had raced ahead of all the rest. The rest of him trailed after. What about Alice, and work, and what about Lily waiting for him with that duck on her tiny nightshirt, not understanding – but the racing part didn't care.

'No, not fine!' Kite was holding Joe's shoulders now, hard. 'I'd be taking you into a *disgusting* war. The death rate among sailors is one in three after a year. Even if you survive, there's damn all chance I could get you back here. So unless you want to abandon your life here and go, forever, towards a thing that will probably kill you, then – no. You just saved my life.' His voice broke. 'Please don't make me take you into a place that will kill you.'

Joe felt like he was being torn in two. He needed to know, *needed* to, because he could see that one day soon, he would give up. He would lie in bed awake at night, watching the purple lights on the gloss-painted skirting board in the bedroom, with no idea why he was awake, no idea why he hallucinated a man who waited for him, no idea who Madeline was or where. It would all stop mattering, and there was nothing soothing about that prospect.

But then there was Lily.

It wasn't a choice at all, not really.

'I suppose you'd better go and help your men, then?' Joe managed. He wanted to cry, but an alarmed part of him pointed out that if his tears froze, he would be out here on the ice blind.

'And find our ship,' Kite agreed. He looked sad, and sorry.

Joe nodded, numb. Making the decision to stay, to not know, not investigate, had cracked something in him. He couldn't tell what, or what the consequences would be, only that there would be consequences. But maybe it was better to just put it all behind him. Lily would be old enough to talk soon. If he felt broken, he would have to learn to live with it.

'Good luck,' he said.

'Thank you.' Kite didn't sound particularly relieved. 'When you get back to the boarding house, don't let anyone talk you out of leaving. All right? You have to get away from this place.'

'Okay,' Joe said softly. He hugged him. It was unbearable to feel the shape of him through their clothes. Kite *looked* like he could kill someone with one good left hook, but up close, he was smaller than Joe. The idea of leaving him on a deck that had to be sanded felt like murder. 'Are you going to be in trouble, for not taking me?'

'No. I can say no one was here. Someone fixed the lamp and left.'

Joe couldn't leave it at that. He searched around for something to say, anything useful. 'You're right. About the Siege of Edinburgh, it's famous. It happens soon. This year.'

'How does it …?'

Joe shook his head a little. 'The French navy shells the city until there's nothing left. Then …' He stopped, because he'd read it not even that long ago. M. Saint-Marie had got together a stack of history books so Joe could learn the world properly. When he'd read them, it had all seemed very factual and ordinary, but now he was talking to someone who had it still to come, all the facts and figures made a knot in his throat. 'They forced all the survivors to dig a long trench outside the city, told them it was for defensive purposes, and then they got everyone in the trench and shot them. It was the end of the war. You need to get out. Take your crew to Jamaica – the resistance was successful there. It's a free state now. Well, free-ish,' he had to add, because the image of Alice was there in his mind, tapping her foot and reminding him that her aunt had sold her for a strip of land on a pineapple farm.

'I'll do my best,' Kite said, and Joe knew that he wouldn't be able to, that the men on his ship would have families and no one would just leave everything behind. Kite smiled briefly, and turned away.

Joe did too. He walked slowly, feeling like there was a chain trickling out behind him, back to the lighthouse, and the more it spooled, the worse he felt.

It was only a few miles to the beach, but it was impossible to see far, so he had to rely on a compass bearing. When he reached the shore, everything was white. Icicles hung from the whale ribs. The dead cormorants were still perched there.

The inn was empty except for the landlord, who had built the fire much smaller than yesterday. He looked alarmed.

'What are you doing back here?'

'The lighthouse is haunted,' Joe said dully.

'Yes,' the innkeeper agreed, as if that had always been obvious. 'But ... everyone's gone up to Stornaway for the winter. I'm just shutting away the last few things.'

'Do you know how I can get back to the mainland?' Joe asked. It was a strange struggle. He felt foggy, like a cloud had come to sit inside his skull, and it was hard to make out the shapes of his thoughts. He rubbed his temple. This was how he'd felt at the Gare du Roi. He wanted to punch himself in the head.

'The mainland! You can't. You'd have to walk. Even if all the ice is solid, which it won't be — you'd freeze before you got halfway.' The landlord paused, impatient now. 'Look, you can't stay here, just go out to the lighthouse and rough it. Have some rum.'

'Thanks.' Joe sat with it and waited for the foggy feeling to go away. He gave his memory a poke, to make sure it was still there. Yes. He'd come from Londres, Lily was with Alice, and he had run out of the lighthouse, scared. He took off the heavy coat and put it on the bar stool beside him. It was warm in here, too warm after the frozen sea.

After a while, he couldn't remember why he'd been so spooked. Thinking about it, he couldn't really bring to mind the lighthouse at all. Empty rooms, maybe; and he'd done something with the door handles. There'd been a strip of red light, somewhere. What had he said to the barman just now? Ghosts? Christ, what bullshit. He must have been having epilepsy hallucinations again. Trust him to walk for miles over ice before he realised that what he was scared of was imaginary.

He scuffed the back of his hair, so frustrated he could have yanked it out. Of all the times to have a recurring bout of amnesia, after two years of remembering well, this was absurd. He wondered if there was just some belligerently unadventurous part of his brain that switched off if he tried to go further than twenty miles from home.

No, said the quiet voice in the cellar of his mind. It wasn't that.

He had no idea why it would say so.

The landlord must have felt sorry for him, because he put a wrapped packet down in front of Joe at the bar. 'Lunch,' he said. 'For your way back.'

Joe smiled and thought, not for the first time, how basically decent humans were. 'Thanks,' he said.

The memory of the lighthouse came back, more or less, once he was inside. Yes; he did remember the spiralling stairway up to the lamps. And the door handles – he'd changed them because they were wooden, because metal ones would burn you in this cold. The lamp room was familiar, now he was here. He pushed up the main switch handle, and the great lamp crackled as it came on. Soon the carbon rods were brilliant, and the light sang out.

Which was odd, because he felt sure he had left the lamp on when he left before. It would have been stupid to try and cross the ice in the dark.

Someone had been here. He looked around the room again, properly, and then he saw the gold coin on the floor by some playing cards. He picked it up slowly. Someone had been here and poked about in the little time he'd been away. Someone had come in with a friend, had a nice card game, shut off the lamp, and vanished.

But when he looked round, there was nobody here. He had a strong sense that he'd lost something important, but he couldn't think what it was.

13

Something banged a long way away. Joe thought at first that it was a lightship firing a gun for a fog signal, but it came again too soon for that.

With his ear to the window he heard it more clearly. It was drums. Winding on his scarf, he leaned out onto the lamp gantry. The drumbeat wasn't fast – it was a march, and it was coming from somewhere so close he should have been able to see something, but there was nothing. The islands were empty.

He listened and felt more and more uneasy. It wasn't like anything he had heard before, none of those cheery army tattoos with their hollow piccolos. It was deep, and heavy, and he could feel it in the iron railing.

He saw the bowsprit first beyond the next island, and then the figurehead. It wasn't a woman or a sea nymph but a man, with a plumed helmet and shield. Part of its side had been blown to pieces, a while ago, because even the torn parts of the wood had weathered. When the rest of the ship glided into view, it was the size of a church, but the only sound it made was the drums, and the wing noise of the sails catching the wind. It cut the forming ice slower and slower, turning so that it stopped side on to Eilean Mòr's tiny wharf. The rail was so high above the waterline that the men had to climb down on netting and let themselves fall the last few feet. Ice crusted the rigging. In the glare of the lighthouse lamp, the ropes cast spider-web shadows right across the deck.

It took a long second to notice that someone had seen him. On the quarterdeck was a woman. She was looking right at him. She had dark hair, very long, and loose because it must have been as good as another scarf in the frozen air. He stepped back from the rail and inside, then ran down the stairs. The first of the men from the ship met him at the door.

'What's going on?'

Two of them caught his arms. He didn't ask what they thought they were doing. They plainly knew what they were doing. When he tried to wrench away, one of them punched him in the ribs.

Someone else was coming now. He walked like an officer, his back straight. His hair was dark red, and there was a burn scar across one side of his face. There was something familiar about him, a gut-deep something, but Joe couldn't trace what.

'*What* is going on?' Joe demanded.

Kidnapped by the Saints, idiot, probably like the other lighthouse keepers.

The man lifted his eyes at the thug behind Joe, who yanked him upright. 'I need an electrical engineer. You're coming with us.' He sounded profoundly tired.

They let Joe bring his bag and then saw him to the ship. There was a gangplank now. When he hesitated by the rail, someone gave him a shove and he stumbled onto the deck. The wood there was rimy, but gritty with sand. He caught the smell of salt. It was strong and instinct said it was something marine and rotting, but then the distant voice of some encyclopaedia pointed out that it was what they must have cleaned with.

A soldier pushed Joe through a delicate glass door under the quarterdeck steps.

The room was long and spartan. It had a bank of obliquely angled windows and a desk, a few cupboards, a table and a lot of chairs, and a plain screen at one end to partition off what might have been a kind of bedroom. On the desk was a light crate, full of hay. In the hay was a small tortoise, looking thoughtful while it ate a segment of orange.

The door clattered again and the man with red hair came through it. The soldier saluted.

'Sit down, please,' the man said to Joe, motioning at the desk.

'What the hell is going on?'

'Sit down and I'll tell you.'

'But—'

'Sit *down*.'

Joe dropped into a chair. He wasn't used to hearing authority in an English voice and it was so strange he wanted to tell the man to knock it off, except it clearly wasn't a joke. When the man sat down, he did it like a gentleman, his ankles crossed, posture neat. He looked like the kind of person who would sit like that even if someone set him on fire.

If he had been French, he would have been well-spoken and well-born. Joe had an uncanny thrill when he realised that, probably, this man was exactly that. It was just that Joe had never heard what that kind of person sounded like in English. He hadn't known there *was* a kind of English that sounded like that. You didn't have princes with cockney accents and you didn't have English officers.

Still, if these people were in the Saints, then they were hardly going to speak French.

'This is His Majesty's Ship *Agamemnon*, welcome aboard. You are here because you're an engineer,' the man said. 'We need you to make guns, electricity, lights; anything to help prevent the siege that's coming in Edinburgh, which is where we're going to take you.' He spoke so precisely that Joe could hear the punctuation.

'You're the Saints,' Joe said softly.

'No, we're the English navy,' the man said. He had taken the flint out of his tone again, but he was still holding it. 'Some rules. If you try to escape, I'll shoot you. If you try to mislead us, I'll shoot you. If you try to involve any of my men in an escape attempt, they will be hanged. If you speak to any of them about when you're from, or what that lighthouse is, in even the vaguest terms, they will be hanged. We can't risk the French learning about the existence of this place.' He looked weary already. 'This isn't bloody-mindedness; if you obfuscate or try to help the French in any way, however indirect, it is treason. You are now subject to the laws of King George, and the naval Articles of War.'

Joe felt as though he had been trundling along, minding his own business, only to have the sky crack and collapse on his head. 'What king? What are articles of – what do you mean, what the lighthouse *is*? It's a lighthouse!'

'Yes, good. Convincing. Keep that up.'

Joe wanted to say that no, he wasn't pretending, he really did not see what was so special about the lighthouse, but he didn't want to hear the flint go back into the man's voice again, or find out what happened if he did spark it. He wanted to say that they couldn't just steal him; someone would come looking, because the last lighthouse keepers had vanished, and he had a master – ex-master – who cared about where he was. But none of it was true. No one was going to look for him. Everyone in Londres thought he had tried to run away to join the Saints once already. They were going to think he'd finally done it.

There wasn't much left to say.

'Well,' he said at last. 'I'm Joe.'

The man stared at him.

'What?' Joe said, uneasy.

The man said something that sounded like a biblical tribe, and then saw how Joe was trying unsuccessfully to arrange the syllables properly. 'Missouri like the river in America; Kite like the toy and the bird.' His eyes went briefly to the soldier waiting behind Joe before he carried on. 'Do you know when you are?'

'What do you mean, *when?*'

'Yes, what year is it?' Kite said, as if that were a normal thing to ask.

'Nineteen hundred.'

'Not any more. You're in eighteen hundred and seven,' said Kite calmly.

More and more, he was reminding Joe of a radio news broadcaster. He could have reported the dead rising through the floorboards and remained entirely factual about the whole thing, before moving on to a segment about the Empress's birthday. 'The break is between the pillars in the sea. People from your time came through them and accidentally built the lighthouse in this one. Which is why it appears ruined in yours and whole in mine. You see?'

'No! What?'

Kite was quiet for a second. Once again, his eyes brushed over the soldier behind Joe. He had apex-predator eyes. 'But you understand why I'm keen to have an engineer from the future.'

Although he didn't want it to, Joe's attention kept slipping around Kite to the rest of the room. The desk had a chart stretched out on it held down with two clean glasses, an orange, and the tortoise; it showed this stretch of coast, hand-annotated and crinkled in the way paper would once you'd dropped it in the bath and let it dry. The ink had run in places and been re-done in brown rather than black. Hanging on the wall was a WANTED poster. It was for Kite himself. Kite must not have wanted it there, because pinned to the córner was a note on blue paper that said, *Do NOT remove (sir)*.

Missouri Kite
WANTED
dead or alive
a hundred thousand francs
to be signed for by
THE WARDEN
of Newgate Gaol
as of December 1806

It was either true, or an extremely expensive, well-constructed hoax. Everything looked right: the things on the desk, the uniforms, the typeface on the poster. But then, Scotland had been cut off from England since the war. It stood to reason that things would look a hundred years out of date if there was still an English navy, or bits of one.

'Bullshit,' Joe said, not as confidently as he would have liked.

'I'm afraid not,' said Kite.

No. Even the Saints used steam engines in their ships. Joe stared around again, desperate for some misplaced electric torch or the clatter of a telegraph hidden in the desk drawer, but there was nothing. The dim lamps squeaked on their hooks as the ship pulled against the anchor rope. They smelled strange, not of kerosene or naphtha but more like the inside of a frying pan that had had the butter burned onto its sides, and on the ceiling, their smoke had made black stains. It was whale oil.

'No,' Joe said, a lot more quietly. 'No, I can't. I'm just a lighthouse-keeper, I don't know how to *build* anything, I just maintain machinery, not—'

'The last lighthouse-keepers explained to me how your system works last week,' Kite interrupted, still and restrained as ever. 'Upon the breaking of an engine, a specialist from the de Méritens workshop will come to repair it. Particularly if the house is unmanned. I broke the engine, and I shot the keepers. Now here you are.' He said it with something like regret. He wasn't even trying to be frightening.

Christ.

'I have a child. If anything changes here, I could lose her. You can't ask me to do this.' Even as he said it, Joe could feel that the idea wasn't sinking in. A hundred years into the past. How could that happen to a person without their noticing, how did you just wander into – what *was* this, even? The Napoleonic Wars? – into *all this,* without some celestial alarm going off and a junior saint hurrying down from the universe's administrative centre to make sure you didn't screw up His Plan?

Joe had never believed in a God who kept a personal eye on him. That was silly. But so was all this. However absurd a reaction it was, he felt betrayed that it had been allowed to happen. It was exactly how he would have felt if M. Saint-Marie had blindfolded him and then directed him cheerily off a cliff. Any second now, he was going to smash in the realness of it, and it was going to be even worse.

Kite studied him. He didn't try to argue. 'Mr Drake,' he said.

Joe twisted back to face him and then gasped when the soldier dragged him out of the chair. Drake took a vicious whip out of the cupboard, and then smacked the back of Joe's head with it. It hurt incredibly.

'We have, at best, a few weeks before the siege in Edinburgh,' Kite said. There was something dead in him now. He was talking to a space of air just past Joe's shoulder. If he had any understanding that Joe's being in pain was anything except an efficient bargaining tool, he didn't show it. 'Either you can agree to do as we're asking you, or I can make you. Which is it?'

Joe managed to nod. It was too much of a shock to speak past.

Kite nodded back as though they were agreeing about when to organise a Christmas party for people he didn't really like. 'Thank you. We'll provide everything you require in Edinburgh.'

The whip-mark howled along the base of Joe's neck. It was coming very slowly, but under the rancid, paralysing fear, he was starting to feel angry. He'd never felt like that before – he hadn't thought he was the kind of person who got angry about things – but here it was, just starting to simmer. A voice in his head that didn't sound like him at all, the one that did numbers and calculations, decided that he was going to screw this man over so far he would end up in Australia.

Kite took another breath as if he had a lot more to say, but then stopped himself. 'It should be a week to Edinburgh, weather providing. I'll try to bring you back here afterwards.'

'Thank you,' Joe croaked.

Australia. That sodding far, Mr Kite.

It was good to know he did have a backbone, after two years feeling sure he was an invertebrate.

'Go down to the infirmary. Mr Drake will take you.' Kite nodded at Drake, who paced over to the door and opened it. The wind outside shrieked. Then, too soft for Drake to hear, Kite said, 'I tried to let you go, before. I'm sorry. I didn't know you'd forget so quickly.'

'What?' Joe said. 'What do you mean, *before*? When?'

'Don't let me keep you,' was all Kite said, at normal volume, because Drake had come back to drag Joe up.

The lighthouse shone in the mist, maddeningly close. The air felt even colder than before. Seagulls wheeled round the rigging, which groaned, the ropes all stiff with ice. Men were talking, but it was hard to hear over the sea.

Drake steered Joe towards an open hatch and a ladder, which led down into what looked like total darkness.

When Joe could see, he found the ceiling was about two inches too low to stand straight. He bowed his head and walked. It wasn't like a corridor; there weren't doors that led off to either side. The way branched and twisted around strange collections of rafters and alcoves where barrels and crates sat stacked or hanging from hooks, unlabelled. One smelled powerfully of salt and chemicals. When he understood what it must be – gunpowder – he had to fight the overpowering urge to run back the way they had come, but then they were down another ladder and into more dark, and a sense of space. He bumped against something with a hard corner. It made him gasp.

A cloud of panic smoked in his chest, and it was a lot of work to push it down. The place wasn't just sparse; it didn't feel safe. The more he breathed, the more he could smell that nothing could possibly be clean and dry at the same time. There were shapes on lines that might have been hanging washing. The floor felt slick. Locked in safety lamps of such thickness that the glass made the flames into pinpoints, the candles swayed. Drake pointed past Joe's shoulder to say, further in.

The infirmary rattled. There were things hanging from the rafters. It looked like an old butcher's shop, although it was clean and, as Joe came in, he had to step around a little boy scrubbing the floor. A woman was sitting with her legs crossed like a schoolgirl on the operating table, a book propped open on one knee and a notebook on the other. There was a lamp above her. To keep it from swaying, she had tied a piece of string to it and fastened it to one of the drainage holes bored in the table. She had a tortoise too, friskier than Kite's and rolling a cricket ball. She looked up when she heard him.

'You're the new man?' she said.

'Yes – Joe. The captain sent me. I'm looking for the surgeon?'

'That's me.' She stretched to shake his hand. 'Mrs Castlereagh. Have a seat,' she said, getting up. The fabric of her dress shushed. 'Mind the tortoise.'

He sat carefully and nudged the cricket ball. The tortoise hurried after it. It had a '2' painted on its shell, or rather, etched on and then coloured in.

Mrs Castlereagh brought across a bowl of water and a cloth. Alice would be furious when he told her that married English ladies were allowed to work, and as proper surgeons no less. Married English ladies a hundred years ago.

She stood close to see the whip-mark and Joe had to look away. He could make out the flower pattern that used to be on her dress, before she'd dyed it the deep indigo it was now. There were still shadows under the colour. Sometimes her arm crossed into his view. She had a slim jade bracelet on.

'Right,' she said at last. 'No need for stitches, so I'll just polish you up a bit.'

When he smiled, the muscles across one side of his face ached. 'Thanks.'

She smiled too and smoothed a damp cloth down the lash-mark. It stung. 'Anything else I should know, any problems you're likely to have while you're with us?' She was business-like, as though kidnapping mechanics from the future were an ordinary part of her week. She brushed the cloth over his fore-head too, looking right into his face. Her eyes were sharp and black.

He had to make an effort not to fold his arms. Of all the stupid things; he'd been able to sit straight opposite Kite, who was terrifying, but show him a friendly woman and he was fighting the need to run away. He had to swallow a mouthful of shame. He'd known that all the stuff with Alice and Père Philippe had bothered him, but not so much that he would start to feel jumpy around *any* women who stood too near. 'Epilepsy.'

'How often does it come on?'

His arms folded themselves. 'I only have auras, not seizures. Once a fortnight or so.'

'Ever puts you in danger?'

'Sometimes. I forget things.' He swallowed. 'I went ashore earlier and I forgot what the inside of the lighthouse even looked like. And I think – I might have forgotten other things as well. Mr Kite was talking like I'd already met him.'

'You did,' she said. Her focus intensified. 'Yesterday. You saved him from the sea; he went overboard in the rip tide after a shore run. He tried to send you back to Harris, but you came back to the lighthouse. He wasn't happy about taking you just now.' She inclined her head. There was an intense precision about her, just the same as a newly-wound watch. It was unsettlingly familiar. 'He told the officers that no one was there when he looked inside, and he turned off the lamp himself. And then of course you turned it back on and he couldn't very well lie any more. We wondered why you'd done it. You're saying you don't remember any of that now? At all?'

'I ...' He was shaking his head before he knew he was doing it. 'No. You don't sound surprised.'

She was quiet to start with. 'You told him you've had memory problems.'

'Oh,' said Joe. There was something frightening about being told things he'd said but of which he had no recollection. His body had been up to all sorts of things without him.

Mrs Castlereagh looked terse. No doubt she was wishing she wasn't medically responsible for a chronic amnesiac.

A light came on in his head. She wasn't familiar because of an aura, she was familiar because she really was. She had Kite's fine manners and the same shape to her eyes too, and when she saw him studying her and lifted her eyebrows to ask why, the similarity was even more pronounced.

'He's your brother, isn't he?' Joe said. 'Kite, I mean.'

She gave him a curious, disconcerted look. 'Yes.'

'Is he going to kill me?' Joe said. His voice had turned small.

'Not if you don't piss about.'

He nodded.

'Go easy for the rest of the evening,' she said seriously. She frowned, like she had no real faith he was made of the stuff that weathered well on warships. It didn't show in her voice any more than Kite's expressions did in his.

Joe moved the ball and the tortoise scuffled after it. He didn't want to get up again yet. It wasn't that he was tired, and still nothing hurt as much as it should have; it was that he didn't know where to go, and even if he had done, he would have staked a lot on its being wet and cold. And here was safe.

'I've been seeing a lot of tortoises.'

'Yes.' She brightened. 'We need to test whether you'll vanish if we change too much and your ancestors are killed. We've got four Galapagos tortoises aboard. They live upwards of two hundred years, so that's easily long enough for the time difference. We have the juveniles here. Missouri means to go to the mainland today to pay a man to look after them for a hundred years and bring them to the pillars at six o'clock today, your time. Our theory is that an intention here should be spooling out already on your side of the gate.'

Joe straightened. 'It is. There's a man with four tortoises at the ... I don't understand, though, what can tortoises tell you?'

'Well, if we kill a little one, we'll see if the older one disappears. Better than doing it with people.'

'Oh.'

A girl in a heavy blacksmith's apron leaned in. 'Ma'am? Captain says it's time to go out to the pillars.'

'Right. Let's see how it goes off, shall we?' Mrs Castlereagh said to Joe. 'Bring the tortoise.'

14

Eilean Mòr, 1807

There were four tortoises in all, and four people: Kite, Mrs Castlereagh, Joe, and a limping Scottish sailor of unclear purpose. The weather was still misty and the land was invisible now, but the gate in the sea was still there, just, infernal in the red danger light from the lighthouse. Standing not far away on the other side was the man from the inn. On a sleigh, in crates, were four boulder-sized things under blankets.

Beyond the lighthouse, the town was a clear run away over the ice.

Kite came up on that side of him by way of showing that he had noticed. Joe looked down.

Together, they all walked towards the gate and the waiting man. He came forward a short way too. When they were close enough to see his face, he looked awed. He put his hand out and Kite shook it. Joe had the alien thought that people here must never have touched each other otherwise. There was no kiss, no hug, nothing. They were all oysters sealed in their stiff manners.

'You're Captain Kite?'

'Yes. You must be related to Thomas McCullough.'

'Jesus, Dad was telling the truth, but I thought, why not go and see. Anyway, I'm Guillaume.'

Kite looked as unsettled as McCullough looked fascinated. 'Yes. I hope you're not too fond of these things.'

'They're not brilliant company, I have to say,' McCullough said. 'But ... why?'

'Because I'm going to shoot them.'

'What! You can't do that!'

Kite ignored him and looked back at the Scottish sailor, who brought out the box with the tortoise marked '1'. Beside Kite, his sister was watching the middle distance, wary. Everything about her said she wasn't sure any of this was a good idea. Joe tried to follow her eye line. There was nobody else coming.

She saw him looking. 'If even one person in ninety years told the French we were doing this, they could save themselves a lot of trouble if they shot us all now,' she murmured.

'No one would believe it,' Joe said. 'And no one's here. I came from the shore yesterday, they've all gone to Stornaway. If there were soldiers I'd have seen.'

'Mm,' she said, but he couldn't tell if she was agreeing or not.

'Agatha, have you got the book?' Kite said to her.

She held up a notebook.

'Then we're ready.'

They were. McCullough and the four grown tortoises were on the future side of the gate, while the rest of them stayed on the past side. The distance between them was narrow enough to shake hands over.

'All right.' She looked happy. She was one of those people who liked books, Joe suspected, that were mainly graphs and numbers. 'Let's have young tortoise number one on our side and old tortoise number one on the future side. Who's doing the honours?'

Kite glanced at the others to see if any of them would volunteer, without much expectation. No one did. He took out his gun and shot the little tortoise in the head.

Joe flinched hard and had to concentrate not to move when a shard of shell slid across and touched his boot. He didn't quite see what happened to the old tortoise. It didn't fade into mist or pop out of existence; it was just gone. So was the crate it had been in. His eye had slid over the real moment of it and he couldn't have said how it had gone except that it had. On the other side McCullough rubbed his eyes.

'Well then. I suppose we'd better get started, if you have to do it?'

Joe stared at him.

Kite was watching McCullough too. He inclined his head slowly. He always moved slowly. He had rusted. 'Could you bring the second one over here?'

'Second one? We haven't done a first one yet,' McCullough laughed.

'Check the numbers on them,' Kite said, quite gently.

'We've got two, three, and four,' McCullough said without checking. 'Never got number one, something must have happened to it before we had them.'

There was a small silence in which there was only the wind singing around the gate.

Joe didn't have many anchor chains to his own character. He hadn't been *himself* for long enough. But one thing he had known about himself for as long as he'd *been* himself, was the epilepsy. Epileptic amnesia, the doctor had said; perfectly common, plenty of people have it. Nothing extraordinary. Even when the Sidgwicks had told him it might be a sign of something else, it had still been epilepsy. A disease with an interesting cause, but still a disease, laced through him as thoroughly as any cancer.

Only it wasn't epilepsy. It was the pillars. It was the future rearranging itself. McCullough had forgotten the presence of a tortoise that was now impossible. Joe must have had a whole life that had become impossible.

He felt himself losing the strength in his knees. If there had been anywhere to sit down, he would have. As it was, he

slumped a little. It must have looked strange, as though someone had smacked him too hard in the middle of his spine.
Mrs Castlereagh noticed and smiled a tiny, regretful fraction.
She must have suspected already. No wonder she hadn't been
surprised to find he'd forgotten meeting Kite.

'Yes,' Kite said. He sounded curious now. 'I just shot it in
front of you. You didn't see?'

'I ...'

Kite pointed with the muzzle of his gun to the blasted little
corpse on the ground. 'About ten seconds ago.'

McCullough looked worried. 'Well, that's something, isn't it.'

'So,' Mrs Castlereagh said, 'let's have young tortoise number
two on the future side, beside old tortoise number two.'

Joe watched the old one hard, because he didn't want to see
the little one die. The gunshot was loud when it came. But nothing happened to the old tortoise, which only hid inside its shell
from the noise.

'I don't like this,' McCullough said unsteadily.

Joe couldn't have agreed more.

'If you could bring the third one over here to the past side,'
Kite said, polite, although everything else about him said, I'm
the one shooting them, you prick.

McCullough looked unhappy and tugged the sleigh across.
His shadow swung in the hellish red light. Mrs Castlereagh and
Joe had to help him lift down the third crate. The third tortoise
was more awake under its blanket. It was eating some lettuce
and it looked at them all interestedly. Once it was on their side,
the past side, McCullough went back to his own side. Kite put
their own third little tortoise on the ground and Joe looked at
Mrs Castlereagh, wanting hard for her to say, no, let me, because
there was something frighteningly disengaged about the way
Kite was doing it. He didn't look away. He even watched the
tortoise while he reloaded the gun, which was only made to take

one bullet at a time and whose handle was like a club in case the one shot didn't hit anyone. But she didn't, and Joe felt the gunshot crackle outward through his ribs a long time after the sound was over. Because of the red light, the blood on the ice looked black.

The old tortoise didn't go anywhere. It snapped its slow way through a piece of apple and blinked at them. Mrs Castlereagh glanced towards McCullough.

'Can you still see him?'

'Clear as day.'

'Let's ... take him back across then.'

They lifted the crate back onto the sleigh and moved it to the future side. Joe waited, his stomach tight, expecting it to vanish. It didn't. The third tortoise stayed exactly where they had left it, chewing.

'Is that it?' McCullough said anxiously.

'Yes,' said Mrs Castlereagh. 'It's what we hoped. Cause and effect only works when there's a time difference. Stick two chronologically related things in the same time, and they exist independently of each other.' She smiled at Joe. 'So you won't disappear, even if something happens to your grandparents while you're here.'

'Um – good,' said McCullough, looking like he had no idea what was going on.

Kite was loading the gun again.

Joe realised what he was doing too late. 'McCullough – *run*, for fuck's sake!'

McCullough only stared at him. Joe tried to run too, to push him, but Kite's free hand clamped over his arm. McCullough finally started to run, but the bullet caught him in the back of the head and he splayed forward over the ice.

'Why did you do that?' Joe demanded. 'He didn't *know* anything!'

'He knew what the gate does,' Kite said blandly.

'Good eating on a tortoise,' the previously silent Scottish sailor observed, pleased. He picked up the rope of the sleigh.

Joe couldn't talk. He had to stare at the pillars in the bloody light, throwing black shadows onto the ice. Both pillars were carved with names, mostly women's: Lizzie, Mhairi, Honour, Anne, Jem, right up and down the length from the sea to as far as the lamplight reached. Some were wind-worn to nothing. A few were much newer. One of those was Madeline. Seeing it at exactly eye level made prickles sweep up the back of his neck.

The masons must have known that crossing to and fro could mean forgetting, or changing the future. They had carved – and maybe this was wrong, but it felt like the kind of thing people would do – their wives' names, in case their wives were gone by the time they crossed back.

Joe drilled down into himself and tried to find a memory of a chisel, stone, ice, even the tiny faint snatch of a dream, but there was nothing.

Not epilepsy. It never had been. The hallucinations, Madeline, the man who waited; he was remembering scraps of the life he'd had before something here changed it all. He closed his hand over the folded postcard in his pocket. *Come home, if you remember, M.*

'Back to the ship then,' Kite said, as if they were coming away from an indifferent picnic.

Joe shut his eyes and wanted to refuse to move, but Kite felt it and pushed him, strong enough to drag him whether he cooperated or not, and in the end, he did cooperate.

One of the *Agamemnon*'s cannons had been run out so that the muzzle reached through the gun port, and sitting on it was a sailor, fishing in a hole in the ice. He had looped the handle of a reed basket over the end of the gun. Joe wondered deliriously if he'd caught much.

Part III

AGAMEMNON

15

HMS *Agamemnon*, 1807

The last fissure of daylight was gone by the time they were back on the *Agamemnon*. Lanterns hung along the sides of the ship and in the masts, sparkling over the frost that encrusted everything. Joe was the first aboard. He could only have waited thirty seconds for the others, but the deck was exposed and the wind was full of ice particles, and it felt like hours. He should have run the second McCullough appeared. The more he thought about it, the less he understood why he hadn't tried.

Four men had begun to turn the capstan. The clank of the anchor chain made him jump. It was slow, and with each revolution, the chain banged, so deep he could feel it through the deck. The weight must have been immense and his teeth itched with the sense of potential energy. If anything in the mechanism snapped, all those men would be torn in half.

An eerie whistle sounded from somewhere behind him. Mrs Castlereagh tucked her notebook under her arm.

'Food,' she explained, and nodded to the hatchway.

Joe was lost within a couple of turns on the deck below. The layout of the entire ship was fantastically complicated. There were lamps, but everything twisted around odd corners and stacks of things that warped the shape of the walls and the spaces between them. He had expected some kind of canteen but Mrs Castlereagh took him down to the gun deck. The cannons were all lashed down and unmoving, and people were using boxes of cannonballs as tables, sitting on the floor. There were hundreds of people. He wouldn't have thought you could fit that many on a wooden ship without its sinking. You only just could. Over the smell of food was the chemical sweetness of gunpowder. There was none out that he could see, but it must have been ground into the floor. It hadn't stopped people hanging little lamps everywhere.

'You can't have a kitchen on a gun deck,' he protested, fighting the need to go straight out again.

'We haven't, it's below, but there isn't enough space to sit.'

Near the far end of the long room was a counter full of bread and bowls of stew. The man behind it lifted his eyebrows when he saw them. Mrs Castlereagh asked for enough for five.

'Can you manage?' she asked, eyeing Joe as if he wasn't to be trusted with cutlery. He realised some of the sailors were watching him. They didn't seem hostile, only curious, and none of them struck him as frightening; they were a real mix, sandy men and black men, women in blue dresses, and one Indian man with a turban but an ordinary jumper, talking seriously over a wooden model of a ship. But Joe looked different to all of them. He was neater, cleaner. His clothes were newer than anyone else's, unpatched. Although he could hear odd strands of conversations, he couldn't understand. The accent was too different, or their English, peppered with infuriating motes that were exactly the same.

Mrs Castlereagh led the way to one of the few real tables, set up in the space where there were no gun ports. By the time they reached it, Kite and a cluster of other people in officers' uniforms were already there.

A roar went up from the other side of the room; a group of sailors was gathered under a blackboard bolted to the wall. In beautiful chalk copperplate, semicircled over two columns, was written *Outstanding Idiots*, followed by dates and names. A pair of sheepish men looked like they might belong to the latest names. Joe tried to make out the looping writing. *Alfred Ayres and Frederick Cooper – caught sleeping on wet boards.* Kite looked that way but seemed not to mind. It wasn't clear what wet boards had to do with anything. He picked up a wine bottle and moved to open it, then clenched his hand – his fingers had been broken and never properly set – and gave the bottle to the woman beside him.

Over by the blackboard, someone broke an egg each over Alfred and Frederick, to applause.

'This is Mrs Wellesley, our first lieutenant,' Kite said to Joe. The woman had just opened the wine bottle.

Lieutenant Wellesley was the sort of person who, on Joe's side of the world, would have been one of those severe schoolmistresses everyone was scared of. She shook his hand. He felt uncomfortable, not sure how he was supposed to talk to her or how she'd become a naval officer when, as far as he knew, women all through history had been lucky if anyone treated them more like human beings than expensive cows whose only relevant bits were the ones designed for the production of more men. But the war must have been going for a decade now: all the men were dead.

Wellesley only nodded once, looking concerned that Frenchness might be catching, then turned to Mrs Castlereagh. 'How was it with the tortoises, Agatha? We were watching through a telescope, but we couldn't see much even so.'

'Very interesting,' Mrs Castlereagh said. She moved her glass forward as Wellesley poured the wine. She explained what had happened. While she did, Joe kept his eyes down. Kite was doing the same. He still had a scarf on, and his coat. It was warmer down here because of all the people and the lamps, but the hatchway at the far end was open. The chill powered in.

Joe wondered about electric heating that wouldn't ignite any stray gunpowder, then stopped, because the ship lurched over a wave and he had to snatch the edge of the table. Cups slid. Kite caught both of theirs. Joe felt ill. Suddenly the stew didn't look like a good idea.

'Anyway,' Mrs Castlereagh was rounding off, 'we've proven that Mr Tournier here won't vanish in the middle of everything.'

The ship rocked again. Joe closed his hands over the edge of the bench and made an effort not to shut his eyes, because he'd heard somewhere that that made it worse, but it was still bad.

Lieutenant Wellesley leaned further forward. 'What I want to know is how that test was even possible. We brought four tortoises and the captain fully intended to shoot three of them, so why did it work?' She had put one hand on Kite's back, protective, and plainly worried about what having to shoot too many living things did to a person. 'There were never going to be four.'

Kite looked like he might have had an opinion, but his eyes went to his sister instead.

'We were only going to shoot them if Mr McCullough arrived with four tortoises,' Mrs Castlereagh pointed out.

'This is giving me a headache,' Wellesley said. Kite gave her a piece of raw ginger. Wellesley dunked it in her wine, then in the sugar pot, winced, and bit a chunk out of it.

'It's fantastic, isn't it,' Mrs Castlereagh said happily, and the others looked bleak and amused at the same time. Kite smiled.

Lieutenant Wellesley tumbled an orange towards him. The tortoise edged after it. 'What are we calling Tortoise Four, sir? We can't call him Tortoise Four. Morbid, given One to Three.'

'Well ...' It was clear Kite thought morbid was everywhere and there was no use in trying to tiptoe around it. He caught the orange and gave it back to the tortoise, very carefully, plainly worried about scaring it.

Mrs Castlereagh looked a little vexed, as if she thought he was just being spacey. 'Sentences perhaps?' she said.

Mrs Wellesley looked like she would have said something if Mrs Castlereagh hadn't been the captain's sister.

'Not Tortoise Four,' Joe said. It would have taken a harder person than Joe not to feel sorry for someone with a sister who made him shoot baby animals and who seemed oblivious to his raging shell shock, even if that someone was a bastard. 'You can't call it Tortoise Four because it sounds like you're trying to say *tortes fortes*. Strong Pies is – not a name,' he finished, because he couldn't think of the English for fundamentally and primordially irritating.

Kite's shoulders tacked into what might have been a laugh. Joe was relieved, too relieved, and he felt utterly weary. The relief must have been from some part of him that remembered Kite from the lighthouse. He wished there was a way to give his brain a slap. It was insisting that he feel things about people he didn't remember.

Other officers pitched in. Joe let himself tip sideways on the bench, full of the strong sense that horizontal was best. If he didn't concentrate, he couldn't catch what they were saying and he let himself sink into hearing only that strange, half-German, half-Scottish rhythm instead of the meanings of the sounds. The wind whirred. There were no windows and all the gun ports were closed, but he could feel how thin the walls were. The cold was stinging his eyes. The sea was getting rougher too, rough enough for them to have to hold their wine glasses. A drift of water splashed down the hatchway. He watched it and felt like he was suspended in cold and bruises and nausea, with no end nearby.

Joe curled forward. At least he wasn't going to disappear.

Alice could, though. M. Saint-Marie, de Méritens. Lily. They would, too, if the English won this war. All of history would be different.

The ship rode another wave and his stomach spun.

Lying still, he could feel the whispering of some unnamed, ethereal rip tide moving from this time to his own, sucked through the pillars. Something that had tided straight through his own skull, and McCullough's, and washed away their memory of everything that had happened when they tried to stand against the flow.

Kite and Mrs Castlereagh were talking over his head now.

'How are you?' Kite said, so softly it was hard to hear him. It was Spanish. Joe was surprised, but he understood. That was unsettling. He'd had no idea he knew anything except English and French. According to M. Saint-Marie, Joe had never left Londres.

Spanish must have belonged with Madeline. He held the idea close, feeling like he had been given another corner piece of a puzzle with no picture on it yet.

Mrs Castlereagh was quiet at first. 'Missouri, we need to know if he can remember.'

Joe froze. The seasickness vanished off somewhere into the background.

'What? I thought we agreed before. If he remembers anything, that would prove the gate does *not* wipe memory entirely—'

'Exactly—'

'Yes, exactly!' Kite said. His voice went high when he was indignant. 'He could go back home, remember all this and— He's *poor*, Agatha. Say he goes home, and he even means to keep the gate a secret; what happens when he's got four children and he's down to the last sixpence? He'll have to sell the information.'

'Right, so we need to know, one way or another. You don't find a mystery bomb and make no effort to find out whether it's live or not, do you? If he can remember, if he's live, he'll have to stay here.'

'And you'll what? Keep him locked in the attic for ever?'

'Yes. Listen to yourself. You're hoping the bomb is just a ball, and that you won't have to defuse it. But hoping for the best is not a strategy.'

Kite was silent.

'And if he remembers,' she added softly, 'there's a strong chance he'll want to help. He'll want to stay. You won't have to keep cocking around trying to scare him into cooperating. The siege is *soon*, he told you that. We need him to help, really help, not just do the minimum.'

'Will he want to? Or will he just be furious and sell us out? Will I end up having to shoot him? I know what you're saying, but if you find a mystery bomb, you don't chuck rocks at it either.'

'You're being a coward,' she said. It wasn't aggressive; she only sounded disheartened from speaking to someone who was less than her. Under the table, Kite clenched his hands so hard that his knuckles cracked. They sounded painful. 'We need to know. Besides, you can't expect him to walk around without being recognised. Someone will know him, someone will tell him.'

'Really?' Kite said, high again. 'Who? Everyone is dead. No one knows anyone any more. I can walk around Edinburgh without being recognised and I'm on WANTED posters all over the Republic.'

'If you can taste sand, I think it might be because you've got your head in quite a lot of it.'

The silence went on for a long time.

Joe sat up. 'What do you know about me?'

They both looked at him like he'd grown another set of arms.

'I know I've been here before,' Joe pushed. 'My wife's name is on one of those bloody pillars. You know me, don't you?'

'Agatha, I swear to God,' Kite said.

Agatha seemed not to hear. She was looking at Joe, with something between dismay and hope etched in the lines around her eyes. 'Have you heard of a ship called the *Kingdom*?'

'I will,' Kite said very quietly, 'have you arrested, Agatha.'

Joe scrabbled for a memory, but no bells rang. It sent a fresh bleakness all through him. Everything from the epilepsy visions – or, the lost part of his life, the changed history, whatever it was – felt so close to the surface that he'd been sure that with one good prod, and it would all open up. The *Kingdom* meant nothing, though. 'No,' he said. 'I don't think so. What's important about it?'

'Sergeant Drake,' Kite ground out, and three marines came across.

'Are you going to arrest her for wanting to help me?' Joe demanded.

Agatha lifted her eyebrow at the three marines, and then clapped Joe's shoulder as she got up. 'Never mind it for now.'

'One more word,' Kite said to her in Spanish. Wherever Joe's Spanish came from, it wasn't his first language. He understood, but not perfectly. He could hear that Kite had a courtly accent, but it still sounded foreign, and more than that, it gave him a buzz of unease, even though he had never met a Spaniard before. Maybe it was just a cultural hangover from the Inquisition, but it felt worse than a vague prejudice. Joe pushed both hands through the back of his hair and pulled hard, wishing he could wrench the memories out.

Agatha ignored him. 'For God's sake, Drake, get back or don't come crying to me next time you're shot.'

Drake and the others shuffled aside, and then looked relieved once she'd gone. Kite nodded for them to sit down again.

Joe waited to see if any explanation was forthcoming, but none was.

'What does the *Kingdom* have to do with anything? Why does it matter?'

'Why are you even asking me?' Kite said wearily. 'You heard me, before. If it turns out you're able to remember anything, we can't let you go home. You could remember the gate, you could sell that information. You should be very eager to remain ignorant.'

'Because I *need* to know! I work for the engine company *because* of the Eilean Mòr light.' Joe pulled out the postcard and shoved it across the table. 'This. This was sent to me not long after I turned up at a train station with no memory. I went looking for someone who might know about this place. I found the de Méritens workshop. When we heard there was a problem with *this* lighthouse, I volunteered to come, to see if I could find out what had happened to me. Or who this person is, who wrote this card. I knew someone called Madeline, I think she was my wife, or my sister, or – I don't know, but M, Madeline, she could still be here! This is my whole life. I have a right to know.'

Kite looked down at the card. 'If you talk about it again to me or to anyone else, I'll chain you to the mast. I hope you won't, though, because I've got a job for you.'

'Is it horrifying?' Joe snapped.

'Depends,' Kite said greyly. He wasn't too proud to show that he was tired. Joe wished that he would be. If he would just do the little show that men always did for each other, pretending to be tough in the face of someone they didn't like, he would have been more manageable. That he didn't care was becoming so disturbing that Joe wasn't sure how to respond any more.

16

Kite took him back to the stateroom. It was busy now, full of officers looking at charts and papers, or making themselves coffee in metal mugs. Another man, the bent Scot who'd come with them onto the ice, settled in the corner with some stitching, his crutch hooked up next to Kite's coat. Just as they arrived, a boy of about fourteen hurried in too and saluted.

'Mr Hathaway,' said Kite. 'You've a new tutor.'

'What?' said Joe.

'You're an engineer; that must involve a good deal of calculation,' Kite explained. 'This is Fred Hathaway, he's going for his lieutenant's exam next month. Annoyingly early,' he added to Fred, who beamed and then remembered to arrange his face in a more officerly way. But Kite smiled a bit too. 'His capabilities are rather ahead of the other midshipmen. Mr Hathaway, you'll look after Mr Tournier for the duration of his stay with us. You keep him on your watch, and you make sure he's in the right place at the right time. The watch schedule is on the door now.'

Joe felt indignant. Kite was the one who'd taken him, Kite was the one refusing to help him remember, and Kite was the one who should have to put up with him. Taking him, ignoring him, and then dumping him on someone else was very much having his cake and eating it.

Joe didn't say anything. Drake, the marine, was in the far corner, watching.

'Mr Tournier, Mr Hathaway. I'm sure you'll enjoy each other,' Kite concluded.

'Oh, excellent,' Fred exclaimed. He seemed not to think that being given a kidnapped man was unusual.

He was a rangy, beachy boy, handsome in a way that would fade fast, but it wouldn't matter; he was one of those people who looked like they might break out into dance at any moment. When he walked, he sprang. Apart from that, he was the image of Lieutenant Wellesley, and Joe wondered just how many brothers and sisters were on the same ship, and whether the navy was too stupid to see what it would do to their families if *Agamemnon* sank, or whether nobody cared any more. 'Let's have a look at the watch rota, shall we?'

Kite stood back against his own desk, absolutely still. He gave Joe a brief wry look, one that said his years of excess energy were so far behind him he probably couldn't have found them on a map now. Joe stared at him hard. There was a special place in hell for people who pretended to be your friend while they were holding a whip over you. To his surprise, Kite looked down like he was ashamed.

While they'd been talking, other children had arrived, boys and girls, all in the same uniform as Fred, and at the mention of the watch rota, they'd all clustered round a chart on the door, but Fred was tall enough to look over their heads.

The chart was a checkerboard of red and green, and full of names. Down the side was a long list of times: all six-hour slots except one in the middle that split into three hours on either side. Joe couldn't work out what it was supposed to be describing. A few groans went round, and a few happy cries.

'Hah,' said Fred, pleased. 'We're on at nine tonight and nine tomorrow morning.'

'Sorry, how are you reading ...?' said Joe.

'We're on a two-set watch. You're in starboard, with me,' Fred explained, or he seemed to think he was explaining. He tapped a green square. 'Red for port, green for starboard. Watches are six hours long. You have one on, one off, at both ends of the day.' He drew his fingertip down the timetable. 'So tomorrow will be good for us, we're not up until nine, but it will be six the next morning. See?'

'A watch is like a work shift?'

'Oh. Yes,' said Fred, looking worried to find that Joe hadn't known even that. 'Does that ... make sense?'

Joe nodded. It did, sort of. He liked timetables, although he could see he was not going to like sailing jargon.

'When you come on watch, someone from the last watch will wake you up quarter of an hour before. Then you get up and go to the mainmast.' Fred smiled. 'Once you get there, the watch officer will tell everyone what to do. Simple!'

Joe decided not to ruin it and ask what a starboard was. 'Sorry, I'm probably not quite – but if you're on for six hours and off for six hours and then on again, surely you never get a full night's sleep?'

Fred seemed puzzled. 'Sleep a bit, work a bit, sleep a bit again; you'll get used to it.'

No wonder Kite looked so exhausted.

The other children were taking seats at the table. None of them were older than about seventeen. Joe felt lost, and then realised with a slow dismay that this was the start of some kind of lesson. Kite was moving chairs; he was putting the ones from his desk at the table. Room for himself, and room for Joe. School; hours after he'd been dragged out of a lighthouse. When Kite said he would be Fred's tutor, he had meant *right now.*

Fred tugged Joe's sleeve to get him to sit down. Joe sat. It was surreal. In passing, Kite gave them a textbook, and then leaned over Joe's shoulder. He smelled of fresh ironing.

'So it's this section,' he said. 'The astronomy stuff there, zeniths and meridians and all that, but it's all basic mathematics. You'll work it out.'

'This is …' Joe was at a total, tumbled loss. 'I'm teaching children now? Why aren't you locking me up?'

'Do I need to?'

Joe didn't want to think about what a cell would be like aboard a Napoleonic battleship. It was cold in here, in Kite's own stateroom. A week in a tiny unheated space buried somewhere in the ship's guts sounded like an efficient way to die before they even reached Edinburgh.

'No.'

Kite was still leaning on the back of Joe's chair, because the ship was really swaying now. Perhaps it was the fight to stay upright, or perhaps he was relaxing a bit, but his shoulders sank into a less officerly straightness. 'Living on a ship is hard. You need friends and people who know you. I don't want to keep you isolated. You have a better chance of surviving if you're involved. I'm not playing games with you, Mr Tournier, I'm just trying to keep you alive. Mr Hathaway,' Kite added to Fred, who had been rubbing one fingertip around the silver ribbon on Kite's jacket sleeve. 'Touching people who you aren't related or married to is …?'

'Creepy, sir. Sorry, sir,' Fred said, not worried at all.

'Yes it is,' Kite said, looking hopeless.

The ship hit a wave at a bad angle and the deck dropped, which flung Kite onto his knees. Joe caught his arm and set him upright, and then thought wryly how hard good manners died even in the face of a psychopath. Kite nodded when he had his balance again. He was shaking; he must have felt seasick too. The thought was less satisfying than Joe would have liked.

'Why doesn't that count?' Fred said indignantly. 'You're not married to *him*.'

'Add bodily peril to the list, Fred,' Joe said, beginning to suspect it wasn't him Kite wanted to dodge.

Fred looked uncertain, then wrote himself a list.

Around them, the children were settling. Given what Kite was like, Joe would have expected a lot of frightened, silent faces. Instead they all seemed overjoyed to be in the captain's stateroom, and when Kite moved to the head of the table, they shut up instantly, but not as if they were scared of him. They only wanted to know what he was going to say.

'Evening, everyone. As you've noticed, we have a new member of the crew. His name is Mr Tournier, and unfortunately he *is* French, but I trust all of you to look after him, and ensure there is no trouble with the men.'

The younger ones looked proud to be trusted, and the older ones sat back a little, pretending not to be.

'He will be making us some machinery that might help us in battle. He has no official rank, but I'd like you to treat him as a petty officer, understood?'

A chorus of yessirs.

'Good. Now, given that, we had better tell him the Articles of War. One article each round the table. Mr Hathaway, you start, please.'

Fred smiled easily. 'Yes, sir. The Articles of War are the laws of the sea. If you stick to them, you'll have smooth sailing, and if you don't, you'll end up looking at a firing squad. That wouldn't be very nice for you probably. Unless you did one of those clever tricks like they do in books and got them to—'

'Hathaway,' Kite murmured. 'What did we talk about not even twenty-four hours ago?'

'Talking too much, sir,' Fred said cheerfully. 'But my sister says it's better to talk too much than not enough. She was talking about you actually, sir—'

The other midshipmen fell about laughing, and one of the older girls threw a pencil at Fred's head. 'Maybe Mr Tournier can build a special filter for you, Fred!'

'That wasn't bad, was it?' Fred said in the rueful way of someone who really couldn't tell.

Kite seemed not to mind. 'Round the table, ladies and gentlemen.'

There were only twenty or so articles, but they were vicious. Sleeping on watch, punishable at the captain's discretion. Drinking, gambling, same. Not reporting information useful to the fleet at the first possible opportunity, death. Sodomy, insubordination, failure to pursue the enemy, incitation to mutiny, death, death, death. Joe might have thought it was all normal enough, given the place and the time, if he'd only read them; but to hear them in children's voices put a spidery feeling down the back of his neck. All the while, Kite watched him.

'Mr Tournier was pressed,' Kite said quietly once the last boy had finished. 'He didn't choose to be here. But he is, and he understands that it isn't anyone's fault. The Articles compel all of us to transport a person of his usefulness to Edinburgh. He understands that we would be shot for failing to do this. He knows too that trying to convince any person aboard, particularly any officers, to help him, will result in that officer's execution. So don't be frightened of him. He won't try to get any of you in trouble.' He had fixed his eyes straight onto Joe for all of it.

'That's probably good,' the littlest midshipman said seriously, a tiny girl who could only have been about ten. Someone who loved her must have been aboard too, because they'd done her hair in beautiful cornrows, studded with silver beads to go with the silver on her uniform. 'I'm exceeding gullible, sir.'

Everyone laughed, and Joe felt cold.

The lesson was all maths and numbers. Kite was teaching them to work out longitude from the stars, and after listening even only for a few minutes, it was obvious that the process took hours. He gave straight data to the eldest, measurements of constellations, and with the youngest it was more of an algebra lesson. They were working with the ship's real location, on the charts that Kite already had out on the desk. The littlest girl looked delighted when Kite let her mark their current location with a cross on the map. It must have been a high honour. Joe felt strangely betrayed. Kite was good with the children. If he'd just been a vicious man, it would have been all right, but watching him be kind made everything that had happened feel personal.

Fred Hathaway was miles ahead of the others. It was fun going through the exercises in his exam book. They were easy enough for Joe to understand, but complicated enough that it was a good piece of mental acrobatics.

After the lesson, Kite hurried the little ones out to bed. It was hard to watch. There were four of them and they went in a line like ducklings. The eldest three, including Fred, stayed for a drink and talked about their families and letters from home. Kite didn't say anything about his own family, if he had one, but he seemed to know all their mothers' names and what their sisters did. There was a wine glass for Joe as well.

In the background, the Scottish man who'd come with them on the ice, and who seemed to be Kite's servant, was sewing. He was called Clay, which suited him, because he was an unhealthy grey colour. His thread creaked through the cotton. Over the smell of the wine, and the young men laughing and the quiet bump of steps outside on the deck, it was homely. The swinging lamps slung shadows up and down the room.

Bells chimed out round the ship. Joe checked his watch. Three hours. He couldn't think where the time had gone. It disturbed him, that he had settled so quickly. He was still on edge, and the whip-mark down the back of his head still ached, but he hadn't been frightened during the lesson and, much worse, he hadn't been angry. He was going to have to learn to stay angry if he wanted to get away from here. Otherwise – otherwise, he would just get used to it. Like he got used to everything.

Joe waited until the midshipmen had all gone and then coughed in case Kite had forgotten he was there, but he hadn't. He glanced over while he gathered together the cups and glasses.

'Don't smoke in here,' he said.

Joe put the cigarette case away.

'Filthy habit,' Clay said unexpectedly from the corner. He shot Joe a dark look, but then he glanced at Kite to see if it was all right and settled back against the wall when Kite smiled. It was unnerving. It was a child's manner in a middle-aged man. Joe's neck crawled again when it occurred to him to wonder if Kite had done whatever necessitated the crutch.

'What the hell have I done to you?' Joe asked him, mainly teasing. If he could get Clay on his side, that would help a lot. Someone with keys and access to desks and papers. He didn't have any kind of plan yet, but access was always a good thing.

Clay gave him a look of such black hatred that it stuck for days afterward. With no other warning, he dipped his hand right into the brazier next to him, picked up a red-hot coal, and flung it at Joe's face.

Joe dived out the way, but the coal hit him on the side of the neck anyway. Even the brief touch burned.

Kite was already across the room, guiding Clay's hand down into the water pitcher. 'Go and get a bandage on that. And then – that reminds me. Lieutenant Wellesley says your cat is stuck in the rigging again.'

Clay made a weird, animal hiss at Joe, but stumped out. Joe frowned. There was something discomfiting about Clay. It made him feel like he would have if the man had been crabbing backwards around the deck with an obviously broken back and every sign of enjoying himself.

'I'm sorry,' Kite said quietly. 'There's no use getting angry with him, he's ...' He touched the side of his own head. 'We play hide and seek when we're off watch.'

Joe couldn't imagine Kite playing with anyone at anything. 'What's his problem with me?'

Kite sank a rag in the water jug, squeezed it out, then handed it to Joe. 'He doesn't like change.'

Joe pressed the cloth to his neck, then looked round when someone opened the door. Mrs Castlereagh. Thank God.

'All done?' she said.

'All done,' Kite said, a little tightly. Joe realised that Kite was waiting for her to bring up the argument they'd had before.

'I'll go,' said Joe. And then, 'Where am I going?'

'No, you're sleeping here or you'll get yourself killed,' Kite told him.

'What? Why? I'm *not* French.'

Kite only gave him a slow, tolerant look which said quite clearly that, given the circumstances, he was willing to give Joe another few hours to catch up on the obvious facts. 'I'd suggest you don't mix too much with the crew, or if you do – pretend to be from Jamaica or something. The officers are fine, they'll look after you, but a third of the sailors are pressed from prison hulks. We can keep them in fair order, but this war turned filthy a while ago now and everyone has very personal grudges towards anyone with an accent like yours.'

Joe stared at him. 'You kidnapped a *third* of your crew?'

'Welcome to His Majesty's Navy,' Kite said, and moved out a chair for his sister.

Mrs Castlereagh told Joe to call her Agatha. She was staying the night in the stateroom as well, Joe suspected to make sure that he and Kite didn't kill each other. With her there, it felt safe – and warm, because the second she arrived, she lit two more braziers and damn it if the coal stores were running out, because everyone would freeze to the floor if they didn't get the room heated up. Kite dipped his head and only looked grateful that she'd taken charge.

She broke out some more wine. After a couple of glasses, she and Kite were telling stories about the Spanish navy; or rather, she did, and Kite filled in the small spaces. Before long, Joe began to see that when she was nearby, Kite deferred to her. It was such a relief to know someone had a leash on the man that Joe wanted to hug her.

Agatha pushed to see how much Spanish Joe could get. Nine-tenths seemed to be the answer and, looking uneasy, Kite told him he had a genteel accent, the kind people learned at boarding school.

'I definitely didn't,' promised Joe. 'My master in Londres bought me before I was even born. Though who knows. Maybe in another version of things.' He hesitated, then told them about the Psychical Society, and the false memories that weren't false at all, that matched up between people who had never met. Madeline. But not the man who waited. He wasn't giving Kite that, not for anything.

Agatha and Kite glanced at each other in their twinnish way. They weren't twins; Agatha was older, Joe's age.

'Is there anything else like that?' Agatha said. 'Things you know but shouldn't?'

'I don't know. I didn't know about the Spanish until today.'

'Don't,' Kite said to her. 'Please.'

Joe was silent at first, painfully aware that they were treating him far better than they had to. He was sitting in the stateroom with the captain and the surgeon, drinking their wine, when Kite could have put him in some dank little cell somewhere. Joe had to screw up a lot of nerve to risk it. 'Look, chain me to the mast if you want, but I can't not ask. Why did you ask me about the *Kingdom* before? What do you know about me, what do you want me to remember?'

'I told you not to ask me again.'

Agatha looked hard at Kite. 'Tell him.'

'No.'

'You,' she said, very soft, 'owe me this, Missouri. You will tell him.'

Joe had seen people struggle less with a crate of bricks than Kite did under the weight of his sister's stare. He'd never known one human being control another so completely. He couldn't tell if she had something over Kite, or if this was just what having a sister was like.

'Why's he owe it you?' Joe said.

'Because he killed my husband, so he owes me for ever,' Agatha said mildly.

The way she looked at Kite then made Joe shrink inside. She was studying him like he was a machine; one that was running down now but still just useful enough to maintain. However relieved Joe had been before to know she had some control over her brother, he didn't feel it any more. He wished that they would just let him go away and sleep somewhere else. He could feel the air crackling between them, and the longer he sat there, the more likely it seemed that he was going to end up electrocuted.

Kite was looking right away now, into the far corner, as if he were trying to will himself somewhere else.

'So the *Kingdom*,' Agatha said. She said it normally, but it wrenched Kite's eyes back to them in the same way a yank on a chain around his neck would have.

Joe shifted, so uncomfortable now that he wondered about pretending to be more seasick than he was, just to duck out. He wanted to tell her to be less savage, but maybe she was right, maybe this was justice.

'The *Kingdom* came from your time,' Kite said to Joe. Every word twisted out like a tooth. 'It's how we know about this place. It sailed from Eilean Mòr in eighteen ninety-one. Surveying for that lighthouse. But they sailed home without going back through the pillars. They ended up off the coast of Southampton in seventeen ninety-seven.'

17

The English Channel, 1797

Kite had been a signal lieutenant on HMS *Defiance* on the day they saw the *Kingdom*. He'd been twenty-five and awake for about six months, because unlike their own captain, Admiral Howe on the flagship did not believe that signalling was only a pointless fad of the Admiralty.

Whenever he did manage to sit down and talk to somebody, he ended up speaking a weird mix of English, Spanish, and naval signal code numbers, so noticeably that the other lieutenants had started drawing out flags on napkins if they had to pass him a note. If he was ever going to hallucinate, Month Six was the time. He was already sure the dragonfly in their cabin was imaginary. No one else ever seemed to see it.

That was what he thought was happening, to begin with: that he was seeing things. It was not such an extraordinary prospect as it would have been on land. Even well-rested people in their right minds saw things in dense fog at sea; Kite had, on several occasions. Towering leviathan things which, of course, were never really there.

They had sailed in inches all day, powered only by the current. The fog was so dense off the Dorset coast that with his hand in front of his face, Kite couldn't make out the anchor design on his sleeve button. The duty watch were taking ten minute turns to ring the great fog bell by the foremast. Five second bursts of ringing, once a minute, every minute. It sounded lonely, and cold.

The noise that blasted through the fog then was so loud it hurt. It wasn't like anything he had heard before. It thrummed in the deck and down his bones, and the men on the quarterdeck smacked their hands over their ears. When it stopped, no one moved. The silence was fearful.

There was a light in the middle distance. It hovered sixty feet above the water, hazy in the fog but brilliant, far too bright to be a lamp. He had a panicky thought about falling stars, but he'd seen those before, and they didn't *float*. A tiny cabin boy rushed away from the rail and hid behind him. The only sound was the sea and a low unplaceable hum. Kite looked around twice, to make sure everyone else was seeing it too. They were. The whole deck crew had frozen.

'I wasn't even christened properly,' someone whispered.

'Quietly,' Kite said, just loud enough to carry across the deck but not beyond, 'send the children below.' He nudged the little boy towards the hatchway. It seemed like the right thing to do, even though God knew a few inches of wood didn't seem like much to put between the children and whatever was behind that awful light.

He stayed there to mark where the hatch was for the children – it was impossible to see otherwise – and then to murmur down to the anxious men who had come to the base of the ladder below. He didn't know what to tell them, except to keep the boys down there. He couldn't say there might be an archangel a few degrees to port.

Fear not, said he, for mighty dread had seized their troubled minds; and well it bloody might. Everyone was staring at the light through the fog, and Kite didn't think he was alone in hoping for a voice, however chilling, to explain itself.

There was no voice.

Christ, you sat there complacent in church while some bore droned on about Eden, or Michael and the sword, and never once did it sound like a thing had happened to real people. It flashed in front of him now as clearly as if he had been there to see it, how Eve and Adam must have felt that day, when a celestial, star-bridging *thing* hammered down from the sky and smashed into the earth just by them, a soldier armed and furious. And God, how negligent it was, for priests to have gone around for a thousand years commissioning artists to paint insipid white-robed fairy-babies with harps when what they should have been warning people about was ... this.

They came to a clearer space in the fog, which gave them a longer view. The light was moving away from them. Under it were littler lights, in the familiar triangle shape that came from hanging lamps on a boom and topmast.

A ship.

Kite could just make out an iron tower and a funnel. It breathed dark smoke. When he let his eyes come back to things in the foreground, he realised that sailors had clustered close, not knowing what to do. He glanced up at the quarterdeck, where Captain Heecham didn't look interested in giving any orders.

'All right,' he said, trying not to show firstly how relieved he was that this wasn't the start of the apocalypse, and secondly how embarrassed he was to have lived for years imagining he wasn't that religious, only to find childhood Catholicism burst-ing back to life right at the most unhelpful moment. 'Back to work. Embarrassing to capsize because we all want to stare.'

There were some muted laughs. He pushed a few shoulders, very gently, because the sailors were slight men, pressed or from long lines of underfed families. He was freshly shocked every few days by how fragile they all were. On the sea, the smoking ship glided on, effortless, on no wind.

The ship overtook them slowly about two hundred yards to port, just in view. There was nobody on the deck, and no sign that anyone on it had noticed the *Defiance*. No reply to their signal flag.

In the deep quiet of the fog, it was possible to hear the flicker-click of moving water over a deeper mechanical snarl. The ship had waterwheels. They were what kept it going, he thought, but the whole thing was so unlikely he had lost confidence in any ability to guess what it might be doing. It had masts, rigging, and sails, but they were furled. When the rocks came sharper and more frequently, the *Defiance* lagged, unable to keep up.

Five knots on no wind, in fog. The sailors were whispering about devices from Hell. Someone thought it must be some advance made by the French. Or both.

'Sir?' the first one said, looking for an umpire.

He shook his head, feeling odd, because an hour ago he would have said that he had a nodding acquaintance with most marine-related things in the world, but the ship was an auto-mated beast unrelated to anything he knew.

Somewhere out in the fog, a cannon fired. It sounded flat: no flintlock. French.

All along the rail, men straightened up fast. Beyond the mechanical ship, still invisible except for the patch of fog its smoke was turning black, there was a French warship, and it had just fired a warning shot. Kite whisper-hissed for the gunners to get below in case they had to engage. Up and down the deck, he heard the other lieutenants doing the same.

A bright light flickered at them from the mechanical ship, about level with the mast. *Flash flash flash, off, flash flash flash.* They had to be signals. Kite had never seen a light code before and he couldn't even start to guess what it said. It was the same three, in sets, again and again. As he watched, a woman in green rushed to the stern with a man, and waved at them before she pushed the man overboard. The man hit the water at a painful angle, but he did surface, gasping.

Just people: normal frightened people. Not archangels or devils. A worried stir went along the rail. The water was freezing. No one could last in it for more than a few minutes.

'Get that man out of the buggering water!' Captain Heecham shouted from the quarterdeck. He was hunched forward on the taffrail, staring like everyone else. He looked like a slouching bison.

Sailors ran for lifelines.

'Where's he gone?'

'I can see him,' Kite said quickly. He followed the man in the water and held his arm out straight to guide the sailors. The man could swim, at least.

A round of gunshots went off this time, a whole broadside, from somewhere beyond the mechanical ship. Kite still couldn't see anything, but he could hear the French ship now – someone was yelling orders. More black smoke poured into the fog.

The man in the sea vanished underwater for a few seconds, but he came up again. Still, the mechanical ship showed no flag. The blinking light signal went on and on.

'Sir, do we engage?' the second mate's voice called from near the hatchway.

'She's got no colours, she could be anyone's!' Heecham bellowed back.

When the man in the water reached the end of the rope, he only rested against it, too tired to pull himself up. Someone yelled at him to tie a bowline knot, but he clearly wasn't a sailor; he only looked blank. Shrapnel tore into the water next to him. The sailors shouted to hurry the fuck up before he was blown apart.

'Quiet!' Kite said to them. 'Quiet, all of you. Sir,' he called down to the man in the water, 'listen. I'm going to tell you how to tie a knot that won't break your ribs when we pull you in, all right? It's not difficult.' Everyone gasped as a cannon ball smashed up a plume of water all of ten feet off the bow. On the quarterdeck, Heecham was still telling the helmsman to hold still, and not far off Kite and the sailors, a midshipman was hauling hard on the signal flag ropes, uncoiling a message up the mast:

URGENT identify yourself

Still nothing from the mechanical ship, no flag to show its nation. More shrapnel.

'Ready?' Kite said, in what he hoped was a calm voice. It was Officer Trick Number One. If you could sound calm enough, you could claim that everything was absolutely fine, even if the man next to you had just exploded, and *people would believe you.*

The man in the water nodded. He was shivering so badly he could barely move his hands, but he was doing a hell of a job at not panicking, and he managed the knot on the first try. The second it was done, the sailors leapt on the rope and hauled him out. Kite leaned down over the side to lift him up. The man folded on to the deck soaked and shivering. Kite knelt to start getting the man's coat off. The water streaming off him was so cold that it hurt to touch.

Through the rails, Kite saw more gun flashes, and then a mammoth fireball exploded across the mechanical ship's prow. The heat blasted all the way to the *Defiance*, along with an acrid smell and plumes of pitchy smoke. Sailors jerked back from the rail, swearing. Something blasted into the water right next to the hull, even bumped it. A chunk of one of those great water-wheels, mangled, and so hot it hissed furiously in the water.

The hull ground along something. The helmsman turned them away.

'Wait, what about ...' The man trailed off. He looked dazed. Hitting the sea would have felt like smacking into something solid from the height he'd fallen.

'We can't sail here blind,' Kite said. He squeezed his hands to make him listen, because the way he was shivering looked more like fear now than cold. 'Come on, let's ...'

'Is he a devil?' someone asked plaintively.

'No, he's just cold,' Kite said with as much authority as he could muster. 'Move aside, come on. Back to work.' He helped the man up as well as he could. 'Are you?' he added, less sure. 'Or – the other thing?'

'No,' the man managed. He looked scared. 'Are you a ghost?'

'No,' said Kite, perplexed. 'I'm a signal lieutenant.'

The man looked even more relieved than Kite felt.

His name was Jem Castlereagh. As soon as he was dry, Kite took him to Captain Heecham who, for all his usual stolidity, listened hard. So did Kite. The two senior lieutenants stood a little distance behind Heecham, the lamplight dotting gleams on the silver stripes on their sleeves.

The name of the mechanical ship was the *Kingdom*. It was not an infernal invention, nor celestial, but one built by ordinary people. It had come from Scotland. It was a vessel surveying for a lighthouse. Jem had been aboard on a government inspection; he was something to do with Parliament and a project to improve lighthouses all round the coast. But then they had begun to see a ghost ship following them.

Jem had thought something odd was going on ashore as well, because when they passed ports, the lights were too few and too dim – but it wasn't until half an hour ago that they had any idea that anything really strange had happened. Not until they realised the ghost ship wasn't a ghost ship at all, but a French battleship trailing them. The French had fired when the *Kingdom* tried to pull away.

While he spoke, Jem studied Heecham's office. His eyes caught on the lamps fixed between the tilting windows, on their uniforms, the papers on the desk. They were remark-able eyes, an earthy shade of bluish-green Kite had never seen before, and which he wouldn't have expected on someone so foreign-looking. But Jem wasn't foreign. His voice was as English as Oxford silverware.

'But why did you think it was a ghost ship?' Heecham demanded. He sounded furious, which was how he always sounded when he was rattled. 'We're in the middle of a war, man; you're hardly more likely to see a *ghost* than the French! And what the bollocking *hell* was that ship? What were those waterwheels, how were you running on no sail?'

Jem showed no ire, nor impatience. He only looked like he would have sold his soul to be anywhere else. 'May I ask what year it is?'

'What?' Heecham snapped.

'Seventeen ninety-seven,' Kite said, with a strange spinning feeling.

Jem nodded. He seemed calm, but it was oil on water. He was still shaking, even though the cabin was hot now. 'Captain Heecham – we left Scotland in eighteen ninety-one. There is no war then. We all thought the French ship was a ghost ship because … because we don't *have* sailing ships any more. Modern ships run on coal engines.' He smiled a fraction. 'I suspect I'm rather lost, gentlemen.'

There was a moment of entire stillness. The only motion was the swing of the lamps on the ceiling, and the tilt of the horizon beyond the windows. Heecham shifted his weight from foot to foot and huffed his breath out. He wanted to roar that it was all rubbish, Kite could see that accusation coiled up in his throat, but they had all seen the *Kingdom*. There was nothing like it anywhere in the world. Kite had heard of engines, but only ones which worked the pumps in mines. They didn't power ships. And there was Jem himself; extremely English and somehow foreign all the same, dressed with Puritanical plainness all in black and white.

'Well,' Heecham said finally. He seemed to deflate. 'We are making now for Southampton, where, if you stick to this story, the Admiralty shall wish to speak to you in detail. In the meantime, Mr Castlereagh, you must consider yourself our guest.'

'Thank you, that's very kind.' Jem sounded mechanical. Kite brushed his shoulder, worried he might be about to faint. He didn't faint, but he caught Kite's knuckles and squeezed them as hard as someone in the middle of an amputation might have. His skin was freezing, despite the brazier beside him. He was going into shock. Kite edged the brazier closer with the toe of his boot.

'How is this even possible?' Jem said softly, to all of them.

'The fog, perhaps. Something eerie about it. One always hears stories.' Heecham had turned angry again. Jem flinched. Kite tried to communicate only with his fingertips that there was nothing to worry about there, that Heecham wasn't angry with *him*, only his own ignorance.

Everyone was quiet. The sounds of the deck came down to them; the thumps of footsteps, muted from the seamen who went barefoot, sharp from officers' boot heels. Kite could feel the rudder pulling to one side as the helmsman steered away from shore.

Heecham sighed. 'Tom,' he said to the first mate, 'get us back on course to Southampton.'

For the first time, Jem really seemed to hear what was being said. He frowned, and sat forward. Kite saw everything in him sharpen. It must have been a prodigious effort of will. 'I beg your pardon, captain, but you must follow my ship. It wasn't destroyed, I saw. They just blasted off one of the waterwheels, they were going aboard with grappling hooks. You *must* get it back. If those people—'

'The French,' Heecham corrected him. He didn't count Frenchmen as people.

'If they got the *Kingdom* in anything like one piece, they could back-engineer the machinery. And if they got the engineers alive—'

'I'm afraid that's out of our hands now. We have no means of chasing them in fog.'

Jem looked between them all. 'Did you say seventeen ninety-seven before?'

'Yes—'

'In eight years,' he said, intense now, 'this navy is going to fight a battle that decides the fate of England. It will be at a place called Trafalgar. It stops a French invasion. But the engineers and sailors aboard the *Kingdom* know that, and I imagine some-one will make them talk. You *have* to get the *Kingdom* back, or you will lose England in eight years.'

There was a little silence. Jem had the most incredible voice, strong as a singer's and low from smoking, unwavering even though Heecham had turned puce.

'Whatever the truth of that,' Heecham said, dangerously quiet now, 'I am the commander here, and I tell you it is *not* in my power to follow anybody in this fog.' He stabbed his finger at the window, where the fog coiled. 'We would run aground, sir, unless you have some wonderful fog-penetrating device about your person we might utilise?'

'I am as you find me,' Jem said, still and calm, and resigned. But the sharpness hadn't gone from him. Kite started to suspect he might be very, very clever. The suspicion made him uncom-fortable. It would have been easier to believe a stupid person without the imagination to lie.

Heecham seemed to be thinking the same, because he was staring at Jem hard now. 'Lieutenant Kite will look after you. These other gentlemen and I will endeavour to think of a way to explain all this to the Admiralty in a manner that does not sound like insanity.'

Kite sketched a bow and waited at the door for Jem, who looked much more aristocratic than he should have been able to in Kite's jacket. As they passed out into the fog again, Jem looked back towards the land, where the French ship and his own had disappeared, his teeth set.

Within a couple of days, Jem proved himself to be sharp as a pin. The sailors, fascinated with him, taught him knots, and he learned so fast he overtook half of them. He managed to get someone to explain how everything worked, every pulley and line, and soon he even had a copy of the lieutenants' exam book and a notebook full of problems from it that he'd solved already. Kite watched him and said nothing, but he noticed the attention, and Jem's unfailing affability with the men. If the French were going to get a spy aboard, they couldn't have chosen someone more charming.

Only, there were a thousand less ridiculous ways to get a spy aboard an English ship. Anyone could sign up. There were plenty of Frenchmen in English service. Officers were tied to particular countries, but sailors were freelancers. They could serve in whatever navy they liked and most of the career men did just that.

Kite started to wonder if the only real explanation wasn't the one right in front of him: that Jem was an extremely well-educated man from the future who had found himself, by some means or other, stuck in the past, and now was doing his utmost to survive life on a warship.

On the morning they were due to reach Southampton, Kite woke up at half past five, half an hour before his watch, to find Jem pressed flat against his chest, his fingers clenched over Kite's sleeve. Kite undid them as gently as he could, but Jem still jumped.

'Ah ... good morning?' Kite ventured.

Jem shook his head. Kite heard the vertebrae in his neck grind. 'I'm sorry. I'm – I woke up, I couldn't breathe. I don't know what's the matter with me.'

'It's all right,' Kite said, not sure how he could possibly look like a solution to that problem. He did not have a reassuring face.

Spray and cold air came down through the open hatch. Everyone agreed they'd rather be damp and breathing than dry and suffocating. Opposite them in the other bunk, the second mate was dead asleep despite being rained on, still in his jacket and coat after the midnight-till-three watch. He was barely an outline in the dark; even with the hatch open, the cabin was always pitch-black at night.

Jem sat up as much as it was possible to, his back against the bulkhead and his weight on his tailbone. It was a tiny space, though, and he had to bridge his knees over Kite. 'I keep etching my initials on everything.' His voice wasn't steady any more. He was right on the edge of tears. 'Bang your head on that third slat there and you'll get JC stamped on your face. I can't stop. It's stupid.'

'Don't sound so surprised about it,' said Kite, shocked. 'Look at what's happened to you.'

Jem had taken Kite's hand and he was wringing his wrist, like a very soft schoolboy burn. He dropped it. 'Jesus Christ. I'm never like this, I'm not – I'm *not* a coward—'

'No one said you were—'

'Not really my most manly hour, though, is it,' Jem said tightly. His voice broke before he reached the end of the sentence. When he cried, it was silent, but Kite heard the fabric of his shirt move as he pressed both hands over his mouth.

Kite caught his arm. For the first time, he was certain that none of it was made up. He'd never seen a person in so much distress and trying so hard not to be.

'Jem, I don't know what things are like where you're from, but this is the navy. People get nervous. We're experts in nervous, we *invent* nervous problems. Battle fatigue, cabin fever, we're all wrecks. Christ's sake, you're a hundred years lost. It is all a bit trying.'

'I suppose.' When he was unhappy, Jem turned even better-spoken than usual, until there was so much cut glass in his voice that speaking to him was more like trying to talk to a chandelier than a person.

Kite rubbed his elbow. 'I've had a distressing thought and if it's right, we can't be associated any more. I do have my honour to uphold.'

'What?' Jem whispered.

'You show, sir, every unfortunate symptom of being from *the army*.'

Jem laughed like he hadn't expected to and then hugged him, hard. Jem was taller and stronger, and for the first time in Kite's adult life he couldn't have got away even if he'd wanted to. It gave him a deep bolt of alarm. But then he saw that what Jem needed more than anything was control over *something*, even if it was just whether or not a signal lieutenant got out of bed on time.

As it turned out, there was nothing for the watch officers to do; the Solent was calm and it would take hours to get into Southampton, because there was construction work in the harbour and they'd have to wait for someone to free up a docking space. So Kite took Jem up to the officers' mess for breakfast, where Heecham's secretary was showing a gaggle of fascinated midshipmen how to tattoo a stretch of pigskin. When someone herded them off to oversee some sailors cleaning, Jem took the needle himself and traced out fine clear lines. It was the lighthouse the architects had meant to build in Scotland. It was beautiful; he could really draw. Kite said so.

'Spend my life looking at architectural plans,' Jem said ruefully. For the fourth or fifth time, he glanced at the window, checking where they were. They hadn't moved. He must have been going mad. No one had said what would happen to him when they arrived, except that Heecham would talk to the Admiralty. That sounded ominous even to Kite. There was every chance the Admiralty would declare Jem a fraud, the crew hysterical en masse, and shove Jem out into the street with nowhere to go. Or worse, into a military prison.

Kite nudged him. 'Put that on me.'

Jem looked round at him. 'What?'

'It's good.'

Jem leaned down a little to catch Kite's eye and make sure he meant it, then held a match to the needle to clean it and turned back Kite's sleeve. It didn't hurt, and Jem did it even better than he had the first time, all razor lines and precise angles, and strange places where stairways went nowhere and something coiled in the sea.

'God's sake,' Heecham growled in passing. 'Tattoos on officers, I should demote you ...'

'It was a psychological emergency,' Jem explained, looking guilty.

'The bloody hell are you doing having psychological emergencies on your watch, Kite? Get the arsing topsails sorted out.' Heecham peered over his shoulder. 'Though I have to say that's very good.'

18

HMS *Agamemnon*, 1807

When Kite had finished, he looked at Agatha. He hadn't spoken for long – there had been a future ship, the French shot at it and took it, the English saved a man called Jem, all as factual as an official report – but he was asking if he could stop now. He had his hand clamped over the tattoo. There was a long quiet, filled only by the click of the coals in the brazier and the squeak of the dim safety lamps.

'Why did you tell me that?' Joe asked at last. 'Was I one of the others on that ship?'

The man who waited by the sea. It would be very, very good to have a name for him. If it was Jem – that would be something. Madeline had faded from his mind's eye, but that lonely figure by the water was something different. He couldn't *see* him well, but he could feel him, as distinct as if the man had only just left the room.

Agatha was sitting back from him. 'No. No, it's nothing to do with you.'

Joe wanted to explode. 'But then why—'

'Enough,' Kite said. He sounded normal, but his hand shook when he set down the wine. When he saw Joe notice, he shot him a flat stare that invited Joe to call it anything other than an injury tremor and see where it got him. Joe dropped his eyes. 'I need to get some sleep.'

'We'd better turn in too,' Agatha told Joe. She sounded hollow.

'What happened to the *Kingdom*?' Joe demanded. He was nearly choking. 'Where is Jem now? Can I talk to him?'

'No, he's dead,' Agatha said. She was twisting her ring finger. 'I told you.'

Joe felt dim. Jem Castlereagh; she was Mrs Castlereagh. 'Jem was your husband? But you said ...'

That Kite had killed him.

Kite ignored him. 'The *Kingdom* was never recovered. It's nothing to do with you,' he said again, and this time, Agatha didn't argue. She'd given up on whatever she had wanted, before. She was sitting straight and brittle, and it looked like only an iron effort of will that was keeping the tears underneath her eyelashes, not falling. Joe had never seen anyone fight so hard not to cry. He couldn't tell if she was fighting because she didn't want him to see, or if she couldn't stand the idea of showing that weakness in front of her brother. He wanted to say she had a pretty good grip on her brother.

'Why won't you just tell me?' Joe asked, with no real hope.

'Because it's better for you that you don't remember,' she said, and squeezed Kite's hand as he went by.

Kite froze as though the Empress had touched him. When he unfroze, his shoulders sank and he went down on his knee to kiss her hand, and Joe saw he wasn't going to get a single word out of them now.

All through the night, the ship lifted and fell. In his hammock, Joe curled up under a blanket and someone else's jacket, which Fred had found for him in the stores. There was a bullet hole in the lapel that made him suspect that the someone had died in it, but the air was so cold that he was just grateful for the extra layer. Now that he was lying down, the seasickness was gone. It was bliss.

Clay had turned off the lamps, but light spilled through the glass double doors from the deck. Shadows went to and fro outside, and voices called down from the quarterdeck – right above them now – and the topmen up in the rigging. It should have been hard to relax, but it was good to have other people in the room, and good to hear that the ship was always awake.

Just across from him, Kite slept like he'd collapsed and died, flat on his back, his hands resting on his breastbone. Joe felt envious, but then greatly to his own surprise, he fell asleep straight away. The motion of the ship gave him dreams of merry-go-rounds. It was the best night's sleep he could remember.

19

Joe's watches alternated between Fred Hathaway and, thankfully, Agatha, who made a point of stealing him to scrub down the infirmary if he ever began to take on too much of a Fred-overloaded look. Before long, the ever-shifting watch system made sense. Completely unexpectedly, he loved it. You did six or three hours, and then you passed out somewhere. Because it was nothing like as long as a normal working day, it was easy to push through. Even better, as his watches began to shift deeper into the night, the strict hierarchy of who was allowed to do what job loosened, and Fred decided it was about time Joe try his bullet-proof cure for seasickness. It was steering the ship.

The rule was that someone woke you up fifteen minutes before your watch. If Joe was lucky, it was one of the older midshipmen, who just gave him a nudge and then vanished; if he wasn't, it was Fred, who banged in and yelled his good mornings, even though there was nothing good about them, or, in the pitch-dark, anything especially morning-like. He would do it even if Kite was asleep, and he did on the day he bounced in to collect Joe for a navigation lesson.

Fred was lighting lamps. The fizz of the matches sounded loud in the quiet. Kite curled up tighter in the other hammock. Joe was sure he had only just fallen into it.

'Fred, put those out, he's trying to sleep,' Joe whispered. 'You oblivious little gosling.'

Fred gasped as if he'd hurt himself, but in fact it was a new burst of enthusiasm. 'I know a goose joke! What do French geese say?'

'Fred!' Joe hissed.

Fred was busy writing on Kite's logbook. When he held it up, it said, HONQUE.

Joe choked, because he hadn't expected to laugh. 'Right, good, mate, now fuck off before someone kills you and I'll be out in a second.'

'What,' Fred said, 'do Indian ducks call white ducks?'

Joe hauled himself up properly and went to see if there was any water left. Not only was there water in the kettle, it was hot, just boiled on Clay's tiny stove; Kite must have put it on for them just before he went to bed. Joe glanced back at him, feeling much too grateful. Hot water wasn't something he'd thought about at home, but it made a continent of difference at three in the morning. He made himself a cup of coffee. There was a lot of coffee on board; the free colonies in Jamaica supplied it. Sugar too; but no tea.

'Go on then, what *do* Indian ducks call white ducks?' he said, so that at least Fred wouldn't reel off onto anything stranger.

Agatha looked around from behind the screen where the washbasin was, in case it was more spelling.

'Quackers!' Fred beamed.

'We could leave you with the French,' Agatha reflected. 'It would be an experiment in mental warfare.'

'Like when *Le Monde* published all that stuff the French did to Lord Wellington, with all the hot pincers and things, and then they sent four thousand copies to Edinburgh!'

Joe glanced at Agatha, wanting to ask if that was true. The part of him that was still raging decided that a dose of hot pincers would do Kite a universe of good.

'Thank you for the light, Hathaway. Now wait outside,' Agatha told him.

'Yes, ma'am,' Fred said, and clattered off.

There wasn't enough water on board for anyone to wash properly, and Joe was too seasick even to shave, so getting ready was just a matter of clambering into borrowed cold-weather gear by the light of Fred's candles. There was a heavy, well-lined coat that was standard issue among the officers, and a safety harness that went on over the top, with sturdy clips that could fasten you to anything close by as the ship ducked and tipped.

The second Joe was ready, Fred, who had hung around just beyond the glass doors buzzing with impatience, seized his sleeve and pulled him out into the frozen night. At the prow, leaning on ropes just above the figurehead, sailors held out lamps over the water to spot anything dangerous in the sea.

Fred hurried him across the deck, too excited to keep quiet. When he was especially happy, he sang. He couldn't sing. It was more like the droning noise Clay's cat made if it wanted to be fed.

'Mr Hathaway, there are people below trying to *sleep*,' an officer snapped from the quarterdeck. 'Keep it down.'

'Sorry, sir!' Fred shouted, and then after another ten seconds he forgot about it and started droning again.

They relieved the helmsman, who gave Joe a sympathy grin when he told them their current bearing.

Because the water was rough, it took two people to hold the wheel. It was hard work, so nobody was allowed to do it for more than an hour, but it was a wonderful hour. Fred showed him how to correct the course on the compass, and how, even once you'd moved the wheel, it took the ship twelve or fifteen seconds to start swinging in the direction you wanted. By the time their hour was up, they were soaked and laughing, and in a flying rush, Joe understood why all these people had signed up for such a wet, miserable, dangerous life. It was the best work in the world.

In the hours off, nobody seemed to mind what he did. At the end of the night watches, the cook put out hot cakes and flasks of coffee. It was unbelievably good, and it meant that there were always people in the mess. People were reassuring, so Joe tended to stay, dozing on one of the long benches, or watching the sailors knit and sew.

Everyone could sew. Fred was making himself a beautiful washbag from silver thread. Other officers made their own shirts. It seemed to be expected, because there were copies of the *Officer's Pattern Book* all over the place – the instructions for making the uniforms, complete with to-scale patterns and lists and lists of directions. Joe always felt too seasick to even contemplate a needle, but it was soothing to watch.

And it reminded him of Lily's duck, embroidered on her nightgown and worn out already from being stroked so much. It hurt to think of that, and of the distance and decades between here and home, but the more he caught himself liking shipboard life, the more he felt certain he needed to keep thinking of the things that hurt. Or he would never get back. He didn't think Alice would stitch Lily a new duck.

At dinner every evening, Kite updated the *Outstanding Idiots* board. The offences were all silly – falling asleep on watch, not getting up when the watch officer fetched you, drinking on watch, and the one man who'd been caught doing something peculiar with the cook's dog. All of them were offences that the Articles of War ominously expected to be punished *at the captain's discretion*. In fact it wasn't ominous: it meant your name on the *Outstanding Idiots* board and two watches' worth of the most undesirable chores. Joe started to look forward to it. On his fifth night, there was a special drumroll before the announcement of Cock of the Week. The honour came with a special hat.

The marines, of which there were many – soldiers, they must have been, because none of them knew a blind thing about sailing – were always set up in a corner with their drums, which they painted beautifully in fine colours, with tiny crests and coats of arms, or ships, or landscape scenes from home. In the absence of any Frenchmen to fight or any disorder among the sailors to break up, there was nothing else for them to do except add pizzazz to special occasions.

'This week's award goes to –' whoops from the marines '– Mr Solomon Vane,' Kite announced, 'for sleeping in the rigging. He will do your bidding for the next four watches, the more airborne the better, given his own assurance of his ability to fly.'

The table next to Joe's erupted laughing. Everyone threw things at a West Indian man, who flapped like a giant depressed fairy. Kite put Vane's name on the board and drew angel wings on either side of it.

'I wish we were on the *Victory*,' Vane grumbled, looking embarrassedly proud as he accepted the special hat. It had a peacock feather in it. 'I'd rather have the lashes. Who came up with all this bollocks about not flogging people? It's not right.'

Joe had seen it happen all week without understanding that flogging would have been the navy standard. He glanced up at the officers' table with a lot more attention than before. Going out of his way to avoid hurting somebody seemed so against Kite's character as Joe knew it that he had to think about it for the next few watches, testing the idea that perhaps, just perhaps, Kite was not as vicious as he made out.

It gave Joe a match flare of hope. It meant that Kite *might* be persuaded to let him go and tell the Admiralty that he'd escaped, and not to spend too much time or effort looking for him. If, if, if, Joe could just bring out that part of him that was kind to children, and preferred an *Outstanding Idiots* board to flogging.

Not the part that had killed Jem. The more Joe thought about that, the more disconcerted he felt, because it was a struggle to marry that Kite with the Kite who put up with Fred and handed out stupid hats. A man with that much range wasn't sane.

The idea of trying to charm Kite was a lot more daunting than steering a battleship had been. It was easy to track him down, at least. He was either on the quarterdeck or, off duty, under his own desk with a hot-water bottle and a romance novel on his knee. The weather was so cold now that sitting on a chair near a window was about as useful as sitting out in the screaming wind. The tortoise sat there too, and the cat, which was a fat fluffy thing everyone claimed was a ratter but whose extremest velocity was an ooze.

Armed with Fred's exam book, Joe hesitated with his hand on the stateroom door. It was a good excuse to talk to Kite, the exam book. Just as Eleanor Sidgwick had pointed out in Pont du Cam, all his science knowledge was in French. He didn't know any English astronomical terms, hadn't even known they existed, and he was having to learn them on the fly. Fred didn't speak French, and sometimes people didn't even understand Joe in English. But Kite did, always – he seemed to understand everyone, even the Indian sailors who spoke a bewildering mix of English and Hindustani.

It still took some nerve to push the door handle down.

'English question,' said Joe. He lifted the book a little.

Kite was already shaking his head. 'I'm alone. I'm sorry, but you can't stay. Use a dictionary.'

'What?'

'We can't have a handsome man with a grudge in a room alone with a senior officer, it's a nightmare.'

Joe was knocked sideways. He'd expected Kite to call bull-shit, but not this. 'Sorry, what? I can't be here in case *I* make an accusation against *you*? Who the hell wouldn't see through that in four seconds?'

'In the best of all possible worlds, they would, but this world isn't that world, and you still have to go away.'

Joe had been about to turn and go, but that last had been a Voltaire joke or he was a porpoise. *The best of all possible worlds* was the catchphrase of an especially stupid hero in an especially stupid book Joe had read at the asylum, from the Classics shelf, because he had run out of newspapers. 'Been bitching about Frenchmen all week but secretly reading French novels, have we, Candide?'

Kite smiled. His smile was younger and shyer than the rest of him; it must not have been out so often. Joe had to as well, and then there was an awkward quiet. It only got thicker the longer it lasted, and trapped all the ordinary things they would have said to each other in different circumstances, and then hardened and sealed them in.

'I'm going,' Joe finished, defeated.

That night, while Agatha was tipping more coal into the braziers and Kite was finishing the ship's log, Joe put his copy of *The Count of Monte Cristo* on top of the blankets in Kite's hammock. He saw him find it before the lamps went out. Kite didn't say anything then, but once Agatha was asleep, he touched Joe's sleeve through the diamond spaces in the hammock and tilted the book to say thank you.

Joe smiled in the dark. The cat bounced up onto his chest. He hugged it and fell into a wonderful, clean, proper sleep like he never did at home. It had been the same all week. He was start-ing to think that the cure for insomnia might be travelling by sea with a madman to talk around. Even though the whip-mark still ached, even though he hadn't changed his mind about Kite, or untied the knot deep in his chest that was the awful awareness he was being taken further and further from Lily with every minute, he felt happy.

Some part of him was aware that Kite was lying awake with the book still resting on his chest, and his hand wringing around the lighthouse tattoo.

20

Southampton, 1797

Once the *Defiance* finally came into port, Kite and Jem waited outside the main office at the Admiralty for a good while. Captain Heecham had gone in first. In the corridor was a window that overlooked the docks. Jem, too anxious to sit down, stood and watched a frigate being refitted. Every time an officer went by, it was with a pause, and sometimes a nonplussed frown. Jem stood like he was someone's son. Kite could see them all running through the sons of every society person they knew, trying to remember if they might have lost one down the back of the smoking-room couch.

Captain Heecham opened the door and told Jem to come through. Jem glanced down at Kite, who nodded to say he would wait, but Jem pulled him up by his elbow.

'And you,' he said.

'But they don't want to see m—'

Jem was already steering him down the corridor. 'Hurry up, don't keep the nice admiral waiting.'

So Kite followed them inside and tucked himself in an unobtrusive corner, but it wasn't unobtrusive enough. The Lords of the Admiralty rotated between ports, and the gentleman behind the desk now was Lord Lawrence. Kite kept his eyes down, but he could feel Lawrence looking at him in the way most people looked at a hair in their dinner.

Lawrence was fully capable of throwing Jem in prison for espionage just to grind Kite under his fashionably high heel. But it was too late to warn Jem.

If Jem found lords of the Admiralty intimidating, or the cavernous office with its frescoed ceiling and leather-topped desk, he didn't show it. He sat in the uncomfortable chair Lawrence pointed to, and smiled when Lawrence's tiger cub came to investigate him. There was no sign of his nervousness from before.

Lawrence asked all the questions he must just have asked of Heecham. Where had Jem sailed from, what was the year, did he know anything of history that they might verify – Jem had thought of plenty now – and whether Jem had a profession. Kite thought he sounded brusque, even for him. He wished he'd never come in. He was rubbing off on Jem like mud.

'Profession – not really,' Jem said. 'I sit in the House of Lords and interfere with other people's professions.'

Kite looked across incredulously, wanting to ask how he'd managed to keep that under his hat on *Defiance*, and why. Heecham would have believed him instantly if he'd known.

Lawrence lit up. Kite saw him shift his grip on his wine glass, from the stem right to the base; someone must have told him it was more gentlemanly to hold the base. Kite hoped he spilled it.

Jem seemed to see at last that they were all surprised. He must have assumed they didn't believe him, because he reeled off his lineage to four generations. There was a duchess and two governors of India.

Lawrence softened instantly. 'Why didn't you say so? That casts things in a different light.'

'Does it?' said Jem.

'I can hardly go around doubting a peer of the realm, sir.'

'Can you not? I do it regularly,' Jem said, and if there had been one atom of doubt before, it vanished now. He had to be who he said he was, or he wouldn't be talking to Lawrence like this, like he was nothing special and this room was on the poky side of ordinary.

All of Kite's organs shrank inwards. They'd shoved Jem into bunks with the lieutenants. He should have had Heecham's stateroom.

Lawrence laughed. 'Well,' he said again, more finally. 'This is rather a difficult situation. I cannot simply let you go into the wider world; the French know, by now, that you exist – your shipmates aboard the *Kingdom* will have told them – and that you are with us, telling us useful things, just as your fellow Kingdoms will be telling the French useful things. There will be a price on your head. However, I do not wish to imprison you either. Would you be willing to enter naval service? At lieutenant. On the proviso that you inform us immediately of anything that might possibly help the war effort.'

Kite shifted, excruciated. Lawrence's rank had gone to his head. It would have made more sense to shackle a racehorse to a milk cart.

Jem, astonishingly, looked relieved. 'Delighted.' He glanced back at Kite. 'I was wondering how I should make a living here.'

Lawrence nodded. 'Captain Heecham here tells me that the entire crew of *Defiance* witnessed the *Kingdom*'s pursuit and capture by the French. That is most unfortunate. Officers, of course, are bound by strict laws and may be trusted to keep secrets, but the men move freely from ship to ship, and indeed from fleet to fleet; some of your current crew will assuredly be working for the French or Spanish sooner or later. We've haemorrhaged men ever since the French banned flogging.' He was speaking more to Heecham now. 'We must therefore take measures to ensure that this does not happen.' His eyes came back to Jem. 'Which leaves you with a responsibility to take every measure to ensure your own safety. You must come up with some kind of history for yourself. I suggest you name a sufficiently distant, obscure colony as your place of origin. You need a new name for yourself too. Every French spy in England will be looking for Jem Castlereagh.' He looked at Kite for the first time. 'I see you've acquired my niece's brother.'

Jem frowned at the odd description. 'He's been looking after me.'

'Well.' Lawrence's face twisted into a peculiar wince that was trying to be a benevolent paternal smile of approval at Jem's continued well-being, soured by his distaste for Kite. 'You shall spend your shore leave with him and my niece at her London residence. You'll be comfortable there. You may go, gentlemen. Not you, Heecham, we need to discuss what shall become of the crew.'

Heecham looked grey as he saw Kite and Jem out again, but he said nothing else except to wish them a good shore leave.

'Wait, sir – what does he mean, what will become of the crew?' Kite tried.

Heecham landed one heavy hand on his shoulder. 'You just look after Castlereagh, Kite. Congratulations, by the way, lieutenant,' he smiled to Jem. It was a pained smile, though. 'On you go, boys.' He vanished back inside.

Something must have been wrong, but there was no time to ask. The *Defiance* was still anchored a good way offshore. The signal flags showed it hadn't been paid off yet; the men were still stuck aboard. That was bad. The first piece of advice Heecham had ever given him had been about getting the ship paid off the second you arrived at a port. Abandoning them for hours or days was the quickest route to mutiny.

'I hope he hurries up and lets them ashore,' Kite said to Jem. 'There's barely any food left.' He remembered abruptly that it wasn't Jem's job to care about the men, or not yet. 'Are you all right?'

'Yes. Are you?' All Jem's ease and confidence was gone again. 'That horrible man rather saddled you with me.'

Kite lifted his eyebrow. 'Oh savage world. I shall collapse under this immense and cruel burden.'

Jem gave him a shove and looked reassured.

*

London, 1797

Two days later, at Agatha's house on Jermyn Street, there was a knock at his bedroom door at seven o'clock. Kite opened it before he was all the way into his shirt, certain it was Agatha's butler – who spelled his name Frome but pronounced it *Froom* thank you very much – coming to tell him off for something, a continuation of a quiet war that had lasted for years, but it wasn't Frome. It was Jem.

All he could think was that it was broad daylight, he was mostly undressed, and the person standing on his threshold was a sheening aristocrat who had probably never been in the sun enough to have even seen freckles before. He dragged his shirt on properly.

'Sorry,' he managed. 'I thought you were Mr Frome. Is everything all right?'

'Tea,' said Jem. He was holding two cups, his sleeves turned back and showing the jade bracelet on his left wrist. Beside him, Lawrence's tiger cub was pressing her face against his pocket, purring. She loved tobacco.

Lawrence had followed them up from Southampton yesterday and invited himself to stay. Project Make Thyself Scarce had ensued, at least at Kite's end of things. Thankfully, Lawrence was taken with Jem. Kite was pretty certain he had only come because he hoped that the scent of actual nobility might be catching. Lawrence was a newly made lord, not an inherited one, and it turned out to his chagrin and Kite's silent pleasure that everyone could tell.

181

Kite had been planning an early getaway to Mr Mahmud's coffeehouse in Marylebone. It would take him well away from Lawrence, and away from Agatha's sugar boycott. He'd been at sea for nine months and all he wanted from life now was quick access to marzipan. Mr Mahmud did marzipan fruit free with the coffee.

He'd assumed Jem would lose interest in him now that he had people of his own quality to talk to.

'They'll be downstairs,' Kite said. 'There should be a proper breakfast by now—'

'Lawrence says you don't eat with them,' Jem interrupted. He gave him a cup and a wry look, as though he was telling a joke they both knew and he was waiting for Kite to join in for the punchline.

Kite had no idea about the joke. 'No, it wouldn't be proper.'

'Apparently your father was a carpenter.'

'Yes,' said Kite, nervous he was being told off for not admitting that he had no business befriending noblemen, even lost ones.

'And your sister seems content with this segregation.'

'Half-sister. I don't know she's noticed. Why?'

'It's stupid. May I come in?'

'It's not very ...' Kite trailed off, because Jem had already settled down in the sunbeam in the middle of the narrow bed. So had the tiger.

'I'm supposed to come up with a new name for myself,' Jem said. He looked worried about it. 'But Castlereagh isn't the name the others will have told the French.'

'Sorry? Why not?' Kite had just sat down on the edge of the bed and the tiger had got her claws caught in the hem of his shirt.

'Because my real one – wouldn't go down very well in ... well, a place like this,' Jem said. 'Castlereagh is my mother's name.'

Kite felt absurdly double-crossed. 'What's wrong with your real one? What do you mean, a place like this?'

Jem only shook his head. 'I've only known you for a week, so I don't – know how you'd take it. Sorry. I'm sorry, I don't mean to sound distrustful, just–'

'No,' Kite interrupted, coming to his senses. He didn't understand what could possibly be so bad about Jem's real name, but it wasn't any of his business to try and poke at it. 'No, you're right not to trust people.' He hesitated. 'So no one is looking for a Jem Castlereagh?'

'No.'

'But – it is Jem?' Somehow that was very important.

'It is Jem,' he confirmed. He sighed. 'Sorry,' he said again. 'I'll tell you one day.'

'No need.' Kite wanted to say he was just grateful that Jem had climbed four flights of stairs to tell him, but it sounded crawly even in his head, so he stayed quiet and drank his tea.

Jem came back every morning after.

Just after Christmas, Agatha sent Jem a note to meet her at a department store. It was an invitation to get a dress uniform made for the Admiralty's New Year ball. A boy delivered it straight to the table at Mr Mahmud's where Jem and Kite were sharing a piece of cake and Kite was trying to find out why Jem had bruised knuckles. Jem said he'd just flung himself into a door at a funny angle like an idiot, but Kite was worried that Lawrence might have done something, and searching about for a way to ask that without asking. It meant he was too distracted to think twice about what Agatha might do, which he regretted later.

Harding Howell & Co. of Pall Mall was bright in the dreary morning, lamps alight inside and out. It was just off St James's Square, and the women coming out were in fur-lined cloaks and deep-coloured silk, comet-tailed by girls or footmen who carried packages tied up with ribbon.

The store was only four sections long, but they were broad, high-ceilinged sections, and mazey. The walls were lined with what scholars in a thousand years' time would probably mistake for funeral alcoves – the whole place had the proportions of a church – but in fact they were for rolls of fabric. Each one had been unrolled just enough to bring a swathe of it right down to the floor, where the edges hung arranged over prettily uphol-stered chairs or over the shoulders of mannequins. They went in order of cost, starting with cotton and muslin, through to painted chintz from India, to silk, brocade, and damask that glinted in the lamplight. Everything smelled of brand-new carpets and fresh-cut fabric.

Agatha had brought her own tailor, his apprentice, and a lot of pins. They had an encampment in a private room. Kite stopped in the doorway, not wanting to climb over anything. Jem had gone ahead to look at the fabric, as easy with the apprentice as he was with Lawrence.

'You run everywhere and then hesitate at the door, you look like a tradesman,' Agatha said to Kite, beginning to laugh.

He edged in by another six inches or so, certain that she would consider it a lot more tradesman-like to nosedive over fourteen feet of teal brocade.

'Is your dress uniform still all right?' Agatha asked. She was, he realised now, halfway through a fitting, in just her stays under the drapery.

For a mortified second he couldn't believe what was happen-ing, and then dragged Jem outside.

'You're coming as well,' she called after him.

'I am not,' he said. People had more properly asked their gardeners to come to Admiralty balls.

'You bloody are. Jem and I will need some human company.'

The tailor's apprentice snorted appreciatively to hear her swear.

'Oh,' she added, 'Jem. You can see the clerk about the dress uniform, just stick it on my account.' She came right out the door, still only in her stays. 'It's under my name, but there's a number as well if they don't believe you.' She gave Jem a slip of paper.

A clerk Kite had seen on the way in walked past, again, quite obviously to get another look at her. A passing old lady snapped open her fan and marched by, steaming. Kite wanted to sink through the floor.

'Thank you,' Jem said. 'Are you sure?' He sounded for all the world as if he thought talking to a basically naked heiress in public was normal.

'Certain,' Agatha said, and finally went back inside.

'Let's go then,' Kite rasped.

He wanted to demand to know what she was doing, but he knew exactly what she was doing. She had a hospital to fundraise for, and she always saw a spike in donations if her name got into the society news-sheets alongside a thrill of scandal. She did it every six months or so. People came to talk to her hoping to know if she was as deliciously risqué as she seemed, only to find that she was herself, quite mathematical and reasonable, and then they donated, going away with what struck Kite as a nebulously righteous sense of having done something *dashed* adventurous but nonetheless quite Christian and proper.

Standing out in her underwear in the biggest shop in London with a beautiful man of intriguingly mysterious origin would do the job.

He wished she wouldn't wrench Jem into it.

He and Jem walked into the next section in silence, and then stopped by a display of fans, all of which cost more than Kite earned in a month.

'She is the sole inheritrix of a very considerable fortune,' Kite said softly. 'Lawrence wants her to marry an earl. People watch her, they're interested, journalists write columns about her. If the wrong person saw all that just now, you will be in every news-sheet in London by tomorrow. And — people will look at you, they'll want to know where you're from.'

'I don't understand—'

'She was just in her corset!' Kite half-exploded, wondering how naked a person had to be in Jem's time before it was pornographic. The way Jem had walked into that room, they must have been down to a hanky and a feather.

'I ... see,' Jem said dully. 'That was stupid of me, wasn't it. I shouldn't have gone in.'

'No, it was bloody selfish of her, she's just using you to get money for the *bloody* hospital — I'm sorry,' Kite cut himself off. He shouldn't be speaking badly of Agatha and he certainly shouldn't be swearing in public, not in his navy uniform coat, which was his only coat. Someone would complain to the Admiralty. He explained about the hospital-fund tactics.

'Quite fun, really,' Jem said, smiling a bit. 'Clever.'

Careless was the word Kite would have chosen. Ever since she had inherited all that money, Agatha was careless. The money was an insulating mass that protected her from everything and he had a feeling she had forgotten that it did not protect other people.

'Yes,' he said. He had to hold his breath when he realised just how bad it was. 'Christ, and you're living with us ...'

Jem was shaking his head. 'It's fine. I'll vanish off to a boarding house.'

'What? No,' Kite said, alarmed. He didn't like leaving the sailors in some of the rougher boarding houses, never mind Jem. And something ignoble in his stomach twisted at the thought of waking up at Jermyn Street to silence and the usual breakfast exile again. 'They're not safe.'

Jem smiled again. 'You'll be stuck with me for a whole voyage soon, remember. And then I'll be possessive and grasping.

Not in a friendly pleasant way, you understand; more a sinister, worrying way that might end with your being trapped in a cupboard on a chain.'

Kite smiled too this time, though not much. In the last month, he had gone from being star-struck by how open and friendly Jem was, to wary of it. It was only that charm they taught people at Oxford and Cambridge. Jem felt obliged to Kite, that was all. Like a fool, he wanted it anyway.

A dapper man near a display of lace had been watching them, and now he came up as bold as an entire brass bedstead. 'Good morning! I couldn't help hearing that your name was Mr Castlereagh,' he said to Jem. He was doing his best to look inoffensive. Kite nearly told him that leaping on the unsuspecting by Men's Buttons wasn't a good start. 'I don't suppose you're any relation of the Castlereaghs of St James's Square?'

Kite thought he might just have taken Jem off guard enough to let something slip, but he needn't have worried. Jem only sparkled at the man. 'I have no idea, I'm afraid. I'm only recently arrived from the Caribbean; why, ought I know you?'

'Oh, the Caribbean? My sister is in Kingston. Where were you, I wonder?'

'I find mystery to be an extraordinarily valuable currency in London, so I hope you won't mind if I don't hand it all over to the first curious person who asks me.'

'Well—'

'Leave him alone,' Kite said flatly.

The man looked frightened and vanished towards the drapery section. There were a few advantages in having a resting expression that looked like you were about to kick someone.

'He looked a lot like a pamphleteer.' Jem had turned off his charm like a lamp.

'He writes for the society pages,' Kite said, feeling murky.

21

HMS *Agamemnon*, 1807

Joe woke up because of what he thought was daylight. The wrong kind of daylight: golden, summery daylight, not the dismal gloom that served now as the sub-Arctic dawn. Then his cogs began to turn and he jolted out of the hammock, onto the floor, just before the fire really caught.

It raced along the ropes, catching the blankets, his own sleeve – he tore his jumper off and stuffed it into a ball to crush out the flame – and across to Kite. It was licking at the lapel of his coat. He must have just come in from his watch, because he was fully dressed.

Joe was paralysed for a horrible second, which was doubly horrible because he hadn't known he was a coward. Furious with himself, he slapped his own forearm, hard. It jerked him out of it and he lurched upright, and pushed Kite away from the fire. They landed on the deck with a thump that wrenched Joe's shoulder.

'What—'

'Fire, there's a—'

'Bloody hell.' Agatha, unlike Joe, had the presence of mind to snatch the water jug and sling it over the worst of the flames. She sounded more inconvenienced than worried. 'There's a sand bucket over there, Mr Tournier, if you wouldn't mind – thank you. No, we'll need more ...' She cast around, then wrenched a whistle from Kite's neck, snapping the chain, and blew it sharp and hard. Then the room was full of people and water and sand, and then only smoke.

Kite was pressed back against the wall. He had turned glassy and unmoving.

'He's not keen on fire,' Agatha said when Joe tried to make her look. She sighed, and then slapped Kite. 'Snap out of it, sailor!'

'Jesus!' Joe yelped, appalled. Twenty seconds ago he would have said he'd have loved to see her do that, but now he caught himself right on the edge of demanding to know if she'd thought about *how* you made someone into a psychopath.

Kite seemed to think it was normal. 'Where did the fire start?'

The answer was clear. It had begun in Joe's hammock. There was even a black smoke stain above the place where the hammock had hung.

'Did you have a candle?' Agatha asked Joe.

'No,' Joe said, beginning to feel panicky. The smell of burned rope and clothes was thick everywhere, and the smoke was sticking to the back of his throat, gritty, and bizarrely homely, because it was how all of Londres smelled. If they thought he was the kind of person who dropped candles and set fire to things, he really was going to end up chained to the mast. 'No; nothing …'

The marines all looked at Kite.

Kite let his neck bend. He was still on his knees. It looked like a lot of work to breathe. There was a red mark by his eye where Agatha had hit him. He got to his feet again. 'All right, everyone, back on watch.'

There was a quiet chorus of yessirs, but some of the men glanced at each other, and at Joe.

'It wasn't him,' Kite said, when he saw how they were hesitating. He pushed his hand through his hair. Joe saw him snatch it back when his fingertips brushed the burn scars on his neck, fast, as though he had touched something unspeakably disgusting. 'It must have been me. Go on.'

They went.

It was the worst lie Joe had ever heard. He'd never seen Kite so much as touch a candle. Kite got up for his watches in tarry darkness. He saw the same thought go across Agatha's face too, but instead of pointing out that there were children who'd said they were on the moon when the cake went missing and were still more convincing, she only nodded.

'All right. Well, I'm on watch in an hour anyway, I might as well be up.'

'Same,' Kite said exhaustedly.

'You get some rest,' Agatha told Joe.

Joe looked between them, saw there was a conspiracy, and kept quiet. When they left, though, he followed Kite, just far enough behind to be out of earshot, hoping that Kite was going to find whoever had tried to set them both on fire.

Kite went down the ladder to the gun deck, down again, down once more, and it was hard to keep up, even following at a discreet distance; he could skip down the ladders facing forward instead of easing down one rung at a time like Joe had to.

The lower decks were windowless and dank, and with their dim lamps, bulky in safety cages, there was never enough light, and never enough heat to dry wet clothes. Everyone hung shirts and jackets from the hammock ropes, but there was no fresh air, and it all stank of damp. In the infirmary, people had been coming in with clothes to wash in vinegar to get the mould off. And of course they left them to dry down here. Damp, and vinegar.

It was a labyrinth of storage crates, stacked so that they made corridors and bypasses around people's hammocks. Joe tripped over a box of chain shot, so heavy it didn't even shift when his whole weight struck it. One chain slithered. He tried to imagine it howling out of a cannon, then decided he didn't want to imagine that. Kite didn't hear it, or at least, he didn't look back. He couldn't hear well, Joe thought; he tipped his head when he was listening to someone in the same way the blacksmiths did if you stood by their hammer-side ear.

There was a tiny door that must have been a store cupboard, because it was barely wide enough for even a small person to slip through. Lamplight seeped underneath. Kite knocked. Joe pressed himself back against a coil of spare anchor chain.

'What do you want?' a Scottish voice said.

'Clay, it's me.'

Clay opened the door. He was sitting on the floor inside, and Joe got a good look at it past Kite. The room was hardly more than a box. There was a mannequin with a man's clothes on it, but not a uniform. The long jacket must once have been very fine, but someone, meticulously, had been unweaving it from the hem up, picking apart the green threads, snipping at the silver embroidery, and now, most of the skirt was just rags. The ends were burned, and on the floor were dozens of used matches, charred into black curves. On hooks on the walls were shirts and cravats that had suffered the same treatment, and now they were hanging above jars and jars of dead matches. There was a stack of empty book covers too; the pages had been torn out. It was hard to tell, but they might have gone into a glass aquarium on a shelf where there sat a very fat, contented-looking rat in a nest of shredded paper.

'Rob, you can't set fires.'

'It wasn't me,' Clay said.

'Yes it was,' Kite said, with tired patience.

'He should be in the brig! He's going to hurt you—'

'Look, I know you don't like having him aboard. I don't like it either, but we need him. Leave him alone. It won't be for long. If you don't agree, I'm going to have to lock you in here.'

Clay was quiet. He was on the edge of tears now. 'Not for long.'

'No.'

'Promise?'

'I promise.'

Like a little boy, Clay put his arms out. Kite crouched down and hugged him carefully. He looked like there was nothing he wanted to do less. When Clay leaned forward, the light inside his cupboard of a cabin shone through the back of his shirt, and Joe wished it hadn't. There were harrows in his back, so deep and broad that Joe wouldn't have thought it was possible to survive them, never mind walk about with a working spine. He looked like he'd gone through a meat grinder. 'Love you,' Clay said in a tiny voice.

'I love you too.' Kite twisted his head to one side and clenched his fist against the doorframe. 'Come up and have breakfast with me later, all right? You haven't told me about the adventures of Charlie for ages.' He nodded to the rat.

'All right,' Clay agreed, soothed. He stroked Kite's arm. 'Sorry. About the fire.'

'No need to be sorry, just don't do again. See you later.' Kite disentangled himself as softly as he could have, and turned away. Joe ducked behind the chain, but Kite reached round and pulled him out by his shirt. 'I'm deaf, not stupid,' he said, with no ire.

'Why's he trying to kill me?' Joe demanded, squashing down the feeling that he'd been caught doing something wrong. He hadn't. It was reasonable to want to know.

'I told you, he's—'

'Clay,' Joe called past him. 'Clay—'

'What?'

'God's sake,' Kite hissed. 'Rob, it's all right, pay no attention. Don't upset him, Tournier—'

'Upset him! He set me on *fire*! That is extremely personal, Kite! He knows who I am, doesn't he—'

'I know who Madeline is,' Kite interrupted.

The whole world spun. 'What?' said Joe.

Kite caught a rafter as the ship powered downhill on what must have been an enormous wave. 'Leave Clay alone and I'll show you what I have of her.'

'What you ... how do you mean?'

'Come on.'

'Are you lying, are you about to chain me to something? Because I'll fucking find a way to ask Clay even if I *am* chained to—'

'Yes, I believe you,' Kite said, weary. 'She wrote a letter, and it found its way to me. You can have it.'

'I can ... but you didn't want to tell me *anything* before.'

'Yes, well, I don't want you to drive Clay mad either.'

'He's already mad. What happened to him, why—'

'The deal,' Kite said quietly, 'is that you leave Rob alone, and you can have this letter. If I give it to you and you then go chasing after him—'

'You'll chain me to the mast, yes—'

'No,' said Kite, 'I'll shoot you in the knee. He was broken in navy service, Tournier, and he deserves some proper care now. I won't have you asking him useless questions. He's nothing to do with you, but you won't believe that until you've chased him half to distraction, and then he'll be even worse, and I prefer not to wake up on fire. Don't you?'

'Yes,' Joe admitted.

'Then we agree,' Kite said, and nodded at him to go up the ladder first.

Back in the stateroom, by the thin light of a single candle, Kite slid open one of his desk drawers and drew out a battered envelope. He stood holding it, and studying Joe.

'This was smuggled out of France two years ago,' Kite said. 'It was handed by one of Madeline's gaolers to an English captain who had no idea what it meant, but he read it out at a pub in Edinburgh because he thought it was so strange. The whole business with the *Kingdom* was kept secret, *very* secret. I bought it off him.'

'Her gaolers ...'

'Read it,' said Kite, who looked like he'd had enough of talking for at least the next week. He held out the envelope. 'But somewhere else, please. You can't be in here alone with me.'

22

The envelope felt like there was a good amount of paper inside. There was no name or address on the front, just *To the English forces* in a clear hand. Joe took it down to the gun deck, to where the lamps were always lit and the sailors who'd just come off watch were having their coffee and biscuits. Until he found somewhere to sit, he kept it pressed hard against his chest, worried that he'd drop it or Kite would change his mind and follow him to snatch it back.

At a spare place at the end of a table, he opened the worn flap of the envelope and slid out the papers. There were about twenty pages of the same neat, clear writing. Even as he glanced it over, checking that the pages were double-sided – and thank God, they were – he felt a fresh round of seasickness. He swallowed it down. He was going to read *some* of this document even if he had to do it stooped over a bucket. His fingertips shaking, he smoothed the pages flat against the table. They made a gritty sound against some grains of old salt there. Two years; he'd been looking for her for two years and here she was.

*

I have entrusted this to one of the guards, who owes me a series of favours. He has promised to send this letter on; to someone in what remains of the English army or navy, God knows where that is now.

So I can address this only to whom it may concern, but whoever you are, a sea captain or a soldier, or some passer-by on the road, you deserve to know why England is lost. My name is Madeline. You will never hear of me, but I am the reason.

I sailed on the Kingdom. Perhaps you've heard of it, perhaps the Kingdom is infamous now and cursed by every Englishman; or perhaps they made it a secret. I'll tell you anyway. It makes damn all difference now. The Kingdom was a small vessel sent to survey potential sites for lighthouses. It did so in the year eighteen hundred and ninety-one. I will not commit to paper how the ship ended up in seventeen hundred and ninety-seven; I'm not certain, and if I were, the worst thing in the world would be for anyone else to find that place and cross. God knows the crossing of seven ordinary souls has wrought enough evil already.

Anyway, I believe we were in this time, your time, for hours if not days before we understood what had happened. All of us remarked on the dimness of the lights ashore, and how sparse the cities appeared on the English and Welsh coasts. But one doesn't pay attention to that kind of thing when one is engaged in a poker match with six other able players and a cabin full of cigar smoke, and one has been talked into betting one's wedding ring, much to the indignation of one's husband.

We even saw the ship that was following us, in the fog. We all came to the perfectly deliberate conclusion that it was a ghost ship. We had an involved conversation about the nature of ghosts. I've never been very pro; I suppose I spend too much time around architectural plans to have much business with the Beyond.

It was not a ghost. It was a first-class French battleship, with a hundred and twelve guns, and we were just off England's south coast when it shot out our waterwheel.

I believe they fired because there was an English ship too. I just caught the name on the prow, the Defiance; I think the French must have thought we were in those godforsaken fog-bound waters to meet her.

Jem was the only one of us who could swim. He didn't want to go; I had to sling him over the side myself. I have no idea what happened to him. I hope the English helped him; certainly sending him to them was safer than letting him stay aboard. I try not to think too much about him.

There was no helping anyone else. Isn't it absurd, how what is usually a negligible aspect of a person's character becomes the deciding feature of his fate? I keep waking up in the night furious about it. If only the six of us had bothered to learn to swim, on some sunny day in Hyde Park or at the seaside, everything would be different.

Say what you like about Napoleon's navy, but they are efficient. The French captain towed the half-wrecked Kingdom to Calais, and us with it. We were all questioned of course, but I don't remember much now. It is, in the main, a blur of panic and sea sickness. I did panic pretty shamefully. But so did the others, at least. We didn't understand what had happened for a while. Silly as it sounds, I think an ordinary person's idea of what is real is too solid an edifice to be blasted apart altogether by one round of shots from French cannon. It took the marines who were our gaolers the entire journey to convince us that it wasn't some sort of ridiculous trick or re-enactment. Looking back, I think it was our very refusal to believe we had slipped somehow by a hundred years that convinced the French we in fact had done so.

At Calais, soldiers bundled us into a coach that drove all night. When it finally stopped, we were deep in the countryside, at a peculiar, half-ruined mansion. I suppose it was the seat of some guillotined nobleman. Fire had blasted one side of it, but the other side was intact, and two soldiers hurried us in as though they were afraid someone might see us. It would have been an extraordinarily beautiful estate, before the Revolution. I still don't know what it's called, but the early-morning sun was making ragged mist-bands across the sloping grounds. The only witness to our passing was a peacock. I don't believe it had seen human beings for some time, because it wore, quite distinctly, the expression of an extremely proper lady who had just been told an extremely improper joke.

Whoever had owned the house before the Terror, he had been a great astronomy enthusiast. The two soldiers saw us to a broad chamber with a domed roof, and a beautiful telescope set up gleaming on a high dais in the middle, below frescoes of the pagan gods, grand and tasteless.

Colonel Herault was waiting for us there. He is a foxy little man, slight, polite in an unctuous, local-vicar sort of way. I ought to have been relieved to see someone in authority, but I've never been as repulsed so instantly by anybody. He struck me as exactly the sort of man who would spend his time now bugling on about Revolutionary fraternity and universal human rights, but who, before the Glorious Eighty-Nine, would have spent all his time pandering and pawing to anyone in a pearl necklace. He isn't like that — really he's rather decent — but I was everything wrong with the English aristocracy then, and not used to seeing beyond a man's manners. Looking back, I can't believe he was so polite as he was.

He smiled at us, then took out his pistol and shot George in the head. I don't know if he knew that George was the captain of the Kingdom or if he chose at random. It was the first time I'd ever seen sudden, impersonal violence, and I think I always thought I would be horrified if I were to see it. I don't know about you, but horror never featured, for me. It was the abruptness that struck me, and rather than wanting to run or scream, I was left only with the huffy impression that Colonel Herault was being very rude.

'That's what happens if you try to persuade me you know nothing useful about your own time,' Herault informed us, like a clerk explaining an obscure contractual clause.

He told us his name, and then he told us his terms. We would live here, in this house, with food, and rooms, and every convenience. In return, we would draw up everything we knew of history between this time and our own. For the first week, we were to do this separately, so we could not confer. If Herault judged that we had not gone into sufficient depth, we would share George's fate. The house was attended at all times by rotating shifts of guards. The consequences of any attempt to escape would be severe.

*

Joe had to sit back. There was more left, a lot more, but enclosed places with no windows were the worst for seasickness, and for all he'd made his bucket resolution earlier, he couldn't carry on. He had to lie flat on the bench and shut his eyes, but his mind was whirring. Seven people on the *Kingdom*; one was Jem. Jem was dead. One was Madeline. George, the captain, had been shot straight off. But the others; God, he could have been any one of the others. She hadn't said which of them she was married to.

Perhaps it was that she wrote conversationally, but he could *hear* her voice. He could hear her making fun of silly novels and see her lifting her eyebrow at things she didn't like. He would have recognised her if he'd seen her, he was sure of it now.

But he had no memory of Colonel Herault, or that grand house with its observatory. It gave him a damp feeling. It was all just gone.

Maybe that was for the best after all. If he didn't remember, then Kite wouldn't feel the need to shoot him.

He jumped when Lieutenant Wellesley gave him a ready-peeled orange and a plate of rice.

'Keep eating,' she said. 'You can die of seasickness.'

'Thank you,' Joe said miserably. Now he came to think of it, all he'd eaten in the last forty-eight hours had been a piece of cake when he had come off a night watch, feeling briefly and euphorically well. Feeling well had lasted fifteen minutes.

She nodded. 'Fred likes you a lot. Don't get yourself killed before his exam, all right?'

'It feels increasingly unlikely that I'll manage that, ma'am,' Joe said. He had to do it in French. He couldn't face English any more. It felt like swallowing cement.

'Don't be silly. Captain Kite's a good man.'

'Your French is good,' he said, surprised.

She smiled. 'My father was the Earl of Wiltshire. We used to live in France six months a year, before the Revolution. Eat,' she told him, and tapped the edge of the table.

23

J oe's next watch started at seven o'clock. He did it in the infirmary, where Agatha set him to cleaning surgical instruments. The letter from Madeline was in his pocket. He wanted to pull it out and start reading again, but he could feel it would still be a bad idea. He could barely stand, and even looking at the row of scalpels for too long was making his head spin.

'Agatha, what happened to Clay?' he asked. Kite couldn't object to that at least. One of his knees panged, a ghost of future pain. Joe had to suck his teeth. It took a certain kind of lunatic to shoot someone's kneecap off.

Agatha glanced up. She was stitching up a carpenter who'd let the saw slip. 'Three hundred lashes.'

'Why?'

'Mutiny. Do you know what that is?'

'Isn't it when someone tries to take over a ship?' Joe said, struggling to imagine Clay doing that.

She was shaking her head. 'It's navy-speak for a strike.'

Joe stared at her. 'You can get three hundred lashes for refusing to work?'

'Not only *can*,' she said. She smiled with no humour. 'The Admiralty is more or less legally obliged to do it. So I suggest you don't refuse.'

The sea was rough. Joe told himself that was why he felt sick. He never normally felt queasy just because he was upset, and had never understood why people like M. Saint-Marie did; he'd just put it down to being delicate. Whatever the reason, though, he had to sink onto his knees and hold the edges of the vinegar bucket, the fumes burning the inside of his nose while spit flooded his mouth.

'Ginger,' Agatha murmured from beside him. He shook his head, because he couldn't even think about eating anything. She set it on the deck beside him and rubbed his back as she got up again. He saw the hem of her indigo dress trail away, stained pale with old cleaning salt.

When the watch was finally over, he went to the gun deck to see Fred, who was running a class about how to tie different knots for the newest round of conscripted men. It was a good, normal thing to concentrate on, and he felt less sick in the cold draught from the gun ports. And the way an excitable Fred kept thrusting new things under his nose, far too many to learn, was reassuring, even though it was driving some of the other sailors so far up the wall they collectively threatened to tie Fred in a knot if he didn't shut up. Joe would have told them off, but Fred was unsquashable.

The sea was getting rougher, and soon, everyone had lost interest in knots and started watching for shapes in the water. One of the older sailors swore it was kraken weather. Joe didn't hold out too much hope for kraken, but the water was spectacular anyway. Fred tugged him up to the rail of the top deck.

The sea was mountainous. There was just enough moonlight to filigree the edges of the waves. Foam and spray poured back from them in white manes. *Agamemnon* would never usually sail in weather like this, Fred explained, but they were in a rush to get back to Edinburgh before the French began the siege. It should have been terrifying, knowing they were sailing in conditions the ship wasn't built for, but Joe had never seen weather like it, and just for now – he knew he'd change his mind once he was cold enough – it wasn't frightening, just exhilarating. It was wonderful not to think about Kite or seasickness, just for five minutes.

Fred pointed to the next wave and recommended that Joe hang on, and he was right; it gathered and gathered, the water rushing upwards towards the crest in ungravitational streams, which tipped as slow as molten iron cooling, then thundered down at them. White water burst right across the deck. The whole prow vanished into it before the figurehead came back up again. Wild things swung in the foam. The tilt of the deck was mad, but Joe couldn't stop laughing.

Fred wondered aloud whether you could predict the motion of a wave, so Joe set off happily on fluid dynamics, which he liked a lot because M. de Méritens had once done an experiment with a whole tank of mercury just to prove a point, and now he always thought of whirling silver whenever anybody mentioned troughs and crests. As he talked, he saw Fred glaze over, and winced. He didn't remember being fourteen, but he doubted you got the kind of mind that lost interest in dragons and started feeling passionately about waveforms until you were at least twenty-five.

'Have a cigarette,' he offered, because in his limited experience, children were instantly impressed by cigarettes. 'I know we can't get warm, but they *smell* of Jamaica. Fools your brain. And you'll think of waveform equations whenever you smoke one,' he added brightly.

Fred took one, stopped, and then began to laugh. 'You won't believe this,' he said, 'but I didn't recognise you until this very instant.'

'What?' said Joe. Fred was odd, but he wasn't enough of a holy fool to forget who Joe was.

Fred didn't have time to say anything, because Kite came out to them. He was just in his waistcoat and shirtsleeves. He must have been frozen; the burn scars had turned silver. He'd run, and he looked scared. Real, honest fear, like Joe hadn't even imagined he would be capable of.

'Tournier, get inside, for God's sake. If you don't die of cold, the next decent wave is going to carry you away.'

'I'm fine—'

'Now,' Kite snapped, a lot more urgent than the cold or the sea really seemed to call for. The topmen in the rigging hadn't even tethered themselves to anything yet. Fred said that was how you knew when things were getting dangerous.

Joe backed away, not sure what was going on. He didn't want to leave Fred with Kite. He lingered not too far away. He couldn't hear anything in the wind, and the rain made a crashing noise as it hit his ear on his windward side, but Fred was talking animatedly now, and he kept pointing at Joe. Kite was trying to stop him.

'—taught me sine waves with a salt pot!' Fred exclaimed, irrepressible. It should have been funny, but Kite was ageing, as though Fred were talking about a penchant for skinning live cats.

'Tournier, what did I just say to you?' Kite called.

'I don't want to drip on the floor, Clay will be angry,' Joe said, not sure why he wanted so badly to pull Fred away, but he did. He couldn't see what had made Kite *run*; Kite never ran anywhere. He imposed a speed limit on officers, even. Running panicked the men. He must have seen something bad, but Joe couldn't tell what. 'Fred, come for reinforcements?'

'In a minute!' Fred shouted, and then swung back to Kite, bouncing. Kite was trying to calm him down. Every line of him exuded the need to keep Fred quiet, but Fred, of course, was ignoring him.

Joe saw something in Kite break. He caught Fred's shoulders and shook him. Joe couldn't hear what Fred said, but Kite slapped him, hard enough to snap his head around.

Joe felt like he was falling, because he knew what would happen before it even started. Fred didn't have the common sense to shut up and cower. Instead, his face darkened, and with the absolute indignation of someone who had never been struck before, he hit Kite back. Kite had slapped him to shock him, not to hurt him, even Joe could see that, but this was a righteous punch in the eye.

Or, Fred had plainly wanted it to be. Kite must have been punched a lot, because he saw it coming and smacked Fred's fist away. He caught his wrist and twisted it up behind his back, but Fred was too far gone. He was yelling and kicking like a much smaller child would have, and if it had ever sunk in that you couldn't strike a senior officer, the knowledge had evaporated from his mind now.

'Kite! You can't do that to him, he doesn't understand!' Joe shouted, frantic to make it stop. 'Come on, you know what he's like, he isn't wired like other people—'

'Tournier, get away from him *right now*!' Kite snapped. 'Get below before you fall overboard, I didn't come all this way just for you to drown like an idiot.'

He wasn't being dramatic. As he said it, the ship hit the trough of the next wave and a wall of water smashed down over them. Kite locked one elbow over the rail and Joe snatched at one of the lines that secured the sails. The weight of the water slammed the breath out of him, and as it receded, it dragged them all hard towards the side.

'I know, but—'

'Mr Tournier, *he's lying to you*!' Fred shrieked. He had lost his ordinary self. He was just enraged. If he had been a toddler, Joe would have called it a tantrum, but on a boy of fourteen it was something else. 'It's not right, lying is wrong, *let me go*—'

'I *will* have you flogged,' Kite said, and Joe couldn't tell which of them he was speaking to now, or both of them.

'Mr Tournier, you're not really Mr Tournier—'

The crest of another wave broke over them. They were riding it well, and it wasn't as frightening as the last surge, but it was enough to make Joe look away.

When he got the water out of his eyes and he could see again, Fred was gone.

Kite was still at the rail, staring into the heaving water.

At least four officers had told Joe what you were supposed to do if someone went overboard. Shout at the top of your lungs, and point with your entire arm, and don't move, or the men with the lifelines wouldn't know where to go.

Kite turned away and put the small of his back to the rail. 'Get below,' he said to Joe.

'He could still be alive, aren't we going to—'

'He can't swim.'

Joe scanned the water, willing there to be even a flash of blond hair somewhere, but there wasn't. He looked at Kite again. It would be utterly stupid to accuse him of murder, even though Joe was certain that was exactly what had happened. An accusation like that – it would be Kite's word against his, and Joe would be locked up for the rest of the journey. Or worse, locked up without kneecaps.

But he couldn't just stand here and pretend everything was fine.

'Is it *that* fucking important?' Joe asked, fighting to keep his voice low. 'That no one tells me who I am? So what if he recognised me? You've *given* me Madeline's letters, for God's sake, and I still don't remember anything! Fred could have told me a name and I'd have been none the wiser, I think that's pretty bloody obvious by now. Something else is going on here, isn't it? It isn't just about whether I remember or not!'

'Your business is not the policing of this ship,' Kite said, quiet and dangerous now. 'Get back to your watch, Tournier. We'll be coming into Edinburgh soon.'

'My God!' Joe heard his own voice go high. 'A child is dead! Were you born a machine, or was there a time when you were human? Can you even remember?'

Kite looked as though he wanted to say something, a dozen things, and all of them filled the air with a charge. For a delirious moment, Joe thought he might explain. But then the charge vanished, Kite shut down, and only stepped silent and fast around Joe to go into the stateroom.

Joe had to stand where he was in the rain, shuddering with rage. When he could think in a straight line, he ran down to the infirmary to find Agatha.

'He's just killed Fred Hathaway,' he said flatly. 'I watched him do it. He pushed him overboard.'

He expected her to tell him not to be so stupid. Instead she only set her hands on the edge of her desk and studied him. 'Why?'

'Fred was about to tell me who I am.'

'Right.' She didn't say anything else. She didn't look surprised in any way.

'I don't understand why that matters,' Joe said into the silence. 'I haven't remembered a damn thing since I've been here, and I'm obviously not going to. Even if I turn out to be Napoleon fucking Bonaparte it wouldn't matter. Agatha, what is going *on*? This doesn't feel like – Kite doesn't give a toss if I go back through the gate and tell the French government in my time! Why would they believe someone like me? And even if they did, all you lot have to do is brick up the bloody gate and it isn't a problem any more. This is personal. He was scared. I *have* something on him, don't I?' he asked. He swallowed, because he was still soaked, and he felt unbalanced now, because his thoughts were arriving while he was speaking, and they were running away from him. 'If I remember – I could wreck him, couldn't I? Personally wreck him. What is it? Did I witness some other murder?'

'Joe …'

'Jesus, did I see him kill Jem?' Joe whispered.

'No.' She was holding her hands out, conciliatory. 'Listen; listen. I know this is all infuriating, but first things first. I need you to tell me what happened to Fred Hathaway. What did Missouri do exactly?'

Joe told her, as measuredly as he could. Afterwards, though, he found that he was trembling, and not with anger. It was something else, and he couldn't tell because he couldn't feel it; his body wasn't connected properly to his mind. From nowhere, he saw that imaginary memory of Lily going under the engine again, the flat crunch, and all at once black stars started to crowded in on his vision.

Agatha caught his elbow. 'You're all right. This is just shock, it's normal if you've never seen someone die before.' She steered him into a chair. 'I'm so sorry this is happening to you,' she said quietly. 'But I think you're tough. You must be, if you were a slave. No?'

Joe shook his head. 'No, I'm useless. Ask my wife. Agatha, you have to do something about Kite. He can't just go around murdering children. I don't care what the reason is.'

'I know, I know. I'll go and see him soon, but I'd like to see your heart rate come down first. Can you hear it?' She was holding his wrist. She smiled like he'd never seen her smile before. It lit her up and gave away her age. He didn't feel nervous to be this near to her now. 'You could have been sprinting.'

Joe swallowed hard. His tonsils might as well have been gravel. 'He's a frightening man, your brother.'

She nodded, full of apology. 'I know. I'm sorry. I made him that way. It seemed like a good idea at the time.'

24

Cadiz, 1777

The *Missouri* had gone down in a storm and taken their mother with it. When her second husband Pedro died five years later, there had been some problem with his navy pension, so they had nothing left to live on.

Agatha was sixteen, and because she was clever in more of a bookish than a common-sense way, she had written to Lord Lawrence. He was her uncle, and until she turned twenty-five, he was in charge of the money she had inherited from her father (her real father, her English one, not Pedro). She had met him once or twice, years ago when she'd been at school in England, and he had always seemed kind.

While she waited for the reply, with every hope that it would be favourable, she taught Missouri English. He didn't approve, but he was a polite child and he learned anyway, although she did overhear him telling his friends that his sister was making him learn a made-up language that sounded like spitting. She couldn't help wondering how it was that somebody who was only five could go round having opinions like a real person.

When the letter came from England, it was a hot day, and they were doing the laundry on their doorstep, beneath the waving lines of other people's washing. Their tenement was in the shadow of the church. The letter arrived exactly on the hour, she remembered that clearly, because the bell had just rung three deafening peals, and like always, she had to dive protectively over the laundry tub as the tower parakeets shot along the alley.

The letter was short.

Lord Lawrence was not bringing them to England.

Lord Lawrence was very sorry, but he didn't see what a carpenter's son was to do with him. Agatha was free to come, of course, because she was real family, and he would see that she had a proper education for an English gentlewoman, but she was not to bring Missouri, who would embarrass the Lawrence name. As she would know, she could get her inheritance from her father's estate when she turned twenty-five, whereupon she was free to do as she pleased, with however many undesirable relatives in tow, but until then, it was his responsibility to safe-guard the family's reputation. He regretted it deeply, but he was sure she would understand.

'Oh, fuck you,' she said aloud.

'Mrs Perez says ladies shouldn't swear,' Missouri told her solemnly. He was wringing out the things she had washed, observed by upstairs's cat. Sometimes it put its paw in the soapy water, plainly trying to see why he liked it so much. It didn't look impressed.

'Mrs Perez hasn't met any ladies except ladies in novels. There's a difference between what a lady can say in a published book and what she says when someone screws her over. Come on,' she said. She took his hand. 'Sod the laundry. We're going to sign on with the *Trinidad* again.'

'I thought we were supposed to be going to the rainy place?'

'Change of plans. We don't like Lord Lawrence any more.'

'Why?'

She taught him some words he probably shouldn't have known.

The *Santíssima Trinidad* was the ship Missouri had been born on, the ship his father had died on, and the ship where Agatha had been a nurse for five years. It was in the dock at the moment, being refitted. Agatha had a happy drop when she saw it. It was home. The size of a castle and by far the largest warship in Europe, it was five decks high, and it carried a hundred and forty guns. Now, the deck was alive with carpenters, the air rich with the smell of sawdust and fresh tar.

The gangway was open, so Agatha shuffled Missouri up ahead of her, and looked around for an officer. The captain was passing. He stopped mid-stride.

'Miss Lawrence! What are you doing here, did we forget some of Pedro's things? I thought we got his sea chest to you safely?'

'No, sir, it's all right,' she said, nervous now that she was here. It would have been better to talk to a more junior officer, someone whose job it was to remember her name. 'But I want to sign on again in the infirmary.'

He frowned. 'I thought there was some provision in England.'

'There isn't, sir,' she said, sprung tight and ready to argue if he tried to say she might like to consider shore work. Shore work would mean some miserable convent hospital surrounded by people she didn't know. And, she was eleven years older than Missouri. People would assume he was her son and take that as an excuse to be repulsive. 'And I can't afford the rent.'

'You're sure you're happy, without protection? It might be better to come aboard as a married woman now.'

'I trust in the authority of your officers, sir,' she promised. It was true; the officers were strict, and she had never had any trouble. Partly, that was because she was tall and flat-chested, and possessed of a sexless straightforwardness that made her invisible most of the time. When it didn't, she found that a lot of difficulties could be solved by stabbing someone with a suture needle and then lamenting how dreadfully clumsy you were. Perhaps you got the occasional punch in the head, but you couldn't go round being precious about things like that. A bit of fighting was improving.

'I'm not asking to be paid, sir,' she pressed. 'I just want a berth and three meals a day for me and my brother. The same as before. As a volunteer.' She swallowed. 'Please. I'm good. If you hire a student instead it'll cost you a fortune and he'll know half as much.'

'I know,' the captain said, waving his hand. 'I'll sign you on as *Mr* Lawrence and then we can pay you for your trouble. Just do me one favour; cut your hair and put on some trousers, and at least the Admiralty inspector will think we've made some sort of nod to the rules when he comes round. And – aha, hello young man,' he added to Missouri, who smiled and hid behind her skirt.

'Thank you, sir,' Agatha said, afire with a disproportionate sense of victory. Lord Lawrence could go and bugger a duck.

Much later, in England, people were shocked when she told them she had joined the navy just to avoid paying rent. But what you had to remember about the Spanish navy, especially in those days, was that they had thought the English habit of sending their sailors out to sea for years at a time was barbaric. Spanish ships only ever did short stints; normally it was about six weeks. It wasn't the punishing life it was for English sailors. A few weeks at sea, a week in port; easy. It had been a good life, and for five years, she hadn't regretted it for a second.

When the war came, it was sudden. The *Trinidad* left Cadiz to escort a merchant ship to Arabia, and when they came home, the British had gone peculiar and declared war on themselves – some of them in the colonies in America, against some others at home, apparently because of tea, which Agatha had to admit did seem typical. The ones in America seemed for hazy reasons to be the favoured side as far as Madrid was concerned, and the short, cheerful runs round Europe and Africa were finished. They were sent to Florida.

She wasn't scared. The *Trinidad* was a behemoth. Nothing had even come close to sinking it. Like everyone else, she was just irritated that they would have to cart a whole army regiment across the Atlantic. That was to say, two hundred people who would be seasick for the entire crossing.

Missouri, who was ten by then, had a lot more in the way of common sense. He studied the troops as they clanked aboard, disapproval etched across him.

'So we're at war now,' he said. 'Does that mean we're meant to start killing people?'

'Well, we might,' said Agatha, who was distracted, because most of the boarding troops were Irish; it seemed mad that they would be part of the Spanish army, but they were wearing the colours and looking cheerful at the idea of a fight. For the first time in all her life with the fleet, she felt anxious about her own surname and wondered if she should pretend to be fully Spanish.

'But the English haven't done anything to us. *You're* English.'

Agatha pulled him against her side. He was small, and it always gave her a nasty stab of guilt if she looked at him for too long. He should have been taller, but for those months they'd waited for Lawrence's reply, she hadn't been able to feed him properly and it had never stopped showing. 'You won't have to do anything, we're just moving the soldiers on this run. And anyway, it's going to fizzle out soon. America's too big, the colonies will never be able to organise themselves properly without London.'

He looked uncomfortable. He was too dutiful to argue, though, and only took himself off to what everyone acknowledged was his corner of the infirmary, along with his exam books and the ship's cat. She stroked them both on her way past and worried that, despite growing up on a ship with a thousand people on it, he was turning out shy.

They arrived at the mouth of the Mississippi in boiling, swampy weather. It kept blowing itself into storms, and as the *Trinidad* and the fleet from Havana furled their sails to keep from smashing into the reefs, the sky roiled muggy grey. A mile from the last British outpost in Florida, the officers sent the children below.

Agatha had seen skirmishes before. What she hadn't seen was a wholesale assault on a port. She hadn't seen the way people on the dock looked when the fleet sailed in. People literally dropped what they had been carrying and ran, and rightly so, because the wharves were in range of the flagship's guns.

For all the British must have known an attack was coming, the place looked utterly unprepared. The wooden church towers were peaceful, and there was a soft haze over the swamp in the distance. They had called in their own troops and allies – there was an Indian encampment just outside the town and she watched as their warriors mounted up to face the Spanish battalions – but there were too few. Maybe a few hundred. The *Trinidad* alone had brought that many men. The fleet had brought thousands.

If it had been a simple matter of chaos, it might have been better. But from this distance, she could see the geometry of the battle plan, the weight of the calculation behind the bang of a thousand soldiers marching. Their jackets were bright white. Immaculate.

The ships were, everyone said, only there to transport troops and set them ashore some distance from the port, but they shelled the town too. One of the officers said something about forcing the pitiful few British ships clear of the bay. She saw people vaporise, and even though it was right in front of her, she couldn't quite believe it. Chain shot was designed to punch through a ship's hull; it wasn't supposed to be used on humans.

The strafe destroyed everything in the harbour. A warehouse exploded, and it must have been a powder magazine, because the flash was pure, apocalyptic silver. She didn't hear it even so, because the thunder of the guns just in front of her would have drowned out God himself.

The guns only stopped when their troops reached the town. She always remembered how the soldiers sounded. It was the way that some of the men were laughing; hysterical, too high. She was glad when an Indian rider powered through some of them. He was the most beautiful man she had ever seen. But then someone wrenched him off the horse by his hair and six men ripped him to pieces. The horse tore away, and then she lost it, black in the black smoke.

She went to find Missouri afterwards on the gun deck. He ran across and hugged her, and then asked, panicked, if she was all right. She didn't understand at first, but then saw she was covered with other people's blood; insufficient though they had been, the port guns were in range. She promised she was, and crushed him close again to prove it. The deck was still full of eye-aching smoke and the tang of gunpowder. The gunners themselves were blank with relief now it was over. Here and there, powder monkeys were coming through with buckets of water, which they tipped over the guns. The metal hissed, and simmering bubbles rushed across the muzzles before bursting away into mists of steam.

She should have been relieved too. But all she could think was that what she'd told Missouri before was wrong. The war wasn't going to be over soon. You couldn't have a massacre like this and expect it all to just fizzle out. They'd be lucky if the British didn't smash up the whole of Cadiz for this.

If he'd been boisterous and full of fight, she might not have worried, but he wasn't. He was quiet and quick to smile. He would grow up to be honourable, and chivalrous. He would hesitate in the face of a desperate man aiming a gun at him, because he would feel too much sympathy. The instinct to be kind, and to negotiate, would slow down the instinct to defend himself. He would hesitate, and he would be shot.

She swallowed hard and tasted grit.

'Miz, come up on deck with me.'

He looked up at her, serious as always. 'Are we allowed to?'

'It's all right, you won't be in anyone's way,' she said, hating what she was about to do.

The guns had stopped firing, but the carnage in the port was still unfolding. The soldiers were still down there, shooting anyone who came close to them, searching houses. She took Missouri to the rail.

He stiffened and tried to turn away. When she caught his elbow to pull him back again, he curled forward against his own forearms. She prised him upright, knowing with an itchy clarity that if she pulled even a fraction too hard, she would break his arm. He was so little.

'You need to see what happens,' she said. 'If you don't know what this is before you have to face it, you'll go to pieces. That's how you get yourself killed.'

A scream came up from the dock.

She wanted to scream too. Every atom in her strained to get him away, to tell him to cover his eyes, and go somewhere else. There was nowhere else to go, though. If she moved them away from the navy, then what? They were in the same situation they had been five years ago. She'd have to work for a pittance at a hospital and they'd live in some disgusting tenement again, and he would end up being someone's stable boy, and all his cleverness would wither, because all that life would require of him was an ability to hold a shovel.

So what she said was, 'Like that idiot there.'

Missouri took it with an eerie placidity. The idiot in question was having his throat cut by a soldier with a bayonet.

'All right?' she said, uneasy. She had thought he would be upset.

'Yes, ma'am.'

'Good.'

She was never gentle with him again. It made her feel evil, but when she met other sisters and other mothers, they all said the same thing. You couldn't forge a sword without hammering it.

25

HMS *Agamemnon*, 1807

J oe and Agatha were still sitting in the infirmary when a boom shook the whole ship. It sounded like a furnace exploding.

Then, from somewhere above them, a drumbeat started, fast. It spread to some other part of the ship, and another. Joe looked blankly at Agatha, who was already pulling fresh linen onto the beds.

'We must be at Edinburgh,' she told him. 'Someone's firing at us. The drums mean battle stations.'

As she spoke, a tiny little boy edged past with a bucket of sand, tipping it out on the deck. Another boy followed, raking it into a fine layer. The first one paused to draw a happy face in it, and the other one giggled.

'Why— sorry, why would the French be at Edinburgh?' Joe asked, numbly, because he couldn't make his brain move beyond the two children. Sand on the deck: surely that meant they expected a lot of blood in here. But the boys were barely older than Lily.

'There's probably a blockade. They do that every now and then,' Agatha said, as if it were only an annoying habit.

Another explosion sounded even closer than the first, and another. Water roared. Joe had a gut-clenching feeling that what he was hearing was cannon-fire tearing up the surface of the sea.

'Why are there children here?' Joe said, even though he could see that was the least of their troubles.

Agatha glanced at the boys. 'Loblolly boys. They help in the infirmary when it's busy.' She seemed to understand then why he was worried, and smiled ruefully. 'It's safe. We're in the heart of the ship here, it's rare to get a shot this far in. Come on, we need these lamps all lit.'

The drums were still beating. Directly above the infirmary was the gun deck, and Joe could hear people running, and the wood-dulled voices of the sergeants. The cannon-fire outside was very close now, or he thought so; he didn't have much experience with the proximity of explosions, but he could feel each blast in the roots of his teeth. The deck was still tipping in the rough water.

Something shot across the ceiling so hard he thought it would splinter. Their own guns. The bones in the back of his neck pulled when screams came from the top deck, muted through two floors.

Agatha touched his arm and looked into his eyes when he lifted his head. 'Keep very calm. If someone comes in who's obviously dying, tell him he'll be fine and make him comfortable. If someone's a real mess, there are pistols in the cupboard — but shoot through a pillow, or the noise will scare the others. They're always jumpy once they've been brought down from the guns. Understand?'

Joe nodded. 'I'll be all right,' he managed, though that seemed amazingly unlikely. He was sure she was lying about the infirmary being safe. The hull *was* thick here, but he had seen those crates of chain shot when he went below to Clay's room. They would slice through any thickness of wood in the same way a hot knife was never going to be defeated by even gallons of butter. 'You should see the accidents we have in the engine yard.'

She clapped his shoulder. 'Good. Your main job is not to have hysterics. You'll do wonderfully.'

Above them, the guns thundered, and the wooden ceiling squealed its protest.

There was an almighty crash. In a second of perfect silence, he heard Kite's voice call clear and calm at the officers to walk and not run.

Men burst through the door, torn to ribbons. Agatha lifted someone on to a table and told everyone what to do, in the tone she would have given directions to the post office. She had a knack for making it normal. Alfie, the little boy with the sand bucket, showed Joe how to tie a tourniquet. All of Joe's nerves were shrieking to get such a tiny child away from everything, but there was no away to get to.

He soon realised Alfie was working on the safe side of things. Not long later, the first children were brought down, the ones who worked feeding powder to the guns. They were as wrecked as the men and women. One girl observed politely that her arm seemed to be missing and would he mind cauterising the wound so she could get back up to where she was needed while the shock was still a good anaesthetic. He started to argue, but Agatha took over, did exactly as the girl asked and then sent her back up with an approving shove.

Joe stared at the ladder where she'd disappeared. He had never heard people talk like that, not even slaves with the nastiest masters and the blackest humour.

As people poured in he caught scraps of news. There had been a direct hit to the gun deck; a cannon had exploded, powder and all. The French were raking the quarterdeck with chain shot and Kite was immortal, as usual. It was hard to hear over the noise of the guns and before long he stopped trying. He didn't have to care. All he had to do was live through the next twenty minutes.

Vane, the man who'd been declared Cock of the Week, swung round the doorway.

'Doctor! There's men in the water, we're bringing them up but they're burned, I don't think we can get them down here.'

'I'm coming.' Agatha caught his shoulder when he started away again. 'You stay down here, you know how to sew, don't you? Joe, you're tall. Come with me, there's going to be some lifting.' She snatched up a gun and took the ladder at a run.

Joe went after her automatically before he understood what they would be walking into. The noise was worse up the hatchway ladder and everything was smoke.

Agatha snatched him out of the way as a gun shot backward, almost right into them, more than a ton of fizzing hot iron. The noise made his ears sing and he couldn't hear anything for ten long seconds, although he saw the ghosts of other guns sling back too, six feet, eight, gunners jolting away from them the second the fuses were lit. In the haze were tiny floating embers, just drifting; they were burning rags of cloth and human hair.

Under all of it, the deck heeled insanely as the ship turned what must have been a clear right angle towards the harbour. Somewhere, a drumbeat kept the gunners loading in time. It was the nearest he had been to hell, and the most grateful he had been to find a ladder that led up into open air. But even the top deck was smoke-hidden. The masts and the men were only partly there, and all there was to confirm that they were real were the officers' orders, the howls, and the terrible drums.

Agatha tugged him. He had no idea how she knew where she was going, but just along from them were men propped against the side. They were soaking wet but covered in burns.

There was a collective yell from somewhere below, and the Union flag floated down just past Joe, the edges orange and burning. A midshipman tore by and snatched the flag, and ran to climb a rope. He managed to fix it back up, but a sniper shot slung him backwards.

The smoke cleared just enough for him to catch a glimpse of the quarterdeck. Kite was standing at the rail, unmoving even though it was him the French snipers were aiming for. He wasn't there for any pressing reason — it was too loud to shout to the gunners — only to see that they were going in the right direction and what the French were doing. He didn't move when the railing beside him exploded upward. Other people were looking at him too, to see if it was time to panic yet. Joe wanted to shout at them that Kite was never going to panic.

Agatha tapped his arm and nodded downwards to make him help with the first of the burned men. She could have carried them on the flat, but not down the hatchway. They straightened up together, carefully with the man between them.

'It's nothing to fuss about, doctor,' the man was trying to say. 'I had a good dousing, the sea put me out.'

'I think we'll have to see about that downstairs, sailor. Joe, take him.'

'Where are you going?' Joe asked, really afraid now. Somehow it had been all right while he was with her, but even the idea of trying to get back down alone was paralysing.

'No one will know it wasn't the French,' she said. She smiled, but her voice was tight, cello strings right on the edge of snapping. 'I should have done it before he hurt a child. I've known he was insane since the fall of London.'

He didn't understand until she turned away to begin the smoky, debris-strewn run towards the quarterdeck, towards Kite, one hand on the gun in her belt to keep it from falling.

26

London, 1805

L ondon fell on the first cold day of October.

At eleven o'clock that morning, when Agatha was on her way to the naval hospital and feeling cheerful about assisting with the amputation of a diabetic's leg, the French fleet were already approaching Deptford. The wind was strong and they were going fast, despite being laden down with cavalry and infantry. Alarms were sounding downriver, but London was going about its day in quite the standard fashion, leaves gusting over the roads and between the spokes of carriage wheels, merchant ships bumping each other on the Thames, adverts for the theatre crinkly from all the rain.

Agatha was thinking about hospital fundraising. She was trying to organise a series of medical lectures for people who weren't students, to raise money for the new ward. Maybe even a lecture for women; hardly anyone in her circle got the chance to see an interesting amount of blood. She could already hear the squeaking noises everyone's husbands would make, but there had to be a gentle way of explaining to the husbands that they didn't have to come.

She was about twenty feet from the hospital's front door when the bells started to ring; first bells from churches near the river, then outward, until they were coming from all around.

It was well past the hour. She stopped, puzzled. Everyone else on the street was doing the same, even the navy officers milling about. It took a long few seconds for puzzlement to turn to fore-boding. The bells kept on, and on.

On the broad way by the riverbanks, people were glancing towards the water, but not with too much urgency. There was a street performer with a full grand piano set up and everyone around him was still clapping and listening to him rather than the bells. Agatha wondered if maybe it wasn't an alarm after all, if the bells weren't just part of some church thing that she'd managed not to hear about.

She was looking round for someone unoccupied to ask when a cavalry regiment pelted down the road. People scattered in both directions, and rather than slowing to let the man at his piano get to safety, the riders steered the horses past him on either side, so close that the reverberation of hooves on the road made the strings hum by themselves. In the middle of the soldiers was a frightened, richly dressed man, and a woman in a purple gown that spilled back over the saddle.

'Was that the ...?' said a girl who had stopped just next to Agatha.

'King,' Agatha said slowly.

From the south, further towards the Thames estuary and Deptford, there was a flash and a colossal bang.

'What was that?' the girl demanded.

'They're firing the land guns.' Agatha caught the girl's arm. She looked horribly young. She could only have been about twenty, slim and well-dressed, and certainly not the sort of person who had been raised to run anywhere. Agatha recognised her dimly, maybe from a party – she was someone's daughter. 'Get home, and pack a bag, and get out of London. I'm not joking.'

The girl stared her.

'I mean it,' Agatha said, and finally dredged up the girl's name. Wellesley; Revelation Wellesley, the Earl of Wiltshire's eldest. 'If they're firing the land guns, then the French are sailing up the Thames.'

A young man in a grey silk jacket looked round and laughed anxiously. 'I don't think there's any need to fret, madam. I'm certain our soldiers are more than up to the task—'

'Don't be such a bloody idiot,' Agatha suggested, and the man looked like she'd slapped him. 'The army is in Spain. Go,' she added to Wellesley, who bolted. The young man stared after her, uncertainty clouding his face. Agatha didn't stay to persuade him.

At Jermyn Street, her uncle was sitting with his feet tucked under his tiger, halfway through a glass of port. When she came in, the servants were clustered in the corridor, taut and anxious.

'Pack a bag each and be back here in five minutes,' Agatha said quietly. 'We have to get out. The French are coming.'

They burst away from her.

'Lawrence,' she said as she went through to him. The tiger flicked its ears hopefully, realised she wasn't someone who might have any tobacco, and sprawled again, tail lashing bright orange on the Turkish rug. 'I see you have ambitions to be Pliny and bathe while Pompeii burns, but now is not the moment. They're firing the land guns at Deptford and I've just seen the royal household taking the King to the river. We have to go. There might still be English ships taking people aboard.'

'Don't be silly!' Lawrence said happily. 'We shall stay and fight, like proper Englishmen.'

'All right, do that,' she said, because she was buggered if she was going to get herself killed over someone she didn't like. 'But the rest of us are leaving for the river in five minutes.'

A cannon blast sounded in the distance, then a whole salvo. If it had come from the land guns, though, they should never have been able to hear it from here. Lawrence looked annoyed, as though it had happened expressly to make her point for her.

'You'll do no such thing!' he snapped, but he sounded disconcerted that she wasn't pleading with him. 'You're being hysterical!'

They both jumped when a gunshot boomed from the street. She went to the window. Smoke coiled in their direction from Oxford Street. She watched for another second, then went upstairs to change. Into something a lot, lot plainer. If they were caught, she did not want to look rich.

She decided she wasn't going to think what might have happened to Jem and Missouri.

Out in the corridor, one of the cook's girls was already packed and waiting, tying and retying her apron strings in a way that looked involuntary. What was almost certainly a bullet smacked into the front door.

'Perhaps the kitchen,' Agatha said, trying hard to look reassuring, and to get her silk-sheets-and-marzipan-spoiled head into something like a useful order. It was a long time since she'd been in proper danger, and now, a slimy fear was slugging up the inside of her ribcage. Maybe she'd forgotten how to function, when things were bad. Maybe she was about to be a hysterical mess.

Lawrence hurried up beside her with a bag, looking flustered. His tiger loped along behind.

They went through the back door, past the chickens in the courtyard, into the tiny alley down behind the garden. More shots went off, much closer now, and more columns of smoke went up. Other people were running too, and soon, the back ways were full. Women in beautiful day dresses were ducking washing lines. Agatha couldn't get past the bizarrerie. It was only just midday, a pleasant autumn morning. They were supposed to go to the theatre tonight.

A monumental noise cracked the sky and the dome of St Paul's disintegrated inwards. There was a strange pause in the alleys. She saw something in Lawrence crumble too. All at once, rather than a stolid politician, or a lord of the Admiralty, he was just a frightened old man. She pushed him ahead of her, then the servants, and seized the hand of the smallest kitchen boy so they wouldn't lose him in the crush. She could smell smoke now.

The docks were howling. It was a noise she had never heard among human beings before, even on that bloody day in Florida. She couldn't count the number of people, but if somebody had said all of London had swarmed on to the riverbank, she would have believed it. She realised what a mistake it had been to come the second she saw the water.

The first ships ahead of them weren't English like she had been praying all the way for, but Spanish. The closest was a leviathan. Four gun decks, black and red stripes, so vast that it didn't look like it could ever have floated, but it did, and the triple-headed figurehead reared sixty feet above the water; it was Christ, God, and an unnerving spectre that was the Holy Ghost.

The *Santíssima Trinidad*. It was their old ship, so close she could see the glints of the insignia on the sleeves of the officers pacing the quarterdeck. It gave her a bolt of homesickness. English officers were gaudy, but Spanish ones wore black, like priests. If she had seen them at any other moment, she would have been overjoyed.

It didn't look like home any more.

The sound coming from it was much worse than the people screaming or the crack of shots. It was drums. It was a deep, ancient sound, and when there was a lull in the chaos, she realised the sailors were singing. A hymn, Latin, one she knew from cathedral masses when Missouri was little. It was a song that came with a vision of people burning at stakes, the hellfire of the Inquisition, the holy fury of a church militant. She had loved it before, in that other life when Cadiz was their home port; it made you feel part of something mighty and celestial, and it had never once struck her as frightening, but even though the guns and the smoke hadn't scared her, that hymn did. She'd never been on the wrong side of it before.

Gangplanks slammed onto the wharf, and a tide of gleaming cavalrymen thundered down. They swerved sharp right along the dock, towards Westminster.

And not a single red jacket anywhere. No English soldiers.

The dust cloud from St Paul's was reaching them. There was so much of it that it cast a sepia fog across everything. It smelled of hot stone.

When a French ship just along from the *Trinidad* swung its broadside towards the crowd, there was a screaming back-surge as the people nearest the water slung themselves around to get out of the way. She flattened Lawrence to the alley wall as it bottlenecked. God, she'd made a mistake. Whichever English ship had come for the King must have gone already. Her ribs started to stiffen with proper panic and she snapped her teeth together, trying to squash it down before it was incapacitating.

And then, just a scrap of colour in among the chaos of French and Spanish ships, there was a Union Jack. An English ship was skimming through. Her breath seized. Yes. She wasn't insane: someone was coming to try and get people away. Through the smoke and the dust, she could see other ships nosing through to do the same.

Lawrence dragged at her arm. His tiger was pressed against her leg. 'Agatha! They're going to fire into the crowd, we have to—'

'No; wait.' Something odd was happening. The captain on the English quarterdeck was signalling with his hands to the

Spanish captain, who was talking back the same way. They bowed to each other. She could just make out their silhouettes in the smoke. 'The Spanish are shielding them. Go. Get on to the quay now!'

'Agatha—'

'Now!' She shoved him ahead of her. She couldn't see the servants any more, but there was no time to think. Everyone else was streaming away. Through a storm of elbows and pushing it took what felt like hours to reach the quay but when they did, she was right; the *Trinidad* had moved to cover the smaller English ship. She hoped to God it wasn't an elaborate trick to sink as many people as possible. The English sailors were already climbing down onto the dock. Someone put her hands on the netting on the hull.

'You have to climb, love,' the sailor told her. He was having to shout. A cannon went off somewhere. She had never jumped like it before. It was so close she heard the shot whine, and she felt stupid until she saw the sailor had flinched as well.

The servants hadn't followed. When she looked back, they were gone. She never saw them again. But the sailor was helping Lawrence onto the ropes now too, and shouting, hoarse already, for the women and children and old people to come first. Nobody tried to argue with Lawrence's tiger, which leapt up after him.

She was one of the first to the top. There was a whole line of men waiting to help them over the rail. An officer with red hair gave her a hand.'

'Where ...?' she said, incoherent from the chaos but aware that they couldn't all stand clustered in one place. The ship would sink.

'Far rail, please, we need to balance everyone out.' He made it sound ordinary.

'Jesus Christ,' she said. 'Missouri!'

'Yes, morning,' he said, easy and self-contained. He smiled as if they had just met in the street, and she stared, because she hadn't recognised him. She had last seen him two years ago, before he sailed, and then, she had still thought of him as a boy. He wasn't any more. 'Far rail, if you wouldn't mind,' he said again.

The far rail was so close to a row of Spanish gun ports she could see the gunners. 'Right,' she managed. She couldn't decide what she was more shocked by: a French invasion, or a failure to recognise her own brother.

No wonder he'd managed to negotiate with the Spanish captain. The man probably remembered him.

She went to the far rail, but hardly anyone else did. Arguments broke out behind her; people didn't want to stand there only to be torn apart if the Spanish captain gave the order to fire. Behind her, the Spanish gunners were talking. One of them called, 'Señora,' and said that it was safe, and not to worry.

She hesitated, and then she leaned over the rail to shake his hand. 'Pleasure to meet you. Have you come from far?'

'Cadiz.' He was curly and cheerful. His hand was grainy with powder. 'You're Spanish!'

'I am, sir.'

He turned back to tell his friends, who came to see.

She knew it was dangerous as she was doing it. The gap between the ships was narrow enough to lean over, but it was a long fall, and anyone in the water now would be crushed between the hulls. But everyone else was watching. She climbed over the rail and hopped on to the end of the Spanish gun, which had been decorated in gold filigree. The Spanish gunners all saw and burst out laughing, but it wasn't mocking; they were cheering her on. A couple of them reached through the gun port to help her.

'Agatha! What are you doing?' Lawrence demanded. He had reddened. He was in the middle of the deck just behind her. 'Don't make such a scene!'

'They'll not want to fire if women are sitting on their guns,' Agatha said doggedly, though she was horribly aware that her legs were showing, and her stockings had slipped down while she'd been running. She looked like a bawd. The thought made her feel little and ridiculous. She could hear her younger self, the one that had worked on the *Trinidad*, sneering at her down the years.

The Spanish gunner climbed out too and put his arm round her, smelling of gunpowder. She kissed his cheek and waved to the people clustered on the English side of the rail. The Spanish men started calling to the women and waving, and finally, people moved across, beginning to smile, nervous but not frightened.

'Hernandez,' a long-suffering voice said behind the gunner somewhere. 'Why is there a lady on your gun?'

The gunners laughed and, this time, she laughed too. In every other direction, from every other ship on the water, the storm of guns was still cracking, people still screaming, the dock still heaving, but the gap between the two ships was a valley of ordinariness. More women came to balance on the guns until sometimes there were two apiece.

'We're full,' Missouri called from the rail. 'Would you like to come back?'

She looked up. He didn't seem shocked or embarrassed, only pleased.

'Oh, no, why?' Hernandez said good-naturedly.

'I'm afraid we must be underway,' Missouri said, smiling.

Hernandez gave him a melodramatic sigh but saluted and ducked back inside. Agatha hesitated, because the jump back to the rail was upwards. Missouri stepped over himself and handed her across. When she looked back, it was a pathetic gap. The hulls of the two ships were almost touching.

'Thank you,' she said lamely.

'Captain!' someone called, sounding nervous.

'*Captain?*' Agatha echoed, shocked.

'Just inherited it,' he explained, then shook her hand. 'Well done,' he said, as if she were another officer, and went away to the quarterdeck steps. A man made a lunge for him and screamed into his face about a wife and children, waving a knife right up under Missouri's eye. Missouri shot the man in the head.

Agatha stood still, wondering if it would even be a footnote in an encyclopaedia article one day. Probably not. A small sensible murder among all the other murders wouldn't be noteworthy, and especially not now it was starting to rain, and not just rain, but hard, stinging rain that ricocheted.

Missouri hadn't broken his pace to do it. He just continued on up the quarterdeck stairs.

She had a crawling feeling that he hadn't seen it properly. Later, he might look at his gun and wonder where the bullet had gone, but he wouldn't recall exactly whose head it was in.

When the shot tore through the quarterdeck stairs, it sprayed Missouri with fire right down one side and slammed him into the banister. She saw other officers freeze – they were hardly more than children, any of them, and they must have been sure he was dead, and for a numb three seconds so was she – but then he wrenched himself onto his hands and knees and told them to get on with their work, thank you, gentlemen. His jacket was still burning.

She managed to get him into the stateroom. He was smaller than her, at least; she could lift him. After scratching around for an alcohol cupboard, she poured out a cup of rum and pushed it into his hand, then started to hunt for something to clean the burns with. Everything in the room was smashed: crockery, furniture, even the windows. The cold sea air and the rain were sweeping in. Chain shot whistled through the pillars of smoke – burning ships, each one of those pillars – and a weird, ringing noise came from the docks. It was crowds of people screaming, but at a distance. One by one, other ragged English ships limped into view, struggling against the wind for the open water ahead.

'We need to clean you up,' she said. She could see his collarbone. If he didn't die of infection, it would be a miracle. 'I'm sorry, but it's going to have to be saltwater. It needs to be clean, or—'

'Agatha! I don't matter!' he said over her, his voice breaking. 'Please. There are men below with their legs blown off.'

'All right,' she said softly.

He was shuddering. Shock.

'Where are we going?' she asked, to try and get his mind off everything else. The shock would be a good anaesthetic for now, but once he settled, he would feel it, really feel it, and none of those boy-officers would know what to do if they had to hear their captain screaming. If she could get him drunk, it would help. She glanced at the door. The boys were clipping to and fro outside, soothed enough for now. Missouri was watching them too.

'Edinburgh,' he said, steady again. 'The castle is fortified enough to hold the King.'

'Edinburgh – why not Newcastle, or—'

'The French are ...' He shook his head slightly. He was about to pass out. He still hadn't made a sound about the burns.

She refilled his glass. He had drunk the first lot at least. 'Don't suppose you've seen Jem?'

'No,' he said, brittle now for the first time. His teeth clacked as he shut them and his shoulders flickered, and she realised, horrified, that he was trying hard not to cry.

Any normal human being would have dropped everything and hugged him, and wanted to make him feel better.

She felt repulsed. The instinct to slap him and shout at him *never* to do that if he wanted not to get shot, that when you let your thinking and clarity go you were dead, was mighty. But it wasn't really crying that was repulsive. It was *any* overpowering feeling, any feeling that prioritised itself over thinking, and she felt just as disgusted with herself as she did with him. It felt like having a ravening cancer, only instead of a thing that ate your bones, this thing ate your heart, made you usefully cool at first, but then cold, and then cruel.

She hadn't known it had eaten so much of hers.

'Pull yourself together and let's get on with this,' was all she could say, even though she could hear it was utterly deficient, and entirely the reason why he could shoot someone in the head without noticing.

He smiled as if she'd said something kind. Sitting there by the wreckage of the windows, in the wreckage of his own flesh, he looked like one of those blasted saints from centuries ago, who would murder all Jerusalem for a chance at heaven's gates. 'I love you.'

She smiled too. Now was not the time to philosophise or reel off into stupid despair about the futility of everything, but again and again, she saw the way that man had collapsed, and how Missouri had just kept walking.

If he remembered, it would be all right.

'Miz,' she said, and felt surprised when her voice arrived sounding normal. 'Did you shoot someone on deck just now? I saw a fight.'

'What? I don't think so. Are you sure?'

'No,' she said, because it was true; already she wasn't sure, and by tonight, she'd have convinced herself it hadn't happened, and it wouldn't matter.

And obviously it didn't matter. The familiar old just-survive-the-day voice in her head was demanding to know why she was so bloody hung up on the death of an idiot who had endangered everyone.

She had always trusted the just-survive-the-day voice. Only, after so long spent not hearing it, she could hear it differently now. It had a hiss to it.

'Are you all right?' Missouri asked. He was watching her, very still, which was disturbing. Nobody should have been able to sit so attentively with burns like that.

'I'm fine. I just forgot how to do all this. I'm having moralising thoughts about the futility of philosophy and human kindness. Say something that will help.'

He smiled a little. 'Perhaps you might squash your delicate feelings down until fewer people are bleeding to death, sailor.'

'Excellent. Thank you.'

She hung for dear life on to the way he laughed, young and honest, even though she knew that one day soon he was likely to do something far worse than shoot an innocent man.

27

Edinburgh, 1807

As Agatha turned away from him, heading towards the human fragments that made the deck look like someone had spilled tar on it, Joe nearly caught her apron string to stop her. A deep part of him couldn't stand seeing anyone walk out into the slaughter like that, but he was too much of a coward. He needed Kite gone and he couldn't do it himself. He swallowed hard, torn between getting the burned men below, and watching her, as if hope was a sort of physical particle, like an electron, that he needed to send her way to help her get through. Up on the quarterdeck, Kite was motionless, watching the French formations through the roiling smoke.

The shot atomised her.

It hit her square and she came apart at the seams. A soft mist pattered across Joe and on the deck. It wasn't as red as he would have thought. The drizzle was already washing it from his hands. He couldn't move. All his thoughts looked normal, not caught up in the anxious whirl they usually were if he was scared. But he still couldn't move.

'Help!'

Joe came back to himself enough to pull the burned man towards the ladder. At the hatch, he looked back. Edinburgh was close. The harbour front strobed as they fired the land guns.

The infirmary was chaos. The surgeon's first and second mates were there, both women in indigo dresses, and Alfie knew what he was about remarkably, but it wasn't enough. Without Agatha, Joe lost the sense of normalcy from before. Along the back were beds full of people too torn up to help. Lieutenant Wellesley loaded four pistols and shot the injured men one by one in the head.

Gradually, he became aware that the guns were firing less frequently, and that the French shots were coming from behind them, not ahead.

Without deciding, Joe dropped the bandages he had been counting out and went back up to the top. He was just getting in the way, and he wanted to find Kite. Really, urgently wanted to find him, because Kite was a murderer who had just seen his sister killed, and it was a small hop from murderer to real lunatic, and Wellesley was in the infirmary shooting people, and there was no one else to stop Kite changing his mind and turning back and getting them all killed for a chance at revenge.

It was an opportunity too. Somehow, Joe was going to have to get round Kite over the next few days. Pretending to be worried about him now was as good a start as any.

Kite was just coming down the quarterdeck stairs. A couple of the younger lieutenants trooped up to him and Joe thought they would have some kind of report, but instead the three of them thumped together in a brief hug that exuded gratefulness to be alive. The littlest midshipman, the one who'd said she was gullible, rushed up and bumped face-first into Kite's chest, in tears. Kite lifted her up and spoke to her too quietly for Joe to hear, then handed her over to one of the lieutenants.

'Oh, Joe. You're alive,' Kite said when he saw him, sounding honestly relieved.

'So are you,' Joe said, relieved as well, against all logic and reason. 'Agatha ...'

'I saw,' said Kite, toneless.

Do it. Pretend.

'I came to see if you were all right,' Joe said, and even though he had been sure he *was* pretending until then, he didn't feel so clear about it now that they were talking.

Kite's wolf eyes ticked over Joe and Joe felt certain he could read the lot, the determination to make Kite like him enough to let him go, muddied by what felt uncomfortably like real worry. 'Thanks,' Kite said.

They were coming into the harbour now. The water was deep, and they drifted right up to the wharf. Men all along the side threw down balls of knotted rope to keep the hull from grinding against the stone. The air was still thick with black smoke. Kite showed no sign of turning them around for another go at the French.

A hissing came from behind them. Sailors were going over the deck with wide brooms, pushing all the pieces of people overboard and leaving red comb patterns behind – it was the brooms that hissed. Kite watched for too long, then seemed to catch himself and put both hands on the rail to keep himself facing forward.

The gangway bumped onto the wharf. Joe expected the sailors to go down, but they didn't; the women on the dock came up.

'We can't go?' he said, not understanding. 'What about the wounded?'

'Not until the ship's paid off. It takes a few days. The surgeons come to us,' Kite explained, nodding to the women. He sounded too normal. He might have just come on to the deck after a morning spent reading the newspaper; there was nothing in his voice, for all he was grazed and smoke-stained, to say he had just seen his sister killed. Joe had a surge of real indignation.

'That's insane. These people need to get away *now*, Kite. Not everyone's a bloody machine!'

But Kite was shaking his head. 'Have you heard of battle fatigue?'

'What's that?'

Kite glanced at the gangway and the surgeons. They looked so clean they didn't seem real. 'During a fight, you want to keep your friends safe, but you can't. When you leave the ship, you just want to hurt everyone, because all these people were tucked up safe and sound while your mates were in bits on the deck. If you have it badly enough, you end up punching someone. Or worse. We can't let people out straight away. They might hurt their families.' He still sounded quite together and presentable. 'I shouldn't be allowed ashore yet either, I expect I'll lose it later. But there isn't much we can do about that.'

'You know you probably wouldn't hurt anyone if you admitted to feeling something right now,' Joe said angrily. 'A stitch in time saves nine?'

Kite looked across at him. The perfect calm didn't break. He decided – and Joe saw him decide – to snap it with perfect precision right down the middle. 'You are so *fucking* French.'

It felt like an electric shock. Joe couldn't remember even hearing Kite swear before. He wanted to back away. If he left things like this, though, Kite was more likely to shoot him behind a shed somewhere than to let him go.

'I'm sorry,' Joe said. 'I didn't mean …'

'What, that the correct response for me now is to go to pieces while I still have a battleship to repair and six hundred living people to worry about?'

'No, I understand. I'm sorry,' Joe said, feeling stupid.

Kite shook his head once and seemed to put it all aside. He looked ashamed of himself. 'How are you?'

'What?'

'First time seeing action is always bad. How are you?'

'Um …' Joe had thought that he was managing, but being asked cracked him, and then he was on the edge of crying. 'Not too good,' he tried to say. His voice came out hoarse.

Kite was quiet, and Joe had to look away to pull his sleeve over his eyes. The tears were leaking now and he couldn't stop them. Kite took an apple out of his pocket, which he showed Joe. 'Can I tell you a secret?'

Joe nodded, feeling like a child.

'If things turn bad, if it looks like the ship will sink, the best and only thing I can do is look calm. Eat an apple, in full view of everyone. It keeps people steady, even when we're putting up a white flag and the officers are about to be arrested as pirates and dismembered in public. We're not in trouble until the contingency apple comes out.'

Joe laughed. It was more of a painful spasm of his ribs, but he felt better.

'Eat the evidence,' Kite whispered, and gave him the apple.

Joe took it and wondered how in God's name someone who was so sporadically kind had murdered a child not even three hours ago.

They stood together in silence while Joe ate the apple. Kite had his back propped against the rail, watching the clean-up of the deck. Sometimes he stopped a passing sailor and shook their hand, very gently, even if they were covered in gore. Some of them cracked just like Joe had and wept, and some, older veterans they must have been, only clapped Kite's arm and told him he'd done well. Little by little, his calmness radiated outward. The panicky zing in the air faded, and the crew became just a group of people cleaning.

The incoming tide of nurses and surgeons and surgeons' assistants from the jetty had ebbed.

'You and I need to go and report to the Admiralty,' Kite said finally. 'Come on. Oh – Wellesley,' he added. She had just appeared from a hatchway. 'If the cook's still with us, tell him to use all the sugar supplies left. Whatever he likes, but make sure everyone gets something.'

'Yes, sir – have you seen my brother?'

'Overboard,' Kite said very low.

She only nodded. She didn't even look surprised. Joe couldn't watch her any more. He was always conscious of how fragile Lily was in the engine yard. It must have been even worse to have a child bouncing around a warship. She must have half-expected this for every single day of Fred's service. He wondered if always being braced for it made it any easier. It couldn't have.

'Sugar supplies,' she repeated.

'Thank you.'

Joe nearly stopped her. He wanted to say, no, you don't understand, *it was him*, but he couldn't. Kite had given him an apple and by some kindly witchcraft, just for this quarter-hour, it made Joe loyal.

As Joe and Kite walked down the gangway, Drake and another marine fell in behind them.

Part IV

EDINBURGH

28

Edinburgh, 1807

The ground felt wrong. Joe was dizzy. He had to look back to prove to himself it was the *Agamemnon* that had been moving, not the shore. When he saw it, he had to stop, shocked. Half the side of the ship was torn out. He'd heard the explosion on the gun deck, but from outside, it looked unsalvageable. A chunk of the stern was gone as well, and the quarterdeck was smashed right down the middle where a mast had fallen. Sails hung now in rags at mad, broken angles. Most of the rigging was torn. The burned ends drifted in the wind, moulting sparks into the grey air.

All along the dock were tents marked with red medical crosses. They were full to the point that wounded men were lying on trestle beds out in the open. Children paced along the lines, selling gunpowder at a tuppence per pinch for fire-lighting. Fires glimmered everywhere. The buildings along the harbour front were mainly rubble, full of people stacking bricks.

Most of the men in the hospital tents had been hurt so recently that they were still screaming. From a distance, the noise sounded like a flock of seagulls. Women in indigo dresses moved through them, reaper-like, sometimes with bandages and some-times with pistols. Just beyond a scruffy customs hut, where the rain was dissolving the chalk list that showed tax rates, a gun on the wharf was still hot; a man was frying eggs on it, which mixed hot oil with the tang of gunpowder. Even after everything, Joe was hungry.

There was no telling where one hospital tent began and another ended, so they had to weave their way through. A preacher intoned hellfire from the one on the left. The path was mud. Someone had laid down bricks and planks so that people could step over the worst of the puddles. Eventually they gave way to a stretch of decking. On either side, the wounded watched them without seeing them. Joe had to concentrate on the wooden slats to keep from staring. He had never seen people ripped apart like that. Arms missing, legs missing, faces burned off, not even bandaged yet. Some of the men in the beds were dead. Ravens circled with the seagulls.

Joe looked back when he heard a splash. They were tipping bodies straight into the sea. There were piles and piles of them, men and horses, all jumbled up together in fishing nets weighted with cannon shot, and mud everywhere, gluey because it was half-frozen.

He saw what a prick he must have looked to Kite, complaining about being taken away from his cosy lighthouse.

All of Edinburgh was uphill. The castle was on another hill of its own, a crag black from the foundries to windward. Everything was black. The church towers; the houses, which leaned into the streets and cast deep shadows in the fading light; the cobblestones. The sun was going down. Joe had lost any sense of what time it was. A cruel steep road led up to the castle walls, lined with soldiers in cockaded helmets whose plumes rippled in the freezing wind. The rain had cloaked most of the city when Joe looked back down the hill, except for pinpoint lights.

The way in was under a low portcullis, lit on either side by braziers whose heat pulsed out and made him want to stop there.

Kite ignored them and went straight through. Joe had expected some impressive main doors, or something definitive at least, but the castle wasn't one single building. It was at least a dozen, all ringed by the curving walls. Torchlight gleamed on the guns aiming out towards the town and the estuary. More guards stood everywhere. They weren't ordinary soldiers. They were all much taller than Joe or Kite, even without the height of their helmets, and they were swathed in furs and tartan. Seeing it on soldiers made Joe's stomach drop.

'What have you got up here, the crown jewels?' Joe said, caught right between uneasy and fascinated. It was another world up here, lowering and dark and silent, with a bleak grandeur he hadn't expected.

Kite pointed to the left. 'In there. With the King.'

'With the ...' Joe stared that way. It was impossible to see the higher part of the complex; there was another wall, and another set of cannon whose muzzles cast stripy shadows on the stonework below. He had to laugh. 'You're joking.'

Kite wasn't laughing. 'Why am I joking?'

'Because that's ...' Joe struggled. Stupid, he wanted to say; obviously he knew England *had* had kings, but if he imagined them, he thought of primitive grubby zealots who insisted that their tiny miserable island in the middle of nowhere was the centre of the world. *God Save the King* was what the Saints said. It was just a fairy tale. 'Britain is too small to have a proper king,' he said. 'It's silly. What's he in charge of, six tenements and a canoe?'

'Really.' Kite sort of smiled. 'That's funny. Good.'

Joe was lost. 'Good?'

'England deserves to be forgotten. You think I took you because I want to preserve a navy that likes beating people to death and a country that made its money from slaves?'

'You could have fooled me.'

'There are six hundred people aboard *Agamemnon*,' was all Kite said.

'England didn't have slavery,' Joe said, confused now.

Kite actually laughed at him. It was a silent laugh. He didn't explain himself. 'What, and I expect King Arthur led us into Trafalgar too, did he?'

'I don't understand what's going on any more.'

'I'm sorry, it's shock,' Kite said. It was the truth; he sounded shattered.

They had to slow down, because up ahead, some men were manoeuvring a cannon back into place. It took five of them to push it up the slope, and another two leading it on ropes. Kite followed the way around left, to a squat, windowless building to one side of the road. Joe hesitated. There were heavyset guards on the door.

'Kite,' he said, because the open gate was all iron bars.

'I'm only going to leave you here for an hour.'

The two marines who'd come with them looked relieved.

'This is a prison—' Joe began.

'Shall we take him?' one of the men on the door asked.

'Yes, please. I'll be back in an hour. Much less, I imagine,' Kite said. He caught the edge of the door. He was barely upright. 'Drake, Pine; go and find yourselves some coffee, you deserve it.'

The old panic vice closed round Joe's ribs again, much harder than it normally did. Beyond the gate, from somewhere down the steps, there was a hum, the nasty wasps' nest noise of too many men in one place right on the edge of fighting.

'Please don't leave me here,' Joe said.

'I won't,' Kite said, unexpectedly soft. He let the strength in his voice go. Without it, he sounded smoky. He must have breathed in more gunpowder fumes in the last hour than Joe had breathed tobacco all year. 'I can't leave you anywhere else for now. It's freezing on the ship. There's a fire in here. Most of the prisoners are French. They're not dangerous, they're just sailors waiting for questioning.'

'Why can't I come with you?'

'I need to say things you can't hear.'

Joe didn't believe him. This was it. Obviously Kite was going to keep him in a proper gaol from now on. What the hell had he imagined, a hotel and some conveniently unlocked doors? The gaol looked like a fortified cave. He would never get out.

One of the guards snatched his arm.

'Careful,' Kite snapped. The man let go quickly. Kite walked away, up the curve of the road, towards the brighter torchlight where he had said the King lived. The guard turned Joe by his shoulder into the prison, and pushed him through a low, heavy door, which thumped shut behind him.

The room was so crowded that at first all he saw was a dim jumble, lit only by isolated candles and the glow of a fire at the far end. There were beds across the whole floor, except where the pallets had been arranged in squares to accommodate a laundry tub. There was no room to stand straight beyond the doorway, because above the pallets were hammocks and hammocks, with just about enough space below to sit up in. Above those, washing lines criss-crossed between empty torch brackets. They were full, and the whole long room was humid from the dampness steaming off them. Every set of bedding and every hammock was occupied. Some people had made tables out of old planks and kegs. There were men playing dominoes, cards, dice, but mostly, they were making things. Tiny boxes were taking shape by the candlelight, and over the low murmur of talk was the rasp of files on wood. Right next to Joe, a man was arranging single strands of straw into a perfect picture of the castle, piece by meticulous piece.

Joe took a step away from the door and almost fell over a boy who had been sitting just behind it. He was holding a chisel. Joe thought he had been trying to chip at the hinge and escape, but he was just carving a picture in the oak. It was a ship, with three masts. He was putting on the rigging now.

'That's good,' Joe said numbly in French.

The boy's eyes ticked over Joe, quick and nervous. Joe was still covered – sprayed – in blood that had dried to butchery brown.

Not knowing what else to do, he eased his way through, in the small hope of reaching the fire. No one paid him any attention as he stepped between the pallets. He had to go down on his hands and knees to get below a cluster of hammocks where seven or eight men were playing cards. When he came up again, a splash of warm water hit his arm from the laundry tub where two boys were struggling with too heavy a load. Someone else told them to watch it.

The closer to the fire he came, the more the air smelled of people and stale straw, and fresh wood, and the closer the men were packed. He got within sight of the grate but no further. Next to him, a man in ordinary, clean clothes was explaining to somebody that he would like the box to be six inches wide, with an inlay of flowers in the lid, particularly irises, which were his wife's favourite. The prisoner he was talking to nodded carefully, but paused over irises and asked with a heavy French accent what that was. The Englishman looked at a loss, so Joe chipped in and explained, and then watched as the Englishman handed over a canvas bag of wood, a tiny jar of lacquer, and six heavy silver coins. He and the Frenchman shook hands, and then he slipped away back the difficult way Joe had come, looking pleased.

'Damn sight cheaper for people to buy from us than craftsmen with shops and rent in town,' the French carpenter explained.

He gave Joe the same anxious look the boy had, then pointed behind himself, to where five others were making an exquisite model of a battleship. Someone was painting its unicorn figurehead. 'For the King,' the carpenter said, with a touch of pride. 'We'll have six pounds for it. Six! We shall be able to set up nicely, once we're out.'

Joe sank down on his knees to watch them work until his knee hurt and he noticed he was kneeling on strands of straw. He brushed them aside. Someone else picked them up and added them to a carefully arranged sheaf, and climbed away again.

Now that he wasn't panicking or busy, he began to feel how cold and tired he really was, and how filthy, and how all the muscles down his back and stomach hurt. There wasn't room to do anything but lean slowly forward to shift his weight. He wanted to look at his watch to see how much time there was left before Kite's hour was up, but he wasn't so tired that he couldn't recognise what a silly idea it would be to take out a modern pocket watch in front of a whole room full of people who scraped half a living from the arrangement of scavenged straw.

Kite was going to leave him here. The Admiralty would want engines, ironclads, machine guns. Kite would be telling them now that it was all possible, and Joe would be here until he agreed to do exactly what they wanted. No; even after. There was every chance he was going to be here for years.

The corner of Madeline's letter prodded his hip. Joe took it out slowly. At least he wasn't at sea any more; at least he could read. He found his place. The Kingdoms had arrived at that half-abandoned mansion, and Herault had given them their orders.

*

Colonel Herault was true to his word. We were kept in perfect isolation for that first week. I wasn't worried for myself. It's easy for a woman to pretend to be an idiot. I had a couple of hysterical fits at the guards, I made my handwriting childish, and I wrote like I'd never really thought of much except nice china, and no one seemed to think that was incredible.

But I was worried about the others. In the desk of the Kingdom's map table, Charles's designs for the lighthouse were tucked away for anyone to find – the architectural plans, and the specifications for the engine and generator. I spent most of the week trying and failing to remember if he had signed his name to them. I doubt the name Stevenson means anything to you, but the Stevensons are, in my time, an empire of engineers, and Charles's particular speciality was lighthouses.

Even if Charles had not put his name to the plans, Herault would know that one of us was an engineer. Even in those first days, the possible consequences of divulging modern science to somebody a hundred years early were chilling. Any moron could have seen that, even then, in that silent, disbelieving, panicky first week.

Our fears were only confirmed when, seven days later, at exactly noon, the soldiers came to take us to the beautiful observatory again. Herault was there. The day before, his men had collected the papers we had written, and now, on the chalk board along one wall, he had written out a neat timeline, stretching from 1797 to 1891. He had used a ruler, even though the line was ten feet long, which I think tells you a lot about him. He had noted the significant things he had learned from our accounts. He had also labelled them with our names. I remember something about those labels made me uneasy, even before he explained why they were there.

He looked pleased, and told us we had done well. It sounds cowardly, but I was relieved, even to the point of joy, that he wasn't angry. One wants to imagine one would be staunchly impervious to feelings of one's gaoler, but I'll tell you now, that's a fairy tale we tell to children to keep them brave. The feelings of one's gaoler become more important than the feelings of God, given that he has a rather more immediate control over one's fate than does the Almighty.

He motioned to the timeline.

An alarming amount was marked on. It was all in English. His English is immaculate.

Circa 1820, ascension of Queen Victoria

Circa 1830, first steam railways; method of mass transportation, run on coal combustion and hydraulics.

Circa 1850, advent of large ocean 'liners'; ships with steam engines and capacity of 1000s.

Circa 1860, advent of the London Underground.

Circa 1870, invention of the 'telegram', a long-distance method of communication via wires.

Most of those bore Charles's name. When I looked at him, he was staring at his shoes. He was plainly on the edge of weeping. I never liked him – men who have to show you all the time how much they know about everything are always tedious – but just then, I understood that it wasn't a trait that he could help, any more than the length of his arms or the colour of his eyes. I tried to catch his eye, but he wouldn't lift his head.

'As you can see,' Herault said, 'much of this came from the excellent Monsieur Stevenson here. So, particular thanks are due.' He shook Charles's hand. Charles looked like he wanted to die. 'Monsieur Stevenson will therefore be given a well-earned reward. He shall have full rations this week. The rest of you will subsist on one meal a day of barley bread and water.'

I suppose I ought to have seen that coming. But you must understand, my time and my world were different. Nobody could go around depriving prisoners of war basic rations – or, nobody except Lord Kitchener and that sadistic lunacy he perpetrated on the

Transvaal. I had never expected physical consequences. Moronic as that sounds.

'There is also the matter of ...' Herault took out the lighthouse plans. He held up the sheet with the engine specifications. 'I believe one of you wrote this.'

'It was Jem,' Charles said quickly. 'The man who escaped, he was an engineer.'

That's the other curious thing about imprisonment. Tiny things take on extraordinary importance. Charles's was a small lie, but it seemed heroic just then. Jem was no engineer; he sat in the House of Lords.

Herault smiled. 'That's unfortunate, because I was going to say that if any one of you can convince me that this document is of your making, then you'll not only go back up to full rations, but you will be allowed certain freedoms about the house and grounds.'

29

Joe pushed one hand over his mouth. Obnoxious as the idea was, he had to wonder if he was Charles. Charles, who knew all the lighthouse specifications and who'd been trained as an engineer. Everyone had said Joe had learned too quickly, at de Méritens' workshop. And then the lighthouse picture on the postcard would make even more sense, because of course Madeline would have thought that the lighthouse would jog Charles's memory.

'Joe.'

He heard it, but hadn't heard his first name often enough in Kite's voice to recognise it. He didn't understand until one of the guards barked 'Tournier' right across the room. Everything in him lurched with hope. He stuffed the letter in his pocket, climbed back the way he had come, and found Kite waiting for him.

'Lord Lawrence wants to meet you,' he said.

Joe crept through, past the two guards, convinced they were going to stop him. Outside was only two yards more, but it was another world; the cobbled sloping road was empty and shining in the rain, and everything smelled of sweet stone. He hugged Kite with all that was left of his strength, so happy to see him that he was shocked with himself. Kite must have been shocked too, because he stiffened, but then he rested the heels of his hands on Joe's back.

'What's this?'

'I didn't think you were coming. Devil you know and that,' Joe said helplessly.

'I told you I was coming back.' Kite's voice had cracked with surprise. 'It's only been fifteen minutes. What happened?'

'No, nothing, it ...' Joe trailed off, not sure what to say. 'They're making things out of straw.'

Kite looked like he had no idea what to do with him, but then he tipped his head to say, shall we go. He only seemed more confused when Joe smiled at him.

Joe started to shiver straight away, but it was delicious after the heat and the stagnant humidity inside. The air was clear, and the sight of Kite had released the pressure on his chest again. A wry little voice pointed out that you were unquestionably in hot water when you were grateful for a *familiar* murderer. Kite pointed to the left to tell him which way to go.

'I hope you've thought about what you might do for the navy,' Kite said. Whoever Lord Lawrence was, he had made Kite small. 'Lawrence isn't someone to mess about.'

Joe nodded. He hadn't dedicated any time to it because he had been thinking about how to get away, but he knew what he would say all the same.

Lord Lawrence was a square man in an old-fashioned wig, the long kind, curling unnaturally over a silk jacket. He wasn't in uniform. Joe knew nothing about the man, but if the room was anything to judge by – oak-panelled, tapestried, and Jesus Christ the tiger rug on the floor had just sat up – it was because Lawrence thought the uniform would look disagreeably trades-man-like. The office must have been partitioned off in haste, just with wooden walls, other voices and steps sounded very close. Despite that, someone had gone to every effort to posh it up. There was a stuffed flamingo by the hearth, feathers rippling.

The tiger, a massive thing with liquid muscles, paced across to have a look at him. It shoved its face straight into Joe's chest just like Clay's cat. Incredibly, the thing purred when he touched its ears.

'It'll be your tobacco,' Lawrence explained. 'She loves anyone who smokes. So: you're our Mr Tournier.'

'Yes, sir,' Joe said, struggling, because he wanted to laugh. The tiger had curled up next him, tail round his ankle.

Lawrence smiled. 'Distracting, ain't she. Good test of character. So tell me, you're – what, a lighthouse keeper, is that right?'

'I'm a mechanic from the workshop that builds lighthouse engines and generators.'

'Well, that's wonderful. I imagine there's very little you'd less prefer to be doing than working for us, but you understand we are preparing for a siege which – if you told Missouri correctly – will finish us entirely if we don't do something significant.'

Joe nodded. He didn't remember telling Kite that, but it was still true. 'Yes, sir.'

'Do you know any details of what will happen?'

'No, sir, I'm sorry. I make engines, I'm not bookish.'

'Mm.' Lawrence studied him. He came up too close to do it and Joe caught the smell of powder on him, from the wig. There was a hunger about him, but not curiosity. It was the way a certain sort of little boy would rush up to the carcass of a dog that had made him jump once, and had just been hit by a cart. A nasty triumph. 'But I hope you have some bright ideas about what to make for us. Lights as bright as the Eilean Mòr lamp would go a long way, you know.'

'Arc lamps.' Joe took a deep breath. This was it. He needed to steer Lawrence away from anything that could really change the world. If nothing significant changed, there was a chance Lily would still be all right when he got home. 'They need a lot of power, and we'd need generators, which I can't make for you in time for the siege.'

'What's a generator?'

'They make power in a way that hasn't been discovered here yet. Electricity. The idea is simple but making one is … we'd need a lot of iron, and I think it's … all going to making guns, isn't it? I saw them taking down railings on the way here.'

'Can you improve our guns, then?'

Yes, God yes, they were still using flintlocks for Christ's sake. The *Agamemnon*'s cannons had barely got off two rounds per minute. He could give them modern guns, electrically lit ships, engines, and he was absolutely not going to.

He was going to have to sell this properly or he might as well shoot himself right now.

'I can give you a way to talk to each other that's far faster than those flag signals you've got, and a lot more secret. You'll be able to convey far more information. They're called telegraphs.'

'How long will that take?'

'With a good blacksmith and the right materials, only a few days.' Joe's heart was going too fast. 'Decent communication will help you. Won't it?'

'It certainly will.' Lawrence was looking right into his face. 'You understand what will happen to you if you're lying?' He said it gently, like a doctor warning him about an operation. But there was that hungry gleam again.

'Yes, sir,' Joe said. He thought of the ruin that was Clay's back, and then had to try hard to stop.

Lawrence patted him. His hand was doughy. 'And no fretting about changing your future, my boy. It's already changed. If you don't make us something, I am going to evacuate Edinburgh of naval forces. So either way, there will be no defeat here.'

It hadn't even occurred to him that it was already too late. God in heaven. 'Yes, sir.'

'Good boy.'

Joe put a smile on his face and tilted his eyes down, even though deferring to the man was starting to feel sticky. The richness of the office and Lawrence's clothes was grotesque after a week on *Agamemnon*, and the more he surveyed Lawrence himself, the more this pallid variety of plumpness had something fungal about it. Maybe that was unfair, but Joe had expected someone different. It was disquieting to see that behind a soldier as upright and war-smashed as Kite, there wasn't an ironclad general or a righteous empress, but this bejewelled, sickly looking mushroom person.

No wonder England had lost the war.

'Now, speaking of defeats, Missouri. Mr Tournier, do occupy yourself with the tiger, she likes you, and I think you'll enjoy what's about to happen.'

Joe found himself looking at the tiger as if it might explain.

'I hear,' Lawrence said to Kite, 'that my niece was on deck during action. Why was that?'

Kite had turned to stone. 'There were burned men in the water, sir, and she had come up to help treat them.'

Agatha.

'Men in the water should be *left* in the water, for exactly this reason.'

Joe couldn't quite believe what he'd just heard.

'They were in easy reach, sir.'

'Don't argue with me.' Lawrence folded his arms. 'I think this is the time to have a little talk about women aboard the *Agamemnon*, don't you? Missouri, you have been expressly forbidden, on a number of occasions, from employing women in active naval service.'

Kite's eyes flicked up. 'There are none on our books.'

Lawrence hit him with the end of his cane. It came from nowhere and Joe froze. Kite didn't even have time to put his hands up. The ivory handle left a graze above his eye. 'No, there are not, because rather than declaring your dead men dead, you continue to take their wages, and filter them down to any number of unqualified women you seem to have collected from wherever takes your fancy. You have a veritable harem. I believe even your first lieutenant is not in fact a real lieutenant at all, but a dead lieutenant's *wife*. Are you going to lie to me about that?'

'Revelation Wellesley runs the ship better than any other lieutenant I've had—'

'And so while I cannot indict you for letting Agatha on the deck, given that she was not *officially* on navy pay, I can absolutely come after you for fraud whenever I bloody like, and I will do so with the most intense joy if this man fails to do as he's promised, understand?' Lawrence pointed at Joe without looking at him.

'No, you won't,' Kite snapped. 'Unless you want the horror of women captains, you're not going to court martial the present ones.'

'Don't be so repulsive, they aren't there for work, they're there for you to stare at and God knows what else. Take that jacket off, it's a disgrace.'

Joe felt something tightening in his chest. Kite slid his coat off, then the jacket, slowly, because he couldn't move well now.

Lawrence went for him. Joe had never seen anyone lose his temper so completely. The walking cane was thin, like a switch, and although Lawrence had been moving at a heavy lumber before, he was fast with it. In five seconds Kite was on the floor.

Without deciding to, Joe wrenched the thing out of the old man's hand, and threw it at the hearth. The tiger snarled and for a sick instant Joe thought he was about to be torn to pieces by a wild animal, but for whatever reason it had of its own – perhaps Lawrence treated it in the same way he treated Kite, or maybe it liked Kite in the same involuntary way Joe did – it caught Lawrence's sleeve in its teeth and slung him aside before coming to nose anxiously at them. Joe kept very, very still, crouched over Kite, one arm across his shoulders to keep him as shielded as he could be. He could feel him shaking, or maybe that was Joe himself.

'Get him out of here,' Lawrence snarled. His eyes kept skittering to the tiger.

Joe snatched up Kite's coat and pulled Kite along with him. He'd never been so glad to get out of a room.

Kite had to stop just outside, on the steps of a chapel. Joe sat down next to him. Opposite them, torchlight beamed down through the high windows of what must once have been a banqueting hall, but now, there were flimsy storey-partions a third and two-thirds of the way up the windows. Inside, there were beds, and women in surgeons' indigo. A girl was singing while she hung up sheets between the rows and rows of beds.

There was no sign of the two marines.

'Who the hell keeps a tiger anyway?' Joe asked at last. His voice sounded wrong. He coughed.

'He served in India,' Kite said.

'Are you all right?' Joe whispered. Sailing through the French assault had been different; that was impersonal violence, and it was easy to imagine that in other circumstances the gunners on either side would get on brilliantly. But what Lawrence had done was rancid.

'Why did you stop him?' Kite asked.

Joe shook his head. 'If you think any normal person can just watch something like that then your idea of the world is even more fucked than I thought. I'd have liked that tiger to eat him then and there.' He hesitated. 'Never been defended by a tiger before.'

Kite smiled. It was the most crystalline cheer, just the very first veneer of ice on the sea. 'It's your tobacco. She goes for it like catnip.'

'Well. Make a fortune at the circus if machine work falls through.'

Kite laughed.

Joe lifted Kite's pistol out of its holster and slid it under his own belt on the opposite side. Now was the time. He could just run. The marines still weren't here. Kite would never be able to follow, not in this state. Dodge down one of those endless black side alleys and Kite would have no hope of finding him. Having no money wasn't such a bad problem, especially at this time of night, when pubs were full and people were tipsy. It wasn't like he was above going home with someone to have somewhere to wait out the frozen night, either. If all the fuss with Alice and Père Philippe had taught him anything, it was not to be precious.

He was just starting to get up when his entire soul cramped. His heart locked and he couldn't breathe, never mind move, and everything in him was shrieking, as if he'd thrust his hand into a fire.

The second he stopped trying to leave, it eased. He stared at Kite, wondering what the hell they'd spoken about at the lighthouse that would have given him a reaction like that to trying to abandon the man.

'Can you get up?' Joe asked, stunned. His heart hurt, the strings inside the muscle structure all too tight still.

Kite hesitated, but then the two marines appeared from another building. They hurried across when they saw Kite and Joe. For the first time since Joe had met him, the slab-faced Drake looked genuinely worried. Maybe, Joe thought hopelessly, it was hard to leave Kite because Kite was just one of those magical people who made everyone love him.

Whatever the reason, the chance had come and gone.

Once Kite was standing, Joe eased his coat around his shoulders. Even the weight of the fabric made him hunch forward. Joe thought he was going to collapse, but Kite only waited and held his breath, then nodded. Joe glanced back at the marines, who looked anxious too, but not surprised. This must have been pretty standard practice for Lord Lawrence.

The cobbles on the sloping road were slick with frost now and, after Joe slipped, they all stepped up on to the high kerb that made a kind of platform for the heavy guns.

'What's Lawrence's problem with you?' Joe asked eventually.

'He's Agatha's uncle. He considers it a personal affront that his brother's widow married a carpenter from Cadiz.' They were passing under the portcullis again. The road they had come up was too steeply downhill now to try and they went a different way, past inns and pubs and shut-up shops. Kite's next breath rattled; between the bruises and the razor air, his lungs were struggling. 'After my parents were killed at sea, Agatha wanted to come to England, but Lawrence wouldn't take her in unless she left me behind. But she wouldn't. We lived in Spain for about ten years before she was old enough to inherit her father's money. We served in the navy there. When she did inherit, she moved us to London.'

Joe was quiet at first, because that was by far the most Kite had ever said to him in one go. He had a feeling it was the most Kite had ever said to anyone in one go. 'If your dad's from Cadiz,' he asked at last, 'how are you called Kite?'

'It's translated. Stupid to try and take an officer's commission in England with a name like Milano. And nobody wants to alliterate.'

'Oh.' Joe turned that around in his mind for a while. 'Where are we going? Not back to the ship.'

'Yes back to the ship. I can't leave them—'

'Kite! Everything's shot to hell, I'm not taking you back there.' He looked at the marines for support. They shifted, uncomfortable, but he could see they thought going back was a bad idea too.

'Everyone else is just as beaten up as us, Tournier—'

'Everyone else doesn't also have to be in charge, you moron,' Joe snapped. Those strings in his heart were screwing tight again. 'You won't sit down, you'll wander around being *nice* to people and then you'll collapse and die, look at the *state* of you.'

'This is normal—'

'What you think is normal is right on the edge of dying.' Joe sat down on a wall. 'I'm not going back to the ship. Try and make me.'

'I've got a gun and two marines,' Kite pointed out, frowning. The two marines were hanging back, though, doing amazing work of looking like two random passers-by who had nothing to do with the argument. Even Drake didn't seem willing to drag Joe anywhere this time.

'Nope, I've got your gun, I took it off you at the chapel.' Joe showed him, then lobbed it behind his own shoulder, where it clattered down steps and cobbles in the steep darkness. 'Next?'

Kite's expression opened out into real confusion. 'That was loaded. Why didn't you shoot me?'

'Tried!' Joe shouted at him. 'Couldn't, nearly gave myself a heart attack. Turns out I'm a good person.'

'Oh,' Kite said. He looked back at the marines, who didn't seem like they had any more idea what to do now than he did. They all turned to Joe again.

'Come on, then; where are we going?' Joe prompted them. 'Fire and hot water obligatory.'

Kite hesitated. 'My sister has some rooms by the docks, in Leith.' He looked at the marines again. 'There'd be room for four.'

'Good,' Joe said. 'Let's find a cab.'

'I don't have any money.'

'Then I'll stop someone.'

'Joe, no one's going to ...'

'Shut up,' Joe told him, starting to feel angry. He couldn't tell who with or why exactly. It was a boiling of a lot of things: the chaos at the dock, Lawrence, the way it was impossible to just hate Kite. He even felt angry about the thing with the women's wages. He wanted to shake Kite and demand he was just good or just a bastard, not this infuriating mix of both.

Joe stopped the first carriage that went past. It was black and sheening with fresh polish. Where the snow motes settled on its sides, they slid and formed perfect gemstone droplets. The horses huffed in the cold.

'What in the world,' the gentleman inside said, quite mildly. He was wearing an idiotic wig, just like Lawrence's.

'I really am sorry,' Joe said, 'but this is navy business and it's vital I get these three men to Leith as soon as I possibly can. It's a terrible imposition, but would you mind?'

The man laughed. 'Well, aren't you charming.'

Joe smiled his charming smile, which was less broad than his real one. Kite was so immune that Joe had forgotten how well it worked on everyone else. He wondered if anybody had ever been brave enough to flirt with Kite, and which ditch they'd ended up in.

'Oh, go on then,' the gentleman said. 'All aboard.'

Even in a carriage, it was a long way. Kite fell still and silent. The gentleman was studying them with frank, pleased curiosity, and he asked silly questions about sailing. Joe watched the buildings glide by. The torches were burning at what the gentleman said was Holyrood Palace, where the Queen lived, and then there was a long expanse of darkness that was its broad park. Beyond that was a strange steep hill, more of a mountain, with one light burning at the top. He closed his eyes after a while. Because the carriage was small, they were all pressed together, knees bumping. Kite's weight against Joe's left side was warm and solid, and he managed not to have any awkward angles.

Now they were safe, something in Joe's brain unwound too quickly and he got the shakes. He had to lock his teeth to keep them from chattering. All his muscles felt weak. He wanted to lean forward against his knees, but there was no room; he'd have been in the gentleman's lap. He wondered exactly how close he'd been to staying in that prison. He could still hear the snick of the men picking up straws. And God, but he could still feel other people's blood dried on to his skin.

And, just to put a cherry on the whole thing, it turned out he was incapable of running away.

What a knickerbocker glory of a day.

'We're here,' the gentleman said. It seemed unnecessarily loud and Joe jumped.

Kite leaned across him to open the door. There was another awkward round of thank yous and don't mention its, and then the carriage was on its way again, the horses white in the gloom. There were no street lamps here, just the lights from windows.

'Thank you,' Kite said when the carriage had gone.

'You'd rather collapse than ask for help, wouldn't you?' Joe said.

'No. I just didn't think anyone would help if I asked.'

'Sometimes people are all right,' Joe said, trying not to sound too dismayed.

30

Agatha's flat was not in the least what Joe had expected. Downstairs, the place was a novelty bar, full of cigar smoke, music, and men dressed spectacularly as rich ladies. Mounted on the wall was a beautiful sniper rifle and a sign which said DOE NOT BOTHER THE SERVATRICES. From somewhere close came the glorious sizzle of meat on a grill. The furniture was all upholstered in velvet. Joe approved. So, he thought, did the marines; they were looking longingly at the armchairs.

Kite went to the bar and spoke to the man behind it, who was dressed in a gown that must have cost as much as all the furniture put together. The man frowned at him.

'I don't know you from Adam, mate.'

'The lady who owns the rooms upstairs, I'm her brother,' Kite said. He pulled out what looked like a Responsibility Card from his pocket, but it was just a ration book with his name on it. 'But I don't have the keys, and I was hoping ... well, that you had a set.'

It was strange to hear Kite talking like a normal human being. He'd switched the naval captain off. He was anxious. Joe stayed close, ready to step in and be persuasive.

The man's expression opened. 'You're Missouri Kite.'

'Yes,' Kite said, not sounding sure whether it was something he ought to confess to or not.

'Jesus,' the man said. 'You just smashed through the blockade to get in here.'

'We – yes.'

'Yes? Be more pleased with yourself, mate. The Admiralty's done bugger all about it, just as well you've shown them how it's done. I'll get that key.'

He looked through some drawers, then gave Kite an old envelope with a key-shaped indent outlining what was inside. 'Come down for a drink, won't you, once you're ...' He studied them both and struggled for something that would be sufficient and polite at the same time. 'Presentable,' he decided eventually. Somebody, he added, would bring up some water. There was only one bath upstairs, but the marines were welcome to use the hot water in the stables.

Hot water in the stables. They had hot water just for people's horses. The marines looked delighted. Kite nodded to say they could go.

There was only one door at the top of the narrow stairs. Kite had to negotiate with the key. When it turned, the room beyond was dark and cold. He passed Joe a lamp to hold against the flame of the one in the corridor. Once it was lit, he took it around the others one by one.

The room presented itself in portions. There was a desk full of books and papers, and a string with letters pegged on it, all in the same handwriting. By the fireplace were two ornate chairs that matched, and one, cheaper, that didn't. That must have been Kite's standing with Jem and Agatha, right there. Joe had to thump his fist against the wall. He had liked Agatha a lot, but after meeting her uncle, and seeing this, he wanted to spit. This was what people in France had fought a revolution to kill off. In fact, this might even be why some of the French captains in the bay had decided to serve. To try and save people like Kite from people like this, before they turned into what Kite was now.

Up a flight of steps was a bedroom. The windows were diamond-paned and unshuttered, and the bay glistered outside until the light inside was too strong and the glass only showed their reflections. Turkish rugs covered the floorboards. Four boxes full of dead plants hung in a corner that would have been sunny during the day.

After a few minutes, a pair of boys came through with pails of water. Joe watched them go into another room down a narrow corridor. There was a rush of pouring water into something metal. They made another two trips, and then Kite shut the front door, looking glad to do it.

'You go first,' he said to Joe.

'No, I'm always last at home, I don't mind,' Joe said, though he was sticky. He was so cold that he didn't want to take any clothes off yet. He was fast finding that, as the temperature dropped, the level of grime he could put up with see-sawed accordingly. 'Anyway, you need to get those cuts clean.'

There was no door, just a wooden archway, and Kite glanced back to make sure Joe wasn't in a direct line of sight before he disappeared inside.

Joe sat on the hearth with his back to the fire. It seemed intrusive to notice, but he could hear the difference between the heavy coat and the thin shirt as Kite took them off. He could hear that Kite was folding everything onto a chair or a windowsill, not just letting it drop. It was taking him a long time. 'Are you all right?' Joe said, starting to worry that leaving Kite alone was nothing but medical negligence.

'Say again? I can't hear very well.'

Joe lost his nerve. Kite was fine. 'I say what happens now?' he asked instead.

'Dinner and sleep.'

With the back of his shirt lukewarm, Joe went to the archway and sat down across the threshold. The room was whitewashed, with bare rafters. There was nothing in it but them, the bath, and a line of soap and razors on the windowsill, which was right down near the floor.

Kite was sitting straight in the bath, facing away. The marks Lawrence had left were vivid stripes. Under those, he was burned. The scars down his face were only part of it. They reached across to his spine in liquid patterns. It was an old wound, but it looked painful. He must have been able to feel it pull whenever he moved. His undamaged skin was translucent. He looked like glass someone careless had left too near a blast furnace.

Joe stretched, sore. He put his head back against the archway. He could have slept like that. From downstairs came a gust of laughter.

'Thanks,' Joe said. 'For not leaving me at the prison. I know you could have done without bringing me home with you.'

Kite laughed. He was pulling his hair out of its plait. That gave Joe a strange stir, because it was something he'd only ever seen women do before. 'You brought me.'

'Well. We must have got on really well at the lighthouse, mustn't we,' Joe said. 'I don't remember, but I'm feeling protective.'

Kite was quiet for a second. Joe saw the bones in his back flicker. 'Could you go away now, please?'

Joe hissed his breath through his teeth. 'I'm not going to make any stupid allegations—'

'Yes; no, but *I'm* in the bath.' He sounded strained.

'My master talks to me in the bath. Not normal?'

Kite inclined his head without looking back and pressed his hands over his face. His breathing was irregular. Joe realised, feeling slow, that for the entire conversation Kite had been crying. 'Not a paragon of normal.'

'Peril of having only a two-year memory,' Joe said, trying to sound as though he'd not noticed. 'People can convince me of anything. I shall sod off.' He wanted to say something else, but he couldn't think what would help. Stuck in his throat like a shard of glass was the knowledge that Agatha had been killed on her way to murder her brother.

That, the practical voice in his head said, would be something to break Kite with later, if he needed to.

When it was his turn, Joe sank into the hot water – it was reddish from the blood Kite had washed off, but still steaming and wonderful – and went right under it for as long as he could hold his breath. A week was more than enough time to miss being clean. Some of the unpleasantness of everything faded away in the steam. He had meant to ask if he could borrow some clothes, but when he looked back at the door, Kite was already there, kneeling to leave some on the threshold.

When Joe put it on, the shirt was so well-laundered that it felt stiff. Once he was dressed he stood in the window to see out over the castle and the city, and folded his arms to feel it tighten across his back. The jacket that went over it was better sewn than anything he had had before, plain though it was. He straightened out its hem to see just how much fabric the tailor had used. It fell in heavy pleats when he let it go. Even M. Saint-Marie's things weren't so fine.

Kite looked different clean and ironed. Out of context, Joe wouldn't have recognised him. He must have been sitting with his back to the fire, because his hair was dry already, and he'd tied it into an untidy knot rather than the uniform queue. It had a curl to it that made him look softer than normal. 'I'll buy you a drink downstairs,' he said. He was gazing at Joe's jacket, then seemed to notice what he was doing and looked away.

'Thanks,' Joe said, and then had a bolt of horror when he understood that he must have been wearing Jem Castlereagh's clothes.

31

London, 1797

The Admiralty's New Year party had taken over the whole of the main hall at the Naval College in Greenwich. Carriages glided down the long drive, between the lawns and the trees full of coloured lamps, and boys waited out on the steps for people's invitations, hats, and coats.

The cold was intense here, because the Thames was only forty yards away and a sea wind was coming in off the water, but inside was brilliant and hot. Free-standing candelabra marked the way into the main hall, which made a corridor of warmth. The gilt at the tops of the columns glinted, and reflections swam in the mirrory floor.

A forty-foot illusion painting took up the whole back wall, full of steps and sky, so that the hall seemed to open out onto a summer morning. At first, it was difficult to tell which of the people were real, and which were paintings. Everything was a whirl of silk and the smell of melting candle wax.

The second Kite and Agatha reached the hall, Jem appeared and hauled him away, stole an entire bottle of wine from a waiter, and set them up in the only two chairs near the fireplace that weren't already filled with rear admirals.

Jem looked well, but Kite had a feeling he would look well enough even if he were in the throes of a malarial fever. There was a nervousness to the way the tendons in his hands moved when he poured the wine.

Kite wanted to ask how he had found the boarding house, because there must have been some shaky moments. He'd written out a manual of things that Jem would need to know – the value of money, how to swear normally, what was and wasn't reasonable behaviour in a boarding-house landlord – but it had not been exhaustive. He would have bet all the marzipan in London that Jem wouldn't tell him the truth, though. He still couldn't persuade Jem that it was all right to be worried, or to have some symptoms of melancholia. Jem seemed to think that a successful human was a thinking machine and anything else was a repulsive failure, even in such extreme circumstances as his own.

Jem noticed Kite was studying him and looked rueful, as though he might just confess to something ordinary. He pulled off his jade bracelet and spun it between his fingers. He did it in the way other people wrung their hands. Kite saw him lose heart. 'Missouri ... there is a woman coming this way with paperwork.'

Kite looked. 'It's a dance card.'

Jem watched her suspiciously. 'Is there a polite code for I'd-prefer-to-drink-this-wine?'

'No.'

He cut his eyes across to Kite, which felt a lot like having the sudden attention of Lawrence's tiger. 'No one's bothering *you*. There must be a hand signal or something.'

'I'm ugly and poor,' Kite provided. He took Jem's wine. 'Do you good. Run free, be with your own kind.'

Jem kicked Kite's chair, but then turned on his charm and seemed delighted to go away with the girl. Dancing would do him good, and talking to women. The women here would be better conversationalists than the taciturn men who usually populated boarding houses, and Kite believed strongly that, whether you liked it or not, five minutes with someone kind and clever was cleansing, like green tea, or confession.

Kite only had time to get a few atoms of enjoyment at the view before Agatha took Jem's chair. He sat up straighter.

'You're looking handsome,' she said. Spanish had two words for *you are*. One, *es*, meant you are always; the other, *estas*, meant you are now, contrary to form. He'd just been *estas*'d. 'Shall we dance?'

She took his hand and led him out to the end of a line. His heart started going harder, and nerves that he didn't feel even when he gave orders to gun crews made his wrists feel weak. He had to keep his eyes down. He could never meet hers for long; she was taller than him, and that black stare reminded him too much of being five and guilty of something stupid.

She put her fan under his chin and pulled upward. 'If you're angry, then say something. You've been boiling since Harding's.'

She was right, but he still had to take a deep breath to work up the nerve. 'Jem's in a dangerous position. A pamphleteer stopped us five minutes after we left you. Jem's name is all over the news-sheets now. *Mysterious gentleman from Caribbean sugar money seen with heiress.* The French have his description, and they know they're looking for someone who just appeared from nowhere one morning ... we're all but advertising him.'

'He was in a dangerous position already,' she said, unexpectedly gentle. 'The Admiralty leaks like a sieve. A man tried to jump him in an alley the day before I sent that note to come to Harding's. Didn't he tell you?'

'What?' Kite said, dismayed.

'So the thing now is to make sure that nothing can happen to him without all of London noticing.' She shook her head a little. 'You're right, anonymity would be much better, but that's off the cards. This was the best I could think of.'

'Oh,' he said. He felt stupidly betrayed that Jem hadn't told him.

'Anyway, I'm hoping that if I'm seen out enough with a devastatingly handsome and mysterious bachelor then the Earl of Wiltshire will give up.' She tried to make it sound offhand, but her collarbones tightened. 'One would think that at my age one would be rather above suspicion on that count.'

It twisted a stiletto in him to hear what she thought she was like, and it twisted even deeper when he remembered how angry he had been with her before. He'd thought she was careless. He should have known better.

'Not the way you wear it,' he said. He glanced over the hall towards Jem. 'Speaking of Jem, he needs rescuing. You'd better sort that out.'

After an hour, he went outside to escape the heat and the friends of Agatha's who thought they ought to make an effort to see what he was like, but who felt worried about anyone without a title. There were long gardens, and a fine walk down to the Thames. The cold was sharp after the hot hall, and the gravel on the path squeaked and splintered as the frost broke. He was only halfway to the river when Jem caught up with him.

'Miz. Are you all right?'

Kite looked back, intensely glad to have been missed and followed, but confused too. 'Just too hot. You? Didn't Agatha find you?'

'She did, but then her paperwork piled up.'

Kite laughed, though it came out forced. They walked for a little while, up the river. There were no lights there except the reflections on the water from the ships. Jem sat down on the low railing to look back at the hall.

'You could have told me,' Kite said. It was too abrupt, but he couldn't hold it in. He nodded at Jem's bruised hand. 'My profession is punching Frenchmen.'

Jem watched him for a few seconds, then sighed. 'I'm sorry. It just seemed so grubby, and in my head you're so pristine, I just wanted not to … to *get* anything on you. Does that make sense?'

'No,' said Kite, but he felt a happy warmth rush right through him.

Jem pulled him close. He was warm, and his clothes smelled both new and of his cigarettes at the same time. Kite didn't want to come up. Jem was holding the back of his neck under his collar, and it felt safe and good.

Jem made a soft sound against his hair to make him look up and then touched his lips to Kite's temple, then his mouth, just ghosts of kisses, before he rested their heads together. Until right then, Kite had always thought of a kiss as a definitive thing, but he couldn't tell what Jem meant by it. He didn't dare ask in case it meant nothing at all.

Lord Lawrence was in the sitting room at Jermyn Street when Kite, Agatha, and Jem got back, both stockinged feet tucked under his tiger. He twisted around.

'You know, my dear,' he said in the careful way he always started his fights with her, so that he would have the appearance of reasonableness later, 'you'll set tongues wagging.'

'They are. It's doing wonders for the hospital fund.'

He frowned. 'Don't be glib, it's unfeminine. The Earl of Wiltshire cornered me today. You've made him deeply anxious, trusting man though he is—'

She was undoing the complicated pins of the jewelled band in her hair. When it came off, it looked heavy. She dropped it in the glass bowl where the house keys lived. It was one of the things Kite loved about living with a woman: they left treasure in odd places round the house. 'Lawrence, that was your agreement, not mine. At first it was something you implied to him, knowing full well I had nothing to do with it, and by a fascinating process of erosion you have convinced yourself in the intervening months that I am now bound to him by contract. I am not, and while I know it would be agreeable to have the Earl on your side in Parliament, there are ways to charm a man like that which do not involve parting with my entire inheritance.'

He was turning red. 'Agatha, don't be absurd. You know fully well a fortune can't really rest in the hands of a slip of a girl.'

'That's by far and away the most flattering thing anyone has ever said to a person of thirty-six.'

Lawrence seemed to see he was losing ground. 'All that aside, girl, you're endangering Jem's life, and perhaps even the war itself. I've been seeing his name in the papers. The papers, for God's sake! Mysterious man appears from nowhere, causes scandal with heiress; after everything I've done to keep him safe, the lives sacrificed, you will not simply *hand* a man with knowledge of the future to the Ministre de bloody Marine!'

Jem frowned and glanced at Kite, who shook his head a little.

Agatha fixed him with a look so narrow it came to a needle point. 'What lives sacrificed?'

'Navy business, and above your head,' he snapped. His hand had tightened around his cane. Kite stiffened.

'I rather think you're making it my business.'

The cane twitched. 'Agatha—'

'That's enough,' Kite said.

Lawrence looked at him as if he'd never seen him before. Trying to convince himself that, really, twenty-five years without a broken nose was a lot more than most men could expect, Kite put himself in front of Agatha and Jem.

'Sir. Look at what you're doing with your hands.'

Lawrence looked. He had shifted his grip on the cane, ready to strike out with it.

'Go away, stay at your club, and calm down,' Kite said, a lot more steadily than he felt. 'I'm sure it will all keep until the morning.'

Lawrence stared at him for a long time. Then his eyes went to Agatha. 'I will have you put in an asylum, madam, if you don't come to your senses. I apologise, Mr Castlereagh, none of this is your fault, but I urge you to consider your own safety, and the reputation of the lady. Good night.'

He stumped out. The front door clicked.

Agatha put her hands against her kidneys. 'Right, I think we'd all better find a way to ensure he can't do any of us any more violence. First concern is you, Miz; he can make life bloody unpleasant for you if he sends you to the Caribbean, so—'

'No, it's you,' Kite said, urgent. 'He's your closest relative, he really *can* send you to an asylum.'

'I'll have to marry Wiltshire, then,' she said, as if it was nothing, as if she'd given up decades ago on getting anything from marriage but a tolerable house and not too many interruptions to life. 'He's timid.'

'Agatha – he's sixty-four,' Kite said softly.

'I'm not prime stock either,' she said, and he realised she was punishing herself for having let it get out of hand. She had clenched her fists so hard her knuckles were marble.

'Don't talk about yourself like that.'

'Marry me,' Jem said. It was a shock, not just because of what he'd said, but because he had been so silent before that Kite had forgotten he was there. 'I'm not sixty-four, and I've no interest in sending anyone to an asylum.'

They both looked up at him. 'What?' said Agatha.

'If that wouldn't go down in your career like a lead balloon,' he added carefully. He hesitated. 'It would help us all. You and I can protect Missouri from Lawrence. Your being in the papers so much – that gives you the power to say whatever you like, loud and fast. Much more than Lawrence. And I have information. If the Admiralty isn't decent to us all, I don't divulge anything. Missouri protects you; if I turn out to be a bad husband then

I've got nothing over him, so he can punch me in the face in perfect conscience. And you being yourself protects me. It legitimises any stories I tell about myself; they must be true if Agatha Lawrence says they are. It's ... a good balance. And needless to say I have no intention of being a demanding husband. Or even in your house, if you don't want me here. I'll sign any contract that ensures you retain sole power over your own assets, then there are no money worries.'

Her shoulders jolted and Kite thought she was laughing, and then, horribly, he realised she was starting to cry. He had never seen her cry. It felt indecent to watch. He stepped right away from them, towards the fire, though he wasn't cold. Lawrence's tiger curled up against his ankle. He knelt down to stroke her, to have some occupation.

'Are you in earnest?' Agatha was asking.

'Yes, ma'am.'

'Why would you do that?'

'Well, I know it must sound premature to you,' Jem said, 'and I've only been here five minutes, but it has been an *important* five minutes, for me. I love you, both of you. What you've done for me – I expected to vanish into an interrogation room somewhere.'

They both turned back to look at Kite.

'What do you think?' Agatha asked him. She was shining.

He hadn't meant to, but all the way home, like an idiot, he'd been stitching a fragile cloak of half-imagined hopes, barely with the substance of thule but there all the same. It dissolved and left him with a nasty residue of shame. Trying on hopes like that was no better than playing dress-up with her clothes. Jem was hers too.

He smiled. 'Sounds good to me,' he said.

32

Edinburgh, 1807

There were a few men Joe recognised from the *Agamemnon* downstairs, along with the two marines, who were clean and hunched over tankards of beer now. Kite avoided them and went to the fire, which was too hot to be anyone else's place of choice. Joe was starting to think that he looked ill rather than just pale. Joe ordered them both some stew and some wine, which was quick coming, but Kite only sipped at the wine and ignored the food. Before long he gave it away to a sailor on the table next to theirs, who was drunk enough to call him an absolute sweetheart. More sober people thumped the sailor and looked mortified. Kite seemed not to care.

The door kept swinging. Deliveries were coming in, crates of them, even though it must have been ten at night by now. The street was full of carts making similar deliveries to all the bars and warehouses along the quayside.

Stockpiling for the siege, of course. How long had the blockade been covering the port? Joe couldn't tell, but he didn't think anyone here could be getting many supplies overland. The French had control of most of Scotland.

Joe watched as a young man carried past a crate of potatoes. The delivery boys were helping, but there was too much for them to get through quickly. Even though Joe only just had a grasp on English money, the price stencilled on the side of the crate looked insanely high. He did some dividing and frowned.

Even if only half a potato per head went into the stew he'd just bought, the price of the combined meals wouldn't have covered half the cost of that one crate. Siege inflation. He pushed his hand over his mouth and wished obscurely that he'd remembered to shave.

Kite was watching him, but he said nothing about machines, or helping, or duty, or any of it. He was just cradling the wine glass in both hands to warm it up. It was red, but icy, because the bottles must have been from the cellar, below the water line.

'Quiet, you,' Joe said to him, to see if he would smile.

He didn't, and Joe realised that he'd misinterpreted. Kite wasn't being quiet for quiet's sake; he was struggling to stay upright. 'When does it start?' Kite asked. 'The siege.'

'I don't know, I'm sorry. I know it's November.'

'It's already November,' Kite murmured into the wine.

The beautifully dressed bartender drifted past with a whicker of pearls and silk, and Joe understood exactly what Kite had said at the dock, about wanting to hurt someone. There was something obscene about how clean the man was, how rich, how perfect. Joe sank his teeth into his lower lip and looked away, very, very bothered by that. He'd never once felt the urge just to hit someone for no reason, but like a scaled thing that had been asleep somewhere deep in him, it shifted, and stretched.

Kite did make it upstairs, but Joe was waiting for it and caught him when he collapsed just before he could open the door. Behind them, the marines shied back rather than help. Kite was heavy, but it was possible to carry him the last couple of yards to the bed. Joe eased his head down as softly as he could. The marines hovered.

Joe sat down on the edge of the bed and opened Kite's collar, and kept still with one hand on his chest to make sure he was breathing.

'Hey, stay away from him,' one of the marines snapped. It sounded awkward.

Joe did as he was told.

There was firewood at least, even if there wasn't much of it. Beyond the window the docks glimmered. Most of the ships were full of lights. Music and voices came up through the floor. It was one of those sounds that would have been quite nice to sleep in, but not above. He sat on the chair by the bed and folded forward to put his forearms on the mattress and his head down, tired enough just to listen for a while.

Despite the time, the clack and hiss of hammers and saws came from the docks. Emergency repairs; there was new tarpaulin across parts of the *Agamemnon*, which was anchored just opposite them, the soldier figurehead right at Joe's eye level. He glanced at Kite when a crane-load of wood banged down on a wharf, but it didn't disturb him. He slept flat, one hand resting on his ribs and the other palm up on the sheet. Joe wished he would move; he looked more like a drowned man than a sleeping one. He was breathing just deeply enough for the candlelight to draw moving shadows in the well between his collarbones, but that was all.

The marines were at the table now, playing cards in silence but getting cross with each other in hand signals.

Joe took out Madeline's letter. He smoothed it out as well as he could against his knee – the pages were suffering now, being pulled from his pocket and thrust back in again – and lit a cigarette.

*

It's contemptible how quickly hunger can affect one. Alone in a room, with nothing else to think about, another day on bread and water is a prospect of despair even after only a couple of days.

I managed to get out of the window on the third night of that second week. I had no idea where I'd go, but I was already starting to feel dizzy, and I thought that if I was going to get away, I was going to have to do it before I was too shaky to run anywhere. I got down to the ground, but it was a long way across the lawn, and before I'd even gone five yards, a soldier rugby-tackled me, took me back inside, and told me that he was going to Educate me with a distinctly capital E if I didn't stay put. Once he'd gone, I broke a vase inside a pillowcase and put a shard in my pocket. Broken pottery is not the best Mrs-Beeton-approved prophylactic, but it's better than nothing.

I stayed awake for the rest of the night, shaking and furious and watching the door and wanting him to come through, because it would have felt better to do something, even if that something was stabbing a man in the neck. I suppose you find it shocking that a woman could be that violent. We are violent creatures, but ours is a rage much more accustomed to suppression than the flabby undisciplined version found in men.

At Herault's next noon session, Charles had top marks again, and there were more points of interest on the observatory timeline. The rest of us were still on bread and water. A week, that's all it really took; a week, and I think the rest of us all felt like there was no getting away, and no useful course of action. While Charles huddled into his coat, we all glanced at each other. The other four already looked worn out and strained.

'But,' Herault said in his maddeningly cheery way, 'I thought you might all like some time together. We've brought you some coffee.'

I could see what he was doing just as clearly as you do. After a week of bread and water, coffee was a phenomenal luxury. The five of us swung round like bloodhounds. It was bestial. Most of what made our thinking human and logical had eroded away already.

It felt very good to sit down in among the observatory's pretty couches (upholstered in fleur-de-lis embroidered tapestry in lapis blue no less) and drink the coffee. Herault and the soldiers had theirs at the next table. We were too aware of them, and silent at first, but they ignored us, laughing about something to do with someone's brother and a pet monkey, and after a while, that invisible wall between tables at teahouses solidified. At last, Frank, the first mate, said,

'You're a prick, Stevenson.'

'I didn't write very much, I swear,' Charles said. He was red. 'I just ...'

'Couldn't help yourself? Madeline must know as much as you but she's kept her fucking mouth shut, pardon my French, ma'am.'

'I think your French is excellent,' I said into the coffee, and like I'd hoped, a sort of wan laugh went through us all.

William, who had been silent until then, set his cup down on the saucer with a clink. He was Charles's assistant, but he was the same age, and probably cleverer, just less fortunately born. For the whole week we'd been on the Kingdom, I'd felt awkward around him. I wanted to sympathise about the patronising way Charles spoke to him, and I wanted to say everyone could see he was brilliant, but coming from me, in my ridiculous Belgravia voice, it would have sounded just as bad as it did from Charles. Sometimes I feel as though the voice of the English upper class has been specifically tailored to sound as though it is addressing a favourite dog, even when it's aimed at people.

I'm not surprised the French killed all their aristocracy, to be honest.

'Look, I think we all need to talk about what we do now,' William said quietly. 'If we carry on with bread and water, we'll go insane or collapse before long. I think every week, we need to elect someone who's going to tell him something useful. Then someone eats properly, and this stupid competition thing he's trying to set up won't work, because we will have decided, ourselves.'

Nobody argued. There was just a silence.

'Well,' Frank said finally. 'Stevenson's had his turn.'

We all laughed again, even Charles, who looked relieved we were joking about it and not throttling him.

'I think we need to let Madeline go next,' William murmured. 'She didn't exactly start out fat and she's less of a way to go before she starves.'

I don't often behave as I'd like, but I think I did then. I wasn't relieved, just offended, and I tried to argue.

'All respect, but do be quiet,' he said gently. He was rubbing the scar over his eye. It was still vivid, a nasty right angle from where some piece of debris had smacked him aboard the Kingdom. 'What does everyone apart from Madeline think?'

'Who put you in charge?' Charles said crossly.

'Shut up,' I said. My voice is good for some things.

Charles shut up.

Frank glowed. I smiled back and had a vision of that night on the Kingdom, when the poker match had boiled down to just the two of us and he'd shaken my hand when I won, like he'd enjoyed being beaten.

'Everyone for,' William murmured, with a sidelong glance at Herault and the soldiers.

He, Frank, and Sean, the engine stoker who never said anything about anything, all hinged their fingertips up to vote yes. Eventually, Charles did too.

I said something unladylike.

'We need to decide what you're going to tell him,' William said, once they had all stopped laughing. 'Just – I think now we can agree it can be anything except major battles of the Napoleonic Wars. Mr Stevenson?'

Charles hesitated, then nodded. 'What about the railway system? It isn't going to do our time a massive amount of damage if the French come up with the Métro a bit early. Maybe they'll be able to move goods faster, but if they invent this stuff then so will our side. Steam engines already exist now, in mines.'

'I don't know,' Frank said. He had a habit of rubbing his jaw when he was worried, and because he hadn't shaved this week, the rough skin on his fingertips made a sandpaper sound. I like him a lot, but hunger grinds your nerves and the noise was so irritating it gave me a flash of rage. 'More freight, more supplies to their lines ...'

'But they'd have to build the railway tracks, and I don't think they'll have the iron for it. Most of it goes to making cannons and shot now, doesn't it?' Charles looked at William, who was encyclopaedic.

'I think so,' William agreed.

'Right,' I said. It was a simple conversation, but hunger had turned my mind to cauliflower, and thinking was stunningly difficult. 'The London railways. I'll ... what should I do, as much of a map as I can remember, how they dig the Underground lines ...?'

'Yes, it was cut and cover in the early days,' Charles said.

'Yes,' I said, 'I know, Charles.'

Sean grinned. I smiled too, because it was news to me that he even understood everything we said. Nobody had said where he was from, but he was a foreigner for sure, perhaps Arabian. I'd seen him write in a script that wasn't Roman. Sean wasn't his real name, certainly. I think it was the name Frank had given him to avoid linguistic embarrassment. Again, I'd wanted to ask him, but it didn't seem right.

Charles coloured. 'Well, you asked—'

'No, she asked how much she should say, not what,' William said. He elbowed Charles. 'Still useless, mate.'

'That's impertinent,' Charles snapped, but not with much strength. He shifted uncomfortably, and the horsehair stuffing of the couch squawked.

William ignored him. 'So we're agreed. Madeline talks about the Underground this week. Everyone else ... try and stick to stuff that doesn't matter.'

'Look, if we're going that far, then why don't we all say useful things?' Charles said. 'Then we all eat.'

'I think he's going to keep prize-giving to one person,' I said. Already, if we mentioned an unidentified 'he', it was always Herault.

'So do I,' Frank said. 'I think we should stick with William's idea.'

'Sean?' Charles demanded.

'Herault's a smug little bastard but he's not stupid,' Sean said, in a totally unexpected London accent. 'He'll keep at this.'

'God, he speaks,' William grinned. He looked honestly delighted. He was always pleased with little things. I loved that about him. I miss it still.

'If you keep quiet mostly, then people listen when you don't.' Sean was full of fun even though he had a feverishness in his eyes.

Looking back, I can see Herault let us do that. There was no reason why we shouldn't nominate a person to be helpful each week; he was getting the information just the same.

It sounds like the right thing to have done, even when I read it back now. It sounds like we sat down and discussed it, and came to a measured conclusion in as fair a way as possible, under the circumstances. I remember going away feeling proud, even though I didn't like being the one chosen to talk. It was all very English, all very neat. I wonder if half the point of letting us sit and discuss it was that we would feel pleased with ourselves and relax.

If we had been less starved and more alert, I'm sure we would have seen the problem a mile away. But we didn't. I didn't. And by the next week, when Herault pointed it out to me, it was too late.

I drew out what I thought was an inoffensive enough thing: a rough map of the London railways, with the stations marked on, and little annotations about how it had been built. I'm just old enough to remember how they'd dug up Oxford Street for the Central Line, and I went into some detail there. I described how train engines worked, not as well as I could, but to a level I thought Herault would believe was as well as I could. I was even feeling pleased with myself, in a delirious sort of way, when the soldiers came to take the papers away on the day before Herault usually saw us, like always.

Someone came to fetch me half an hour later.

Herault was in the observatory with coffee and cake. Cake; it had only been a fortnight since I'd eaten properly, but it already looked like something from a fairy tale, the kind of beautiful food one ought never eat, lest one were trapped in the underworld. It was hard not to feel that it was, really, exactly that. Somehow if I ate with him, then I was his.

'Mademoiselle,' he said, pouring out the steaming black coffee. I'd not told him that it was Madame. 'Come and have some coffee with me. What do you call it? Afternoon tea? Can't stand tea.'

I sat.

'Cake?'

'No, thank you,' I said, doing some interior shrieking.

'All right. You've produced that fascinating map of London train stations.'

'Yes,' I said slowly, and glanced back, worried someone was coming up behind me. I was sure that it would be his style to smile at one while somebody else bashed one over the head with a brick. I thought, even then, that I was there because he found the map too obscure.

'Some of them have wonderful names. This one here. Elephant and Castle, why is it called that?'

'Oh. Um … it's a, what do you call it, a corruption. Infanta of Castile. Catherine of Aragon, I think that must be.'

'Ah. And this one: Waterloo. Beside … what you've marked on as Waterloo Bridge? Why is it called Waterloo?' he said pleasantly.

'Waterloo, I believe, is a town in the Netherlands.'

I can't make any excuses. I was hungry, yes; I was concentrating hard on not snatching up one of his stupid cakes. I'd nearly fainted when I lifted the coffee cup, because the scent of it was so rich that it felt like trying to breathe marzipan. 'There was a famous battle there,' I said.

'I see,' he said, smiling. 'But there is no such place in this time, so it was named ... well, recently, for you.'

'I ... suppose.'

You won't know this. I don't think it will ever happen for you now. But in my time, in that future which no longer exists, Waterloo was a great battle between England and France, at the end of this present war. England won. Yes, I know; imagine England winning anything.

'And this station here, Charing Cross, beside which you have marked Trafalgar Square. Again, it isn't called that now. Trafalgar is, here and now, a nondescript cape of land in Spain. Why is the centremost square in London named after it?' *He was twinkling now. He never was stupid.*

'I don't know.'

'Do you know what's interesting about Trafalgar? The Spanish one, not the London one.'

'No.'

'Nothing. But it is only about – oh, fifty miles down the road from Cadiz.' *He inclined his head.* 'Cadiz is the home harbour of the Spanish fleet, and indeed one of the home harbours of our fleet, since the alliance with Spain. A favourite hobby of the British navy is to blockade it.'

'How ... vexatious.'

I was hanging on to the hope that he couldn't possibly reason out the existence of two major battles from only a pair of names on a map of London. As I say, though, he was never stupid.

'Yes, it is, but do you know which direction the wind blows, out of Cadiz?' *He was laughing.* 'Which direction one is almost always obliged to sail? I'll tell you, it's towards Trafalgar.'

'If you say so.'

'I do.' He smiled again. 'Waterloo, a battle which you won; you must have or you wouldn't want to enshrine the name. Trafalgar; a sea battle, I suspect. Trafalgar would be … quite a natural place to have a sea battle, if ever the Coalition Fleet were to try and break out past the British during a blockade. Tell me about Waterloo and Trafalgar, mademoiselle.'

'I had no idea what they were until you told me just now,' I protested. 'May I remind you I'm sixty years too young to know all this? They're just − places, I don't know why they're called that.'

'Oh, that's a shame,' he said, entirely serious and completely insincere. 'No extra rations for you then. That's very frustrating for you, you must be hungry by now.'

I gripped the piece of broken vase in my pocket for a second, then jolted forward and slashed at him with it. I was just too slow, and instead of catching his neck, I only got his cheek. He shouted and I went for him, but the soldiers caught me and pulled me back.

'For God's sake!' Herault yelled at me. I always remember what he said, because he was actually shocked. 'Mademoiselle, all I'm doing here is my duty! I haven't hurt any of you, I haven't treated you badly, I'm making you uncomfortable, nothing worse! Have you any idea how many millions of people live on the rations you feel so deprived with? I did, when I was a child, for years, because people like you took everything.' There was such hatred in his voice. It's stark to me, even now. I'd suspected for a long time that poorer people resented people like me; it's why I was cautious around William and Sean. But I'd never understood the furnace heat of it. 'So contain yourself, please! You are safe and warm and dry, and if you're hungry, it's your own fault. There is no need for savagery.'

I didn't argue, because even though I'd been angry a few seconds before, I felt sorry now. I felt like I was talking to someone who had been wounded by people who looked just like me.

He pulled his sleeve over his bloody cheek. One of the soldiers touched his arm to ask if he was all right. 'Just put her somewhere, please. I don't want to see her again. Tell the others that the first one who can properly describe the battles of Trafalgar and Waterloo will be given full rations for a fortnight.'

33

Edinburgh, 1807

Cigarette ash dropped on Joe's knee. He scooped it up and scattered it out of the window, which was old and stiff, and opened only a few inches. He hardly noticed himself doing it, his head still with Madeline in that strange chateau in France. Maybe he was wrong about Charles. Maybe he was Sean. That certainly fitted the way Joe looked. And then there was William; Joe had that same scar, the little mark over one eye.

He didn't see that Kite was awake until he got up and went to the door.

'Hold on, where are you going?' Joe said.

'Away from that,' Kite said towards the cigarette.

'It's no better downstairs, don't – look, gone, see? Don't.' Joe went after him. 'You shouldn't be standing up. It's only a cigarette; why does it bother you so much?'

Kite didn't push him very hard. It was meant to make a point, not hurt, but it did hurt; it banged him into the wall and sent a thick airless ache through his ribs.

'No, all right,' Joe heard himself say. He touched Kite's knuckles. 'Come on, it's all right.'

Kite let him go and stepped back. 'Sorry,' he whispered.

'I've sailed for fifteen minutes and I nearly punched the bartender just now, you're doing well to speak in sentences.' Joe breathed slowly to make Kite do the same. He let the quiet spin, waiting for Kite's lungs to take on the rhythm on their own, not just because he was forcing it. In his hands, Kite's were shaking. Too much energy. It had to go somewhere. 'Come on, we need to go out for a walk. A long walk. What's that hill called, in town?'

'Arthur's Seat?'

'Let's climb it. See in the morning from the top.'

Kite looked out at the dark for a long time, but then nodded. The marines stared claymores at Joe, who pretended not to notice. He realised it was a stupid idea as soon as they were outside. It was foggy, and the hill was more of a mountain, with only one steep track up. Even by the time he hurt all over, the light at the top didn't seem any closer. In the fog it was only a halo haze. The longer he looked up at it, the less it looked like something they could reach, and the more like an incurious angel.

'In your time,' Kite said. 'You said it wasn't only you, with epilepsy. The forgetting. You said it was common.'

'Yes, it's … well, the doctors said it was common. They said it happened in clusters. Started about two and a half years ago now, three. Why?'

'Something happened here, three years ago. It will have affected the future a lot. You'll be angry when you hear, but – I'll tell you if you want to know. It's the only thing I can give you, to …' he lifted his hand a little ' … return the favour,' he said.

'What could have changed the whole future that much?'

'Trafalgar.' Kite's hand went to the burns across his face but like always he pulled it away before he could touch them. 'The *Kingdom* came from a future where the English won the Battle of Trafalgar. London didn't fall, the French fleet never made it to Calais to ship the army across to Kent and Bristol, they didn't invade, none of it. Your time was under English rule. But then we lost.'

Joe almost laughed, but only almost. 'Jesus. And she was only trying to tell Herault about railway stations.' He held up Madeline's letter to show what he was talking about.

Kite nodded, but not like he blamed her.

34

Offshore, Cadiz, 1805

Everything had smelled of paint and turpentine that afternoon. They were repainting the hulls. The *Belleisle* was even having to redo the rings around her masts in yellow instead of black. Kite swapped his jacket for a brush and a can. He liked painting. It was simple, and it was obvious when it was finished.

Suspended on a rope swing below the furled sails, he could feel a tiny breeze that didn't reach the deck, where the heat haze swam. Other people on other ships had noticed too and the masts swung with men on ropes, which gave the fleet a festive look, as if it were made of dangerously high carousels. Like he had done every five minutes, despite always promising himself he wasn't going to look again for at least another hour, he glanced at the flagship. It was conspicuous for *not* flying any flags. No supply orders, no post, no invitation to cross between ships.

The golden dome of the cathedral at Cadiz showed, just. He had been trying not to stare at it as much as he'd been trying not to stare at the flagless masts of the *Royal Sovereign*. As of this morning, he hadn't been ashore for twenty months and two days. He had never wanted to with any particular exigency, but Cadiz was different. It wasn't home; he'd moved too often to have a home except wherever the majority of his clothes were, but it was a place he liked, and whenever he did look, he wondered if the same priests were there. He had started, since getting here, to want to go to a real Mass again, in a real church instead of the bleak grey English ones with their boneless English parsons. There was something off-putting about faith with no backbone and only just enough teeth to get through a cucumber sandwich.

Just around the arm of the bay was the French fleet. They had been there for thirty days. They hadn't moved once, not even to scout. They weren't bothering to fire on the English frigates that scudded up to look at them. Their officers' wives had even taken to climbing down to see the English officers' wives as they rowed out to go shopping in Cadiz. It was a weird little piece of friendliness in the middle of what was otherwise a strict blockade. If a single man had been on one of those boats, it would have been blown out the water. But everyone had decided that there had to be a line, and that line was pissing off the women.

Above him, the two sailors filling in the next stripe up were muttering that it was nothing but a way to pass the time. He flicked paint at them.

'Get on with it.'

'Yes, sir,' one of them said quickly.

Usually the trouble officers had was making the men listen. Kite would have liked it if they'd listened less. He had never done anything noteworthy; they had no reason to be afraid of him. The point wasn't inherently sensible either. They were painting because all Nelson really wanted – and Kite could never decide if he found it dandy or endearing – was that nice checkerboard effect that came of having black hulls with yellow stripes. When the gun ports opened, they hinged black squares into the yellow, and he liked the masts to match.

Tom mooched up from the cabin, in gallant disarray in the heat, and slouched forward against the taffrail just opposite Kite's swing. He must have stood in the same way at another rail before this one, because his waistcoat crumpled into already established creases.

'Afternoon,' he said. 'Why is … why?' He waved his hand at Kite's paint can. 'Have we not sailors, lieutenant? Have you not that paperwork I made up earlier?'

'I was tired of waving at the *Orion*, sir,' Kite said, and there was an assenting mumble above him. Something under his chest turned unhappily. Jem had waved back early that morning from the other deck. They could only make each other out properly with telescopes. It had been a relief to see that Jem was alive and with all the right limbs, but it was a short-lived relief.

'So we're painting,' Tom concluded. He seemed to search for something constructive to add. He didn't find anything.

Kite caught himself rubbing at the tattoo under his sleeve, full to splitting with the need to say *something* to Jem. It was getting so urgent he was willing to try smoke signals.

'Captain, may we not—' one of the sailors began.

Tom looked up. 'May we not go across to other ships even though there is no signal flag on the *Royal Sovereign* suggesting that we might be permitted to ship visit?'

'The ladies are doing it,' the sailor said hopefully.

'Not any more. Banned since Tuesday,' Tom sighed. Not far from them, the *Royal Sovereign* rode a bump in the sea and swayed. 'For God's sake, what does Lord Collingwood *do* all day? I've known barnacles with a greater need for society. It's all very well saying we must be in a state of readiness instead of cluttered about on boats between ships, but three weeks not talking to anyone? He's either got a very amusing dog or an exceptionally beautiful cabin boy.'

'It must be the dog, he'd have to speak to a person,' Kite said. The usual rule about keeping your opinions of senior officers to yourself had eroded around the time the sugar had run out.

One of the sailors made a small annoyed sound as he strayed outside the lines for the paint. Kite passed up the jar of turpentine. His fingers felt sticky when he let go. The open sea shouldn't have been stuffy, but the air felt just as close out here as it did in tiny baking alleyways. The sailors had even given up on fishing off the guns. There was nothing to catch; the only things that ever passed through here were jellyfish, which put off everything else. Across on the *Orion*, someone had stretched a washing line between four open gun ports. He could see the shirts pegged on it. The sea was too calm to spray them.

Down on the deck, the sailors were doing decent work of keeping busy, but everyone had slowed down almost to nothing. The heat was rippling and most of them had their shirts tied round their waists. The black men were tanned so dark their tattoos were lost, and the white ones were burning. The bosun, with exactly nothing to do even though he was on watch, was propped against the base of the mast with his rifle, in case there were any birds to take a shot at, but there weren't. Trying to get rid of the lethargy that had been creeping over him all afternoon, Kite let himself down beside him, even though he had nothing particular to say. He was starting to feel like it was better to be silent in company, at least. The bosun glanced at him and they knocked their knuckles together. Kite made scissors and the bosun made paper. Rock, scissors. Rock, rock. The bosun kicked his ankle.

Across from them, the *Agamemnon* creaked unpromisingly. The bosun glanced that way too and they both sank into a more depressed silence. It was obvious even from here that it was rigged badly, but there was nothing to do about it. You couldn't signal across to someone else and complain. It wouldn't have helped, anyway. *Agamemnon* was a horrible piece of shipwrighting. It wasn't old, but whenever Kite saw it, new bits of it were falling apart.

Although Kite didn't know till much later, the shameful state of the *Agamemnon* was why its captain hadn't asked many questions of the six peculiarly well-qualified men who'd signed on two years ago in Portsmouth, when usually he couldn't get anyone better than the local drunks. It was why he hadn't cared that they had no real references, and why he'd believed them when they said they'd deserted from the French navy because they just didn't believe in Napoleon any more. Qualified hands were qualified hands.

'Sail,' someone called, uncertainly, from the bow; then, 'Sail!'

Everyone swung around, searching the horizon. Kite wished they were allowed to put up a signal that said they would all like to personally shake the hand of the first French captain who tried a run on the blockade.

'It's the *Victory*! Lord Nelson's here!'

Tom shot down the quarterdeck stairs. 'What's the signal, can you see?'

Kite had to frown into the heat haze to see *Victory*'s mast. The flags there said, *We have sugar. Come for dinner.*

Tom thumped his shoulder. 'Thank *Christ*.'

Nelson was waiting for visiting officers on the deck, looking scruffy and only a little more substantial than a collection of dandelion feathers, but cheerful all the same. *Victory* had pulled in just on the far side of *Agamemnon*, so it didn't take long to cross. A couple of men helped them over the rail. Kite wove through the crowd, catching other people's shoulders when they passed too quickly, and then smiled when he found him.

'Jem.'

Jem whipped round and snatched him close. He felt more fragile than he should have, but Kite couldn't tell if he really was, or if it was only that, being older, Jem had always been the same size, while Kite himself had broadened in the last couple of years. Jem gripped his shoulders to get a proper look at him.

'You look terrible – what's Tom done to you?'

'Are you all right now?' Kite demanded. 'Your last letter; you said you'd had an accident with the guns and then you didn't say anything else.'

'I didn't want to fuss,' Jem said easily. He smiled and hugged him again, and bumped their foreheads together. Kite shut his eyes. His whole chest hurt with the effort of not weeping. He wasn't very successful and he had to put his head down against Jem's neck. Two years; he felt like he could breathe again. Jem pressed one hand over the back of his skull and curled forward over him. It was all right, though. They weren't the only ones. Some triplets had just found each other, and even Tom had to push his sleeve over his eyes when he managed to collar Jem's captain, a sweet man called Codrington who'd got them all hopelessly lost in Canada once.

'Gentlemen!' Nelson was tiny and therefore invisible in the crowd, but he had a clear voice. 'I'm delighted to see you all so pleased with each other, but before I forget, I've brought the post.' He burst into his merry laugh as he was mobbed.

The stateroom tables were laid out with water jugs and bread, and real butter. Most of the captains and first lieutenants were there and more besides. Formality was out the window faster than orange peel. It felt more like being in a coffeehouse than a fleet flagship, and because there were so many of them, it was even laid out that way, with ten or twelve tables. There was easily space; *Victory* was a first-class ship of the line, and the stateroom was twice the size of *Belleisle*'s.

Tom arranged them in a square, he and his brother Ru on one side and Kite and Jem on the other. Further down were officers from Jem's ship and from Ru's, all familiar. Despite all the doors and windows being open, the room was too hot, and before long Kite had to pull off his cravat and open his collar. Jem did too, then produced a needle and ink from his pocket and claimed Kite's arm. He put a new star on to the tattoo whenever they met up. He was two off finishing Orion.

When the food came, there were pomegranates and pears, real grapes, duck, *wood-pigeon* for God's sake, things Kite hadn't seen for years. The sun set fast here and, when it did, the servants came in with lamps. The silverware reflected the lights and the bright buttons on their jacket sleeves. Kite was strict about it with the men, so he didn't have much of a head for wine. He leaned gradually against Jem. It brought him nearer the tiny crackle of the cigarette Jem was sharing with Ru, and the sweet smell of the tobacco. From the other side of the room, the Grenadier fife and drum song broke out, with dirtier lyrics than usual.

Jem had one hand on his thigh, stroking the edge of his thumb to and fro over his hip. Kite was on the edge of falling asleep after the second glass of wine. The idea of getting up, never mind going back outside, finding a boat and rowing back to the *Belleisle*, was starting to take on the same enormity as a journey to Brazil. He hoped someone organised was going to invite them all to stay here overnight. There was nothing in the world more appealing than settling down in a hammock with drunk conversations seeping through the grain of the deck, breathing the rich smell of old sherry.

'Hammocks going up below, gentlemen,' someone called.

Thank God.

'Do you want to share? Then we won't have to fight for two,' Jem said.

'No.' Kite straightened up. 'Too hot. I'll fight.'

'What? I haven't seen you for two years.'

'No,' Kite said again, and smiled so that he wouldn't look miserable. He'd requested to be transferred to the *Belleisle* because he'd hoped that his psyche, always lazy and suggestible, wouldn't be up to staying in love with someone it hadn't seen for years. It had turned out to be a lot more determined than he'd thought.

The feeling was so deep-rooted now it might as well have been hunched up round all his organs and staining his blood, a pestilential thing staring hard at his sister's marriage. Given one single hour alone and drunk enough, and he would assuredly say something that led to a punch in the face. Whatever Jem – poor decent kind Jem – had meant that night by the river, it had not been to provoke this creeping, deformed devotion.

'Miz,' Jem said, frowning. 'Come on.'

He would just have to be offended. Kite shook his head.

'Can I have that cigarette back?' Ru asked. 'It's wasted on you, Jem, you smoke so much I bet you can't even taste pepper, never mind—'

The shots came straight through the window at the back of the room. They blasted the far wall. He didn't see it but it must have been chain shot, to do to the room what it did. He had been flung ten feet backward into the wall and his lungs wouldn't fill properly. When they did, he choked and realised there was too much on top of him. Broken chairs, part of a table.

Something was hissing right by his head. He thought it was the cigarette, but when he looked, there was a cannonball sitting on the deck, perfectly intact and still glowing red from the furnace. The floor began to catch fire while he was staring. He found a water jug and upended it. The steam roared.

The whole thing belonged so much to action on a gun deck that he couldn't remember where he was. When he did, he stood up unsteadily and looked around the wreckage for any sign of Jem. It was impossible to tell what was furniture and what was a person at first. Splintered bones and splintered wood looked alike. Smoke poured up from the fires, which were everywhere because the brandy bottles had exploded and ignited. He waited until he could tell people moving apart from the flickering shadows and the shapes in the smoke. There was no use shouting. All he could hear was a dull howl.

He started to move the fallen tables. Towards his side of the room there were more people lurching upright than nearer the windows, but not all of them. Tom was there, torn in half, still alive.

'Help a fellow along, Miz,' he said, quite himself.

Kite shot him, and then couldn't look under anything else in case he found the same again. The ash in the air was sandpapering the back of his throat.

Jem kicked away a table and rocked to his feet with one hand clamped around his arm, which was bleeding. Kite could see but not hear that he was swearing. Jem caught his shoulders and asked if he was all right, then saw Tom's body on the floor, the gun still smoking in Kite's hand, took it off him and flung it away. It bounced off the wall near to where Nelson had been sitting. Parts of him were sitting there still.

Jem must have been trying to talk to him, because he turned him by his elbow and touched his own lips to say watch.

'Where's Ru?'

Casting around, it was by accident that they found Admiral Collingwood too, slumped just beside him. Collingwood was trying to talk to Jem. Ru was dead.

'Lord Nelson, what about ...'

'He's dead, sir.'

Collingwood stared between them. 'Right. I see. That was the ... where did it come from?' he said helplessly, and he looked like an old man, though he wasn't yet sixty.

'*Agamemnon*,' Kite provided. He could only hear his voice inside his own skull. But now Collingwood had asked, he knew; he had seen the flashes from six of *Agamemnon*'s gun ports, but the memory was only just fighting to the surface.

'Where's Captain Brown?' Collingwood looked around, then stopped when Kite pointed. 'You're Kite. You're the Spaniard?'

'Yes, sir.'

'You have command of *Agamemnon*. Get over there and find out what the hell is going on. And do it quickly. We can't afford to leave *Agamemnon* behind when we sail, we need her guns. Jem, you …' He was staring at someone's body. 'I suppose you're going to have to take over *Orion*.'

They helped Collingwood up, but he collapsed again and didn't wake this time. Jem motioned to get out and organise the boats. Kite eased away through the mess of pieces that had been people a minute ago. The doors were wrecked. Men were coming from the deck to help. Someone caught his arms and tried to stop him walking, and he had to explain, without really hearing his own voice, where he was going. When he looked back, he had left perfect black bootprints across the deck. Blood or wine or tar, he couldn't tell.

Jem caught up with him and they waited together for the boats to be ready. *Orion* and *Agamemnon* were in opposite directions. Kite sat down on some ropes. He felt like he was about to faint.

The sun had set but it wasn't wholly dark yet. A cloud bank had turned most of the sky orange and smoky, like something gargantuan was burning in it. Jem sat down next to him.

'You said this would happen,' Kite said.

'What?'

'You said we could lose at Trafalgar. Trafalgar is forty miles away from here. The French are going to run the blockade any minute now and we'll catch them at Trafalgar.' He looked up. 'And if we lose, they'll get to Calais, and they'll take the army across to London.'

'We might not lose.'

'With about six senior officers left alive to cover twenty-six ships?'

They both fell quiet again.

'Who's first?' a sailor said from behind them. He must have tried to say it before, because he tapped their shoulders to make them look back. He did it carefully, like he was worried they might crumble if he pressed too hard. Kite frowned and felt how stiff the ash was on his skin. They were both grey from it.

Jem brushed his sleeve. 'Go on.'

'I'll see you ... well, in Portsmouth.' He shook his hand, briefly, because there were sailors watching and none of them would feel better if they thought he was convinced he would never see Portsmouth or Jem again. His throat hurt. 'Good luck.'

'And you. Miz,' Jem added as the boat was lowering. He had come to the rail. 'Go straight there. Better to get it done quickly. I'll go over to *Belleisle* and get your things sent across.'

Kite sat down so he could look up without overbalancing. 'Collingwood should have sent you. You'd have it sorted out in ten minutes.'

'No, he shouldn't. If the choice is someone who looks chronically lost and someone who looks like he personally oversaw the Inquisition, I know who I'd bet on.' He dropped his voice. 'If they're scared enough of you, there's a chance you won't have to do it. Someone might come forward.'

The sailor with Kite glanced between them and plainly wanted to ask, do what, but Kite hadn't the energy to say it.

The further from the chaos on *Victory* the boat lowered, the clearer he could hear the men trapped by their officers on the gun deck of *Agamemnon*. They were bellowing to be allowed out. The sound carried over the muggy water. Jem was right. Kite wanted to think that if you presented frightened men with a reassuring person, they would tell the truth, but it wasn't true. They only felt safe enough to lie. 'First time in my life I've been accused of being looks over substance.'

Jem laughed his smoky laugh and stayed at the rail, but the sunset was on the wrong side and before long Kite lost sight of him.

Kite was still climbing the ladder on the *Agamemnon*'s side when a shout went up from the mast, and then whistles and drums. The French were on their way out of Cadiz. The flagship, lit up with so many torches it was possible to see it clearly even as it rounded the bay, was a titan flying Napoleon's colours.

Someone leaned through an open gun port and grabbed his arm. It made him jump and he almost punched the man in the face.

'Sir – sir. Where's Captain Brown?' It was a lieutenant, too junior to have gone over to *Victory*. He glanced back as he spoke, plainly expecting someone to ambush him and shove him into the water. Kite could just see a protective wall of marines behind him. He looked terrified.

'Dead. I'm replacing him. I'll be through in a minute.' He wondered whether the rungs above him would hold up against the weight of a whole person. They didn't look promising.

The young man either didn't hear or didn't care. 'It's – we can't – what should we do?'

He was perversely glad to have something to concentrate on. 'Did you close off the gun deck as soon as it happened?'

'Yes, sir, of course. No one's gone in but me and the marines. Certainly no one's gone out.'

'How many men are there?'

'Forty-five, sir. Everyone else was above; there was a play. We were all ...' He was starting to cry. He could only have been seventeen.

'All right. Bring them up on deck and get together a firing squad.'

'But we don't know which of them — it only took three or four to load and fire six guns, but half of them are accusing the other half and—'

'There's no time to sort them out,' Kite interrupted. Across the fleet, sails were already unfurling. The bang of canvas had a muffled water-echo from here. 'The firing squad is for all of them. Then we need to be underway.'

35

Edinburgh, 1807

From the top of Arthur's Seat, the city lights were so many spilled cinders. Joe and Kite had sat on one of the stone outcrops for about half an hour, enough to cool down. They had raced on the last stretch of the way up. Joe had always thought he was quite fit, walking everywhere through London, but Kite won by fifty yards. The electric fizz had gone away from him now. Joe had been glad to lose. Straight ahead of them, across the city, torchlight blazed at the castle, which was gaunt and full of strange angles.

Joe watched Kite in the moonlight. He had his hands crossed palm up in his lap, his forearms facing upward, the lighthouse tattoo stark against his skin.

'Are you cold?' Kite asked.

'I'm frozen to this rock,' Joe admitted.

They set off again. At first, Kite walked a little way from him. Joe chased him and took his arm. Kite let him, and leaned against him a fraction, plainly glad for someone to walk with.

The mechanical voice in Joe's head said, *And now I can snap you in half whenever I like.*

Lily. It was not a bad thing to want to get home to your little girl. It wasn't.

When Joe woke, dawn had broken and seagulls were crying to each other from the roofs. Downstairs was already full of the sounds of people who had been up and about for a while. He lay still for a few minutes, soaking in the light. He couldn't remember the last time he'd woken up in daylight. He was too early for it even in the summer normally. Closing his hands through folds in the blanket, he turned onto his chest and breathed. The weak sun soaked through the back of his shirt.

Kite was asleep, though not easily. He was hot, his collarbones strained and shining, but sleep had paralysed him too well for him to have pushed off the covers.

Joe moved them, then opened the window an inch to let in the air. He couldn't bring himself to throw water over the last glow of the coals. Heat was too valuable to just throw away. When he looked back, Kite had shifted onto his side. He still didn't have any colour. The things he slept in were all thin cotton, and they made him look hopelessly fragile. They showed where his bones were.

The scrap of cannon fuse he tied his hair up with had dropped onto the floor. Joe picked it up and then swayed when he straightened.

At first he thought it was just wooziness after too long on the ship, but then the familiar epilepsy fog came down with its pure wonderful brilliant euphoria and he was right where he always wanted to be: on that pebble shore in grey weather, while the man who waited by the sea was just ahead of him.

The vision lasted longer than it ever had. The man was skimming pebbles on the flat surf, slowly; before he threw each stone, he waited for the ripples from the last one to fade altogether. It looked like one of those dull rules people made up to complicate dull games and pass the time. There was a sad patience to him. He was close enough to touch.

But he must have been a memory of someone Joe had known well, because the things he would have noticed about a new person – hair, height, build – were somehow not there at all, even though the man himself absolutely was. Wherever Joe knew him from, he had seen him so often before that day on the beach that he had stopped perceiving any of it.

And then the room was just itself again.

Joe blew his breath out in a rush. The vision was gone, but it left him full of happiness, like always, powerful as opium. This time, though, it came with a bitter edge. Something had been wrong that day, badly wrong. He could almost remember.

Seeing him again gave Joe a glimmer-hope that he had been wrong before; that it was all there in his mind – buried, but possible to excavate.

It had to be Jem. It couldn't be coincidence that this had happened the morning after Kite had told him another story. But he hoped it wasn't. Jem was dead, and Joe wanted desperately for the man who waited to be waiting still.

Joe eased out and lifted the door a bit as he pulled it, to keep it from scraping. There were two new marines on the landing. They didn't say anything, but they followed him downstairs.

Breakfast was a lot better than he'd hoped. Eggs, toast, real butter; after six days of ship food and seasickness, it was the best meal he'd ever had. It was ten o'clock, and though the breakfast crowd were still there, some of the tables by the windows were free now. He sat with his hands around a cup of bitter coffee and watched the harbour. Not much was happening. No ships could get out, so no one was loading. Some had been there for so long that the frost on their hulls was as thick as snow, the rigging turned to monstrous spider webs. The sharp winter shadows showed all the hulls that hadn't been repaired properly yet. Some had been torn open and just patched over for now with canvas. Some had new planks, at least, but they weren't tarred.

Someone on the quay slung a hawk off her arm and it wheeled up to chase out the colonies of seagulls in the masts. They burst in all directions, wailing.

Across the room, the two marines were sitting side by side at another table, watching him, though they were talking to each other. He gave them a cheery smile and took out Madeline's letter. There was only a little of it left. Maybe, maybe, the last of it would say what had happened to the Kingdoms, or even which of them he was. She had known, after all; she had sent him the postcard.

*

Two weeks went by and nothing happened, then three; nothing, not even our hateful little timeline seminar. I started to chatter to the guards in my appalling French through the door, just to talk. And then halfway through the fourth week, we were summoned to the observatory, and there was food: an amazing buffet of real meat, real vegetables, real everything. Wine, tea, coffee, even smart uniformed waiters who served things to us on silver plates. Herault, I was starting to suspect, was a thwarted thespian. I would have poked fun, but I was too astonished to say anything. Instead I just ran straight into William, who had held his arms out.

He felt too thin even through his warm clothes. I saw him think the same thing about me.

Charles, of course, had a healthy glow. He might even have put on weight. It was Herault's doing, not his own, but I hated him anyway. But then he burst into such wretched tears that I don't think any of us had the heart to be angry with him any more. Sean patted his arm and Frank told him to buck up, looking so pained I thought he was on the edge of weeping too. We all were.

'This,' Herault told us happily, 'is a leaving party. One of you has been so helpful this week that I've decided to let that person go free.'

My guts clenched, because I had cracked four days ago. I'd written down everything I knew. It's unforgivable; no one hurt me, the guard never did educate me, but I was just so hungry I couldn't think any more. Maybe it was me; maybe it was Charles.

'William,' Herault said.

It was the last name I expected him to say.

'Here's a bag. There's food in there. The soldiers will take you to Paris, whence you may go wheresoever you choose.' He beamed. 'Congratulations.' He and the guards all applauded, and two soldiers led William away from us, to the front door. William looked back at us, wretched, and that was the last I saw of him.

There was silence after that. None of us moved. It was a kind of shell shock.

'Well?' Herault said. 'Come on. Eat! That could be you one day soon.'

Frank, Sean, and I were all so hungry there was no sensible choice but to do as we were told. Charles poured out four glasses of champagne, his face set. He handed them round.

'Maybe better to be drunk now,' he whispered.

We all sat down together, just like we had before, when we came up with our first stupid plan. We drank the champagne in silence, listening to Herault and the soldiers talk and joke. They were genuinely happy, relaxed; I thought of what Herault had said, about just trying to do his duty, and how he was doing it in the lightest way he could. I think the most frustrating thing about it all is that he was right. He could have put all of us on a rack or started chopping off fingers, but he never did.

I studied the others. Frank, who still had his sailing jumper, was too small for it now; it hung loose off his shoulders. Sean normally had a lustre, but he was losing it. Even Charles, well-fed as he was, looked wrong close up. He was healthy, but it was hollow health, and now that he had been crying, I could see what he had looked like when he was little. After a while, I squeezed his hand.

'I wrote about Trafalgar and Waterloo as well,' I said, because it felt important now to tell the truth.

Sean nodded. 'Me too.'

Frank and Charles looked up at the same time. They checked with each other, and they had opposite reactions. Frank pressed one hand over his eyes as his shoulders tightened, and Charles looked relieved.

'So he got it from all of us,' I said softly. 'Not just William. We must have all said the same thing. That's ... why he's so sure it's true.'

'What's William going to do in France, now?' Sean said. He was frowning at the bubbles in his champagne. He hadn't drunk any. 'He's English. Is he going to be all right?'

'We can't do anything about it,' Charles said. 'So it's pointless to worry.'

Sean looked very tired of him.

'They're going to go after Nelson and Wellington,' Frank said softly. He clenched his hands over the sleeves of his jumper. He didn't seem as though he had heard what the other two had said. 'Jesus Christ.'

'They know who Nelson and Wellington are anyway,' I said. 'That's common knowledge even now. Isn't it?'

'Maybe,' he said, looking reassured.

'If they know when and where they have to win, that's that,' Sean said. There followed a quiet in which he refilled all our glasses.

'I'm sorry,' Charles said in a brittly steady voice, 'but I don't think I can ... bear this any more. I want to try and get home. We know it wasn't the fog that brought us here—'

'Quiet,' Frank whispered.

'We all know it wasn't the fog that brought us here,' Charles ploughed on, 'it was those pillars. Nobody builds a fortification like *that wall unless it faces something they must keep out. We get back there, we could still get home. Before he changes anything.'*

'Are you suggesting telling him even more?' Frank snapped.

'No, I'm suggesting we escape.'

'I tried, they caught me,' I said.

'You were by yourself,' Charles told me. He had a feverish shine now. 'Look, we agree a time. Two o'clock in the morning, tonight. We all have windows. Get out of them, meet on the lawn in front of this room. I'm a coward, I'll crack if he does anything worse than he already has. I think we all will. We have to go.'

A pause.

'Cheers,' Sean whispered.

I chimed my glass against theirs, and didn't say that the guards had put bars over my windows already.

I saw them go; Charles, it turned out, was only a few doors along from me, and I saw a flash of white as he edged down onto the little mantle-roof of the bay windows below. He sprayed gravel awkwardly when he landed on the path, then shot over the lawn to meet the others. Not long later I heard yells and gunshots. But I think they got away, because I never saw any of them again.

Earlier this evening, Herault arrived with an expensive bottle of wine. We're friends now. I think he's forgiven me for growing up like a princess, and I've forgiven him for doing his duty for his country.

'Mademoiselle,' he said, glowing. He has always called me that, all down the years, though I'm forty now and it sounds absurd. He's trying to be kind. 'It's happened. Trafalgar is won, London is taken, and the war is over.' He tinked our glasses together and managed to look rueful, despite all his joy. He has such unexpected grace sometimes. 'I'm so sorry, mademoiselle. Well fought.'

So I thought I had better write it down; how I lost us all. I shall hang myself tomorrow morning. I don't expect it shall help anything — I'm afraid it's all past help now — but it will be justice at least. Perhaps, just perhaps, the other Kingdoms made it across to you in England. Perhaps they will help put it right. If not; God help you, because the Terror is coming for you.

*

'No. What?' Joe said aloud to the last page of the letter. There was nothing else. But she couldn't have hanged herself. She must have found the other Kingdoms again.

'It's only coffee.'

Joe jumped. 'Mother of God.'

He hadn't seen Kite arrive, or set the coffee cup down next to his hand, but he was sitting just opposite him with a plate of toast. He looked bad still. Anyone else would have slumped forward, elbows down on the table, but he stayed fire-iron straight. Joe nearly told him to relax and then realised just in time that, after that beating from Lawrence, Kite wouldn't be able to slouch for weeks.

'Sorry. I was reading. What happened to the Kingdoms, did they get away?'

'Must have,' said Kite.

'What about her?'

'I never met her,' Kite said, shaking his head.

Joe lifted his hands and let them drop again. 'You gave this to me because you knew full well she never says anything that would really tell me who I am or what happened to me, didn't you.'

'Yeah,' said Kite. He did look ashamed. 'Sorry.'

Joe ground the heel of one hand into his forehead, because he was getting a headache from frowning at the letter. 'No. If

I was going to remember, I'd have remembered. But ... none of it rings a bell. Not the chateau, or Herault, or any of it. I think it's just gone. You can relax, at least.'

'Mm,' said Kite, who didn't look like he was ever going to relax again.

Joe sipped the coffee. 'How are you feeling?'

'Better. Thank you, for ... last night.'

'No, it was good. Amazing view.' Joe gave him the coffee to share and watched him take it. His bad hand had seized up. 'Why cigarettes?' Joe asked. 'You were fine, until I lit a cigarette.'

'Jem smoked.'

'Oh.' And here was Joe, wearing Jem's clothes. Even though it wasn't his fault, he felt guilty. 'Sorry.' He hesitated. 'Agatha must be bringing it all back.'

'Agatha would be ashamed I was taking it out on random mechanics. I'm sorry.' Kite watched the docks for a little while, and Joe thought for at least the tenth time that the way he talked about his sister was how most people talked about royalty. The devotion and the fear were servile.

'I know you're going to call me too French again, but it's all right to be sad, you know,' Joe said quietly. 'She was your sister.'

Kite set his teeth and Joe thought he wouldn't say anything, or that he was going to snap, but then something in him cracked. 'It isn't all right,' he said. 'She isn't *mine* enough for me to be sad about.' He shook his head slightly. 'A few years ago the old Queen died and London was full of people watching the funeral carriage. Half of England was just – distraught. Like it was any of their business. It was disgusting.'

'You knew your sister, though.'

'She's not that kind of sister,' Kite said, with a tightness that said he had finished talking about it.

Joe decided it was worth pushing just a little further. Part of him was appalled that anyone could have been made to feel that way about their own sister, and part of him, the mechanical voice, noted in its cold dead way that the more upset Kite was, the less he was going to be keeping a proper eye on Joe today. 'Well, maybe people told you she wasn't, maybe Lawrence convinced you you were about on a level with her footman, but that's not true, is it?'

Kite wasn't having it. He only studied Joe. 'You look better.'

'You look like hell.'

'I'm much improved by candlelight,' Kite said, with a tiny sparkle, and smiled when Joe kicked him under the table. The smile faded too quickly. When he took a deeper breath to speak again, he held it for a long time before he used it. 'Right. We're going to find a blacksmith. You can start ordering in what you need.'

All the peaceful ordinariness of the morning broke.

'I can't do this,' Joe said softly. 'I know there will be the siege, I know people will die, but she's my *daughter*. She might never exist if you make me do this.' He touched Kite's broken hands where they rested on the cup still. 'I could just – escape. No one would know you let me.' He squeezed gently, and let his fingertips creep over the first lines of the tattoo where the lowest tentacle of a kraken circled the bone in Kite's wrist. 'Please.'

Kite looked at their hands for a long time. For a teetering second, Joe thought he was going to say yes. But then something behind his eyes shut down. He took out his gun – he must have had a second one all along – and rested the muzzle against Joe's knee.

36

The cold was wolfish. As they walked uphill into town, it felt worse than it had even at Eilean Mòr. They passed other men in uniform who touched their hats. Too many; they should have been at sea. The city was flooded with red and blue jackets. Red for soldiers and marines, blue for the navy. Boarding house after boarding house. The port was blockaded, of course; nobody could get out. The two marines followed them, not close but not far either.

Joe usually had a good sense of direction, but once they were in Edinburgh proper, he was lost. It was a tangle of marble monuments and chaotic tenements. He got a glimpse downhill once, when they were near the castle, and saw the slums – a labyrinth of wooden buildings clustered around wells in muddy courtyards where chickens and goats scratched, and people had hessian sacking instead of front doors. And then they turned a corner and they were on a broad stone bridge, and on either side were warmly lit inns and shops that sold specialist whisky.

Up a flight of more than a hundred steps was a whole street of blacksmiths.

The workshop Kite chose was back from the road through a twisting little passage. Inside, the workshop smelled of hot metal and the forge, where the coal was cherry red. The blacksmith was a large woman in a heavy apron, hammering out a sword on the anvil. Joe could see the shape already. It sparked under every hammer blow.

She looked like she might hit them with the hammer too, but she must have been expecting them, because she dropped the sword into a cooling barrel and came across to shake Kite's hand. With evident pride, she offered them some tea. Kite looked impressed. Joe didn't understand at first, and then realised that India was on the far side of France. It must have been hell to get anything from there to here.

While they drank the tea, he looked around at the equipment. The place was well supplied. The walls were covered in racks and racks of hammers and tongs, pincers, some big enough to make an iron hull for a ship and some small enough for jewellery. The forge pumped out heat and red light, which gleamed on the claymores laid on the workbench. She must have had a commission for a whole regiment.

'Has the *Ajax* been in?' Kite was asking. He was holding his tea in both hands. The two marines were doing the same, and they kept giving the smith adoring looks.

'Ah, no. Sunk off Calais. How's your sister?'

'Lost in action.'

'Fuck. So what are we making?' she asked, as if they'd been talking about bad weather before. Kite inclined his head at Joe.

'Can I explain what this is or are you going to shoot someone?' Joe said to Kite.

'No, tell her,' Kite said, without any hostility. He was sitting with his back to the forge. Joe would have been ferociously hot after ten seconds, but Kite was still wearing his jacket.

'Right,' said Joe, and explained what telegraphs were, and how Morse code worked.

He'd had to learn to code as part of the lighthouse-keeping exam. Anyone de Méritens sent anywhere near a lighthouse took it, and after he'd learned, Joe had found the whole transmitting system so fascinating that he'd taken some telegraphs apart at work just for the novelty.

They worked in the same way that arc lamps did: with a spark gap. But where, in a lighthouse, you ran electricity through the two electrodes to get a continuous spark – the light of the lamp – you just needed little blips if you wanted to talk to somebody. If you sparked *your* spark gap on and off, the electromagnetic field could affect any wire coils nearby. If you gave it enough electricity – 10,000 volts, say – it would affect a coil miles away. The machines were beautiful: all delicate copper coils in the transformers, and electrodes that looked like ball-bearings on sticks. Despite everything, he found himself enjoying drawing the parts out, and showing them how the circuit worked. Kite and the blacksmith listened in silence. One of the marines crossed himself.

'So, once this is done, you should be able to communicate … eh, over about twenty miles. They did it from France to a lighthouse in England a couple of years ago.'

'Twenty miles,' said Kite.

'It's not far, but it'll do you for the siege,' Joe pointed out, and then realised that Kite had meant twenty miles was long, not short. 'I need to make a battery, don't I,' he added, more to himself, and looked around a bit aimlessly. 'Where do we get sulphuric acid?' He paused, because a home-made battery was only going to manage about ten or twenty volts. 'And – a *lot* of copper wire.'

It was hard to explain wireless telegraphy to someone who didn't know what electricity was, but Joe decided to give it a go. He put Kite's compass near a test circuit, hooked up to a battery made of coins and saltwater, to show him how the wires produced an electromagnetic field that would skitter the needle. Kite was still looking at it when Joe came back from the forge, turning the circuit off and on to watch the compass needle move. He seemed to have an infinite concentration for that tiny motion. It wasn't wonder, or even interest. He looked grim, and Joe could see exactly why. A child playing with potatoes and some bits of wire could have worked it out, given enough time. It must have been maddening to see it done in the course of a day, after suffering for years.

'Cheer up,' Joe said, angry to be feeling for the person who was forcing him to do all this at gunpoint. 'It's not your daughter you're killing, mate.'

Kite looked at him down and up, very, very slowly, as if Joe had just waltzed in dressed as Marie Antoinette, complaining about the absence of cake. 'Get on with it.'

Between the clips and thunks of hammers on metal, he kept thinking how McCullough had come out to the pillars with the tortoises when Kite had only intended to ask his grandfather to look after them. The intention alone had been enough to conjure a whole new future.

This wasn't like that. There were a lot of steps between these telegraphs existing, and changing history. The tide of the war changing wasn't inevitable just because he'd made them – or not like giving McCullough's grandfather the tortoise instructions had been inevitable once Kite had decided to do it. This was different.

It had to be different.

The steel pieces hissed and oxidised in the cooling barrel. They were only shapes in metal. But they were shapes that shouldn't have been thought of for sixty years. A pressure settled on the back of his neck and seeped between the bones. Kite watched him with his endless patience for three days. At the end of those days, the parts weren't just shapes, but working machines.

37

'They work,' Joe said. 'When can I go?'

They were by the docks. One telegraph was set up on *Agamemnon* in Kite's stateroom, the other in the office of a severe man called Lord Howe at the castle. Joe had drawn up two codebooks and the first message had gone through clearly. *Does it work then?* from Howe. Kite had looked at the clicking machine as if it were hurting him, replied that yes it did work thank you, and left it straight away in the hands of a delighted Lieutenant Wellesley. Joe followed him, childishly hurt that, after everything, Kite didn't even seem pleased. He caught up with him on the gangplank.

Kite swayed back from his hips when he stepped onto the wharf, letting the wind push him as he slowed down. He had never really stopped looking ill. 'The blockade, Tournier. I can't send you anywhere, you'd be killed trying.'

'We got through.'

'We had no choice. We had to get you ashore. Sixty-four people were killed.'

'Are you really trying to blame me for that?'

'No,' Kite said, 'I'm explaining why I don't want to do it again.'

'I could go over land.'

'There are French garrisons all the way to Glasgow.'

Joe fought the urge to hit him. 'I speak French and I can lie, what's the problem?'

'One slip and they'll have you. Your French isn't their French, even I can hear that.'

'Well, the blockade isn't going anywhere.'

They had been walking along the dock, not into town. Now, they were among ramps where half-made hulls stood partly under tarpaulin, and then past a building so long Joe couldn't see the end of it. The doors were open, though, and inside, dozens of men were working on enormous stretches of rope, as long as the building. It smelled of tar. Just up ahead was a wooden bridge between the sea and an enclosed part of the dock. It was perfectly rectangular and empty; or, Joe thought it was empty. He jumped when something grumbled in the water. A pair of men had wound a pair of wheels on either side of the pond, which lifted a net and, in the net, half a woodland's worth of trimmed-down pine trunks rolled together and round each other. The noise was like God's own wind chimes. Masts. The pond must have been part of the process of treating the wood. Joe had no idea.

'It will be. I just need to talk to Lord Lawrence. I can't break a blockade without orders.'

'My daughter might be disappearing while you're fretting.' Joe heard how unfair it was while he was saying it. Lawrence had beaten Kite half to hell while Joe stood there; God knew what he was like in private. No one in their right mind could call how Kite must have felt about that man *fretting*, but the control Kite had over his own voice was maddening, and the longer he kept it up, the harder Joe wanted to hack it down. Even as the anger started to boil, he could feel that if Kite would just say, look, I'm terrified and I need another day, he would have calmed down. 'Go and talk to him now.'

They both glanced towards the sea, because a ship had just fired a training round. It was a monster next to all the frigates around it. The *Victory*. It was even more battered than *Agamemnon*.

'If I go there now, he's going to shoot me in the eye,' Kite said patiently. 'Just give it a few days.'

'There's going to be a siege in a few days!'

'Just – there is nothing I can do to get you home now this second. I'm sorry.'

Joe caught his arm and spun him back. 'You've got no intention of letting me go, have you? And it's nothing to do with whether I'm useful or not. You're punishing me.'

'What?'

'You don't think I have the right to go home,' Joe said, not caring that some people on the dockside were looking at them now. In fact, he was glad. When he wasn't being anyone's captain, Kite was quiet; exactly the kind of person who hated public scenes. 'Your sister is dead, and so is Jem, and I keep on and on about my family. No?' he said, because Kite had been shaking his head. 'You can say honestly you don't hate it?'

'Of course I hate it!' When Kite snapped, he lowered his voice rather than raised it, but it felt like whiplash all the same. 'I know officers who didn't ask for leave for their children's funerals, and that isn't extraordinary; it's just how it should be or there would be no navy. Family is a luxury, and watching you chase after them at the expense of the well-being of thousands of people is repulsive. But I'm not punishing you for anything, Tournier, I physically have not the means to help you now this instant.'

Joe was savagely glad to have got something out of him at last. 'I'm not *repulsive* for wanting to go home, Kite. I'm normal. You're lonely. You don't object to me because I'm endangering anyone, you object because I'm *not* lonely and I *have* a home to go back to.' He had meant to stop there, but it was the mechanical voice that took over then, because he was furious, and he knew all of Kite's weak places now, and exactly which sticks to shove into them. 'You wish I was just as lonely as you, because then I might stay. I remind you of Jem and you were in love with him. You had to be, the way you pine and sulk. But I'm not Jem, and you're a nasty creep with a disgusting little crush that's grown on you like rot. Grow the fuck up.'

Kite slowed right down. He watched Joe for too long. Joe stiffened, waiting for a punch in the face, but it never came. 'If I send you off without approval from Lawrence,' Kite said, inhumanly level, 'he'll send someone after you. They'll hurt you, and I don't mean a knock to the head. They'll hurt you until you swear honest fealty to the King. Whether you like it or not, it *is* for me to say what's safe and what isn't, because you are a member of my crew, and I am responsible for your life. You're not going anywhere until that blockade is cleared. Do you understand?'

Responsible raked its fingernails along a nerve Joe hadn't even known he had. Responsible was for slaves. You didn't keep promises to slaves.

'I understand,' Joe said.

'Good. I have to buy a mast. Do what you like for now. Keep with him,' Kite added to the marines. 'I'll see you back at the house for dinner.'

The mechanical voice was raging.

I'll fucking show you responsible.

Joe turned off onto a random street and walked until he found what he was looking for: a woman putting out washing. He slipped through the open door behind her and through the house, out the front. Nobody noticed. He waited, but the marines didn't come after him. Then he walked as quickly as he could to the castle.

He had been too disorientated and too tired to notice when they'd first come up, but there were barricades on the road

– star-shaped hulks of wood spaced far enough apart to admit people but not horses. There was traffic on both sides; carters from the city were stopping to unload onto carts that must have been running the rest of the way up to the castle, and then having to go through the precarious business of turning around at the front of the queue.

People were ducking through the horses and the wheels. Close to the barricade, children held signs saying they would courier packages up for much less than the official carts did. Joe went through slowly, part of a single-file shuffle. The points of two star-arms met just above his head. They'd been salvaged from ships. One of the beams still had rope loops pegged into it, the kind that ran along all the ceilings on *Agamemnon* so you could hang hammocks. He glanced back down the hill in case the marines had guessed where he was going. The crowd was full of men in the same red jackets, but none of them were hurrying. Slimy unease turned over in his stomach again even so. Kite had known what he was going to do, he was sure.

He gave himself a shake. Kite was not omniscient.

He followed the way round, up the steep hill and past the forbidding guards, until he found the Admiralty's surprisingly small building opposite the prison.

He had no idea if Lord Lawrence would be in and he thought that, if he wasn't, he'd have to bribe someone or do some sneaking. But when he asked the servant inside, the servant stared at him for too long, then nodded and saw him up so quickly that Joe wondered if the man was worried about voodoo curses waiting to be deployed on the unobliging.

At the top of the stairs was a library. Lawrence was the only person there, settled in an armchair by the fire, with a bottle of red wine open beside him. His tiger was there too. She loped across and rubbed her head against Joe's hip. Tentatively, Joe stroked her neck.

325

'What are you doing here?' Lawrence frowned. 'Aren't you supposed to be in the gaol?'

'I was under guard, sir, but I wanted to see you.'

He lifted his eyebrows. They were black, and they looked too dark with the grey wig. 'Why?'

Why? Well. What I'd really like you to do, you see, is arrest Missouri Kite and chuck him in a cell as he richly deserves, and in the inevitable chaos that will ensue when your soldiers come for him, everyone will forget about me for at least a minute. That's more than long enough to get on my way to Eilean Mòr.

Or maybe I won't be so lucky, maybe you'll be organised and you'll hand me to some other captain to look after, but whoever that is, I'll take my chances. Maybe I can't talk my way round Kite, but that's because he's a block of cement. Other people aren't.

You aren't.

Watch.

Joe took a deeper, slower breath. 'I have to report a murder. Kite killed a midshipman.'

Lawrence sharpened. 'Midshipman.'

'Frederick Hathaway, sir. I think he was the Earl of Wiltshire's son.'

Lawrence lost the reluctance in his manner instantly, just like Joe had known he would. 'You saw this?'

'Yes, sir. It was stormy, and I was playing with Hathaway, we were looking for shapes in the water. Kite came out of the cabin to talk to him. I looked back at the wrong moment. He pushed him overboard. I pretended not to have seen.'

'Why on earth would he do that?'

'I wish I knew; he'd scare me less.'

Lawrence only paced. He was one of those men who made far more noise than he had to, and his steps banged as he thumped over the Turkish rug. He walked without bending his knees much. When he reached the table, he picked up the brandy decanter.

'And you tell me this why?' he asked abruptly as he poured out a measure.

Joe felt strange. It should have been difficult, coming in here and talking to an important man he didn't know, but it wasn't. After all the time he'd spent sidestepping around de Méritens and sweet-talking M. Saint-Marie, after coping with Kite, it was nothing. 'He's either mad or going mad. I understand why I was pressed, I can't argue that and God knows I want a free England.' The patriotic rubbish came easily after all the insanity the Saints spouted. *God Save the King!* 'But I think he's going to shoot me before I can get the job done.' He inclined his head. 'If I wanted to run away, sir, I could have done it right now. I don't.'

Because if I go now then Kite will come after me like a prince of hell.

Lawrence nodded slowly. 'You could have,' he agreed. He watched him for a long time. 'You are right about Missouri, naturally. Anyone could tell you that. But this doesn't mean you'll be freed for your trouble. I ought to put you in the gaol right now, in fact. He took you out without my permission.'

'No, sir, I was hoping it would mean I would work under your supervision rather than his. As I say, I *want* to help.' He shifted in what he hoped was an awkward way. 'But you don't seem the type to hold a pistol to a man's kneecap.'

And you're much stupider than Kite. Anyone with a temper like yours is a moron.

'Oh, he is delightful, isn't he,' Lawrence said irritably. 'It's what comes of letting carpenters' boys become captains – Agatha wouldn't be told, of course. She paid for the commission. I hadn't the heart to stop her.' He snorted his breath out again. The longer Joe was with him, the more he seemed like a stunted buffalo. 'I'm sure we can arrange something less ballistic. Have you made the machine I asked for yet?'

'This morning. Two machines, they communicate with each other. One is on *Agamemnon* now, one is in Lord Howe's office. They work. They'll allow the navy to talk to the land without signal flags over about twenty miles.'

Lawrence lifted his peppery eyebrows. 'Twenty miles. That's quite something, lad.'

'It's standard,' Joe said. 'I've given Mr Kite the specifications.'

'Good. Very good. And I hope you'll be able to make us other things too?'

'Yes, sir. I mean to.' He held Lawrence's eyes, clear and straight. 'But if you put me in the prison, he'll know I spoke to you. He doesn't seem like the kind of man I'd like to give a warning to.'

'Ah, how nice of you to be concerned about me.'

'I'm not. I'm very concerned about me.'

Lawrence seemed to take that as the sign of an honest man. 'Only sensible. Now, can I trust you to take yourself back?'

Lily had laid more sophisticated traps. 'No.' He made himself look worried. 'I got a bit lost on the way here. If you'd send someone with me I'd be grateful.'

'Good,' Lawrence laughed. He shook Joe's hand. He had warm dry palms, unscarred, and a firm handshake. 'Very good. Now let me see you out. Under no circumstances tell him that you spoke to me, do you understand? He'd kill you.'

'Yes, sir.'

'Good boy.'

See? Easy.

Joe went straight back to Kite's rooms, where Lawrence's men left him and where he could hear voices arguing through the door. When he opened it, Kite and the two marines looked around.

The towers of Robespierre Bridge were mostly taken up with the space required by the pivot of the bascules. When the bridge came up, counterweights swung down inside the towers in arcs, in twin chambers the size of concert halls. He'd been there once, on maintenance work. The bridge staff had forgotten about him and a tall ship came unexpectedly downriver. The bridge had begun to lift, and the bascules silent, had reached halfway down the room before Joe saw. They had already covered the door. There was a space of about four feet wide at the very far end of the chamber that was safe. Despite knowing that, he hadn't trusted it and flattened himself to the wall, expecting to be crushed. He hadn't been able to move for a while afterward.

This felt like that.

'I lost you two,' he said. 'I've been looking for you for an hour, where did you go?'

'You disappeared down through someone's garden – sir, he was trying to—'

'It was a girl selling apples. I went to get some and when I looked back out you two had buggered off.'

The older marine had turned red. 'You didn't come back out. We looked for you.'

'I thought you were right behind me. If you'd walked *with* me instead of prowling around behind me like a pair of bloody hyenas—'

'Sir!'

Kite let the silence go on for much longer than he might have. Watching him consider was worse than hearing him speak.

'Sir,' the marine said, much more softly.

'Call off the others.'

They went, fast.

'I *was* looking for them,' Joe said, copying the man's urgency. 'I was – it was ten seconds and then they were gone.'

Kite studied him for a long time and Joe looked back, though the air was fizzing.

'All right. Have you eaten yet?' Kite said.

Joe nearly collapsed. 'No.'

'Come on then.'

Joe picked up his coat again and struggled to grip, because his hands were shaking. 'Don't do anything to my kneecaps, please. Or to theirs.'

'I'm not going to. What did you do?' Kite said, starting to smile.

'Nothing. What I said.'

'Mm,' he said.

Joe faltered, because he'd expected him to ask more and argue more, and be angrier. Uncomfortably, he realised that Kite sounded a lot like he knew exactly where Joe had been and who he'd spoken to. On the chance that it was only the lethargy of grief and tiredness, he locked his teeth together and followed him downstairs. The house felt too hot now. Sweat slid down his spine. By the time it reached his waistband it was unpleasantly cold.

A distant boom sounded from the harbour. It wasn't their own guns; the French were doing drills, just on the horizon. Joe looked towards the castle and wondered greyly what Lawrence would do now, if there would at least be time to eat first. Downstairs they were serving something whose name Joe didn't know, but it smelled rich and good.

When Kite tried to pay, the bartender waved the money away. He was the man from yesterday, and Joe wondered if he was the owner, to be working such long hours. It was brave in daylight in front of all the marines, too, dressing like that, but no one seemed minded to arrest him.

'On the house.'

'Thank you. Why?' It was only the simple way he talked, but over small things Kite could sound like a child.

'That ship whose mast you got on your way into port? Sank this morning.'

'Good,' Kite murmured. Some men whistled and clapped. He lifted his glass to them. He didn't mind the attention, but he didn't like it either. He wasn't Captain Kite now, just Missouri – he'd switched over as soon as he'd let the marines go. Joe wished, fierce, that the captain side of him would reappear soon. He didn't want to see Missouri taken away.

'There's a free booth,' the barman said to Joe. 'Better hide him before he breaks in half.'

'Thanks. Ah ...'

'Hetty.' It was a bit sharp, defensive.

'Joe,' said Joe, pleased. He caught himself smiling his charm smile, and the mechanical voice saying how useful it would be to know someone who lived downstairs, with all the keys, and who had enough money to wear pearls, with perhaps some spare goodwill. He glanced at the front windows. No one coming yet.

'Any chance you mean to run the blockade?' Hetty said hopefully to Kite.

'I'd love to. But no orders.' Very occasionally, he let a Spanish accent slip through into his English. Joe had thought it was random at first, but he was starting to see that it happened when Kite wanted you to know he was telling the absolute truth.

'Damn orders, the Admiralty's just the bunch of cowards who wasn't good enough to go to sea.'

That got a round of applause from the people near enough to overhear.

'Yeah, *de accuerdo*,' Kite said, but he was already walking away to the booth.

'How about King's fucking English?' someone said to him, then yelled when Kite smacked him face down into the table. The man's friends looked at him like he'd walked out in front of an omnibus.

Joe winced and went after Kite. In the booth, Kite sat back against the cushioned wall, into the watercolour light. Faint

331

freckles traced the bones around his eyes, and there were purple marks under them, so dark they could have been bruises.

Outside, a flash of red passed through all the rainy greys and browns in the street. A small party of marines was coming down the hill, with an officer in a black uniform Joe didn't recognise. He watched them come on, past all the boarding houses they might have been aiming for.

'Did you go and see Lord Lawrence earlier?' Kite said, from nowhere. It wasn't accusatory. He only sounded interested.

'What? No!'

'That was silly of you, wasn't it,' Kite said into his glass. 'Thought I'd be being shot around now.'

'Don't be dramatic. He wouldn't shoot you, he just wants to lock you up and give you a scare.' Joe could feel himself going red. Acting was much harder around Kite than anyone else.

Kite looked at him as if he'd started howling at the moon.

'Why would you sit here and wait, if you thought Lawrence was coming for you?' Joe demanded, angry again, but this time it was a hollow, worried anger that came of the suspicion he'd done something truly stupid.

'Mainly I'm too tired to get up.' Kite sounded like he was joking, but his focus had gone far away. He was holding the tattoo under his sleeve. 'That bed is murder.'

Joe turned the glass around on the table between his fingertips. He could feel the seconds dying. The kitchen girl came out to give them some bread and Kite smiled at her, polite rather than flirting. She smiled back, flirting rather than polite. Kite looked away.

The door smacked open. Joe pushed his fingernails into the spaces between the knuckles of his other hand when he heard a hard voice ask for Captain Kite. Kite glanced that way, not surprised. He was relieved.

38

Joe understood.

It was an efficient and unfussy suicide. Kite wasn't the sort of man to shoot himself and make his sailors find the body, or worry that he'd vanished. Lawrence could do it and all the rest would be the Admiralty's problem.

Joe didn't know what he'd expected. Something satisfying. Fury. A chance to say, got you. Not this rotting feeling that he'd attacked a wounded man. He felt sick, worse than sick. Panic was wrapping itself around all his insides exactly as it had on the steps of the castle chapel. He had honestly thought Lawrence would just lock Kite away for a while. He hadn't meant for Kite to die.

The mechanical voice inside his head hissed. It should not have been difficult to cause the death of a murderer who was holding Lily to ransom, it just shouldn't, and who gave a toss *what* Kite had said or done on that lost night at the lighthouse. There was *nothing* he could have done to deserve this ridiculous attachment.

Knowing that made no difference. Like before, Joe's throat had closed up, his heart was squeezing, and his fists had clenched themselves so hard he could feel his nails making marks in his palms.

Hetty was pretending not to know who the soldiers were talking about. The officer in black pounded his fist onto the bar. Hetty flinched and nodded towards them.

'Missouri Kite,' the officer said when he saw them. 'You are under arrest at the pleasure of His Majesty and the Admiralty of Great Britain and Ireland for the murder of—'

Something in Joe's head shut down, and something else snapped awake. Whatever it was, it wasn't *him*. It was something else; someone else.

He punched the man in the face. It hurt a lot and he wished he had put his sleeve over his hand first.

The marines started to draw their swords, but the men who had cheered Kite were already up and some of them had guns. Joe hadn't hit the officer hard enough and the man wrenched out his own gun. Joe bumped back against the edge of the table.

'I'll shoot him through your eye, I swear to God.'

Joe wanted to tell him to get on and do it, but his voice wasn't working. He stayed where he was anyway. A feverish part of him observed that he looked far too scared to convince anyone he'd stand there long.

A shot went off behind him and the officer collapsed. It was so loud it was agony. He had to smack his hand over his ear. When he looked back, the muzzle of Kite's gun was resting on his shoulder. Kite let it drop while the smoke was still breathing. It smelled like fireworks. Joe thought he was going to tell the sailors to let the marines go, and go with them anyway. He hadn't killed the man, only shot him through the shoulder; although with a bullet the size of a marble, it was horrific all the same.

'Disarm those men,' Kite said. 'Are there any signal lieutenants here?'

'Sir,' someone volunteered towards the back.

'Put a signal on *Agamemnon*'s mast. Anyone who wants to break the blockade should come now.' Then, much lower, 'Joe? Are you all right?'

'I'm …' Joe had meant to say fine, but found himself shaking. He looked down at his hands. He felt disconnected

334

from himself, but he couldn't have said where the loose coupling was.

Kite was holding his shoulders. 'It'll go off in a minute.'

Joe nodded, acutely conscious that he must, to Kite, look so pathetic that he deserved to be shot. 'Sorry.'

'If you don't freeze the first time someone points a gun in your face, you're mad,' Kite whispered. He bent his neck to catch Joe's eyes, so that their foreheads almost touched. 'I met a man once who didn't. Turned out he had fifteen women buried in his garden.'

Joe laughed, which came out more like coughing. Kite smiled too. The shaking went off. Joe let his breath out slowly. He nodded when his lungs filled properly again.

'Why did you *do* that?' Kite asked. There was real indignation under his voice. 'You could have been killed.'

Joe shook his head. He still didn't know, but the more he thought about it, the more unnerving it was. Getting up and punching that man had felt like being a marionette someone else was moving.

The carpenters had been working on the *Agamemnon* since it came in. The hole over the gun deck was covered and tarred. The dock had been sluggish five minutes before, but now, men were flooding to the gangplanks and the boats. Other ships had put up the same flags as the ones on *Agamemnon*'s mast. Drums rolled out everywhere and people shouted through the doors of boarding houses. Half of Edinburgh must have been waiting for the order.

'Is there a plan?' Joe asked. He was waiting with Kite by the rail on the quarterdeck, feeling out of place, because people who weren't officers weren't generally invited onto the quarterdeck. But Kite had asked him and he was hoping he wasn't meant to stay there all the way through.

'It's easy to break a blockade, you just have to get on and do it,' Kite said, distractedly, because he was showing one of the midshipmen a piece of paper. It was the semaphore code. A few seconds later, new flags started to run the mast. When Joe looked to either side, other flags, answers, came up from other ships. There were twelve in all.

The semaphore conversation went on as the flags changed. There were only nine different flags; everything was made of those, with different numbers corresponding to different words. A wrong one must have gone up, because Kite waved at the lieutenant and tapped two fingers against his palm, then three, to correct it. From the open doors of the stateroom, Joe could just hear the hesitant dits and dahs of Lieutenant Wellesley telegraphing the army office at the castle. The conversation had been going on a little while, and already, there were soldiers in red jackets marching down from the steep road up to their barracks. This was history changing; it had to be. Joe couldn't remember how the Siege of Edinburgh had begun, but he didn't think it could have been with the smashing of the French blockade.

He bent forward over his arms. He didn't know if he would be able to get through another battle.

Lieutenant Wellesley came out and waved up at them. She looked worried.

'Something funny's happening to the telegraph,' she called.

In the stateroom, something funny was indeed happening. The telegraph was receiving a signal, beeping and clacking, but it wasn't the army office at the castle. The coding was fluent and smooth, fast. And French. Joe went to it and bent down to make sure the paper stayed straight as it emerged from the transcript reel.

—*signs of action in the harbour stop might be a drill stop but Agamemnon has hoisted her colours stop*—

'Christ,' he breathed. 'They have these too. This is the French signal. They're talking about us, they've seen us.'

Kite had come down after him. 'Can they hear us?'

'They'll hear us if we start coding again. I didn't give you a modulating frequency because I didn't think anyone else would be on the line.' Joe held his hand out to stop anyone asking him what a modulating frequency was and listened again.

—*message received Angleterre stop take up position by the headland* ...

And so Joe listened and wrote things down, and drew out the French battle plan right there. He handed it to Kite. Kite took it, expressionless for a full five seconds while he read. But then the mask broke and when he lifted his eyes, there was hope in them, real hope. It took years off him. He shook Joe's hand in both of his.

'Thank you,' he said softly, and set something down on the floor by Joe's boot. He stepped up close and spoke right by Joe's ear. 'This definitely isn't a bag with a French uniform and a map in it, and you definitely shouldn't take it and go now.'

Joe stared at him, then at the bag. The others were still busy with the telegraph; Lieutenant Wellesley and an excited midshipman even younger than Fred. Kite squeezed his hand one last time and let him go with the very smallest glow of a smile.

Clay burst in. Joe had never seen him move so fast. 'This,' he said, one finger right in Kite's face, 'is *mutiny* and you fucking *know it*!'

'Yes, it is. Go ashore with Mr Tournier, you don't need to be here.'

'I'm not going anywhere with him!' He smacked Joe in the chest.

'Joe – can you take him and the children ashore, please.'

'Mutiny,' Clay said in one of his eerily adult moments, 'is what got me where I am. That said, I'll enjoy it if they flog *him* round the fleet,' he said to Kite, and smiled in a sick, mad way.

'No, you wouldn't, you'd be bored. It takes ages to give some-one three hundred lashes,' Kite said, but he was set and pale in the way he always was when he was in pain. 'Joe, don't listen to him, it's fine. Please – get ashore. We're leaving in about twenty seconds.'

*

Southampton, 1798

Jem and Agatha were in Bath for a honeymoon, so Kite had gone back to Southampton to see if there was anything to do. Refitting a ship was mainly just carpentry, but he liked it; hammering in some pegs for a few hours a day was much better than sulking around Jermyn Street by himself.

He got off the coach from London stiff and hungry, and feel-ing that odd catch between irritable and sad that long journeys always provoked. The cold trip out to *Defiance* on a rowing boat was a prospect that loomed more than it should have. It was only gradually that he noticed the docks looked wrong. There was no one working, and no boats coming to and fro from the ships at anchor. At the jetty which would have taken people out, there was a rope line, and a sign.

Ongoing mutiny on Defiance. Any incoming officers, report to Admiralty.

'No,' he said aloud to the sign, not understanding. He'd seen mutinies before, but only on ships with bad officers. Everyone loved Heecham, and Tom and Rupert Grey were universally popular lieutenants. *Defiance* was the very model of a cheerful ship.

'Oh, Kite,' someone said, and he twisted around to find Heecham stumping towards him along the wharf. He looked miserable. 'What a mess. Come to see them take her back?'

'Pardon, sir?'

Heecham pointed with two fingers to a ship Kite hadn't noticed, just setting sail. It was the *Calcutta*, and on the deck were at least two hundred marines. They were fixing their bayonets. 'The Admiralty wants to keep the men quiet about Castlereagh and the *Kingdom*. Lord Lawrence left them out there all this time with no food. They mutinied yesterday to demand supplies, like he bloody knew they'd have to.' He coughed, but it was more of a sob. 'Captain Bligh's got orders to take a few men, the ringleaders. But the rest of them are not going to get off that ship alive if a single man tries to fight. And if they don't try to fight, Bligh shall have to say that they did.'

'I don't understand,' Kite said, numb. 'No one would have believed them. This is ridiculous.'

Heecham gave him a hollow look. 'Missouri. They would all have told exactly the same story. They would all have talked about Castlereagh, named him even. The French would have snatched him within a week.'

Kite almost laughed. 'They already tried! My sister just married him to keep it from happening again. If someone kills Agatha Lawrence's husband, the proportionate response would be – destroying Nice.'

Heecham dropped his face into his hands and wept with an awful shudder. Kite gripped his shoulder, hating Lawrence more than he had hated anything.

There was nothing to do but watch as the *Calcutta* drew up alongside *Defiance*. Someone on *Defiance* put up a white flag on the yardarm. Heecham put his hand over Kite's eyes and told him he'd seen nothing of the sort. The marines boarded anyway, and then there were gunshots.

When the shots stopped, they trailed away together, and drank in silence at a dockside bar.

A week later, the four men who'd written the demands to the Admiralty and organised everyone were flogged around the fleet: three hundred lashes each. It was the kind of sentence the Admiralty only ever handed down if the mutiny had been violent, if officers had been killed. Usually a straightforward mutiny about food was just embarrassing. Not this time. The story was of foul malcontent, nefarious plans. Anything shocking to distract from any mention of the *Kingdom*. When Kite read the news-sheets afterwards, it had worked. Not a word about the *Kingdom* or Jem had made it out.

Three of the men died, but one didn't. Kite watched, because he felt like he had to. Heecham had to leave halfway through to be sick in the sea.

39

Edinburgh, 1807

Joe herded the children down the gangway ahead of him, shocked by how many there were – about forty. They were all grumbling about being made to go, even Alfie, who complained that he wanted to be allowed to do his duty thank you very much. On the dock, Joe lifted him up so he could see the ships go out.

'It's a mutiny, lad,' Clay told him. 'Don't want to get caught up in that. Even if they win, they'll all be shot.'

Joe kicked his ankle. 'Can you shut up about mutiny?'

'Mutiny on *Defiance*, they shot everyone,' Clay said implacably. He gave Joe a poisonous look. 'Mr Castlereagh was too secret, so the Admiralty killed everyone who'd seen the *Kingdom*. Let us starve till we mutinied, then they shot everyone. Except me and the other people who organised it. Flogged round the fleet. They didn't expect me to make it.'

Joe frowned. 'I thought Kite did this to you?'

Clay frowned back. 'No. Mr Kite looked after me.'

*

London, 1798

Clay had woken up in a bright, white room in a single bed. Someone touched his shoulder, and a glass of water appeared in his hands. He took it carefully, not wanting to spill it on the crisp linen. It wasn't his. It must have been expensive. Whoever owned it would be furious. When he tried to sit up, he screamed. A voice, a familiar one, told him everything was going to be all right, but even while it was happening, it sounded like a memory, because he couldn't think of anything except how his entire body seemed to be on fire.

Of all the people in the world he could have expected to see, Heecham's youngest lieutenant wouldn't even have been on the list. He was the one all the men were afraid of because he always looked like he might kill someone. Clay wondered if that might be true, and tried to edge away, but then he had to do some more screaming.

'No – no, it's all right,' Kite was trying to say. 'You're safe.'

Clay sat propped panting against the cold wall, not sure what was going on, or what might happen next. He wished Kite would take the glass of water away. The glass was very thin. Easily smashed.

There was a tiger sitting next to him.

That couldn't possibly be real.

'If you could try and drink ...'

Something was wrong with him, really wrong, but he couldn't remember what it was. He remembered being ill for a long time, and he sort of remembered a carriage, but the greater part of him shied away from getting at anything too clear. It would be bad. There was a strange, howling blackness where the normally-thinking part of him had used to be.

'You can touch her, look,' Kite said. The tiger was real. It pawed at the sheets next to Clay's hand. Clay wondered feverishly if Kite had always been mad or if it was a recent thing.

Not wanting to, but scared Kite would do something nasty if he didn't, he put his fingertip out and brushed the tiger's head, then took his hand back as fast as he could. Why Kite wanted him to make friends with a wild beast he had no idea, but he was pretty damn certain that he had more chance of staying alive now if he did as he was told. He glanced at the door. It was propped open, just, but then there was no telling how many locked doors there were between here and any way out. And there was the problem of not being able to move.

'Are you hungry?' Kite asked.

'No.'

'You need to eat.'

Clay stared at him and wondered what he would do with a refusal. More dark, more hospital, more – that black storm in his mind howled and burned and raged when he tried to touch it – bad stuff. 'All right,' he whispered.

'All right, good,' Kite said, looking pleased. 'That's good.'

Kite seemed not to understand that any thinking person would do as he was bloody told whether he felt sick or not in the face of a tiger and a madman who kept a tiger. A bowl of fruit was forthcoming. Clay picked at it, having to force things down. He didn't know what half of it was: foreign something. Kite was foreign, someone had said that. He glanced up at Kite every few mouthfuls, waiting for some sign that this was enough and he could stop, but Kite only watched him, and it became horribly clear that he meant for Clay to get through the whole bowl.

About halfway through, the door opened. Clay looked up, hoping that whoever it was might take Kite away or at least distract him, but the hope died. It was that Castlereagh man. The one it had all been for.

Without deciding to do it, he slung the bowl at the man's smug head and launched himself after it, scratching and screaming and then crying when Kite lifted him away.

'Clay – Rob! Rob, it's all right ... please, it's all right ...'

'It's his *fault*! If someone had just shot him then none of it would have *fucking happened*!'

Stumping steps on the stairs, devil's hooves, and then the door opened again, and a fat man in a long wig was in the frame. 'Who's that? What's all the noise?'

'The result of your clever plan,' Kite growled.

'How dare you! This is *my* house—'

'No, it's my wife's,' Castlereagh said from somewhere. 'And since this man's injuries, devastating as they are, seem to be the price of my life, the least I can do is give him a room while we're on shore leave.'

Kite nudged the door shut with his elbow. Anyone else would have kicked it, but that was one of the things that made him unsettling; he was calm. You knew where you were with someone who yelled and swore and slammed doors, that was why everyone loved Captain Heecham, but Kite – something about that eerie restraint had always given Clay the shivers.

The other two kept arguing outside, but inside was quiet. The tiger hopped up on the bed, offensively orange. Clay pressed his hands over his eyes in case it started to get too interested in those. And then the voices in the corridor were going away, banging down the stairs again, and everything was silent, except for the scuffle of the tiger in the white room as it bounced to the floor, and the click of its claws.

Kite never left him, and sometimes there was more food to choke down and an evil woman who did things to his back that made him shriek. In the evenings, the fire turned Kite's hair devil red. After a while, Clay realised that he was in hell. But, as hell went, it was all right. Kite was an anxious sort of devil, one Clay liked before long. Castlereagh never reappeared, frightened off maybe.

Clay decided to kill him one day. He felt much better after that.

*

Edinburgh, 1807

'Clay,' Joe said. 'What happened to Jem? Did *you* kill him, did Kite cover for you?'

It was useless. Clay was playing rock paper scissors with Alfie, not listening.

It didn't matter any more anyway.

The dock was in happy chaos. If someone had told Joe the day before that half of Edinburgh would stream out to cheer on a naval battle on its own doorstep, and that people would have found, at five minutes' notice, Scottish flags to fly and thistles to sell at little side stalls to wear as good-luck charms, he would have said they were demented. But there was a festival joy all along the harbour.

Sailors were still pouring onto the ships, and surgeons in indigo were setting up tents at intervals of about a hundred yards, ready for the wounded. Pipers and drummers had gone out onto the wharves. Either they had all decided to play the same thing, or the song was the obvious choice; Joe didn't know it, but the pipes were so piercing even the French ships must have heard them. The sound ghosted up around the masts in an eerie wail. He had meant to run straight away, but he stood rooted, because now that he was listening, it was familiar.

There was a human roar as the ships let their sails down and caught the wind. The French were tacking landward, in exactly the formations they had discussed on the telegraph. The harbour must have been in range of their long guns, but nobody seemed to care. Joe had never seen a crowd of people behave like it. Not a single person ran away when the first rounds fired. Instead there was a surge towards the sea. Joe saw a cannon shot hit a medical tent.

Still no one ran.

Instead, the harbour erupted. The drums went up again, but this time it wasn't so Scottish-sounding. Because the singing started a good way off, he didn't recognise the Marseillaise at first. But by the time it reached *aux armes, citoyens*, it was all around him. Until then, it had been a dull song you had to mumble around the Emperor's birthday at Mass and sometimes at an international cricket match. He knew the lyrics more or less, but he hadn't given them much thought. He'd never really heard what it was: a blood song, full of impure gore and slaughterfields. It was a song to rip a man's throat out by.

It was a new one on him, singing the enemy's own national anthem at them, but whoever had thought to do it was right; it was unnerving.

He turned away. Clay seemed not to notice, even though Alfie waved.

It felt like hours before he found a post house. He stole inside, then stole a horse. No one questioned it; he had seen a man sweeping in the yard, but everyone else must have gone to the harbour.

He'd thought that finally being on his way home would feel fantastic, but even after he was out of the city gates, it didn't. He felt like something in him had been anaesthetised and cut out.

Part V

NEWGATE

40

The Glasgow road, 1807

Joe rode out of Edinburgh among a train of ordinary people heading east with geese and baskets, but the throng thinned only a few hundred yards up the road as they turned off onto footpaths through the fields. After a mile, he was the only one. Kite was right: there was a French blockade across the way ahead, made of ten-foot hopjacks like the ones outside the castle. He approached it with his hands up and off the reins. Once they heard his voice, they lowered their rifles. He told some lies about reconnaissance, and then pretended to be angry when they asked him about passwords.

'I've been in that shithole for six pissing months, how am I supposed to know your poxy password? Do I *look* Scottish to you?'

They let him through.

He kept on in the dark and didn't stop until after midnight, through two more roadblocks. He had to pay a bribe at one for having no papers (Kite had given him money too), but they pointed him to a garrison, a remade Roman fortress another mile on. It was a bleak tower on a hill, where, somehow, there was mist and rain at the same time. He was so cold now that he couldn't tell if he was gripping the reins or not. Staying outside for the night was out of the question.

The guards stopped him at the gate and asked why he hadn't got papers, in the bored way of people who saw incomers without papers all the time, so he snapped in a way he hoped was officerly and they let him in faster than before.

The courtyard was full of heavy artillery. The guns were sitting on their chassis, lined up among wooden boxes of ammunition and spare parts. They were bulkier and even more unwieldy than the English guns. These ones didn't even have flintlocks, only fuses. It was a miracle they ever hit anything. Sore, with his ribs aching, he led the horse around the curve of the path, hoping to come across a stable soon. Someone had chalked *Stable* and a stick horse on the wall beside an arrow, so that seemed promising. Someone else, in differently coloured chalk, had added the inevitable.

A stable boy was dozing on some hay just inside, but he jerked awake when he heard hooves and hurried up to take the reins. Joe gave him some money and asked where to go. There was a side door. There were so many soldiers billeted there that they had set up camp beds in rows down the hall like a hospital and even then most people were sharing. He managed to tuck himself alone into a corner away from the fire where no one wanted to go.

He lay looking at the window. There was a thin moon outside. It vanished slowly and drizzle pattered on the glass. Inch by inch, he felt safe. There were whispers all around, but they were ordinary and homely; someone was arguing about why the army would go to hell if collar stocks were abolished, and someone else was hoping they would be allowed leave soon, because it was his daughter's birthday in three weeks and he had missed the last one.

The rain gusted again and turned to hail. It was so cold the tip of his nose was numb. The men in the beds all around him had pulled the blankets up over their heads. Mattresses squeaked as people tried to curl themselves up into as little a space as possible.

Because he had done all this week, he thought he would sleep, but it was back to the usual now; when he did doze, he jerked awake in a borderless panic. He knocked his hand hard against the wall. It was made of narrow Roman bricks, etched with graffiti from centuries of people who must not have wanted to be sleeping here any more than he did.

He tried to tell himself that it was all right, that Lily would be at home waiting. There was no reason why she shouldn't be – nothing had changed yet, really – but he couldn't calm down. He sat up and hugged his knees.

Kite was going to die soon whether the French took Edinburgh or not. He walked into fires and nobody stopped him because they all thought that was what he was for.

Joe thumped his own heart, wishing that the tightness over his ribs would stop screwing itself down and down. He had been fine on *Agamemnon* – not to mention at Kite's rooms, sleeping across from someone who made a habit of threatening to shoot him. It had been so good he'd thought the sleep problems might finally be over.

He pushed his hand into his pocket and took out the lighthouse postcard, feeling tired and wry to have to use it as a sleep talisman again. He tipped it towards the nearest light. It was dim, but because he knew what the words were already, he could make them out.

Dearest Joe,
Come home, if you remember.
M

He had read it hundreds of times, thousands, but this time was different. The world shifted. Always, without question, he had thought it was from Madeline. But he had read Madeline's letter, seen pages and pages of her clear strict handwriting.

This wasn't her writing.

It was Kite's.

The same egg-white horror which had slid down his spine that day at the Gare du Roi was back again now. He curled forward, wanting to scream.

Someone was pacing up and down the lines with a candle. He'd been aware of it before, but he glanced up when the candle reached him.

'Tournier, is it?' the man with the candle said.

Joe realised too late that he should have said no. The man dragged him up by one arm and wrenched him out of the hall.

The man with the candle dumped Joe in a chair in front of a desk. At the desk sat a neat, sharp man in a French lieutenant's uniform.

'I'm Colonel Herault, I oversee naval intelligence,' he said politely. 'You are Joseph Tournier?'

Joe sat back from him. It was uncanny to meet someone who he'd read about. Herault was just like Madeline had described him: slim and foxy, a bit too proper in the way of a really working-class person who'd polished themselves up. Then, immediately on the tail of that oddness, Joe felt exposed. He was one of the Kingdoms. Herault knew exactly who he was; Herault had seen him before.

'I suppose I should say it's ... nice to meet you again.'

'Again?' Herault looked blank. 'I don't think we've met.'

'We have.'

'What? When?'

Joe frowned, because he couldn't see any reason for Herault to lie about it.

'We haven't,' Herault told him, laughing a little. 'I assure you, I'd remember. Now: *are* you Joseph Tournier?'

'There are a thousand Joseph Tourniers,' Joe said slowly. 'What do you want?'

Herault showed him a piece of ticker tape from a telegraph. It had been printed with neat letters rather than just stamped with dots and dashes.

Message from a Scottish source. They have a future engineer.
This man will be on the Glasgow road from Edinburgh tonight.
Name Joseph Tournier, foreigner, brown hair green eyes, 6ft,
scar above left eye.

'Sounds like you, doesn't it,' Herault said, quite sympathetically. A broad fire crackled behind him.

Joe gazed down at the piece of paper.

Herault didn't know him.

Joe wasn't one of the Kingdoms. Kite had fed the whole stupid thing to him to distract him.

Of course he bloody had.

Which meant Joe could beg ignorance now. 'What's a future engineer?'

'I think you know, M. Tournier.'

'I don't.'

'Well, of course you say that. Let's see what you say after a while in Newgate.'

'Newgate's in London,' Joe said, a chasm opening in his chest. It was too much, piling up on too much. M was not Madeline but Missouri. He, Joe, had clearly never been on the *Kingdom*. He was right back to where he'd started, with no clue as to what had happened to him or why, and now here was a man who was going to take him to a gaol six hundred miles away. 'What's the point when there are prisons in Glasgow?'

'It'll be much harder for them to break you out of Newgate,' Herault said cheerfully. 'I don't believe even the notorious Captain Kite will be able to do much about Newgate, do you?'

'Captain Kite like the pirate?' Joe said, letting his voice mist helplessly. It wasn't difficult to sound helpless.

'Captain Kite like the pirate,' Herault agreed. 'Where did he *get* you? He can't have just stumbled over you.'

'I don't know what you're talking about. I don't know any pirates!'

Herault sat back in his chair, which was irritating, because he was acting the part of someone who felt comfortable, rather than someone who was. 'Do you know what I think? I think if you are who my source says you are, then I don't need to interrogate you to confirm it. All I need to do is blare out where you are in a national newspaper, and wait for an extremely well-known pirate to come and fetch you. You're worth a lot to him. Telegraphs! It took us years to work those out. You must be the very devil with future devices.'

Joe forced himself to fall still inside. 'I really ... don't understand what's going on, sir.'

'No, of course, of course, you're just a random passer-by who is unaccounted for in any of our garrison records and exactly answers a very precise description.' He smiled. 'You know what happens to pirates, when we catch them? And they *are* pirates. England is not a state any more, M. Tournier, it does not have officers who I must treat as prisoners of war. It is a group of bloody-minded savages who don't know when to admit they've lost. When I catch Missouri Kite, I shall have the pleasure of seeing him tried for treason against the Emperor, and then I shall have a nice champagne on the balcony of Buckingham Palace while he's torn apart by horses in the courtyard below. How would you like to be on that balcony with me?'

Joe arranged his face into baffled blankness. After sitting opposite Kite – Kite who really was balancing right on the edge of full-blown madness, Kite who had lost everything and who was turning piece by piece into a glass man – Herault wasn't sinister. He was about as frightening as a theatrically untalented puppy.

'If you say so, sir.'

'Where did Kite get you?' Herault said again.

'I don't know your Captain Kite. My master was called M. Saint-Marie.'

'Was,' Herault snapped.

'He died. I was – I was running away. I was trying to get to Edinburgh, they don't have slaves there, and ... I thought that was why you took me.' He lifted his eyes. 'It's not, though, is it. This ... Kite person? I'm not a pirate, sir, I'm ... please. Maybe I deserve a brand for trying to get away but I'm *not* – that.'

Herault was staring at him hard, but it was with the intensity of a person covering over some doubts. 'Where were you running from?'

'London, sir. Clerkenwell.'

'And you got all the way up here.'

'Yes, sir.'

'What street did you live on?'

'I don't know, sir, I was kept in the cellar. I can't read.'

'Kept in the cellar,' Herault echoed flatly. It was the way people talked about misfortune when they hadn't had any, like you must be making it up because, to them, it sounded so grotesquely unlikely. It struck them like a particularly disgusting piece of fiction, one that literary critics in *Le Monde* would say was a pile of depraved rubbish and which ought never to have been published.

'It was quite a nice cellar,' Joe offered. 'He gave me paints and things.'

'Just drop it, Tournier, I know it's you. I have your name and your description.'

'Sir, I ... far be it from me to tell you anything, but there *are* a thousand Joe Tourniers, and most of them look just like me.'

Herault stared at him for a long time. 'I'm sure you'll reconsider after a week in Newgate,' he said. 'And even if you don't, Kite will come for you.'

Joe lifted his eyes properly. 'Colonel, Captain Kite isn't going to come for me. Captain Kite doesn't know me.'

'We'll see,' Herault said tightly.

Joe didn't know what to hope for: that Kite would stay away, or that Kite would come.

All he could think of was two teams of horses waiting outside Buckingham Palace.

41

Edinburgh, 1807

There were fireworks on the deck, and a lot of rum going round. Kite had given up on keeping anything like a proper watch going. All of Edinburgh seemed be out on the docks tonight. There was music and more fireworks and the occasional squeak of someone too drunk falling in the sea, both from the jetties and the ships. And bonfires everywhere; people were burning the wreckage of the two French ships whose powder magazines had exploded.

They had taken a ship called the *Angleterre*, and given the atrocious state of *Agamemnon*, everyone had moved across, along with what must have been half the crews of the rest of the fleet. The hold, delightfully, was full of coal, so now there were braziers everywhere.

Kite felt hollowed out. There was nothing left to do.

He had nabbed the desk and the far end of the *Angleterre*'s stateroom before anyone else could, which was just as well. Over the other side of the room, around a mahogany table, a group of captains and officers from other ships were in the middle of an involved-looking card game, coats slung over the back of the ornate chairs. Some of them were snugged up under velvet throws. The French captain had been living quite a nice life.

Had been; Kite had shoved him in front of a firing squad, along with all the French officers. The man had seemed to think that was unfair, and remained unpersuaded even after all the

English officers pointed out that a lot worse was waiting for them in London if ever they were caught. Kite thought that was boorish of him. If you were going to dismember people outside Buckingham Palace, it was silly to go round being surprised when someone shot you.

The French sailors had been pressed firmly into English ranks.

'Wellesley! Almond croissant?' someone called.

His insides constricted. He had been trying to avoid Wellesley.

He put the cross of his rosary back into the candle again. It was haematite, because the wooden ones always got burned or broken.

'Have you seen Mr Kite?' Wellesley's voice asked. She sounded like she was halfway through a croissant.

'He *was* here, we must have put him somewhere. Oh, bugger. Fold.'

'I'm here,' he called past the oriental screens. Cowardly to hide. Smoke rose delicately from his arm as he pressed the cross against the tattoo. There were already two burned crosses over most of the lines already.

He hadn't really decided to get rid of it. He had just known he had to, as soon as he sat down. Normally he couldn't be anywhere near open flame without dissolving into shuddering moronhood, but this was different, maybe because it was to a purpose. The important fact wasn't that he was burning off a tattoo. It was that Joe was gone, and he wasn't coming home again.

Wellesley came through. 'Has Clay's cat put something in the fire again? I can smell— Jesus Christ! What if that goes bad!'

'I burned half my face off without too much difficulty, I think I'll be fine,' he said, half-smiling. 'Are you all right?'

Wellesley stared at him. 'You're not even drunk.'

'No?'

'Can you drink something please, sir,' she said, with a mix of rage and helplessness all battened down. She reached over to pick up the rum bottle from the edge of the desk, then froze when Kite flinched right back from her. He lifted his hands a little, trying to say without having to find the words that his nerves were frayed to oakum.

'Just the bottle,' she said carefully.

Kite gave it to her.

'Look, I can see this must be Mrs Castlereagh-related, and I suppose in theory that this particular moment is a ... a small lull, in which you might choose to go to pieces *somewhat*, but could you possibly rein it back in from flaying yourself? You know, pull it down to shouting at the mids or crying in a corner?' She sounded strained.

From beyond the screen came a collective groan as someone produced an unlikely hand. 'I'm fine. You'd be a lot more annoyed if I *were* having hysterics in the corner.'

'Should I be fetching an indigo to relieve you of duty?' she said sharply.

'You bring an indigo in here and I'll throw her at you.'

'Well, that's not very attractive, is it.'

'Wellesley. You mean to suggest I might be – *homely*?'

She gave him a patient look, but she was starting to laugh. 'Are there bandages in the desk?'

'Sorry?'

'There must be.' She came round and opened desk drawers until she found them. Kite jolted away when she tried to take his wrist. 'You can't leave that to the open air.'

Reluctantly, Kite let her have his arm. Wellesley got the bandage on quickly and neatly. He wished he could just be honest with her. She was one of the few people he knew who wasn't scared of him. She was six foot two, so to her he must have seemed small and manageable. He caught her watching him sometimes on the quarterdeck in the way he would have looked at a china figurine.

'Are there any orders yet, from the Admiralty?' she asked as she passed the bandage around his arm.

'No orders, hence the evening off. But apparently we're all getting an official pat on the head for acting so promptly on their command to break the blockade,' he said, smiling. 'You should join that poker game. Fleece them and buy some wine.'

She ignored him. 'That's quite something to pull off, sir. All-out fleet-wide mutiny and then making the Admiralty pretend they ordered it.'

'I imagine Lawrence will be by later to shoot me unofficially,' Kite forecast. He wondered how soon you heard the hellfire snickering round your ankles after you died. Not instantly, it couldn't be. It had taken the angels nine days to fall to Pandemonium from heaven, and Earth was halfway, so it stood to reason you got a half-week of peace and quiet en route.

'If you could pretend to be one or two atoms worried?' she said.

He frowned. 'What for?'

Clay sloped in and looked cross. 'Get rid of one, 'nother one turns up twice the bloody size.'

'Just the way of it,' said Wellesley, unmoved.

Clay scowled. Kite set both hands on the arms of the chair, ready to get up fast if Clay decided to go for her. 'Watch it or I'll sell you to the French and all.'

Kite froze. Something awful was snaking around the inside of his skull. 'Rob.'

'What?'

'What do you mean, you sold Joe to the French?'

Clay gave him a cold look, sane and measured. 'I put the code onto the machine thing and they answered.'

42

Santíssima Trinidad, the Irish Sea, 1807

They were sailing. Joe could feel the water bumping the
hull. He was lying on a bunk with a high side, knocking
against it sometimes. The cabin held eight or ten other beds, all
fitted to the walls at odd angles to account for the inward slope.
It was right in the prow of a ship, and it was dank. Crumbling
patches of wood, white with brine, made even reading the graffiti difficult.

The room must have been below the waterline, because it was
so cold. He tried to get up and found he was manacled to a slat
in the ceiling. When he called out, someone from somewhere
above, maybe at the top of a hatch he couldn't see, told him to
shut up.

He felt hazy and panicky, and when he touched his head, it
hurt. That was right; someone had hit him.

After the fort on the Glasgow road, there had been horses.
Colonel Herault had taken him to Glasgow with six men, going
hell for leather through the witching hours. They'd come to
the city in the early morning, the horses steaming. Joe had felt
bruised in places he didn't know he had. Everyone was tired, so
he tried to make a run for it, but they caught him and someone
smashed him over the head with the butt of a rifle.

He only remembered the docks in a drugged-feeling way.
Herault rode past frigates being refitted and brand-new ironclads where welders were soldering the pegs into towering

waterwheels, sparks everywhere and men with soot-black arms and masks on high, high ladders glancing down at the uniformed soldiers riding by. Past all of it, to a tall ship that could have held *Agamemnon* three times. Five decks, more than a hundred and thirty gun ports – Joe lost count – and a monstrous figurehead with three torsos: a crucified Christ, wearing the crown of thorns; God; and a thing half-hidden in a shroud like a leper. The ship was the *Santíssima Trinidad*, the Holy Trinity, so it must have been Spanish once, but the captain was French.

And then there were chains, and the darkness below deck, and endless eerie safety lamps, and all the while Joe couldn't shake the image of that shrouded figure carved into the prow. It all rolled into a fever nightmare.

They were moving fast now, too fast; he could feel it. When he put his hand on the wall, he could feel something else too, a thrum that had never been there on *Agamemnon*.

Engines.

43

HMS *Agamemnon*, 1807

'How in God's name are we going to get into Newgate?' Wellesley asked into the long quiet.

It was the morning after Joe had been taken, and he was headline news in *Le Nord*, which the smugglers got into port like clockwork at nine every morning. There was a press in Glasgow, and Kite suspected that the garrisons between there and here were under orders to let the papers through, certainly since the French had begun to use them as a kind of ammunition. Every week, there was another report of an English officer being torn to pieces outside Buckingham Palace, or another pocket of resistance in Cornwall being rounded up and shot. Today, the headline announced that the honourable Colonel Herault had caught one of the Republic's Most Wanted, a pirate engineer responsible for supplying the English with new technology. One Joseph Tournier, now on his way to Newgate Gaol.

'Easy,' Kite said. He pointed at the WANTED poster hanging on the wall. The one she'd forced him to put up, for a joke, and which she had brought in here from *Agamemnon* as a matter of principle.

Missouri Kite
WANTED
dead or alive

a hundred thousand francs
to be signed for by
THE WARDEN
of Newgate Gaol
as of December 1806.

44

Newgate Gaol, 1807

Joe hadn't known how wrecked London had been in the taking. St Paul's was rubble. There was scaffolding everywhere, and every house was new-roofed, because there had been so many fires. It was beginning to get dark, but there were no street lamps, just pollards of twisted metal where they used to be. People had pulled them down during the siege, to make it harder for soldiers to move at night. Instead, there were cheap paper lamps outside the shops, and even paper in a lot of the windows.

'The glass monopoly went to a workshop in Paris,' Colonel Herault said when Joe asked. 'Too expensive to ship, and you get your windows broken if you use illegal glass.' He gave Joe a quizzical look. 'Least of your worries.'

Joe knew that. He felt like he was in a dream, though, and irrelevant things mattered a lot. His brain was trying to cram in everything it could before someone shot him.

He watched a girl waxing one of the paper panes and thought it seemed a lot more deliberate than a trade decision. No lamps, no windows: no lenses. He wondered how much spectacles cost now, or microscopes. It was a brilliant way to stop people learning, advancing, anything.

They were selling newspapers in French too: but wide-spaced, easy French, with friendly labels at the top that said they were for learners. On the front page, there was a bold sign that said:

Remember!
It is ILLEGAL to possess WRITTEN ENGLISH.
The amnesty for books ends
ON THURSDAY.

Bad. And yet; people here looked a lot better than they did in Edinburgh. There was plainly enough food, enough fabric. He found himself scanning Herault. The man was pin neat, well-kept, but he had a strong local accent: he was unashamedly from Nice, not Paris. About Kite's age. Joe had a hard time imagining that anyone like Lord Lawrence would be allowed to get anywhere at all on the French side of things. He'd have been guillotined years ago.

Maybe this was just what it took, to make people unlearn that vile, diseased way of thinking, the one that put the Lawrences at the top of the world.

The Cour de Cassation was still called the Bailey. There was an iron gate that said so, and just along from it, grim and grey and hung with the Tricolour like everything else, was Newgate Gaol. It was in sight of the natty apartments around the Postman's Garden and the bishop's palace behind St Paul's, and it sat sullen as if it knew it was out of place.

They went in through a side door and arrived in a small office that looked like it belonged to a lawyer: all neat bookcases and maps on the walls, and the warm smell of polish. An interior window looked down into what must have been the Bailey court, empty and dark. On the shelf below it was a whole row of cement casts of people's heads. The eyes were all closed and the expressions were sometimes twisted. Some of them were marked up with dotted lines and measurements; whoever owned the office liked phrenology.

'Fellow there should have been hanged at birth,' one of Herault's men said idly. 'Look at that skull.'

The cast in question had a low brow. Joe had to look away. He wasn't normally squeamish, but he didn't want to see a row of hanged people's faces.

'Oh, it's all horseshit,' Herault said. He patted Joe. 'Look at this one. He'll go down for high treason and he looks angelic.'

Joe had to dig for his own voice. 'I still don't know what you're on about.'

'We'll have a talk soon,' Herault said easily.

Joe thought he might fall over. He hadn't been allowed to get up for the whole voyage here, four days even with engines, and there hadn't been much food. He was shaking now. The chains were clinking. They felt incredibly heavy. Carrying their weight pulled a nasty ache right up into his shoulders.

A man who looked like a vicar arrived, but he was some kind of guard, and after a murmured conversation with Herault, he led Joe away without speaking.

After that, Joe was lost. There was gate after locked gate. The man who looked like a vicar unlocked each one, brought Joe through, and locked it straight after them again with the rhythm of a person just stupid enough never to find it boring. The passages were narrow and very, very cold, with high windows that had no glass in them, just bars.

They came out into a broad yard. Because it was sunken under street level, it was like being at the bottom of a well; the sky looked distant above the grey roof, and the walls seemed to go up and up. Tiny windows punctuated them here and there, so small it was impossible to see into the rooms. People were traipsing to and fro, some in little groups. There weren't many. The well-shape of the yard must have funnelled the cold, because it was worse here than out in the street. Their breath steamed.

'Exercise yard,' the not-vicar explained. 'And through here is the main ward.'

Ward, like a hospital; but he just meant wing. It was for felons, apparently, but Joe had no idea how that was different to anything else. It was much more crowded inside. There were no cells, just an open space. Mats like hammocks hung from hooks in the ceiling. Dozens. There was a fire, and a long table, and men eating. None of them had anything else to do. Some were playing dice. There wasn't even the frenetic industry of the gaol in Edinburgh Castle. Everyone looked vacant.

'Can you pay for your own food?' the not-vicar asked.

'What? No.'

'You've missed dinner then.'

Joe wondered what would happen if he collapsed now. That might call Herault's bluff; Herault was clearly trying to scare him into cooperating. Or maybe they would just leave him in a heap. There were men hunched against all four walls, and in the corridor, and in the next ward beyond that, which was identical to this one. He looked down when he realised the not-vicar was unshackling him.

'What happens now?' he asked. He heard his voice cracking.

'Now you await your trial. Or whatever it is Colonel Herault means for you,' the not-vicar said, and vanished before Joe could scrape together words and grammar to ask when that would be.

Joe dropped down at the end of a table near a man who seemed to have stopped eating. 'Have you finished that?' he asked.

'Yeah,' the man said vaguely. Joe hesitated, because he'd expected to be blackmailed for it, but nothing was forthcoming. The man looked too listless to bother. Later, a guard tried to – inmates were supposed to pay for bedding, thank you – so Joe said he'd got syphilis. The guard beat him up instead, but on balance, he thought it was all going a lot better than it could have. He curled up in one of the strange mat-hammock things, holding his ribs and hoping they weren't broken. No. Not as bad as it could have been. And better than the queasy darkness in the cabin on the *Santíssima Trinidad*.

For the hundredth time, he wondered if it was Kite who had told the French where to find him; just a simple piece of revenge, for running off to Lawrence, and for all that foulness Joe had snarled at him about Jem.

Nobody made anyone get up in the morning. You could sleep all day if you wanted, so Joe stayed where he was, hunched under a blanket. But the guards kept turning people out of their hammocks, and it took three or four before Joe twigged that they were dead. He watched as they carried someone out in a sack. A minute later, there was a thump outside. They were dumping the bodies in a storage block, just over the courtyard. He looked around slowly. Now that he was really awake, there was a lot of coughing. Typhoid. Or something.

Stiff, with unpromising twangs going through some bones, he limped to the table, where the guards had put out breakfast. Someone must have insisted that bread and cheese at least had to be free, because nobody tried to make anyone pay for that. He forced himself to eat. It made him feel sick, even though he was ravenous, so he stuck to a few mouthfuls every ten minutes, and kept to it until he'd cleared a plate, because if one thing was certain, it was that he was going to be in one of those sacks soon if he let himself stay so weak.

On the fifth day, Colonel Herault asked to see him. The not-vicar took Joe out of the felons' wing and up to a cosy office with a pretty view of the ruin of St Paul's, and an impressive fire. The corridors were labyrinthine, and even with the cathedral for a reference, he couldn't work out where the office was in relation to the front door. Herault looked cheerful when someone came in with coffee. And milk, and sugar.

'Well, you've seen what the prison is like,' Herault said, pouring the coffee, which steamed. He handed over a cup and watched Joe hold it for a short while before he continued. 'If you don't want any more of that, you'll need to tell me a few things. And then we can talk about pleasanter accommodation for you.'

'What things?' said Joe, and swallowed, because he hadn't spoken for a week and his voice sounded wrong. Looking down at the coffee, he noticed his own hands; the webbing between his fingers was cracking, painful now he was holding something hot. He must have been allergic to something in the acidic prison soap too, because there were angry marks right down the heels of his hands and the sides of his wrists.

'Drink your coffee,' Herault said.

Joe sipped it. After a week of bread, the flavour was so powerful he couldn't swallow at first. But when he did, the heat spread down his throat and through his chest. His ribs still hurt, but holding the cup against his breastbone helped. He stared around the office. Ordinary things, like the books on the shelves and the steaming cafetière, looked foreign.

'So how do you like Newgate, Tournier?'

Joe forced himself to brighten up. 'It's not so bad. Free food and a bed. Not too much bother from the guards.'

Herault looked taken aback. Kite, Joe thought, would not only have beaten him at poker, he would have had the whole table and the full tea service off him after about twenty-five minutes. Then Herault caught himself and lifted something from his desk drawer.

Joe nearly jumped out the window.

It was a bomb. A delicate clockwork bomb, made with a stick of dynamite and what was unmistakably a modern watch

– Joe-modern, not now-modern. People had pocket watches here, but they were bulky things and inaccurate. Nobody had invented bimetallic mainsprings yet, the little mechanism which allowed watches to shrink down into something small and elegant.

'A friend of mine made this for me,' Herault said, winding up the watch. Once it was ticking, he came around the table, put it in Joe's hands, and then retreated behind the desk again. 'She was very clever.'

Joe stared down at it. He had worked in artillery. He knew how much dynamite did what amount of damage, and this much was just about enough to blow him to pieces, but only to shower Herault with gore. 'What is it?' he asked, and was impressed that his voice didn't shake. The watch was set at two minutes to twelve. Two minutes.

'Oh, just a toy really.' Herault put up an umbrella and sat with it balanced against his shoulder. It looked ridiculous, but an umbrella would save his expensive uniform from the red mist that would be Joe in a minute and forty-three seconds.

Joe wanted to sling the bomb at him and run. He laughed a little. 'I like your umbrella, sir.'

'Yes, so do I,' Herault said, and spun it. 'Monsieur Faveau,' he added to the not-vicar, who was just outside the door, 'if Tournier here tries to harm me in any way in the next – er, minute and thirty seconds, you are to shoot him in the leg immediately, is that all right?'

'Yes, sir,' the man said.

The fear was bubbling up inside Joe even though everything depended on not showing it. He was about to cry, or yell, or something, he could feel it coming.

Don't be so fucking French, said Kite's voice in his head, so clearly that Joe wondered deliriously if telepathy was real.

Joe wasn't sure that even Kite would be able to sit here holding a live bomb and keep a straight face.

No; he would. He would be eating the contingency apple, but he would look calm until he exploded, and he would do that because if you were going to explode, it would be embarrassing to do it after you'd gone full headless chicken. That wouldn't help anyone. What would be the point? If you made it to the good place, a saint would be along to poke fun, and if you didn't, there would be plenty of time for headless chickening there.

He lifted the little bomb up to see underneath, and turned it around twice, pretending to be interested in the watch.

'This is beautiful. I've never seen a watch like this. Is it silver?'

'It is platinum.'

If he closed his eyes, he could feel Kite's hand on his back, and far from a bad thing, it was steadying. Say something *useful*.

'I've heard of that. My master bought me for platinum.'

Fifty seconds left.

'Did he really?' Herault said.

Joe nodded. 'I was quite expensive.' He sipped his coffee again. Oh, God, he could smell the metal on his palm where he'd gripped the bomb. 'I had like a breeding certificate and all that.'

Herault frowned. 'A certificate.'

'I'm a d'Lioncourt,' Joe said proudly. He didn't know if the pedigree line went back this far. In his Londres, a d'Lioncourt slave cost more than a town house in Kensington. They only ever changed hands between royalty. But there *were* pedigree lines in this time, there had to be. Slavery had been around for donkey's years even now. 'He said that was good. Is it? I don't know, I feel like he might have been lying to me, to be nice. He did that a lot.' Joe looked into the middle distance and tried to conjure up someone he loved, in the way people of the kind he was pretending to be loved their captors: fierce and hopeless, and beaten.

For the first time since Joe had first dreamed him, the man who waited by the sea was there when Joe wanted him. He was facing the water and entirely distinct, just beyond Herault. He was skimming stones the same as before, but finally, Joe could see him clearly. He had red hair; deep, church-window red.

Herault took the bomb out of Joe's hands and pulled out the connecting wire. He put it to one side, and stayed standing by Joe, scrutinising every inch of him. Joe stared up at him numbly, not sure what had hit him harder, the sudden impossibility of exploding in twenty seconds, or the understanding that the person he had been looking for for all this time, for every minute that he could remember, was Kite.

'You were holding a bomb just now, Tournier. It would have killed you.'

Joe almost didn't have it in him to act any more, but then Kite's voice was there in his head again, snapping that if he was tired of acting then he was tired of breathing and to stop being such a whiny little fuckwit.

He jolted right out of the chair. 'It's a *what*? Why would you *give* that to me?'

Herault was deflating slowly in front of him.

Joe started to cry. It was no effort at all. 'What are you *doing*? For God's sake, I don't know who you think I am, but I'm *not* him!'

'No,' Herault sighed. 'I don't believe you are.' His eyes ticked over Joe. 'You didn't happen to pick up that purity certificate when you left?'

'No!'

'Shame. Look, stop that please,' Herault added, looking embarrassed to have a crying person in his office. 'Right, this is what's going to happen. You're going back into the felons' ward for now. I'm going to find a buyer and I'm going to sell you on, and you shall be bloody grateful I don't shoot you for wasting my time.' The longer he spoke, the more annoyed he sounded, and the more he took on the terse look of a man who was worried he had cocked up catastrophically.

'Yes, sir,' Joe whispered. Sold on; not ideal, but it was progress. He could get out of a normal house a hell of a lot more easily than out of prison, and he came from the Missouri Kite training school of applied savagery.

The edges of the vision – the memory – were still with him. Kite was still waiting by the sea, as patient and as silent as always.

45

London, 1807

K ite hadn't thought he'd ever see London again. It was all the same and all different. Spanish frigates harboured at Deptford; the dry docks were full of warships he knew very well indeed, because they had once been English – the *Bellerophon*, the *Mars*, more – but repainted and given new French names. He had never had time to feel the loss of them before, but there was nothing else to do now.

'Quieter than last time we were here,' he said to Wellesley.

She was standing with him in a green silk dress. He'd never seen her out of uniform, not since she first came aboard, and now the dress seemed as stupid on her as it would have on a lioness. You didn't *put* people like Wellesley in dresses.

With her perfect French, she would pretend to be the dead captain's wife when they docked. If reward collections here worked anything like they did in the English navy, then she would be able to take him to Newgate herself, and speak directly with the warden; he would give her a prisoner receipt, and the docket to collect the money from the Admiralty. After that ... she'd told him how she would get to Joe, but everything was falling out of his head. He'd never worried about dying in action, but dying in front of Buckingham Palace had a gravity that the quarterdeck didn't.

He watched the ruined dome of St Paul's creep nearer. Joe would be all right. He had an amazing knack for being all right.

At the docks, Wellesley was enjoyably French at the customs men, and they got by without any trouble. Once they were past, they moved in a tight phalanx towards Newgate; six of *Agamemnon*'s crew in French uniforms they'd taken from the pressed men, flanking her and Kite.

'I'm not leaving you there, you know,' she told him.

'You have to. Collect the reward money, get Tournier, and get out. I thought we'd agreed?' he said tiredly. He'd been afraid something like this was on the way.

'No. You agreed and I made a humming noise,' she said. 'We can do it. Forty men; it will be straightforward enough.'

'And how many of those men will die in the process? You can't risk a single sailor, Ray; we haven't got the *people* to replace them, never mind trained people.'

'Well, we're not leaving you there to be executed.'

He turned to face her. They were on a ruined street that had never been properly cleaned up; the rubble of blasted buildings still sloped towards the pavements, and here and there, groups of unoccupied children hung around, playing cards at brick tables. It had taken him the whole length of the walk to recognise that it was Oxford Street. 'I killed your brother,' he said.

'Yes, and the moon is assuredly made of cheese.'

Kite had no idea what he'd ever done that would have made her that loyal. He wanted to catch her sleeve and shake her, but he couldn't bring himself to. She was taller than him, and probably stronger, but there was a special side-chapel in hell for men who decided it was all right to lay hands on women, *any* women. It wasn't about being stronger. It was about everything else. In the end he had to put his arm out ahead of her to stop her walking.

'I threw him overboard before we came into Edinburgh.'

'Stop it. Why would you?'

Kite shook his head slightly. 'He had ... one of his turns. He hit me. I suppose it was just battle fatigue, but I snapped.' He looked up at her and held her eyes for a long time. 'I'm sorry, but I did, and you should be leaving me here.'

'You wouldn't just ...' She looked less sure, and he didn't blame her. Even aside from what he was saying, he looked exactly like the sort of person who might murder someone. He always had, but the burns made it look especially convincing now.

'I did.'

'Why?' she said again.

He shrugged, because he knew it would make her angry, but he felt disgusting doing it, especially because he could have explained exactly why.

*

Edinburgh, 1805 (twenty-five days after Trafalgar)

It had been a nightmarish journey from London to Edinburgh. The sea had turned rough, and Kite would never usually have worried, but six in seven – *six in seven* – of the men had been killed either at Trafalgar or at the evacuation of London, and now most of the people raising sails and tying lines were not sailors at all, but women and children who Revelation Wellesley, his dead first lieutenant's very young wife, had conscripted to the cause. There was a moment off Newcastle when he was certain they were going to sink. He never once got sight of the *Orion*. He'd signalled to other ships, but no one seemed to know if she'd even made it past the line at Trafalgar.

He had never been so happy to see a harbour when they came into Edinburgh, or more surprised to make it to one. Even one in a state like this.

It was crowded to the point that it was impossible to dock at a wharf. They had to anchor a little way out and send boats ashore to request medics, who, thank Christ, had been waiting on the harbour. The School of Surgeons was only a couple of miles away and they seemed to have sent every single student and alumnus they could lay hands on. A vicious wind tore into the damaged ship from the north, which spun them in loops even at anchor. It was hard to get people aboard. He spent about an hour helping nurses over the side, and then collapsed on a doctor. The doctor took him firmly into the stateroom to look at the burns.

People were in and out all the time. Heroically, Agatha and Ray Wellesley had gone straight ashore and managed to buy space at the already crowded boarding houses on the dockside for the wounded men. Wellesley had come aboard with a rope of pearls and sold it for them. He still couldn't believe she'd done that. She had nothing except those pearls and one change of clothes, but she seemed to think she was only doing what anyone would.

Able people would have to stay aboard and help with the repairs. Messages came up from the infirmary and its overspill on the gun deck; they needed cleaning salt, urgently, or there was going to be cholera. The mainmast was loose in its socket. The Admiralty had taken over Edinburgh Castle and they were calling all able officers to get up there for a briefing, but the doctor threatened to hit Kite with his instrument case if he made any noises about being able. It was a relief. When he did manage to get away from the man and his odious salt solution, which hurt a lot more than getting the burns in the first place, he could only just walk. He hated letting the sailors see him like that, but there wasn't much choice now.

He limped onto the deck to make sure everyone had enough in the way of warm clothes. With the death toll from Trafalgar, and from London, one thing they did have in abundance was spare coats. Then he stopped.

Sitting on a cannon with a little boy was Jem. They were talking over what seemed to be a set of salt and pepper pots, and a copy of the lieutenants' exam book.

'So that's where that odd number comes from,' Jem was finishing. 'It's because of the curve of the wave, which is why it's related to *pi*. Hardly beyond the wit of man. Want to try a cigarette?' he added. 'Nice blend, from Jamaica. It smells of warm weather even if it doesn't do much for you.'

The boy laughed, delighted with him. Kite waited while Jem showed him how to roll a cigarette, and then, stiffly, sat down beside them on the gun.

'Aha,' said Jem softly. 'Here he is.'

Kite couldn't say anything at first. All he could do was slump against Jem and try to reassure himself that he was real, not a battle-fatigue hallucination. Jem gripped his hand. 'What are we doing?' Kite managed at last.

'Waveforms,' Jem said, sunny as ever. 'And this young man is going to remember them now because they will be inextricably linked to the far more memorable memory of his first decent cigarette. I'm clever that way.'

'You're ridiculous,' Kite told him. 'Don't let children smoke.'

'I like it,' the little boy protested. Then, brightly, 'Are you Captain Kite? Did you really sail into battle with fifty dead people hanging off the yards?'

'I – what? No,' said Kite. 'Who said that?'

'Everyone,' the boy said happily.

Fantastic.

'Better run away,' Jem said in a stage whisper. Once the boy was gone, Jem put his head against Kite's. He talked quietly; he'd been here two days, one of the first to arrive. *Orion* had brought the King, which was why it had been so far ahead. Shore was chaos; there were message boards right along the docks, full of notes so relatives could find each other; the army had opened an office just to deal with getting people back together with their families. And people, brilliant ordinary people, had set up more message boards detailing spare rooms and attics where refugees from London could stay. Kite didn't hear half of what he said, because he was deaf on one side and had been for days, but it was still good to watch him talk.

Kite had forgotten that that little boy on the gun with Jem had been Fred Hathaway. It had stayed forgotten right until that moment he had seen Joe give Fred a cigarette.

Usually, Joe was different enough that Kite didn't struggle too much to see him as someone new. Every so often, though, he was still Jem.

Only he wasn't Jem any more. He was a desperate man with a child to get home to, and if Fred had told him who he was, he would have seen straight through all of Kite's stupid threats and walked away in broad daylight without giving them an atom of help, knowing that Kite was incapable of hurting him.

*

Newgate Gaol, 1807

Kite waited by the window of the warden's office with two of *Agamemnon*'s men in French uniforms, feeling exposed all the same. Wellesley had insisted on hanging onto him until the warden arrived to sign the docket that would allow her to collect the reward money, and then – well, then she'd have to leave him there, he'd vanish into the prison and that would be that. She had turned very quiet after he told her about Fred, and he did not doubt that she would be happy to leave him now.

There were plenty of other considerations he ought to have been giving his time to, but his overriding thought was that he wasn't used to land any more. Even at Edinburgh, he usually slept on the ship. He didn't like how solid ground was. Normally, if everything was perfectly still, you were becalmed on the Pacific and you were looking seriously at the prospect of starving to death. It gave him a knee-jerk anxiety.

Sergeant Drake, from the marines, was one of the disguised men. He seemed to see that Kite was teetering, and put one hand on the small of his back. He was usually a granite man, but he offered him an awkward little smile now. Kite winked. Drake looked reassured.

When the warden did arrive, he was a dandy with a streety Parisian accent, which he exaggerated in the way of someone extremely pleased with himself for not being an aristocrat.

'Madame!' he exclaimed *at* Wellesley rather than to her, and then did a funny skipping retreat when she stood up and turned out to be so much taller than him. Kite could have laughed. He loved watching people meet Wellesley for the first time. 'I hear you brought in Missouri Kite on behalf of your husband, the captain of the ... dah-dah-dah, where is it – *Angleterre?*'

'I did.'

'Amazing,' he said happily. He skittered over to look at Kite, who couldn't help thinking of a discombobulated daddy-long-legs. There was an urge to be careful with him but also to throw him out the window. 'And we're sure it's him?'

'How many other redhead Spanish pirate captains are there kicking around the North Sea?' Wellesley said drily.

'Are you really Spanish?' the warden said to Kite. Kite could follow his French, more or less. Joe had got him used to it, with that strange, Anglified future French. The grammar got turned around, or something subtle but significant, and it made a bridge between English and this Parisian thing. 'Silly of you to join the English fleet, don't you think, given that your side won?'

'In hindsight it was something of an error,' Kite agreed in Spanish, to prove that he could.

The warden laughed as if a wild animal had spoken to him. He turned back to Wellesley. 'Excellent! I'll sign the docket for you, madame. I think this merits a proper glass of wine, don't you?'

She smiled. Kite was still struggling to find the magnificent green dress anything less than offensive, but she was playing the part well. She even sat differently; usually she had the tall person's inclination to curve forward, but she was resting against the corsetry now, bolt upright. 'Indeed it does, sir; and, while we're here, and since I find myself rather newly wealthy, I was wondering about the purchase of a slave or two. Perhaps I could look at some before I go to the Ministry to retrieve the reward money?'

The warden looked delighted. 'Oh, absolutely. But wine first. What kind of slaves?'

'Well,' she said. 'I have to say, I have been hankering after a handsome man to be decorative about the house. Dark and pretty, perhaps?'

Kite frowned, because he hadn't thought this would ever happen; that she might just be able to put Joe in a room with all of them at the same time. Which meant there was a chance of getting out of here. He swallowed hard, because hope was worse than fatalism.

'Absolutely, absolutely – oh, here's Colonel Herault,' the warden added as a side door opened. 'He wants to have a look at our pirate; Herault, meet Missouri Kite.'

'Isn't it interesting,' Herault said, 'that you turn up just after I put an advert in the paper about your man?'

'What man?' Kite said. 'What paper?'

Herault swept his eyes over him slowly, taking him in, the cuts, bruises, the chains, and then tilted them towards Wellesley. He didn't say anything, and only folded down into the armchair not far from Kite. When the warden burbled that they were going to sell some slaves to the lady, Herault glanced at Kite and lifted one eyebrow.

'Are you indeed,' he said.

46

Newgate Gaol, 1807

After the dimness in the yard and on the stairs, the light in the office was rich. It looked to Joe like a room trapped in amber. There were a lot of people there now; Colonel Herault in an armchair by the window, a flouncy man who might have been the warden, three other men who must have been prisoners from the state of them. Joe glanced at them uncertainly. One of them gave him a thin smile. All of them were in their twenties or thirties, and remarkably good-looking. The warden hurried across and shuffled Joe into line.

And there in an armchair was Revelation Wellesley, looking entirely unlike herself in a green silk dress. She had changed the way she held herself too; she was quick and precise on *Agamemnon*'s deck, but she looked languid now, and she had taken on a glassy, arsenic-brightened quality just like a certain sort of rich lady always had.

'My goodness,' she laughed, sounding like an idiot. Joe could have kissed her. Her French was brilliant. 'You really do have a good selection. How is it that so many lovely slaves have committed crimes?'

Slave auction. Right. Jesus, could people just walk in like that? And where the hell were they going to get that kind of money? The English fleet seemed to have sixpence between them, and even then, it was probably a fake sixpence off an illegal mint.

'Oh, sometimes we sell debtors to clear their debts. Minimum ten years of service,' the warden explained, jolly. In the corner, Herault was leaning against the arm of his chair, clipping a cigar.

Joe hadn't seen because he was on the periphery of the lamps, and very still, but Kite was there too. He looked terrible, new cuts and bruises everywhere, chains on his wrists, and he wasn't wearing enough for the cold. Joe looked away. Too fast: Herault had been watching him, and he noticed. Joe frowned to ask why he was being stared at. Herault made a vague spinning motion with one hand. Just going along. But he glanced back at Kite, and for no reason that Joe could see, he flicked the chains. Kite flinched, then looked annoyed to have flinched.

'This lady wants to buy one of you,' the warden continued, and smiled in the hopeful way of someone who wanted them all to look much more thrilled than they were. 'Say hello.'

There was a murmured chorus of hello-madames.

'Well?' Wellesley said in her exquisite French. 'What's your going rate?'

'Fairly standard,' the warden began.

'Fellow on the end's an unconfirmed d'Lioncourt,' Herault put in. Joe couldn't believe this was happening, but then, if Wellesley had walked in here with Kite as a prisoner, with her French like it was, in that dress, then there was no reason for anyone to believe she was anything other than what she said. The wife of a captain or an officer, she must have told them. Even if Herault had been waiting for Kite, it was pretty bloody convincing.

Wellesley snorted. 'No pedigree certificate, no worth. And he's in a hell of a state.'

She haggled. The warden and Herault assured her that she was being silly, and that she was out of date in her notion of the worth of a slave. She assured them just as civilly that she knew the price of a slave perfectly well, thank you, having consulted the financial papers that morning for the stocks.

In the end she bought all four of them for not very much. While she wrote out what might have been a cheque, and the other three men nodded at each other, anxious because of course they had no idea if they were going to somewhere better or worse than Newgate, Herault came up to Joe. He gave him a long, appraising look.

'Your lucky day, Tournier.'

Joe kept his eyes down. 'Yes, sir. Madame seems like a wonderful lady.'

Herault still didn't seem to have finished appraising. 'Before you go, just something to ask. Do you know this man?' He nodded towards Kite.

'I ... no, sir. Why?'

'That's all right then,' he said, and shot Kite.

Joe didn't see where the bullet hit. All he saw was that Kite collapsed. Joe's lungs stopped working.

'I beg your pardon,' Wellesley snapped into the silence. 'What the hell was that for?'

Herault was still watching Joe.

Joe copied the other prisoners. He let his eyes go wide and his expression still.

'He's alive,' Herault said. 'But I'll shoot him in the head unless you tell me where he got you.'

'Fuck it,' Wellesley said in English, and Joe had never seen anyone look as surprised as Herault did when she took a gun out of her pocket and shot him in the chest. 'Someone get the captain. Come on, Tournier, and you three – now, move, hurry up—'

Joe fell down on his knees to catch Herault's shoulder. 'What happened to the Kingdoms? You let them go, where did they go?'

'Let them go?' Herault said faintly. He was already deathly white. 'No ... no. We shot them. And then Madeline ... hanged ...'

'Tournier,' Wellesley snapped, and wrenched him away.

They were outside. Outside, just like that. There was a tall gatehouse that led out onto a tiny cobbled street, a portcullis above the gateway: the main entrance of the Bailey. There, just along the road, was St Paul's; and the busy crossroads just beyond, full of people who probably didn't know they were walking right above the underground tunnels of the prison.

Joe couldn't think. He could hardly speak. That she had managed to pull off something so ludicrous had made the world spin, and so had how precarious an idea it had been. It had relied, completely, on his having said nothing to Herault – on his lying right from the start, even. Kite must have known he would, but that was unsettling, because Joe hadn't known what he was going to say until he was saying it.

He expected someone to yell and chase them, but no one was yelling or chasing. There was just Wellesley behind him, steering him away from the gaol and into the street, past St Paul's, away, away. Some of her men were leading the other three Newgate prisoners down different roads. He heard a faint whoop that must have been one of them finding out that the Agamemnons were English and that English law didn't do slavery.

Someone had carried Kite out of the room, but he was walking now, one sleeve bloody. It was just his shoulder. Joe ran to catch up, put his arm around him, and nudged away the marine who had been helping before.

'Back to the ship in twos and threes,' Kite said quietly.

They did as they were told. Within a few seconds, everyone had melted away in different directions. Kite pulled Joe into a side alley.

Joe snatched him close and breathed in against his hair. Kite was the only clean thing he'd been near all week, and he smelled perfect. Linen and gunpowder and tobacco — Joe's own tobacco. He'd left it behind on *Agamemnon*.

It must have hurt, but Kite didn't complain and only rested against his chest. For the first time since they'd met, Joe realised that Kite was smaller than him. He could put his head against Joe's neck without stooping. He managed to make it feel like he needed the shelter a lot more than Joe did. It gave Joe a hot rush of protectiveness, and the second that arrived, he felt stronger and less lost.

'Thank you,' Joe managed.

'Very little trouble, as it turns out,' Kite said. He was alabaster from blood loss, and his hands were cold. 'Right. You know the way north?'

Joe didn't know what he'd expected him to say, but it wasn't that. 'You're letting me go,' he said stupidly.

'Let you go, I can't get rid of you. Do you know the way? Better not come with us, we'll be chased all the way to Edinburgh.'

'I — yes. I'm from round here.' Joe nodded to the left, and then had to cough. His throat felt like emery paper. 'But Kite. You know me. How? I'm going to forget anyway, you might as well ... for God's sake, this postcard, it's from *you*, I don't understand ...'

It was hard to tell if Kite had heard. 'I think I'm going to faint.'

'You have to ... you can't know what it's like, to have children,' Joe said, begging now, though he wasn't even sure what he was begging for. Not information any more. 'Look — if you need me. I don't know where I'll be, but find the Psychical Society. They're at Pont du Cam. Cambridge, I mean. That's forever money, they'll outlast any changes we've made here.'

Kite nodded, but Joe still couldn't tell if he had understood. Joe was about to say he'd better take him back to the ship, but Drake, the marine, must have seen how bad the gunshot wound was, because he was coming back now, hurrying towards them through the alley.

'Sir, are you ...?'

Kite looked like he wanted to speak, but he buckled into Drake's arms.

'Don't you dare run,' Drake said to Joe.

Joe didn't want to. But Kite was as safe as he was going to be and Lily might have been disappearing while he hesitated, and although the panic pressure that had always come with trying to leave was still strong, it wasn't paralysing any more.

Joe managed to get to the porch of a church with no windows before he had to stop, the world gone too blurry for him to walk.

47

Eilean Mòr, 1807

When Joe let himself into the lighthouse, it was exactly as he'd left it. He had thought he was tired and hungry, but he couldn't sit down. Instead he spent the next half-hour tidying, then cleaning the brine from the windows and easing heat into the engine to unfreeze the pipes, all the while feeling more and more urgent, because he knew he had to go back to the mainland, but he couldn't stop.

But then there was nothing left to do. He stood with his hands against the wall where the heavy-weather gear hung, his head close enough to them to smell the wax on the nearest jacket. When he lost the circulation in his fingertips and they needled, he straightened up, put the gear on and started the howling walk to the tiny harbour.

He took a hammer and chisel with him to the stone gate in the sea. He wrote *Alice* and *Lily*. The dust spiralled away on the wind. He touched the first few letters of *Madeline*. And under Madeline, *Jem*. It was all there; he felt like he had all the pieces, but he couldn't match them up. He was never going to know. It was too cold to stay standing there. He took as deep a breath as he could, then stepped through and didn't feel any different at all.

Part VI

HOME

48

London, 1903

There was a Christmas song on the phonograph and it danced through the house. So did the twins, who had tiny holly crowns made of silk leaves. Joe laughed when he saw. Toby was chasing them through an obliging assault course made of his cavalry regiment. Joe had a child's-eye view because he was sitting under the dining table, fiddling with the hydraulics of the porcelain Taj Mahal fountain. It was a monstrosity, but Toby had brought it back from the Punjab as a present, so here it was, only a bit worse for wear from travel. Fifteen bottles of wine were waiting on the side for when he had fixed the valve in its base.

There was a roar when George won and five or six men swept him up and exclaimed what a good officer he would make one day. Beatrix drifted away with her head down, and Joe realised with a pang that she was already used to being left out. He put his arms out. She came to see under the table too.

'You are destined for better things than horses,' he said, in the hope that firmness made things true. 'Will you help me fix this?'

She nodded. He could never tell if she understood exactly, or just understood enough to know that she was being asked a question. He brushed her hair back. It was black and smooth, tied up in a knot with a ribbon now, but he couldn't shift the impression that it was curly. That was a leftover from the epilepsy hallucinations of another little girl, one who had been his, not Toby's. He tried not to think about her too much, but she felt real, and whenever he came up from the hallucination – it still happened every month or so – it took him hours to get over the crushing panic that he must have left her somewhere. Being told by doctors and everyone else that she was imaginary didn't help. He'd even sewn a duck on Beatrix's nightdress because it had looked so wrong duckless; the little girl in the hallucinations had one. That was before it had dawned on him that sewing things on the clothes of other people's children was creepy and that he was making Toby nervous.

Beatrix reached for the screwdriver. He gave it to her. 'You can do this screw, all right? This way round. Good girl.'

She nodded again. He watched her while he guided her hands, aware that she would only have to decide to get up suddenly and she would bang her head against the underside of the table, but unlike George, she was a still child. She would sit exactly where you left her, for hours, uncomplaining.

George squeaked and laughed as Toby put him on his shoulders. Beatrix watched, then looked down into her lap and turned the screwdriver around twice. She was pretending it was more interesting than it was. Something in his heart splintered.

'Toby,' he said.

Toby leaned down, which tipped George upside down. 'Hello?'

'Take Bee for a spin too. She's left out.'

'Wha-at?' Toby laughed. He dumped George into Joe's arms and scooped her up. 'Left *out*? Never!' He galloped away.

George looked annoyed, but was soon placated with the screwdriver, which he seemed to like.

'Doorbell!' one of Toby's friends called. 'Shall I get it?'

'I will,' Joe said. He needed to stretch. 'Who are we expecting now?'

'Carol singers probably,' Toby offered. 'Shouldn't think Kahn and Co. will be in for half an hour yet, they're coming from some blasted heath in darkest Willesden.'

'Tell them to bugger off,' Joe and Toby's father rumbled from the next room. He pretended that he didn't speak English, although Joe had noticed there was a distinct correlation between his English abilities and the increased potential of mince pies. 'It's awkward being privately serenaded by an entire choir.'

'Humbug,' Joe said, but he went.

'Bug,' said George to Alice, who passed them on the stairs with a tray of differently shaped pastries.

'How's the fountain?' she asked Joe.

'Fit for a very tasteless maharajah in about ten minutes,' he promised, awkward, because he didn't know what to do with Alice minus Toby. Married people were closed off; you couldn't get to know a person's wife without someone else looking at you funny, and so although Alice had been his sister-in-law for years now, Joe had no idea what she was like, apart from incredibly elegant.

And he knew she didn't like him. She had never said she thought he was an embarrassment, the permanent bachelor who didn't have his own children or his own life and who kept clinging onto hers and Toby's, but he could feel it coming off her sometimes.

'Horrible, isn't it,' she agreed.

Joe smiled a bit. Agreeing with him was, for her, a mark of overpowering Christmas cheer and goodwill to all men.

'Ooh, are those the pie things?' his father called hopefully.

'She doesn't understand, Ba,' Joe called back, 'you'll have to try harder ...'

'My English is fine,' his father huffed, although since he also swore up and down that King Edward was a fine figure of a man, Joe suspected that it was code for appalling.

Joe opened the door, still laughing, but then stopped, because his heart vaulted.

There was no choir outside. Only a man. There were burn scars across the left side of his face and he looked as if somebody might once have abandoned him in the Arctic and left him to find his own way home, but he was well-dressed and he held himself so straight he must have been from the army or the navy. Joe had met too many of Toby's military friends to place him, but that didn't stop him feeling happy to see him.

'You came. I haven't seen you for ages.'

The man looked alarmed. 'Pardon?'

'Come in, it's freezing,' Joe said. 'Sorry – you're going to have to believe me, I'm very glad to see you but I can't remember where we know each other from. Are you from the regiment? No, you can't be,' he corrected himself, puzzled. There were no white people in the regiment. The army grouped soldiers more or less by colour. Toby was too noticeably Chinese to go in with a white regiment, so he had gone in with the Sikhs. He always said he was lucky not to look more like Joe, who would have been dumped into a regiment full of hopeless Eton boys and dead years ago after some heroic stupid charge.

'No, the Psychical Society.' The man was well-spoken, officerly. 'Eleanor Sidgwick is coming too, but I'm the placeholder. She just called on someone else on the way. She gave me your Christmas card for proof. We don't ... know each other,' he added.

'Sorry,' Joe said, though he was still sure they did. He had to crush the feeling down. 'I've got you mixed up.'

'It's all right. You're ...' He had to glance again at the envelope, then turned it around helplessly for Joe to see. *Mr Tchang*.

'Jang,' said Joe, charmed because the man had looked so worried by the spelling. 'It's just how the French write Chinese, I don't know how they came up with something so odd.' He put George down. George ran off, following the sound of Toby tickling Beatrix in the next room and cavalrymen horsing about. 'Do you work there? At the Society I mean.'

'No, just visiting.' The man handed over the envelope and didn't come up the step. His hands were in a bad state. There were scars across his fingers, one of which was crooked, broken and not healed properly. 'Chinese, you said?' he asked. Not in the accusatory way bigots asked. He was handling the idea with such care he seemed afraid Joe might take it off him.

'That's right. Anyway.' Joe opened the door wider. 'Coming in? We've got about forty people already and we're still expecting the other half of a cavalry regiment.'

'Who is it?' Alice called, on her way down the stairs again. Behind her, a couple of her friends were stretching to hang up mistletoe on the gallery banisters, laughing.

'Someone from the Psychical Society, Eleanor's late.'

'Anyone capable of unequine conversation is extremely welcome,' she said.

'See?' said Joe.

The man smiled, at least, and finally did as he was told. He glanced up when from upstairs came a cheer that sounded a lot like they might have got the Taj Mahal fountain working. It didn't make him jump, but he was on edge. Joe touched his arm to try to bring him back. He would still have sworn to a jury that they knew each other, but it must have just been an epilepsy illusion, because he couldn't recall a particular conversation. Knowing that it was only a misplaced impression did nothing to smooth it over. 'So Eleanor wandered off and left you, did she?'

'She pointed me in the right direction.'

'She's a bit … yes,' said Joe, not wanting to say bad things about her. 'If you'd like to stay overnight, there's plenty of room. You don't have to decide now; decide after some wine.'

'It's all right, thank you, I'm staying in Knightsbridge.'

'But wine?' Joe pressed, wanting to make him sit down and fighting a rush of anger with Eleanor for having left him alone. It wasn't her fault; the man seemed steady and it was only a fractional brittleness that said he wasn't. Joe wouldn't have recognised it if he hadn't seen it before at one time or another in half the people upstairs.

'Please.'

'More reliable supply in the kitchen,' Joe said, because it seemed better not to put him in front of all Toby's loud friends, or even the eager intensity of the Society scientists.

The man looked relieved, then laughed when Joe tucked a sprig of silk holly into his breast pocket. They were easily the plainest people in the house. With so many of the women in bright dresses, and the vivid-sashed uniforms of the cavalry officers, there wasn't much else in the way of grey and white but them. Joe was even more glad of him than before.

However much Joe promised himself he was a perfectly worthwhile person, it was difficult not to look at Toby's friends and feel like a coward for not serving. To be clearly demarcated as such in black tie was uncomfortable. It didn't matter that he oversaw the workshop that made the artillery they used. It always niggled, and worse because he couldn't remember why he hadn't signed up too. Toby was good at telling him about the life he'd forgotten, and Toby said he had forbidden it because you couldn't waste a good brain on cavalry, but Toby was also prone to telling whichever story he thought would go down best.

The kitchen was large enough to stay at one end of it without disturbing everyone else too much. Joe poured two glasses, mismatched because all the matching ones were upstairs now, then put the pan back on the stove, where Alice poured in another bottle. Her dress was a brilliant peacock blue whose shade changed all the time.

'Hot, careful,' Joe murmured as he handed over the glass.

'Thank you.'

'I'm Joe,' said Joe.

When the man said his name was Kite, it sounded familiar. Joe wished the déjà vu would go off. It had never lasted this long before.

While they talked, Joe stoked up the fire behind them. The kitchen used to be two rooms, knocked through now, so it had two hearths, one at either end. The front door opened again and a new clatter of soldiers came through and raced upstairs. Some of them had brought husbands and wives, and Alice went out to see them properly. Kite watched as if he'd never seen so many people in a house at once. He relaxed little by little and Joe felt relieved. Toby's crowd wasn't for everyone. They had a sweet but clumsy unconsciousness of how much space they took up, and how it could feel threatening to anyone less strong or less young.

'So what brought you to the Society?' Joe ventured.

'I was looking for someone I used to sail with. He told me to look up Mrs Sidgwick because he didn't know where he'd be living. And then I didn't get much further. I've been staying in her attic.'

'Find him?'

'Yes, he's well,' Kite said, but not as though he wanted to dwell on it. It must have been a lie, unless the friend didn't have a spare blanket to sleep on.

Someone upstairs dropped a glass. It made Kite jump. If he was absolutely still, if you'd taken a photograph of him, he looked like a powerful man. Moving, there was a china fragility to him.

'Look,' Joe said, 'this is none of my business, but are you all right? I mean generally.'

'Yes, thank you. I think that lady is looking for you,' he added, as politely as if a grown woman had come in, but it was Beatrix, with her wandering walk and the expression that worried Joe so much — the one that said she was never sure if she would be welcome.

He couldn't remember her ever having not been welcome, but he was painfully conscious that what was the most unmemorable and passing half-moment for an adult was the formative turning point of a small child's life. He picked her up and made a fuss of her, even though he could feel that it was unkind to do that in front of a man who spent Christmas in the attic of the first obliging stranger he stumbled across.

'This is Beatrix,' he said. 'She's my niece. Say hello, Bee.'

She opened and closed her hand. Kite looked worried that he was going to frighten her.

'She gets a bit neglected,' Joe said, wanting to explain himself. 'She's got a twin brother. He's loud and she fades into corners if you're not careful. Don't you?' he added to her.

She nodded. He tickled her to make sure she knew it wasn't an accusation, but she only looked down at her own chest.

'Old soul,' Kite said.

'Yes.' With a fresh ache, Joe missed the little girl who had turned out to be a false epilepsy memory; missed her just as if she'd been real, and taken away. He hugged Beatrix closer. Stealing the twins helped.

Unfortunately, this meant he talked about them all the time, even though he knew that for any thinking adult, there were types of yeast more interesting than other people's children.

'I think she's going to be clever,' he said, though everything in him yelled that everyone who had ever loved a child always thought it was the next Mozart. 'God, I'm sorry. I bore on about them all the time, I plan not to and then it just sort of comes out, it's unbearable.'

'No. I think you're right about her,' Kite said, and Joe tried to imagine how anyone learned grace like that.

Beatrix patted his shoulder, worried now, and he realised she had come to fetch him because dinner was ready. Cutlery and glasses clinked along the corridor; the maids had gone.

'Come on, she's right. Better get up there before the gannets from the maths department pilfer everything.'

Kite looked unsettled when Beatrix leaned towards him.

'You can hold her,' Joe said.

'But – I might drop her.'

'Don't be stupid,' Joe said, and put her in Kite's arms.

Kite held her properly, like she was precious, and for her part, Beatrix looked pleased with him. She put both her hands over one of his and rubbed to see if the scars would come off, and squeaked interestedly when they wouldn't. He crooked his fingertip over hers, just, still afraid that he was going to hurt her. Beatrix curled against his chest. She must have felt safe. She was too used to being hauled around by people whose minds were on other things. Joe had to push away the urge to put his arm round them both. He couldn't tell where it came from, or why it was so wonderful to see Kite with her. Clearly the epilepsy was determined to have a party tonight too. He shoved his hands into his pockets. If he could just *not* do anything insane or sinister in front of this poor man, it would be a good night.

Kite gave her back in the doorway rather than put her down. Joe smiled, but Kite didn't stay with them at dinner. He sat with some cavalrymen who spent the whole evening boasting to him about some charge or other in the Sudan, but he seemed to mind that less than a small child and overfamiliar strangers.

Joe kept finding his attention straying down the table. The cavalrymen had managed to engage Kite a lot more than he had and now, they were laughing together. He kept deciding to concentrate on something else, but within a few minutes he was listening again, jealous.

He couldn't shift the certainty that he knew the man. He couldn't remember how. All the tired old dream-images were suggesting themselves for the job. Names on pillars, the sea, a book in French. They were so worn out he could see through the fabric of them. It made him sad, because shamefully, they were the brightest things he had.

He had to leave the room to try and make his brain reset itself with a change of scene.

Under the sweep of the stairs was a cupboard with low rafters and floorboards that still smelled new, because it wasn't used for anything. The glow of the candle was good, and so were the striped shadows the light made in the rafters.

He liked it because it was a door to nowhere, and he kept looking at doors to nowhere as if there was something just past them he couldn't see. It was maddening, but it was good at the same time, to feel like there was somewhere else, waiting.

The cupboard was like a ship's cabin too. He loved ships.

He had a vision of sitting at a table aboard an old ship, the wood creaking with the tide just like the stairs above him were creaking now, sharing a cigarette across a table full of fruit and baklava, while someone leaned against his left side. He could remember being happy; the kind of happiness that hurt because it couldn't last and tomorrow it would be gone.

'You're going mad,' he said aloud, and got up fast, though he wanted to stay and see more imaginary things. He surprised Kite, who had just been coming down the stairs.

'I doubt you're mad,' Kite offered. He must have heard him through the knotholes.

'You're not going already?'

'It's past eleven.'

'Let me walk with you,' Joe said, in every bleak expectation that Kite would say no.

'Thank you,' Kite said. He smiled. 'Just as well. I don't know the way.' He gave Joe the card of a Knightsbridge hotel.

'I'll get you there, come on.'

'Why did you think you were going mad?' Kite asked as they went out into the cold, Joe still shrugging into his coat.

'I ... see things,' Joe said. He shook his head. 'Hence the Psychical Society. It's just epilepsy visions, but they're ...' He trailed off, feeling stupid. 'I get déjà vu too, a lot. Even now. I feel like I know you. I'd swear I do. I've been jealous about you all evening.'

Kite didn't veer away or look doubtful about being taken through London by a madman. 'From where?'

'I don't know,' Joe said tiredly. 'Like I say, it's just déjà vu. I have hallucinations too. A lighthouse. Having dinner on an old ship.' He sighed. 'A man who waits by the sea. I mean it's clear, very clear. I can see him skimming stones.'

'Yes. That's right.'

Joe looked up sharply. 'What?'

'Yes,' Kite said again. 'You're not mad.' He looked as afraid as he had holding Beatrix. 'I lied before. You do know me. It's you I came to see.'

Joe's breath caught in the back of his throat and so did all his words. 'I can't make any of it join up, it's – more real than dreams but not so real as real.' He caught Kite's arm, probably too hard. 'Please. Do you know what happened to me?'

Kite nodded. He let his breath out slowly. 'I'll tell you what happened, and you ask me anything you don't remember.'

49

Edinburgh, 1805

It was only a few months after the fall of London that the order came from the Admiralty. Someone at the whaling station on Lewis and Harris had sent round word that the French seemed to be building some kind of tower on a rock out to sea, supplied by ships like no one had ever seen. Once *Agamemnon* was refitted, they were to investigate straight away. Kite didn't see at first that Jem had dropped down onto the floor. He was bent forward with his hand against his chest, his colour gone. It took him a minute or so to say anything and when he did, he promised it was only nerves, and then explained what the tower was.

Jem knew what had happened as soon as he saw the lighthouse. It took a while to find where the time difference was, that it was between the pillars in the sea, but when they went through, the town turned from a healthy whaling station to bones on the beach and one lit lodging house.

'What the hell are we meant to do about that?' Kite said finally.

Agamemnon was waiting in the lee of the lighthouse island, unable to get any closer because of the rocks under the surface of the sea. Kite and Jem had rowed out, and now the boat was rocking just on the future side of the pillars. If Kite leaned to the left, to see outside a pillar, the lighthouse looked ruined. Lean to the right, to see it through the pillars on the past side, it was brand new and not even quite finished yet. The new one was on the wrong side.

Jem was quiet and tight. He was holding the oars, because Kite's fingers were broken. Kite couldn't remember breaking them, but they were getting painful in cold weather. 'We sailed through here in the *Kingdom*. None of us realised anything was different. I always thought it was that fog. You know, when ... you found us.'

Kite didn't know what to say. He knew what he wanted to say, but it was all questions. Just what Jem's life had been before: had he been married; did he have children. The things Jem had never told him. But none of that would have helped. 'We need to find a way to brick it up. The French are going to find it, if we're not ...'

Jem looked at him slowly. 'Say again, sorry?'

'I say we need to close this off somehow.'

'My son will be twelve by now.'

'Oh,' was all Kite could say.

'Or maybe not,' Jem said. He was staring at the whaling station. 'I came from an England where we won at Trafalgar. This will be an England where we didn't. London will be French. God knows how that will have changed people, families ...'

'You never talked about yours.'

'My what?'

'Family.'

'Well, damn all use, was there.'

Kite had to look away. Jem had settled and made the best of a bad job, he'd always known that. Hearing about a son, though, felt like taking chain shot to one of the foundation supports of their own ramshackle little family.

'I was married. She was – she is, called Madeline. She was aboard the *Kingdom* with me, the French took with her with the others. But we had a son. We left him behind, at school. I thought I'd never see him again.'

'Well, here we are. Do you want to try?'

Jem looked up. 'I have no idea how things have changed. And anyway, I lived in London.'

Kite couldn't bring himself to argue for it any further. Jem wanted him to, he could see that; he wanted to be persuaded rather than suggest it himself, and a better, more chivalrous person would have done that for him, but drowning would have been easier.

Jem swallowed. 'Miz … thing is, if we were to go through, if we went to London, they would have records. Of everything that's *going* to happen to us, in our time, in Edinburgh. We could check. We could see if there are things we can change.'

Kite didn't say that there were libraries in Glasgow, and there was no earthly need to go all the way to London for that. 'Yes.'

'It will all be different obviously. Edward won't be there.' But his eyes were full of begging.

'He might be,' Kite heard himself say. His whole mind was going numb, etherising itself. 'We can't know until we check.'

'Even if he is, I don't see how he could know who I am. Everything's different.' Jem's voice was shaking. His heart was already there, hundreds of miles south.

'We don't know how it works,' Kite murmured.

'Do you really think he might …?'

'Maybe.'

Jem looked at him properly, shining now. 'Will – shall you come with me?'

Kite didn't want to meet Jem's son. He didn't want to have to trail back to Edinburgh, alone, to explain to Agatha that obviously Jem had stayed in the future after all, with the family he had chosen, and not the one that had been thrust on him by circumstance.

As if *wanting* gave him some God-given right to get in the way. Jesus Christ. Jem deserved to go home, to his real home, after all this time.

'Of course,' he said.

An hour later they were on a steamship, chugging away from the future-side whaling station. Kite had heard about engines before but he had never imagined what they were like. Noisy, grimy, and very fast, even though there was no wind. It took them round to Glasgow, where finally the time difference was unavoidable. Machinery dominated the docks. The shipyards were like nothing he'd seen. They were building ironclads there in scaffolding, titanic things with propellers four times the height of a person. Cranes moved to and fro everywhere, and men – welders, not carpenters. An impossible number of people. Jem didn't let him look for long and went straight to the railway station.

Kite had never disliked anything as instantly as he disliked the trains and the rivers of track. An engine was steaming in just as they came out onto the platforms and all at once he understood why Jem had never minded sliding under the guns to fix chassis axles. Next to these colossal machines, a cannon was tiny.

The train had slowed to a crawl, easing forward inch by ponderous inch. But when it hit the buffers, it banged, hard. He couldn't even guess how heavy it must have been. Only a few people stepped down.

Jem climbed the three-step ladder up to the door and pulled it open, then dropped back down again to hand Kite up first. Kite waited for him at the top, looking around. The corridors were about what they were on a ship, but taller. Glass doors joined the carriages. Jem touched his elbows and steered him to the right, to an empty compartment, which was like a small cabin with upholstered chairs.

'First class,' Jem explained. 'I can't sit on a train for twelve hours on a bench in third.'

Only twelve hours, all the way to London. How long did it take to ride from here – what, a week?

Kite sat down slowly, then let himself tip forwards and raked his hands through his hair. He could have slept there and then, though it was only seven o'clock. Jem rubbed the back of his neck and pulled him harder and harder until he dropped sideways over his knees. Jem took his scarf off and put it round Kite instead. It was dark tartan. It still smelled brand new under the soft overlay of tobacco, not quite his yet.

He heard the door open once, but if anyone said anything he didn't catch it. When he woke up properly, it took a long few seconds to understand where they were and why. He wasn't good at sleeping in snatches. Coming out of it was close to vertigo. He had to close his eyes again and wait for it to go off. Jem had bent over him to keep him from the glare of the gas lamp, which was much brighter than oil.

'Food. With cutlery and real glasses,' Jem said against his hair. He spoke like he was kneeling on the edge of a black pool and coaxing up something shy from fathoms deep.

He sat up. Jem looked relieved and Kite realised it hadn't quite been expected. He hadn't made any close acquaintance with a mirror since Trafalgar, but although all the burns and bruises were a painful nuisance, it hadn't occurred to him that he looked so bad he might die for no real reason in a chair somewhere before dinner.

'Stop looking at me like that, I'm fine. I'm just still on the watch rota.'

'No, I know.' Jem poured out a glass of wine each from a bottle with a French label. The plates were proper crockery. He frowned and put the bottle down.

'All right?'

'Just fuzzy.'

'I'll find you some water.'

It was strange but not unpleasant to walk down the gangways and feel everything moving. A few more people had arrived somewhere along the way. They were dressed differently than the same people would have been at home. Women's dresses had turned cumbersome and taken a step in the direction of the seventeenth century, all corsetry and rigging. Men had turned plain, unless all of the ones he saw had a particular taste for grey.

When he came across the steward, Kite showed him some ordinary coins and asked if they were all right here. The steward hesitated, then took out a booklet full of densely printed numbers. He read down, paused, looked embarrassed, then took out a miniature key and unlocked a miniature strongbox, which was full of stacked coins and newly minted notes. There was a great deal of change. When he produced two glass bottles of water, he did it with much more of a flourish than Kite thought he would have a minute ago.

Kite managed to take both the water and the change without moving his face or looking at the money, and get all the way back to the right carriage. Once the door was shut behind him, though, he stood against a wall and pulled a coin out of his pocket again. It was new and shiny. One franc, eighteen ninety-nine; on the back was a man super-arced by 'Napoleon IV' in copperplate.

'Jem. Look at this ...' He stopped, because he had made Jem jump when he opened the compartment door. 'Sorry. This is for you.' He gave him the water. 'But look at these ... Jem?'

'I forgot you were here,' Jem said.

'Agatha does too. But—'

'No – I mean ...' He struggled and then shook his head when Kite put the coin into his hand. 'Sorry. What am I ...'

'Is this normal?'

Jem gazed down at the coin for too long. 'No. It should be Queen Victoria.' He glanced across at last and smiled. 'Still, if the French want anachronistic, we can bloody give it to them. Pretty sure I know enough to discover electromagnetic motors early.'

Kite wanted to say he didn't know anyone else who could take such enormities so sunnily, that it was a sort of gift, but framing it would have been trite.

Jem looked into his wine and a frown traced a line between his eyebrows, pulling at the scar over the left one. 'Who did I say the Queen was a minute ago?'

'Victoria.'

He pushed his fingertips over his forehead. 'Sorry.'

'Does it hurt?'

Jem touched the scar. 'No. I don't think it's this. It's just … fog. It's been coming on since Harris,' he said, and stopped on a strange tone that wasn't quite finished. Kite waited for him to add something else, but he only drank the last of the wine and set down the glass. 'Dear God, I can tell I'm going to be boring tonight. You haven't got cards or – obviously you've got cards,' he laughed when Kite took the pack from his pocket.

They bet with buttons. Jem picked them up all over the place. Whatever he was wearing, he always had a reliable supply in his pockets.

'Only nine ships left now,' Jem said after a while. 'If nothing else, we'll be on shorter stints. Home more often.'

Kite nodded.

'You'll have to come and stay with us on your next leave.'

'Mm.'

Jem kicked him. 'Why are you so determined not to?'

'Look. Agatha doesn't want to share her very tiny apartment, or her husband.' Jem and Agatha had bought some rooms in Leith, bartered with Agatha's jewellery. They were basic, hardly bigger than the tenement apartment in Cadiz, and they were above a bar of extremely questionable morals. Agatha had been nothing but cheerful about it, and quick to stress that it was extraordinarily lucky to have found anywhere at all in the refugee-flooded city, but he could tell she was falling into a kind of shock, and he didn't blame her. She had never expected to be poor again. 'So it would be far better for your marriage and for the health of my sister's tolerance for me if I die in a hedge before I come and stay with the two of you.'

Jem didn't laugh. Instead he watched him for too long, then dealt another round. He didn't look angry, but he never did, and Kite could never tell when he was. He must have been sometimes.

Despite not having taken out a cigarette since boarding the train, Jem still smelled of them; the heady sweet Jamaica blend was in the grain of his skin now, and even in the cold weather – even if he was cold himself – it seemed warm. By long association now, though it wasn't there, Kite always caught gunpowder with it. More and more, it brought on a strange feeling that Jem was always right on the edge of igniting.

Jem laid down a card. 'You're coming home with me after this.'

'I just told you—'

'I'm not negotiating. At least two hours every night with a proper roof and a proper fire and real food, whenever we're on shore. I cannot – I *cannot* live any more counting the number of times I've seen you by the stars on your arm.'

Kite sat still at first and couldn't speak, because his throat had closed, then went round to him and hugged him. Jem kissed him once, very soft, and paralysing until he did it again and Kite got back enough control over the nerves in his hands to pull him nearer. After a second, Jem locked the carriage door and lifted

Kite into his lap so they could sit chest to chest, his hand over the tattoo as though he wanted to rub it out.

The steward rang a bell down the carriages half an hour before they came into London. Kite was already awake. He put together everything that they'd scattered about, which wasn't much, then pressed one hand to Jem's chest when he showed no sign of coming to by himself. When he opened his eyes, he looked disorientated.

'Nearly there,' Kite said.

'Oh … right. Thank you.' He sat up gradually and looked around, then seemed to come back to himself and put away the blankets and the bunk, and went out without saying where. When he came back he was neater. An inspector came soon after him and asked to see their tickets. Jem handed them over and the inspector clipped out the 'Glasg' of Glasgow. Jem took them back slowly, not as if he were sure what was going on.

'Jem. Are you all right?'

'Sorry? Yes, I … not really, I … this is ridiculous, but where have we just come from?'

'From Glasgow. From Eilean Mòr, the lighthouse. Do you remember?' Kite said quietly. It had been a bad hit Jem had taken, the one that gave him the scar – even being clipped by a recoiling gun was bad – but Kite had never seen anyone suffer the effects so long afterwards.

'Yes. Yes, what … were we doing there?'

'Looking for your son. Finding a couple of libraries, maybe.'

'Jesus Christ,' Jem said, himself again. 'What the hell was that?'

'You just forgot for a minute what—'

'That's not normal, that's never happened before.' Jem's voice broke halfway. 'Everything was gone, I didn't know who I was bloody talking to, not since I woke up!'

He pushed his hand over his mouth. Kite levered it away and put both arms around him. Jem hugged him tight. Outside, the limits of London were sliding by, tenements and washing lines, and then houses with gardens. There was a strange brown mist in the streets. He thought it was smoke at first, but there was too much of it. Nearer the station, tributaries of track ran together and, beyond them, dull grey walls and wires stretched overhead, some singly and some in tentacular clusters that wound down wooden poles. He couldn't see what they did. Unease hit the seabed under his diaphragm. They looked like totems, the kind the Caribbean maroons made, that might have been memorials or KEEP OUT signs. He wouldn't have known it was London if Jem and the timetables hadn't said so.

Jem gripped his hand as the train glided into the platform. When it stopped, the jolt jerked them sideways an inch.

'Gare du Roi,' the guard called. 'Gare du Roi, all change!'

'Miz, I think ...'

'Hold on,' Kite said, worried now. He was closest to the door and the latch wasn't obvious until he saw a sign that said you had to push down the window and open it from outside. It meant leaning awkwardly. Once the door was open, he stepped back to let Jem go first. 'What's wrong?'

Kite saw it go from him this time. He stopped still on the platform and stared at the people going past, his eyes sliding over Kite as much as they did anyone else. He jumped when Kite touched his arm. He didn't recognise him.

'I'm sorry, this is – but could you tell me where we are?' Jem said. He sounded different. It was a French accent. When Kite told him, he shook his head. His shoulders had gone back, taut; he didn't like talking to a stranger. Kite put his teeth together and tried not to stare. It wasn't a lapse. Everything that made him Jem was different. Even his expression wasn't right. He held his face open usually, but it was locked now. It was how people looked in the parts of the docks you didn't go if you were in a uniform, where it was only stevedores and carpenters, and women who watched you too hard over the slick noise of the fish knives.

Feeling like he was sinking, Kite asked his name. There was a long pause before the wrong one arrived.

Joe.

The panic came down slowly, not in a normal flustering rush but like something very, very heavy. It had solid edges. Kite could think past it enough to get them into a cab and to a hospital, where the doctor at least seemed to take it seriously. He waited, but before long a nurse came to say, crossly, that visiting hours were over thank you.

He stayed the night at the first place he walked into, an inn called the Coeur de Lion. The chatter at the bar was English and the men were rough; mostly they were filthy and still wearing tool belts. They talked about tunnels and drills. There were newspapers strewn about, so he found a corner and read one start to finish. It was in French, but easy French, and full of pictures. Mainly it was news from Paris. The Emperor's brother had been typically silly; society parties; abolition rally. The Saints had blown up something, again, in the Premier Arrondissement.

He felt better for having had to concentrate on something and slid the paper under his coat to show Agatha later, but it still made him jump when a girl cleared her throat next to him and said the room was ready. He saw her wondering whether to ask about the burn scars, but she was too polite, and only gave him the new candle that came with the room and explained that he could have another on Wednesday, if he stayed, or before for three sous, and he had to pretend to know whether or not that was reasonable.

In the morning, the doctor explained the transfer to La Salpêtrière, which had been Bethlem when Kite had last read about it. There were strictly no visitors except on every second

Monday, so he had to negotiate and managed ten minutes, but Jem, or Joe, had no idea who he was and didn't want to speak English. Kite explained that they had been on the train together, but he could see it wasn't sinking in. He tried again the next day. One of the doctors didn't like having unashamed English people there and had him arrested. He spent a night in a police cell. By the time he got out again, Joe had gone home with a family who said he was theirs.

The address was easy to find after he'd bribed a nurse for it. It was a shabby town house in Clerkenwell. He introduced himself in the evening to the landlord, who gave him a cup of tea for his trouble.

'It was very good of you to follow it up,' the man said. He had excellent manners, but through their weave shone a match head of suspicion. The more English Kite spoke, the less M. Saint-Marie seemed to want him in the kitchen. It was a calm caginess; not rude, but how Kite would have been if an obvious highwayman had thumped down opposite and put his boots up on the table. He would not, he had said right at the start, fetch Joe; there had been enough confusion already.

'I just wanted to be sure he's – where he should be. Has he lived here long?'

'Always. He grew up in this kitchen. He's where he belongs, I can assure you. I imagine you need to be getting home now?'

'Not till tomorrow,' Kite said, and inclined his head to say he hadn't missed the hint. 'Does the name Castlereagh mean anything to you?'

'No.'

'Was his family always called Tournier?'

'I believe so. Why?'

'On the train, he said his name was Castlereagh.'

'Well, everyone lies on trains,' Saint-Marie said, quite gently, though he tipped his shoulder to say, particularly if they've been accosted by an English thug. 'If you were hoping for a reward, this isn't a wealthy family, I'm afraid.'

'No. I'd just like to see him, that's all.'

'I'm afraid not,' said Saint-Marie.

There were footsteps on the stairs and Joe came down with a basket of laundry. 'It's freezing up there, can I sit in with you and steal your marzipan?' he asked Saint-Marie in French, and then paused when he saw Kite. He didn't recognise him.

'Well, good night,' Saint-Marie said to Kite. 'Don't let me hold you up.' He saw him to the door. Once it had shut behind him, Kite heard Saint-Marie tell Joe he'd been some kind of beggar. He let his head bump against the wall. He could see horribly clearly what had happened. Joe Tournier was who Jem Castlereagh would have been, born into a London that had fallen to Napoleon. Jem's London was lost, and so was Jem.

Could he really kidnap a man who was taller than him and get him all the way back to Eilean Mòr, all without hurting him? Even if Jem's memory were guaranteed to return, he didn't think he could do it.

'He's still there,' Saint-Marie murmured. 'Let's call the gendarmes.'

He tried to talk to Joe again the next day, one last time, was arrested again on suspicion of conspiracy to steal a slave, spent two days in another police cell, and came out having decided, leadenly, what he would have to do. He had wondered about sending a letter – that would get through the front door, at least – but Joe had no reason to believe a random letter from a stranger. In the end, he went back up to Eilean Mòr and straight back through to the present side, back round to Stornaway. Trying not to think about it too much, he went to the post office and wrote a letter for them to hold until 1899. The woman at the counter looked suspicious of a scam, but promised to follow the instructions.

Agatha had got up an experiment with a frog and a Leyden jar when he came back to her rooms in Edinburgh. She had an apron on over her ordinary clothes. He put his bag in the corner and sat down on the spare stool. He was there for three or four seconds before she saw him.

'Jesus! I'm putting a bell on you,' she laughed. 'How was it, what did you find?' She looked properly. 'What have you done with Jem?'

'I ... don't know.' He was quiet for a second, because he wanted to say, just let me keep it for another five minutes, but it wasn't his.

'Missouri.' It had a rattle to it, like she was shaking a tax box at him.

He explained as much as he understood. It left him hollowed out. He felt like that man from the story who, because he couldn't pay in coins, had to pay with an equal measure of flesh flensed off his chest.

'That's it?' she said at last. 'You left him there.'

He nodded.

Downstairs somewhere, doors clattered open and voices drifted up the stairs. They must have just opened the bar for dinner. Very different to that grand house on Jermyn Street, this, but of course the English banks had collapsed. They had no money now.

Agatha smoothed down her skirt, tipping herself towards the light while she made sure there was nothing on it. Since he could remember, she had worn white, or patterned white, but the navy women now were dyeing their dresses dark blue, like officers' jackets. She put her wedding ring in the top drawer, and locked it. When she came back around the desk, she slapped him so hard he fell onto his hands and knees.

'Get out,' was all she said.

50

London, 1903

The frost fair glittered. Around the stalls, electric lights that ran on an elderly generator loud enough to hear, over the hiss of chestnuts on hotplates and the plinking song that came from the bicycling fortune teller's music box. Joe and Kite had made a couple of circuits through it while Kite told the story.

They walked while Joe tried to think what to say, which took a long time. It was all true, he could feel that; he had recognised it while Kite was saying it. Once or twice he could have joined in but didn't, because his voice had gone somewhere else.

The Clock Tower sang out midnight, and then so did St Paul's and all the carillons of other bells along the river. He stared at Parliament. He could remember it in ruins.

It was like trying to remember a dream. It all ran together in a blur of sounds and engines. When he looked back towards the cathedral, he had a vivid memory of printed signs saying when confession was available and Mary with an electric halo, but he couldn't have said when it had been, or what he had done before or after. Beside him, Kite was quiet, and different, because he wasn't just a beaten-up sailor any more; knowing what he had looked like before the burn scars made them a translucent mask over someone who was still handsome.

The cold was rising off the ice. He could feel it getting under his sleeves and the hem of his coat, so he stopped to buy some of the chestnuts, which were covered in hot sugar, and gave them to Kite to hold. Kite bumped his shoulder against Joe's to say thank you.

'You came to make sure I had a family, didn't you?' Joe said. 'Not kicking about by myself above a shoe shop or something.'

Kite didn't say yes or no, or what he would have done if there had been a lonely shoe shop. 'I came to say goodbye. The gate is being bricked up, there will be no way through in a fortnight's time.'

Joe looked away and over the ice. Kite offered him the chestnuts. 'Thanks. Do I seem the same, in any …?'

Kite nodded. 'I think you're the same thing in three different lights.'

'But we're not talking about morning and evening light, are we,' Joe said, because although he couldn't remember anything specific that Kite had said to him in the past, he had a good idea of the shape of his conversation. 'It's more along the lines of ultraviolet, infrared and visible, isn't it. And don't say you don't know what the electromagnetic spectrum is, it's impossible to sit in a room with me in any iteration of myself and not get onto it at some point.'

'Yes I know, because my sister had to rescue me once from Someone's X-ray experiments. What sort of lunatic makes a fluoroscope in the shed?'

Joe sort of laughed and choked at the same time. He couldn't tell if he remembered, or if he could just imagine it well.

'Was it hard this time?' Kite asked after a while.

'No. I lost my memory while I was in Harris. The vicar there took me in until the sea ice melted and then we went to a doctor in Glasgow. Toby and Alice came up to fetch me.' He frowned when he remembered how things had been when he'd left. 'How is it in Edinburgh? Was there a siege?'

'No. It's all right. Better.' Kite eased away and walked further from him, just out of reach. 'Although I hope we aren't making everything even worse than before by bricking up the gate.'

'No, that sounds sensible – why would it?'

Kite pointed upward. 'The design of all the light bulbs just changed while we were standing here.'

'It ... has,' Joe said slowly.

'It's all the people going to and fro at the gate. I've tried to stop the crew going ashore too much, but we have to make supply runs and everyone wants to see what a hundred years in the future looks like. I think there's a lot of flotsam from both times floating around between the two now. It must affect things.' Kite was watching the string of lights above them, like he was daring them to change again. 'We keep getting visits from the future-side whalers. They know what the gate is, more or less, so they keep coming to lecture us about modern shipbuilding.'

Joe laughed.

Kite smiled too, and Joe suspected he had a soft spot for the whalers. 'But, every time someone from your side comes to my side, something changes, doesn't it, however small, because they shouldn't be there. I've been worried all week that someone from your side will call the wrong person from my side a moron and I'll wake up to find everyone here is speaking Russian or Hindustani or God knows.'

'I'm sure it'll be all right. We can live with different light bulbs,' Joe said, although now Kite had pointed it out, he felt uneasy.

At Knightsbridge, the hotel room was airy and simple, with a broad fireplace and coal in the grate, waving heat across the hearthrug. Kite stayed downstairs to fetch some wine – the night manager was keeping it hot – so Joe went up alone to stoke the fire. He had flames flickering over it again by the time Kite opened the door with his elbow and came through as if it were Joe's space and not his. He set the wine glasses down carefully on the table where, anticipating the wine, the housekeeping people had left a bowl of oranges and a sharp knife. He took an orange and began to cut it up, and shied back when Joe touched his arm.

'Do you mind if I take the wine with me? I can sneak out with the glass I think, then I'll be out your way,' Joe said, aware how monstrously strange it must be to have him in the room at all, when he remembered being Jem Castlereagh and Joe Tournier but wasn't either of them.

'No – stay. You'll freeze.'

Joe didn't point out that Kite could hardly look at him. Kite was better when you didn't call his attention to himself. More and more, Joe had a feeling that when he wasn't standing on a quarterdeck, what Kite most wanted was to be allowed to sit quietly in the corner of a conversation and go unnoticed. 'When's your train?' Joe said instead.

'Seven. In the morning.'

It gave Joe an unpleasant bolt of alarm. He had hoped Kite would be around for another week yet; or not even hoped, expected, because it was hard to travel anywhere between Christmas and New Year. 'I'll – are you okay at railway stations, do they make sense?'

'No, they're terrifying, but it's all in English now, so that helps,' Kite said. 'I can't accidentally go to Paris.'

There was a painful silence.

'I can see you off?' Joe offered.

'No, I'm all right.'

Joe was starting to feel urgent about finding a reason to see him again. 'I could bring you something to read for the way? There's a lot you'd like, published lately. Nothing that can hurt.'

Kite shook his head. 'No, better not. I'm honestly contorting myself into passions of anxiety already about things changing.'

'Passions of anxiety. You.'

'But thank you.' Kite tipped some of the orange slices into a wine glass and slid it across to Joe. He looked, now, much more like someone who had been in a war than someone who was in the middle of one. His hair was short, and the scars down his neck had turned silver. There weren't any new ones. He raised his eyes when he felt Joe looking at him. He was so familiar and such a stranger that it was like meeting an actor. He was the man from the sea, the one who waited, and looking at him here, Joe could finally remember the beach. It was where Jem and Agatha had been married.

He could remember that Kite had slipped away after the celebrations, which had been on the deck of the *Victory*. He must have thought he was giving the newlyweds some privacy. It had always been impossible to make him understand that he was wanted; having been told all his life that he was nothing but human jetsam attached to his famous sister. So they'd run down after him onto the beach. The three of them colliding had sent them all tumbling into the sea.

He could remember grasping Kite's hands, unbroken then, and promising there was always space for him, and how Kite had never believed it, though he had pretended; and how Agatha, guiltily, had been glad her brother had never believed it. In bed that night, she'd confessed how badly she wanted something – someone – who was just hers, not who she cultivated for her brother's career or the benefit of a hospital.

He could remember how his heart had splintered when he understood that, far from having made the three of them a proper family like he'd meant to, he'd just taken two people who belonged to Kite, and made it so that neither of them did.

'I'm not going to see you again, am I?' His heart was juddering. 'After this. That's it.'

'No.' Kite was quiet for a second. Joe thought he was going to change the subject or close in on himself again, but he did the opposite. 'Are you all right? You've gone white.'

'Of course. I'm ...' He trailed off, because he wasn't. 'You could stay.'

'I can't. I'm on leave for now, but I have to be back next week—'

'You can't tell me all this and then just vanish!' What had begun as the steam from a small worry was building and building, powering whole pistons and mechanisms that were well on their way to firing full panic.

'Then what am I supposed to do?' Kite said, quite gently. 'I can't stay here, I have eight hundred people to look after. You have people here who need you too, the twins and your brother. I don't know what—'

'Then take me with you,' Joe said, before he had decided to. He swallowed hard. 'Look, those visions – those *memories*, those are the best things I have. Please.'

'Your family, Joe—'

'You're my family! You were family before any of them. I've missed you even when I didn't remember you. Everything I've done since losing you has been about getting back to you. And I know I've left you behind before for other families, but not this time. I can't do it again.' He swallowed when he noticed how much he was saying *I*. 'Sorry. If you don't want me to – look, I'd understand if you said you never want to see me again. I didn't mean to just invite myself.'

Kite said nothing for a while. But then, 'Seven o'clock, platform three. King's Cross.' He inclined his head, careful and full of courtesy. He was holding himself at a distance from the idea. 'I'll expect you if I see you. Don't worry if you change your mind.'

Joe pulled him close. Kite turned to stone, but little by little he unstiffened, and hugged him back.

Home was a painting. There was a thinness to everything and sometimes he could see the canvas through it. He walked around the whole house, all the way up to the attic; the same attic where Joe and Alice Tournier had lived, in that other version of now, where M. Saint-Marie had not gone home to France, fed up with all the post-independence paperwork and restrictions designed to discourage Parisians from moving here, and left it to Joe. The view beyond its round window had been of a London blackened by the steelworks. Now, the towers were sandy-coloured, even in the dark, uplit by the street lamps. He stood in the place where Lily's crib had been. The attic was just an attic now, full of the accumulated rubbish of past Christmases.

It had been real. There had been a real little girl who he'd fought to come back to. Kite was real, and had waited for him years ago by the sea.

He went slowly back downstairs. He passed the sun room, where the fire was still burning and their father was still going strong with the mince pies, and the regiment were ineffectively hushing each other as they sang a drunken song about a lion and a unicorn.

'Boo!' Toby caught him from behind and squashed him into a vice of a hug. 'How are you, small bear?'

Joe was older, but he was a head smaller. Toby was a monster person. 'I'm all right.' He hesitated. 'This is going to sound mad, but I need you to tell me whether or not someone was really there, or if I was just hallucinating.'

'Who's this we're talking about?' said Toby, who did a good impersonation of someone who found epilepsy visions only of mild interest. It wasn't true, but he didn't know Joe had heard him talking to Alice at night.

'The man who came here today, the one who wasn't from your regiment, the sailor. White, red hair. I think he sat with Sanjeev.'

Toby nodded. 'Burn scars.'

Joe sagged. Toby squeezed him again, more gently this time. 'Friend of yours?'

'Yes. I thought ... well, he serves in Scotland and I thought I'd go back up with him for a bit.'

'Send me a haggis.'

'Will do.'

'Everything all right?' Toby said, scrutinising him now.

'Yes ... yes.' Joe looked up at him and wanted to say, I remember that in another life, you died in a field just beyond the Scottish border. But that changed; because a hundred years ago now, there was no siege at Edinburgh, no massacre. No genocide that set off the fury of the last surviving dregs of the English army, who became the Saints. They don't exist any more. They didn't shoot you this time.

It was all there, like a map.

'Love you,' he said.

Toby kissed his forehead. 'I love you too, you tiny oddball. Last glass of wine?'

Joe agreed. Toby walked him to a sofa, both hands on Joe's shoulders, probably to keep him from changing his mind.

'What happened to the Taj Mahal?' Joe asked, because there were just a lot of empty wine bottles now where it had stood.

'Is that the start of a joke? I don't know, what *did* happen to the Taj Mahal?'

'No, the ... model, the fountain.'

'What?' Toby said, looking confused in the edgy way he'd carried around with him ever since he and Alice had had to fetch a memoryless, bewildered Joe from Glasgow.

'Nothing,' said Joe. He wondered if it was possible to drop a brick in 1809 and, by some convoluted process of history, cause a demented potter not to think of making a ceramic Taj Mahal fountain a hundred years later.

Like an oil-slick layer, Joe became aware of a new memory, of Toby bringing back chintz for Alice, not a tasteless fountain. But that oil-slick memory was very, very thin. Everything else was still there underneath.

George and Beatrix were still playing by the fire. Alice's rule, which worked amazingly, was that they went to bed when they were tired, whenever that was, but on the condition they were quiet after eight o'clock. Once Toby had gone to talk to other people, Joe knelt down with them on the hearthrug and built forts for a while, wondering if they would notice when he was gone. Briefly, maybe, but it would be fine. Alice loved them, Toby loved them; even Joe and Toby's father adored them in his gruff way. He pulled Bee into his lap anyway, to try and soak in the memory of holding a child. He wasn't going to have one of his own now.

He must have dozed off.

The clocks struck three, and he became aware that the room had quietened enough for him to hear the hall clock tick. The room was empty now, the embers of the fire clicking, the few candles left on the mantel burning down to pools of liquid wax. Someone had already taken away most of the decorations. No more festoons of holly looped along the ceiling; there were just a few clusters of ivy and bells around the mantel mirror. The detritus of the party was gone too: the wine glasses, the mince-pie plates, everything. He twisted around, worried that someone had asked him to help and he hadn't heard. Alice said he had an unnerving way of ignoring people sometimes – particularly, she pointed out, if he was listening to an epilepsy hallucination.

426

He stood up, lifting Bee with him, because it would disturb her less than setting her down. He was going to have to get some proper sleep if he was going to get to King's Cross for seven. King's Cross, which had once been the Gare du Roi.

Vaguely, he wondered why Alice hadn't come in to take the twins from him. She didn't love leaving him with her children, but maybe she was cheerful enough not to mind for tonight.

He put Bee to bed, then George, set an alarm for six and fell into bed himself in the next room. His quilt cover was different to the one he'd woken up with. Another dropped brick in 1809, probably.

5 1

J oe woke up at half past five because the house was too silent. They had employed a full staff over Christmas; with eleven people from the regiment staying for the week, it was too much work for just Joe and Toby and Alice by themselves. All week, the cooks had been up at five, and Joe had woken to the cosy sound of pots clanging in the kitchen directly below his room, knowing he didn't have to use them or wash them up. There was no clanging now; no doors opening and closing; nothing. And there was a strange tight feeling in his stomach. He'd had bad dreams, but he couldn't recall them.

He went to look around downstairs, which was all dark. And deserted. His heart starting to squeeze, he went fast up the stairs to the master bedroom that had once belonged to M. Saint-Marie and was now Toby and Alice's.

Empty. There were sheets over the furniture.

Joe was normally good at functioning even when he was feeling panicky, because he'd had so much practice. Now, though, he felt sick, and he had to lean against the wall for a second before he could get together the nerve to look into the twins' room.

They were there. Bee heard the door open and sat up.

'Morning?' she asked, full of faith that he would know best, however tired she was.

'I ...' He sank down on to his knees beside her small bed. 'Bee. Sweetheart; can you remember where your mum and dad are?'

She looked blank. 'Mum?'

'Yes, dolly, where is she?'

Bee blinked once and then looked away, and clapped absent-mindedly. She was too little.

Joe was torn. He wanted not to let them out of his sight, but he wanted to know as well if there was *anyone* else here, because at seven o'clock he was supposed to be on a railway platform.

'Don't move,' he said, and hunted through the whole house.

It was all empty. There was no sign of any party, no sign of the regiment, no sign that anyone had used the kitchen yesterday. A plate and two babies' bottles stood on the drying rack. That was it.

Joe stopped halfway back up the stairs and told himself aloud to pull it together. When the Taj Mahal fountain had gone missing yesterday, he *had* remembered why. He *did* know where Toby and Alice were, he had to; his memory would have changed, but the new layer would be thin.

Unless he was wrong; unless he had dreamed a wonderful life where everyone was here, and where the man who waited by the sea stopped waiting and came to the door.

'Come on,' he said softly into the candlelight. 'Where are they? You know.'

Bee must have known that something was the matter, because she came to the top of the stairs now, towing George. They were too tiny to speak properly, but they had a shared burble that both of them seemed to understand, and when they found him, they both looked anxious, watching him like a pair of baby owls.

'Toby is ...' Joe said aloud, and left a quiet to try and force his mind to fill in the gap.

Toby is dead.

Toby has been dead for a year.

Toby and Alice died of malaria in India.

Even though they were here yesterday.

The new memory already felt more solid. The older one, the one of last night and the party, and Kite, was already starting to fade. He had looked after the twins alone this year, always afraid that one of Alice's relatives or a lawyer, or *someone*, would power in and declare that a single man had no right to bring up children by himself.

'We have to go,' he said to them. 'Right now. Come on, let's get you dressed.'

Maybe it was a dream, maybe he would get to the station and there would be no such person as Missouri Kite – who the hell was called Missouri anyway? – and he would have to trail to the hospital to report that his brain had absolutely buggered itself this time. If he had to say it aloud, that a man he recognised from epilepsy hallucinations had come to find him from ninety-five years ago, it had the ring of obvious madness.

Or maybe it wasn't, and some accidental conversation at the Eilean Mòr gate had changed the world overnight, and George and Bee might vanish as thoroughly as Alice and Toby before he even reached the station.

He had to swallow a rock of gritty panic. 'Quick, now. We're going on a train, won't that be fun?'

They both gave him a look that said they had noticed he was imminently hysterical, but they were willing to bear with him for now.

They let him bundle them into clothes and coats, sat helpfully still while he laced up their shoes, and then stayed on either side of him, one to each hand, as he ran out into the road to hail an early cab.

52

King's Cross, 1903

Horrors went through his head on the way to the station. Kite wouldn't be there; or after everything, he, Joe, would disappear, and perhaps there would be a tingling a few seconds before it happened and he would know it – or worse, he would see Beatrix and George go to dust in front of him.

And even if everything was all right, even if he wasn't insane and this was all real, Kite had not signed up for two children along with the crazed mess that was hardly anything more to him than an unnatural *thing* stitched together from the remnants of his friend.

It was too early for the commuter rush. The station was eerie, and where the trains sat breathing steam at the platforms, they loomed spectral. Joe walked as fast as the twins could go across what felt like the acres of concourse to platform three. He could feel his own pulse banging at the bones deep inside his ears. He knew what he was going to find. No Kite, no one waiting. The man from the sea would be imaginary. Yesterday, the party, life before, would be an epilepsy dream.

There was a man with red hair reading a newspaper, leaning back against one of the brick pillars. He was barely more than an outline in the vapour.

Joe had to get close to him before he was sure.

Bee lit up and hurried ahead of him. Kite must not have been able to hear very well at all now, because Bee tugged at his hand before he noticed them.

'Hello,' Joe managed, and thought he was doing very well not to cry. 'I'm sorry about the children. I – I had to bring them. I'm sorry. Things have – changed overnight.'

Kite was watching him with well-controlled alarm, but alarm all the same. 'Where's their mother? Does she know they're here?'

'She's dead. I woke up in an empty house. They've been dead for a year. Alice and Toby, they ... but you met them, right? Yesterday, at the ...'

'I did. I did – Joe, you're all right.' Kite grasped his shoulders and gave him a shake, only light. 'You're not mad. You can just see things changing.'

'Yes,' Joe managed. He looked helplessly at the twins. 'I think these two are mine now.'

'Good. Right, let's go then,' Kite said, as if the unexpected addition of a pair of toddlers was not a thing that could possibly worry anyone. He lifted up Beatrix and asked her how she was, like he would have asked an adult.

'Very well, thank you,' she said, and Joe stared at her, because he had never heard her do that. She gave him a pointed look that made it clear she had only been waiting for someone who would listen.

It took until well after midnight to reach the Eilean Mòr gate. Even though Joe had brought enough money to get them all there in the relative comfort of first class, he had dreaded it, anticipated tears and God knew what, but George had been immaculately behaved for the entire journey. Joe suspected that he was trying to impress Kite. On the way out to the gate over a black sea, something in Joe's chest screwed tighter. He'd forgotten how far out it was. An hour in which they could still just disappear. He had to bite his lip the whole way, ordering himself not to weep with the useless terror of the journey.

Kite must have noticed, because although he said nothing, he sat close and shared his brandy flask.

There was building work at the gate. The two pillars were surrounded by scaffolding now, and something was going on underwater; it looked like they were on their way to building an artificial island. There would, Kite explained, be a new tower to enclose the space, but it would be solid, with no doors. It wouldn't last for ever, but it would be good for five hundred years.

Joe couldn't believe it when they were through. Nothing was different and everything was. The *Victory*, a leviathan shape on the far side of the lighthouse, looked like a floating castle. Beatrix straightened up in Kite's lap, and George grasped the bow, vibrating with excitement. They were both wide awake from having been bundled onto the boat in the dark.

Joe had to dash one hand over his eyes.

'They gave you *Victory*,' he said.

Kite glowed. 'She's perfect, isn't she. Newly refitted.' He leaned down to make sure Beatrix could see. 'What do you think?'

Beatrix opened and closed her hands on his sleeve, the picture of frustration. 'How, how to say – a *da* boat?' She spread her arms out.

Either Kite was on her wavelength anyway, or he had a few words of Chinese. 'Battleship.'

'Battleship,' she repeated.

'You know it's news to me that she even talks,' Joe said, knocked sideways.

Beatrix patted Kite's arm to make him lean down to her. 'Other one name?'

'*Victory.*'

Beatrix slid down to talk to George in their twins-burble. Joe could only understand a little of it, but he had a feeling they thought the ship was alive because Kite had called it she. He took a breath to explain, but then stopped. It was a good thing to believe.

He held himself just about together until they were on board. The sailors took over the children immediately; there was, incredibly, a nursery, because the women brought their children with them now. Joe stayed long enough with them to see that it was a bright, cheery room, warm and well-lit, right in the heart of the ship, next to the infirmary where no shots ever came through. There were matrons on duty, though all the children were asleep. One of them put the twins into a spare hammock. George looked like he'd never seen anything better in his life, and then fell asleep so abruptly he might have been knocked out. Beatrix sat quietly, bobbing to make the hammock swing. She giggled when the matron gave her an extra push. Joe had never seen them so happy to be put to bed. He kissed them both, and then found that he was shaking with the sense that he'd forgotten something, some danger that would still loom up and snatch them. The matron lifted her eyebrows at him.

'Nothing worse for disturbing sleep than hovering fathers.' She made it sound like an unfortunate medical condition.

He had to laugh, or sort of. He couldn't help wondering if they had made it through with plenty of time to spare, or if there had only been forty seconds before one or all three of them winked out of existence, the inevitable outcome of some innocent conversation on either side of the gate, a dropped watch, a penny spun at the wrong second.

Kite touched Joe's back, just between his shoulder blades. It stopped all those what-ifs hurling themselves around.

'Night, Bee.'

She looked past him and smiled, and saluted at Kite, who must have just done it towards her.

The way into the stateroom was familiar. He'd walked this way before, he knew it, and when Kite opened the door, he knew the room. He knew the tilting windows, the dining table, the desk, all so powerfully that he could smell the wine and the cigarette smoke from that last night off Spain, before Trafalgar, before the shots had come in.

It was all beautifully repaired now, and on the desk was a gleaming bronze telegraph. But it was still itself, warmer and brighter than the cabin on *Agamemnon*, and somehow, it had soaked in all the good things that had happened far more than the bad.

Home. It was coming up through the deck.

He had to sit down, because all the strength had evaporated from his knees. When he looked up, Kite was sitting next to him, very still, not touching him. He looked anxious.

'I know it must have been bad, leaving. But – I swear, they're safer here than—'

'I know,' Joe said. He started to laugh, because when he said *I*, it felt different now. He knew who that was. 'It all looks a damn sight better than the last time we were here, doesn't it? Much nicer now it's not on fire.'

Kite did his unbearable trick of turning to glass. 'You remember that then?'

'We were sitting here, with Tom and Rupert Grey.' Joe studied the dust in the air. He could nearly see their ghosts in it, the lamps that night in the heat, the glitter of the wine glasses. 'I think that was the happiest I've ever been. I'd been *sick* missing you, it was making me crotchety with the men, I could hardly sit still more than fifteen minutes for that last six months. And then there you were.'

When Kite cried, Joe's whole chest hurt. Joe pulled him close, and even that didn't feel near enough. He kissed him once, very softly, for permission, then again when Kite leaned up to him, cradling the nape of his neck where the bones were fragile. His fingertips already knew the pattern of the burn scars. And then it was all there, everything, and all of him: Jem, Joe Tournier, Joe Zhang, different and not, three winking facets of a person who he wasn't sure had a name. Whoever he was, though, he had a surge of joy when Kite sank forward against his shoulder.

He put his head down a little. Kite smelled of cedar, from the sea chest his clothes lived in. Joe touched his arm where there was a new burn, too precise to be accidental. There were hints of cruciform shapes in it. Kite took it back and folded it close to his own chest without looking up.

'Can I do something new on your other arm?'

Kite hesitated.

Joe caught his hands. 'I'm not leaving again. You're not going to get rid of me now. And the twins have adopted you.'

'All right,' Kite said, but not like he believed it.

Joe decided it didn't matter. There was all the time in the world to make him believe it.

ACKNOWLEDGEMENTS

As always, thanks to my brother Jacob for keeping me sane and telling me how to fix my stupid plots, even though he's always busy with things that matter much more. Also to Alison and Sara Helen, my brilliant editors, who took me seriously when I insisted that the introduction of giant tortoises to nineteenth century Scotland would definitely solve everything. Huge thanks to Jenny, my agent, who stuck with this project even when everyone else thought it was ridiculous, and worked on it above and beyond the call of duty for years. Thank you to the Arts Council, who funded the 2018 project which took me aboard my first tall ship, *Atyla*, and thanks even more to Darwin 200, who gave me a place aboard *Pelican of London* in 2020.

And special thanks to Pete Best, the bosun aboard *Pelican* and the most incredible and helpful expert in tall ship sailing anyone could ever want (that is, when he isn't hatching some horrendous plot to do with bananas).

A NOTE ON THE AUTHOR

Natasha Pulley studied English Literature at Oxford University. After stints working at Waterstones as a bookseller, then at Cambridge University Press as a publishing assistant in the astronomy and maths departments, she did the Creative Writing MA at UEA. She later studied in Tokyo, where she lived on a scholarship from the Daiwa Anglo-Japanese Foundation, and she is now an associate lecturer at Bath Spa University and panel tutor at the Cambridge Institute of Continuing Education. Her first novel, *The Watchmaker of Filigree Street*, was an international bestseller, a Guardian Summer Read, an Amazon Best Book of the Month, was shortlisted for the Authors' Club Best First Novel Award and won a Betty Trask Award. *The Bedlam Stacks*, her second novel, was published in 2017, followed by *The Lost Future of Pepperharrow* in 2020. She lives in Bath.

@natasha_pulley